THE SOCIETY

Also by Michael Palmer

THE SOCIETY

Michael Palmer

Severn House

This first hardcover edition published in Great Britain 2006 by
SEVERN HOUSE PUBLISHERS LTD of
9–15 High Street, Sutton, Surrey SM1 1DF,
by arrangement with Century and Arrow,
a division of the Random House Group Ltd.

British Library Cataloguing in Publication Data

Palmer, Michael, 1942-
   The society
   1. Serial murder investigation - Fiction
   2. Managed care administrators - Fiction
   3. Suspense fiction
   I. Title
   813.5'4 [F]

ISBN-13: 978-0-7278-6361-4
ISBN-10: 0-7278-6361-4

Printed and bound in Great Britain by
MPG Books Ltd., Bodmin, Cornwall.

To my sister, Susan Palmer Terry, and all those others who have battled against breast cancer

Acknowledgments

In preparing to write *The Society*, I used my mailing list and web site to hold a contest in which I asked my readers to share accounts of both their misadventures and gratifying experiences with managed care. There were many, many entries. In the course of reading this novel you will encounter a number of these stories. In fact, I did not find it necessary to make up any! So, special thanks to all those who submitted their tales, especially finalists Dr. Louis Borgenicht, Fay McEleney, Lisa Reagan, Vicki Kozlowski, Martha Ficklin, Dr. Jack Langley, John Lynch, Dr. Lamont Weide, Bev Spellman, Judy Converse, Dr. Mark Dahl, Jill Adams, Laurie Peterson, Geoffrey Kent, Dina Mason, Doug Ansell, Melissa Smith, and Jodi VanMeter.

I feel so fortunate to have the friends and experts in my writing life that I do.

Jane Berkey, Don Cleary, and Peggy Gordijn at the Jane Rotrosen Agency continue to be there for me at every turn.

Bill Massey and Andie Nicolay at Bantam have shepherded this book through each step.

Susan Terry, Daniel Palmer, Robin Guilfoyle, and Mimi Santini-Ritt have been my special readers.

Lt. Cole Cordray, Eve Oyer, Officer Matthew MacDonald, and Dr. Bud Waisbren have given me technical help.

Paul Fiore has helped keep me in shape for the rigors of novel writing.

Bill Wilson and Dr. Bob Smith have taught me patience and given me the ability to write 500 pages one page at a time.

Luke remains the enduring constant and life force behind every thing I do.

THE SOCIETY

Prologue

4,013,864.

Marcia Rising tilted back in her chair just enough so that neither her chief financial officer Leonard Smith, seated to her right, nor Executive VP Dan Elder to her left could see what she was writing on her legal pad. She was expected to take some notes at these meetings, anyhow. After all, she was the boss. Smiling inwardly, she added an ornate dollar sign in front of the 4. At the far end of the broad mahogany table, Vice President Joe Levinson droned on. Levinson was the cost-containment officer for Eastern Quality Health, and as such was responsible more than anyone except Marcia, herself, for the managed-care company's strong financial picture. But as a speaker, he was as animated and vibrant as drying paint.

'...We took last quarter's slumping numbers as a strident warning – a shot across our financial bow, if you will – that we had to renew incentives among our employees and physicians in the area of cost containment. The in-house contest we ran was most successful in this regard. Almost immediately there was a twenty-one percent increase in claims rejected outright, and a thirteen percent increase in those surgical claims that were bundled for payment together with at least one other claim. There were some complaints from doctors, but nothing Bill's physician-relations people couldn't handle...'

Four million ... thirteen thousand ... eight hundred ... sixty-four.

Marcia wrote the numbers out longhand, then she added touches of calligraphy to the figure, which was her salary for the preceding twelve months. Factor in her eight million in unexercised stock options, and she was well into the upper echelons of female executives in the country. The numbers had a delightful rhythm to them, she mused, perhaps a conga. She imagined a kick line of her nineteen hundred employees, snaking its way through the building.

Four million thir-teen kick! ...

Marcia was more than pleased with the way her officers had responded to the recent dip in corporate profits. Her philosophy of one set of premiums and coverages for companies with younger, healthier employees and another for those who might have a more risky, older crew was infallible.

'If they don't get sick, they can't cost us,' she had preached over and over again to her minions.

Let some other company cover those who are running out of time or won't take care of themselves. Every dollar spent researching the demographic makeup of a company (blacks get more hypertension, diabetes, and kidney failure; Asians are ridiculous hypochondriacs; Hispanics have too much alcoholism, drug addiction, and mental illness; thirty-somethings are okay, forty-somethings are not) would return hundreds in the form of payouts that Eastern Quality Health wouldn't have to make.

Eight hun-dred sixty-four kick! ...

'...And so, as I see it, our company has weathered a passing financial squall,' Levinson was saying, 'but there are major storm clouds on the horizon for the entire industry. Still, our ship will remain seaworthy so long as we never lose sight of the fact that our business is all about health – that is, the health of Eastern Quality.'

To laughter at his rare humor, and a smattering of applause, Levinson bowed slightly and took his seat. The meeting was, to all intents, over. Marcia stood and encouraged her officers to maintain their vigilance, to bring problems and ideas to her attention sooner rather than later, and never to lose sight of the goals of Eastern Quality Health – not to be the biggest HMO, but rather to be the most efficient. Then she crossed to the door of her suite and shook the hand of each of them as they left. Finally, she settled in behind her desk and gazed out at the reflecting basin and double fountain that graced EQH's fifteen-acre campus on Route 128, eighteen miles north and west of Boston. The setting sun had already dipped below the tree line, yielding to a still, cloudless evening. Arranged neatly in labeled wire bins on her desk was two or three hours of work she expected to complete before going home. Seldom was she not the last EQH employee out of the building.

Marcia brushed a minuscule crumb from her Armani jacket and started with a review of reports from the team of attorneys handling one of several suits pending against the company – this one centered on confusion over whether or not a particular policyholder had the coverage for a bone marrow transplant. EQH's position was, of course, that she did not, although, as of the woman's death six months ago, the question had become moot. Still, her annoying husband's unwillingness to accept the truth was prolonging a resolution. Marcia dictated a carefully worded letter demanding that the lawyers stand firm at a settlement of $50,000 with no admission of culpability. It was to be that, or nothing.

Outside her third-floor window night settled in as she reached for the next set of reports. Finally, at nine, she gathered her things in the Moschino briefcase her husband had given her, straightened her desk, then her skirt, and headed out to the elevator. Floor two of the garage, the so-called officer's parking lot, was accessed only via the elevator, and only with the aid of a pass card. Marcia pulled her overcoat tightly about her and stepped out into the raw March night. She knew what vehicle each of her upper-management officers drove, and took pains to encourage them to choose automobiles reflecting their personal success and, through that, the success of EQH. Besides her Mercedes SL500 Silver Arrow convertible, there were still two cars in the lot – utilization management director Sarah Brett's Infiniti, and chief of physician relations Bill Donoho's Lexus. Marcia made a mental note to reward them both for their diligence.

She was nearing her car when she felt more than heard the presence of someone else in the lot. She whirled at the sound of footsteps. A man, fedora brim pulled down to the bridge of his nose, hands in his trench-coat pockets, had left the shadows and was approaching her.

How in the hell had he gotten out here? she wondered angrily. This was absolutely the last screwup for Joe O'Donnell. If you couldn't trust your security chief, who in the hell could you trust? First thing in the morning, O'Donnell was history, and none of his whining about five children was going to save him this time.

Marcia's pulse shot up at the sight of the man, then slowed as she took in the situation with the quick, analytical thinking that had become her trademark. There was a security camera sweeping the lot from just above the doors to the elevator foyer, so maybe one of the two guards on duty would spot the stranger. Managed care was at times a controversial and emotional business. Her executive officers were encouraged to have a legally registered handgun. Hers was locked in the glove compartment of the Silver Arrow, but if this was trouble, there was no way she could reach the car in time. She peered through the gloom trying to get a fix on the man's eyes.

11

Dammit, O'Donnell!

Less than ten feet away, the intruder stopped. By now, Marcia was certain that this was no one associated with EQH.

'Who are you?' she demanded. 'How did you get out here?'

'Mrs. Rising, I have something for you.'

A woman! Marcia felt her pulse surge once more.

'Who are you?' she said again, her voice breaking.

The woman – slender with a narrow face and eyes still shielded by her hat – withdrew her left hand and passed over an envelope. Her calmness and the coldness in her voice tied a knot of fear in Marcia's chest. She stared down at the envelope, which she now held.

'Go ahead,' the woman urged. 'Open it.'

Marcia fumbled the envelope open and withdrew two cards, each three inches square. On one, carefully printed with some sort of marker, was the unadorned block letter *R*. On the other was a *T*.

'What is this? What's this all about?'

She stumbled backward toward the Mercedes, the letters and envelope still reflexively clutched in her hand.

Before her, the woman calmly withdrew a pistol from her coat pocket, its muzzle covered by what looked like a rubber nipple.

'My God, no!' Marcia cried. 'Don't do this! I have money. Lots of money. I'll give you whatever you want.'

'This won't hurt as much as it should,' the woman said, firing from four feet away into the center of Marcia's chest.

The CEO was reeling backward when a second shot, fired almost from the hip, caught her squarely in the throat.

The woman slid the silenced pistol back into her trench-coat pocket and turned toward the door.

'Sleep tight,' she whispered.

Chapter 1

'*Drained.*'

'*Wiped.*'

'*Fried.*'

'*Burnt.*'

'Oh, that's a good one.'

'Okay, whose turn is it?'

'Dr. Cameron's.'

'Hell no, lass. Not me. I just did *tuckered out.*'

'Then it's Dr. Grant's turn.'

From his position across the operating table from his partner, Will Grant surveyed the three nurses and, finally, the anesthesiologist.

'You sure?' he asked.

'It's you, all right,' the scrub nurse said.

'I can't think of any more.'

'Well you damn well better, laddie,' Cameron said, his Highlands brogue as dense as it had been when he moved to the States a decade and a half ago. 'Give me a sponge on a stick please, would you, Mary? Thank ye. Now, Will, today's word was your idea. T'would be a travesty for you to lose the whole shibickie and end up buyin' the beers for this motley crew.'

Before he could reply, Will yawned widely enough to displace his paper surgical mask off his nose.

'Seems like I should have picked some word other than *exhausted*,' he said as the laughter died down. He turned his head to allow the circulating nurse to reposition his mask. 'But it was the only one I could think of.'

'No surprise there,' Cameron said. 'We should allow "Dr. Will Grant" as a legal answer to this one because, laddie, you define the term. I couldn't believe it when I heard you were covering again tonight.'

'Four days of alimony.'

'What?'

'Every extra call night I take from you guys translates into four days of alimony paid – more if I get a case.'

'Which you almost always do. Well, we're getting ready to close. Sir Will, my trusty assistant, do you have any reasons why we shouldn't go ahead and sew up this lucky bugger?'

'Stomachs R Us,' Will said. 'You did a really nice job getting that tumor out, Gordo.'

'You forgot to add "as always." '

'As always. How about *prostrate*?'

'Debbie did that already,' the circulating nurse said. 'I've been keeping track. *Fatigued, winded, frazzled, run down, wilted, sagging, flagging, weary, sucking wind, tired, overtired, dog tired, dead tired, worn out, prostrate, whipped, spent, leaden, run down, pooped, too pooped to pop, baked, toasted, enfeebled, haggard, tuckered out, plumb tuckered out, drained, wiped, fried, and burnt.* You only have until Dr. C. gets the last clip in.'

Will flexed his neck muscles, which, after a three-and-a-half-hour case, felt as if someone had injected them with Krazy Glue. It was only a slight exaggeration to say that the last time he hadn't been some form of exhausted was eighteen years ago when, at twenty-three, he started medical school. Med school, internship, surgical residency, vascular fellowship – he often wondered if he had known, really known, about the call schedules; and the interminable hours in the OR; and the early morning emergencies; and the office practice; and the continuing-education responsibilities; and the staff meetings; and the mushrooming malpractice premiums; and the ambulance chasers, and the diminishing financial returns brought about by managed care; and ultimately the divorce and supplementary nights on duty to make ends meet, would he do it all again the same way. The answer, as always, was yes – except, of course for the managed-care part.

'Last clip coming down, laddie,' Cameron announced, lowering the final surgical clip dramatically toward the incision.

'*Petered out*,' Will blurted at the last possible second.

Silence held sway as those in OR 3 polled one another.

'We'll give it to you, Will-boy,' Cameron said finally, 'as long as you assure us your answer isn't merely a description of your sex life.'

Fredrickston Surgical Associates was a four-person group, head-quartered in the Medical Arts Building, a block away from Fredrickston General Hospital, a fully designated trauma center thrity miles south-west of Boston. The four surgerons rotated call with three others, although in any given seven-day stretch, Will would take on one or even two nights in addition to his own. Today, Tuesday, he finished seeing patients in the office, then trudged back to the hospital through the raw, gray afternoon. James Katz and Susan Hollister met him for sign-out rounds outside the surgical intensive-care unit. Katz, now in his late sixties, was the patriarch of the practice, if not the entire hospital. He was as stiff in his manner and speech as he was in his posture, and to the best of Will's knowledge, no one had ever mentioned him telling a joke. Still, the man was universally beloved and respected for his dignity, his skill in the operating room, and his ability to teach residents and other physicians.

'Weren't you just on call, Will?' he asked.

'That was two nights ago, and it was incredibly quiet. Steve Schwaitzberg wants to chaperone some sort of overnight with one of his kids' classes.'

'Is he going to pay you back with a night?' Katz pressed.

Whether it was his liberal politics and interests, his relaxed dress and manner with the patients, or his inability to keep his marriage together, Will sensed he had, for some time, been Katz's least favorite of the three younger associates. Still, the two of them had always been on decent terms, although there was invariably some tension when the subject of Will's extra call nights came up.

'He probably will pay me back,' Will said, knowing – as doubtless did his senior partner – that the truth was being stretched.

'Don't you see the twins on Tuesdays?' Susan asked.

As reserved and conservative as Gordon Cameron was flamboyant, Susan had preceded Will into the practice by two years. A competent surgeon, she was quite slender and attractive in a bookish way, but to the best of Will's knowledge had never been married. For several years, she had been dating a businessman – at least according to her she was. Will had never met the man, nor had Gordo. And from time to time, Cameron would speculate that Susan's businessman was, in fact, a businesswoman. Regardless, Susan had gone from being reserved and somewhat distant from Will before his divorce to being a concerned friend, worrying about his health, his children, and even his social life. One of the rare times Will had allowed himself to be fixed up was with a former Wellesley College roommate of Susan's. Had he taken years of acting lessons, he couldn't possibly have been less himself than he was that night.

I'm just not ready, he reported to Susan after the spiritless evening. *We didn't have anything in common. She was a human being.*

15

'I do have the kids, yes,' he said, 'but tonight's our regular night at the soup kitchen, so I'll just take call from there until I bring them home. Speaking of the Open Hearth,' he added, determined to divert the subject from his taking too much call, 'we're always looking for volunteers to serve.'

'When I resign from the symphony board, I just might take you up on your invitation,' Katz replied sincerely.

'Me, too,' Susan added with more sparkle.

'I didn't know you were on the symphony board,' Will said.

'I'm planning on being on it someday.'

'All right,' Katz said, 'let's get on with this. Will, it's a good thing you enjoy your work, because you certainly do a heck of a lot of it.'

Jim Katz had seven patients in the hospital, Susan and Will three apiece, and Gordon Cameron, who had already gone home, two, including the case he and Will had done earlier in the day. The trio of surgeons that included Steve Schwaitzberg had another five. Schwaitzberg had signed his three out over the lunch hour, and the other two would do so by phone. Twenty patients in all – a load by modern standards. Insurance restrictions had seen to it that most of them had received their pre-op evaluations as outpatients, and had been operated on before they had even seen their rooms or met the nurses who were going to be their caregivers. The moment after their surgery was completed, they were being primed for discharge. Actuarial tables compiled by the managed-care and insurance industries had demonstrated that such policies saved money without causing a significant rise in post-op complications. Will's experience with his own and many other practices had shown that a good number of patients would gladly beg to differ with those statistics.

At Susan's urging, they saw Jim Katz's group first. He would never complain about his workload or diminishing physical capabilities, but the three younger members of the group had each seen evidence that layers were peeling off his stamina and abilities in the OR, and they sought to protect him in any way they could. All went well until the last of Katz's patients, a sixty-three-year-old diabetic man whose gallbladder Katz had removed the morning before.

'So, Mr. Garfield,' Katz said, checking the four small incisions he had made into the man's abdominal cavity, and nodding approval of the way they looked, 'is your wife on her way here to get you?'

'She just called from the parking garage, I shouldn't worry,' Garfield said.

'Good, good. And the nurses have given you my discharge

instructions? Good.'

Will didn't like anything about what he was seeing and hearing. Stuart Garfield was doing his very best to mask it, and maybe he didn't even realize it was happening, but he was experiencing some shortness of breath. Susan nodded minutely that she had noticed the same thing. The managed-care companies decreed that a night in the hospital or even less was to be the standard of care for the laparoscopic removal of a gallbladder. Katz did not consider that the man's diabetes was reason to argue for more, and it wouldn't have been except for the distension of the veins alongside the man's neck and the slight bluish cast to his lips – both subtle signs of evolving trouble.

Nonchalantly, Will sidled over to the bedside, slipped his stethoscope into his ears, and listened through the man's back to the base of his lungs. Rales, the crackling sounds made by fluid filling the small air sacs, were most definitely present. Stuart Garfield was in early heart failure – a potentially serious condition in any patient, but even more so in a diabetic who, with little warning, perhaps by the time he and his wife had reached the highway, could be in full-blown pulmonary edema – a terrifying, life-threatening emergency. Will motioned Katz over to the doorway. There was no easy way to present the findings, and with a physician as forthright and honorable as Katz, it wasn't smart to try.

'Jim, he's in some congestive heart failure,' Will whispered. 'Neck veins distended, rales at both bases, a little blue around the gills.'

Katz sagged visibly, crossed to the bedside to listen, then returned to the doorway.

'I knew I shouldn't have been rushing him out,' he said, shaking his head in dismay.

'Listen, don't be hard on yourself. We're making rounds together as a team. This sort of thing is why we do it. Thanks to our friendly neighborhood insurance companies, the pressure's on all of us now all the time. They tell you that the average surgeon gets his gallbladder patients out of the hospital on the first post-op day, or even the day of the procedure. You know darn well that if you keep yours in an extra day or two, you're going to be right down on the HMOs' list. They don't ignore these things.'

'Just the same,' Katz said wearily, 'thanks for saving my bacon.' He returned to his patient. 'Mr. Garfield, I'm going to wait for your wife to get up here, then we have to talk.'

★   ★   ★

'I've never seen him so glum,' Susan said, as they headed off to see the first of her patients.

As the sole woman in the group, Susan had proclaimed herself the mother hen, dedicated to keeping Gordo's weight under control, seeing that Will got enough sleep and met someone special, and insisting that Jim Katz cut back on his many obligations.

'We more or less grew up with the problems of managed care,' Will said. 'Jim's had to adapt to them. He gets sort of wistful when he talks about the time when you simply diagnosed a surgical problem in a patient, cut it out, and cared for the person until they were ready to go home.'

'Ah, yes, the good old days before one-size-fits-all medicine. My mom is embroiled in a battle with her HMO right now. She's got huge fibroids, complete with pain and vaginal bleeding, and her GYN wants to do a hysterectomy.'

'Makes sense to me.'

'Me, too, but the evaluators at her HMO say the procedure is unnecessary. What's more, they performed their magnificent evaluation of her over the phone. No one from her HMO has ever laid eyes or hands on her, but they're the ones making the decision.'

Will hoisted himself up haughtily and adopted a dense British accent.

'I'm not a doctor, but I play one on the phone.'

'Exactly. So Mom has pain every time she takes a step, and her doctor says the fibroids would make it impossible for him to feel a malignancy if one were there.'

'Goodness. She still in Idaho?'

'Forever.'

'And you never had any desire to go back there to practice?'

'How can I know I exist if I can't see myself in store windows when I walk down the street?' Susan's dark eyes smiled. 'Besides, what do I have in common with Demi Moore and all of those other big-name transplants from Hollywood?'

'You should bring your mom's case up at the Society meeting Thursday night.'

'Um ... the truth is, I hadn't decided if I was going to go. Will, I appreciate your enthusiasm for the Hippocrates Society, really I do, but after almost a year of going every month, I just haven't gotten caught up in it. I'm definitely upset with managed-care companies' policies and regulations and all they're doing to the way we practice, but I just haven't been able to get as ... as fired up as the rest of you,

18

even with my mom's recent problems. You know me. I'm pretty reserved about most things – not shy like some people think, but not that outspoken, either. And excuse me for saying so, but you people are fanatics.'

Will laughed.

'Hey, now, I wouldn't go that far. How about committed?'

'If that makes you more comfortable.'

'Listen, Suze, we need everybody we can get at these meetings. There were over a hundred docs there last time. A hundred! The papers are really starting to take notice.'

'Will, I'm on two committees in the hospital and a couple at church. The people on the desk at my gym don't know who I am, and I'm afraid my boyfriend may be headed there, too.'

'I understand. Just do your best. I may tell your mom's story anyway.'

'You have my permission.'

'These companies have ripped the heart out of medicine, Susan. They have to be stopped.'

'You just be careful not to rile them up too much. You wouldn't be the first doctor they've squashed.'

'I'd like to see them try,' Will said.

Chapter 2

Ashford was a bedroom community located almost midway between Fredrickston and Worcester. Beeper and cell phone at the ready, Will checked out with the ER and surgical residents and headed west through modest late-afternoon traffic. He knew that he was hardly the only divorced dad forced to drive to the house that had once been his to take his children out for dinner, but that knowledge did nothing to assuage the weirdness he invariably felt in the situation – especially when the doorbell was answered, as it was tonight, by Mark Mueller, once a friend and financial adviser to him and Maxine, and now, for more than a year, her live-in.

'Hey, how's it going?' Mueller said, knowing better than to attempt a handshake.

Mueller, though about Will's height and build, had a full scalp of curly hair, which invariably made Will reflect on the modest but relentless recession at the corners of his own. Max had explained that she and Mueller were too much in love not to live together but that the cost of marriage, in terms of lost alimony, made nuptials a fiscal impossibility.

Will stepped into his former foyer.

'Kids ready?'

'Danny's just finishing up his homework. Jess is ready, though.'

Will smiled to himself. Could any pair of twins ever be more different from each other – or more wonderful in those differences? Jess always ready, Danny last minute or beyond; one meticulous, one scattered; one serious and intense, one flaky and wildly imaginative; one (Jess) an athlete, the other already credited with several community-theater productions.

Damn you, Max.

'Hey, Dad, who loves you?'

Jess, in jeans and a bulky sweater, came racing around the corner and dove into his midsection.

'Who loves *you*, baby. Everything okay?'

'Fine. Tammy got sent home today for throwing spitballs. Cody Block said he likes me. I got an "A" on my Morocco project. Are we going to the Hearth or your place or a restaurant?'

'Hearth.'

'Great!'

'Danny, let's get –'

The shoulder-first assault from behind, with more force than any ten-year-old should be able to generate, nearly knocked both Will and Jess over.

'Open Hearth night, right?' Danny asked.

'Right on.'

'Um ... Max wants them home by nine,' Mueller said uncomfortably.

Will's eyes flashed. His thin smile said many things.

'Nine it will be, Mark. She at the gym?'

'Office. She should be back soon.'

'Nine. Come on, guys.'

'I keep telling you, I'm not a guy.'

'All right, come on, girls.'

'Daddy!'

Will, two classmates, and a saintly psychiatrist had started the Open

Hearth Kitchen during Will's sophomore year in med school. The idea was to survive two intense years of basic science studies by involving themselves in a project centering on real live humans. Almost immediately, the other students and faculty joined in, helping to make their efforts a success. A dynamic, visionary young director and a committed board saw to it that the merchants, schools, churches, and residents of Fredrickston and the surrounding towns understood the place and embraced it. Now, after sixteen years, there were times when volunteers had to be turned away, although none of the thousands of diners who had patronized the kitchen ever were. Three hundred and ten was the record for dinners served on one night, but with the economy continuing to nosedive, that record seemed likely to fall before long.

No matter how hard it had been to take time off from work, Will seldom missed the monthly board meetings, and almost never his serving obligation – the first and third Tuesdays of every month.

The rugged, three-story clapboard structure occupied a corner lot in the most run-down part of town. Maxine had tried insisting that the area was too dangerous to keep 'dragging' the twins to, but in this debate, unlike most of the rest, Will had prevailed.

'Okay,' he said, easing his four-year-old Wagoneer into the small parking area, 'you guys know the drill.'

'I'm doing dessert,' Danny called as the two raced up to the kitchen door.

'You did it last time!'

As he often did, Will paused to survey the building and to reflect on the years since the project's inception. In the beginning, a nearby Episcopal church had rented the first floor to them for next to nothing. Now, the Open Hearth Kitchen, a tax-exempt corporation, owned the whole thing. Belief, perseverance, fearlessness – over the intervening years, the Open Hearth had come to mean so many things to him. Now his involvement was limited to board of directors' meetings and those two nights a month as a server. His energy – what there was left of it – had instead been channeled into the Hippocrates Society and its quixotic mission of reclaiming medicine from the HMOs and insurance companies.

Belief... perseverance ... fearlessness.

By the time Will entered the kitchen, the kids were each involved in animated discussions as they worked. He smiled at the ease with which they had made themselves part of the gang, and the genuineness with which they had been accepted. In all, this night there were sixteen volunteers and five staff. No army had ever functioned with more efficiency and esprit.

'Hey, Will, wassapnin'.'

'Same old, same old, Beano. How about you?'

'Can't complain. Your kids are really something. Two minutes and they're already up to their elbows in whatever needs doing.'

Benois Beane, forty-something, had been the Hearth's director for going on five years, during which he had continued to expand the agency's programs, instituting a Meals on Wheels service and an employment counselor. He had also taken it on himself, following an offhand remark by Will, to ensure that no one called Will 'Doc.' Many knew he was a physician, but there was no reason at all to advertise the fact. The last thing he wanted was to dilute the dual pleasures of serving food to those who needed it and introducing his children to people who were light-years from the tree-lined privilege of Ashford.

'Beano, the place is looking great.'

'Yeah. Thank God for all those churches and synagogues.'

'I suppose that *would be* appropriate,' Will said.

Beane took a moment to find the humor, then his ebony face crinkled in a broad grin.

'Good one,' he said. 'I almost missed it. Forgive me for saying this, Will, but you look as if you've been working too much.'

'Hell no. By my standards I'm exceedingly well rested. See me tomorrow morning. By then I'll be looking as if I'm working too much. What you're viewing now is totally fresh Grant.'

'Fresh Grant,' Beane echoed. 'Sounds like something we should have on the menu.'

By five-thirty when the doors opened, at least fifty were lined up to be served, a number of them with young children in tow. A goodly percentage of the patrons still had a roof over their heads, but for them, food and heat were getting more and more difficult to manage. The twins had settled their conflict in house and were working side by side at the dessert section. Will, an apron tied around his waist, strolled among the tables with a soapy-water spray and a towel, chatting with the diners and cleaning up after they had left. At one table, where a particularly grizzled down-and-outer sat alone, picking at his beef stew and rice, Will stopped.

'How're you doin'?' he asked.

The man, with metallic-blue eyes and a nose that had been broken probably more than once, forced a weak smile.

'Can't complain,' he said.

'Name's Will.'

'John. John Cooper.'

'I haven't seen you here before.'

'Haven't been.'

'Well, you picked a good night to start. Beef stew is about the best thing we do.'

'It's very tasty.'

'Listen, John, I don't go around advertising the fact, but I'm a doctor. I work at the hospital. Stop me if you think I'm out of line, but I'm concerned about those lumps on the side of your neck.'

Cooper didn't bother reaching up to touch them.

'What about 'em?'

The lumps, markedly swollen lymph glands, were trouble. Will's quick differential diagnosis included several types of cancer, as well as scrofula – a form of tuberculosis.

'Has any doctor checked them out?'

'Can't afford no doctor.'

'You have Mass Health? Any kind of insurance?'

Cooper shook his head.

'Will you come see me and let me check those over, maybe run a few tests? It won't cost you a thing.'

'Maybe.'

'I promise I'll take good care of you.'

'That's nice of you.'

Seldom more than a couple of tables behind, Will could see enough from where he stood to know he would be hard-pressed now to catch up with the influx.

'Listen, John,' he said, 'I'm going to send Ben Beane over to talk with you. He runs this place. He'll help you fill out the forms to get some state insurance, okay?'

'You mean welfare?'

'Insurance – the sort everyone in this country deserves to have. I don't like to put labels on things, but what I'm talking about isn't welfare. Wait here. I'll get Ben. He'll explain everything, and he'll also give you my address. Okay?'

'If you say so.'

On the way over to find Beane, Will paused briefly to wipe down two tables. Most of the patrons of the Open Hearth Kitchen were respectful of the place and quick to do whatever they could to keep the tables ready for others. But some weren't.

23

'Beano, I need your help with a new guy.'

'The one you were talking to?'

'He needs to come see me about some big lumps in his neck. Can you give him my address and have your people start him on the bumpy road to Mass Health coverage so we can get some tests done?'

'I would,' Beane said, 'but the dude just got up and left.'

Will raced to the front door. A mean wind was sweeping through the blackness. There were a few patrons shambling toward him, but John Cooper was gone. Impotent with the situation and peeved at himself for possibly frightening the man off, Will was still on the staircase, peering down the street, when his cell phone went off. The display showed an ER number.

'Damn.'

'Will, it's Lydia,' the surgical resident said. 'Rescue just called from an alley downtown. They're working on a guy a couple of kids found there, beaten up pretty bad. Mid-forties, robbery probably. No ID, no BP to speak of. He's frozen, but they assure me he's still alive.'

'ETA?'

'Ten minutes.'

There was no sense in trying to find out the location of the alley, even though it might have been nearby. In the field, the paramedics and EMTs were better and faster than he could ever be.

'I'll be there,' he said, sensing the familiar adrenaline rush and accelerated thinking that accompanied a possible surgical emergency. 'Have the CT scan people ready to do his head. Call someone in if there's no one there right now. Two lines in, large bore, cath his bladder, get bloods off including a *stat* alcohol and drugs of abuse panel, type and cross-match for six units and have them be ready to do more. As soon as the bloods are off, give him a jolt of glucose. Don't bother waiting for the sugar result before you do that. Just in case, alert anesthesia and the OR that something may be brewing.'

'Got it.'

'Oh, and, Lydia, if he's as cold as the rescue people say he is, please have the nurses get a warming blanket ready and heat up some Ringer's lactate solution.'

Of all the Tuesdays he had taken call while volunteering at the Hearth, this was the first time he was faced with an emergency that demanded his immediate return to the hospital, ready to race up to the OR. He went back inside, looked over at the kids, and, as he was doing for the emergency at FGH, sorted through a dozen different courses of action at the same time. Finally, knowing there was no

24

other way, he swallowed his pride and frustration, and called Maxine.

Lydia Goldman spotted Will and the twins approaching down the hallway and raced to meet them. A third-year resident, she had never handled emergencies calmly, and Will was pleased to have learned some weeks ago that she had been accepted into a plastic-surgery program in Kansas.

'This is real trouble, Dr. Grant. His core temperature is fifty-two. He's been beaten to a pulp. BP isn't readable. I'm getting set to put in an arterial line.'

'Deep breath,' Will said, 'now slow exhale. Kids, this is Lydia. Lydia, Dan and Jessica. The guy's alive, right?'

'Yes, but –'

'Hold it for a second. Jess and Dan, I'm really sorry about having to cut off the night so early. Mom will meet you over there in the waiting room. I've got to get to work helping Lydia with her patient.'

'Can we watch?' Jess asked.

'Yuck,' Dan said.

'Another time, I promise. I'll see you both on Saturday. I love youse guys.'

'Da-ad.'

'I know, I know.'

Will kissed each of them on the forehead, then followed Lydia into the ER. The unconscious, middle-aged man had been stripped and placed on a large warming pad. Two nurses were adjusting his IV lines and monitoring equipment. He had been beaten badly about the head, face, and chest, with some fresh bruising on his abdomen as well.

'Order some neck films, Lydia, just in case.'

'Oh, my, I'm really sorry I didn't do that.'

The woman, a knowledgeable-enough resident in spite of her lack of cool, flushed at having made an oversight. Will paused to settle her down.

'Lydia, we do this as a team so that together we might think of everything, okay? Self-flagellation does nothing to improve our focus.'

'O-okay. I'll be right back.'

She raced off to get spine X-rays ordered.

'Arterial line,' Will called after her, already examining the patient as he approached the bedside.

No extremity fractures... pupils slightly dilated, not reactive to light

... probable orbital fracture on the right ... chest appears intact, moving air poorly with grunting respirations ...

'Julie,' he called to one of the nurses, 'please call anesthesia down here to put a tube in this man.'

Abdomen somewhat distended, dull to percussion ... fluid? ... blood? ...

Will set his hands on either side of the man's abdominal wall and felt the muscles beneath them tighten. Even comatose there was some reaction from John Doe. Light pressure had caused enough pain to break through his depressed consciousness.

'It's in here,' he said to no one in particular. 'I'd bet the ranch on it. Listen, everyone, as soon as we have cervical spines and a CT scan of his head, we're going up to the OR. Someone alert them. Lydia, you'll assist, so go scrub as soon as you can. Tell them we're going to explore this fellow's abdomen.'

'Do you want antibiotics?' she asked.

Will glanced up at her and pumped his fist just enough for her to see.

'Way to go,' he said. 'Order whatever you think would be best.'

'Julie, two grams of Mefoxin IV, please,' Lydia said.

In minutes, the broad-spectrum antibiotic was in, and the anesthesiologist had placed a breathing tube down John Doe's trachea. Next he inserted a third intravenous line via a 'blind stick' into the internal jugular vein.

'Temp's seventy-two,' a nurse announced. 'BP is still in the twenties.'

Will glanced down at the man's abdomen, which was more distended than even a short while ago.

'Let's get him over to X-ray right now,' he said. 'We're running out of time.'

This was medicine the way it was meant to be, Will thought, vigorously scrubbing his hands with a hexachlorophene-impregnated brush. A patient in big trouble, a surgeon and his team prepared to act. No forms to fill out; no panel to go through.

He wished things with Maxine had worked out differently and that he didn't spend so much of what little free time he had alone. He wished he had the kids more and the money and time for a memorable vacation with them. He longed to spend more time in the gym. But one thing he never wanted to change was the rush of this moment, focusing years of training and experience into the awesome

26

responsibilities of being a surgeon.

Using his knee, he shoved the lever to the right, shutting off the water. Then, hands up, palms facing in, he backed into the OR, accepted a towel from the nurse, and dried his hands. Finally, he slipped into a sterile gown, allowed it to be tied, and thrust his hands into a pair of size 7½ gloves. Time for battle.

John Doe was stretched out on the table, covered with drapes that exposed only his abdomen, swabbed in russet antiseptic. Will could see and feel that the area had become even more distended. Just before he had entered the operating suite, he had received the blood-alcohol report – negative. That result, coupled with the negative head CT, strongly suggested overwhelming infection or massive blood loss into the abdomen as the cause of the profound shock and coma.

'Ready, Ramon?' he asked the anesthesiologist, who peered over the drape separating his work space from Will's and nodded. 'Ready, everyone? Lydia? Okay, number-ten blade, please, Jennifer.'

One by one Will sliced through three of the four layers of John Doe's abdomen.

'Suction ready,' he called out just as the fourth layer, the thin peritoneal membrane, parted beneath his blade. Under pressure, volumes of foul-smelling brown liquid spewed out of the abdominal cavity, a good deal of it overwhelming the suction and flowing down onto the floor. Will stepped back just in time to keep from irreparably soiling his trademark OR footwear – red Converse Chuck Taylor high-top sneakers.

'Whew!' the circulating nurse exclaimed. 'Deodorizer?'

'Why not. And a pile of lap sponges, Jen, and more suction.'

The circulator placed two drops of deodorizer on every person's mask. One by one, Will inspected each organ – large and small bowel, kidneys, pancreas, liver, spleen, stomach, and gallbladder, even though the source of the problem was already quite apparent. Scar tissue from chronic inflammation caused by gallstones had shut off the blood supply to the large intestine, causing a foot-long section of it to become gangrenous and finally to split, spilling feces into John Doe's abdominal cavity. Septic shock was the result.

'Lydia?' he asked. 'Where to from here?'

The resident's eyes were red from the onslaught of the fetid spillage. Will suspected that at least a corner of her brain was imagining life as a plastic surgeon – bowel contents versus Botox. No contest.

'Isolate the diseased intestine, staple it off with a GIA stapler,' she said, 'then control bleeding, irrigate the abdominal cavity clear with warm saline, and then go after the gallbladder first.'

'The artery we need to tie off to get the gallbladder out?'

'Cystic.'

'Excellent. Go ahead and locate it. You sure you want to go into plastics?' Will could tell from her eyes that she was missing the glint in his. 'Don't bother answering that,' he said.

He guided her through the removal of the gallbladder and then did the colon removal and colostomy himself. If by a miracle Mr. Doe survived this ordeal, the colostomy could be reversed some time in the future. With heavy bacterial contamination, it was best to leave the skin incision packed with dressings rather than to suture it closed. The scar would be impressive, but that, too, could be revised down the line. At the moment, it was life versus death, with death holding most of the high cards.

Finally, it was done. A procedure fraught with potentially fatal pitfalls had just been completed quickly and virtually without a hitch, and every person working in OR 3 at that moment felt part of it.

'Great job, Will,' the anesthesiologist called out as he lowered the drape. 'You can take out my gangrenous intestine anytime.'

Several nurses and Lydia echoed the praise.

John Doe still remained teetering on the edge of death and was facing a multitude of potentially lethal complications if he managed to survive the hours immediately post-op. But Will felt exhilarated. The hundreds of decisions he had dealt with, instinctively or after deliberation, were holding up.

He helped transfer the man to a recovery-room bed and watched approvingly as the nurses reconnected the myriad of fluid and monitoring lines.

Maxine, the exhausting hours at work, the alimony and support payments, the periods of loneliness, the truncated time with the twins, the pressures from managed care – as long as practicing medicine could deliver as it had tonight, he would somehow find the strength to deal with the rest.

Chapter 3

At five in the morning Serenity Lane was dark and still. Posed in front of the vast picture window over the kitchen counter, Cyrill Davenport carefully fork-split a Thomas's English muffin and set the toaster oven for precisely two-point-five. Davenport was nothing if not precise – obsessive, he knew some at the company called him, but he didn't care. He was the president and chairman of the board of the Unity Comprehensive Health HMO, and they weren't. He could see little through the darkness beyond the window but had no trouble envisioning his yard – nearly two rolling acres of grass, gardens, walkways, majestic boulders, and ten varieties of mature trees. Not bad for someone who had to wheedle a scholarship just to attend a small state school. Now the student center at that school bore his name – his and Gloria's.

It had been a mistake to include her name on the building, he thought now. He unwrapped a soft pat of custom-prepared butter, sliced it precisely in two, and spread each piece in concentric circles beginning at the center of the muffin halves. If he had donated a detox to the school, Gloria's name should definitely have been on it – but otherwise, most resoundingly not. The Cyrill Davenport Student Center – that's how it should have been. He poured eight ounces of the chilled orange juice he had squeezed the previous evening into a Waterford goblet and sipped it down as he finished the muffin. No matter, he acknowledged. Gloria gave great parties, kept a magnificent house, and handled the help impeccably. So what if she was too sloshed most of the time to be much of a wife?

Davenport pulled on his overcoat and set his dishes in the sink. This day was to be a most significant one for Unity Comprehensive Health. Depson-Hayes, one of the largest electronics-manufacturing corporations in the Northeast, was on the verge of shifting its total coverage package to Unity. By mid-morning, the announcement would be made, and the seven different HMOs that had been covering the D-H employees – including several who had been pressuring Unity to join in their merger – would be shit out of luck.

It had taken statistics and promises – a boatload of each – to convince the health people at D-H that care would not suffer despite a striking reduction in the premiums they and their employees would have to pay. Now it would be up to Davenport's lieutenants to see to it that Unity's hospitals and physicians made good on those promises. Davenport knew he was asking the impossible, but this was one instance, like horseshoes and hand grenades, where close would be good enough. There could be problems and complaints from the D-H policyholders, even serious ones – just not too many of them. Fortunately, although he would never broadcast the fact, both the state and federal governments had taken significant steps backward when it came to holding HMOs responsible for medical catastrophes incurred by their insured. Clearly, the powers that be understood that the HMOs and other health insurers were merely trying to make the system work by keeping costs in line. If the physicians and hospitals in the old fee-for-service system hadn't lost sight of that goal, fee-for-service would still be the standard of care in the land.

Davenport flicked off the kitchen and hall lights and slipped out the door into the garage. As he was shutting the door behind him, he swore he heard Gloria's prizewinning snoring emanating from the master suite, upstairs and at the far end of the house.

The broad garage door was closed, and Gloria's neat little white BMW roadster was in its customary spot, but his Cadillac Seville was missing. Suddenly nonplussed and anxious, Davenport hit the button on the wall beside him. As the automatic door glided upward, he sighed with relief. The silver Caddy, an absolute joy from the day six months ago when he decided to make the switch from his Lincoln, was parked a dozen or so yards down the drive, right by the walk to the front door.

Curious.

Davenport distinctly remembered driving into the garage last night when he returned from work, and also closing the electronic door behind him. Only Gloria, their garage-door service company, and their attorney knew the keypad password. Not even their grounds-keeper, Julio, had it.

Davenport glanced at his Rolex. Almost five-thirty. He had a mountain of work to get done before the others arrived and this most significant of days got under way. It had to have been Gloria, he decided as he stepped out onto the drive and shut the garage door behind him. She obviously ran out of booze late last night and in a moment of clarity decided to take the heavier, safer car to get restocked. Davenport grimaced at the image of her fumbling with the keypad in the Caddy, then finally giving up, leaving the car where it was and entering the house up the front walk instead. The notion of her driving sloshed, which she was even before he went to sleep, produced a knot in his throat. Gloria was capable of doing damage that not even their ten-million-dollar umbrella liability policy could cover. He wondered how the neighbors would feel having some homeless, crippled accident victim take over Sycamore Hill.

With images of another trip to rehab suddenly occupying his mind, Davenport slipped the key into the ignition and turned it. The Caddy purred to life. He put the car in reverse, checked over his right shoulder, and gently depressed the accelerator. The journey to Unity Comprehensive Health lasted just four feet. Cyrill Davenport heard the explosion a nanosecond before he and the Cadillac were blown to bits. All twenty-three windows on the south side of 3 Serenity Lane shattered.

In the second-floor master suite, Gloria Davenport, her blood-alcohol level still three times legally intoxicated, opened her eyes a slit and tried to make sense of the noise she had just heard and the chilly air she was feeling. Then she pulled the covers over her head and sank back to sleep.

Chapter 4

The jangling phone slammed into Patty's dream like a wrecking ball, shattering a scene in which she was flying, arms outstretched, over the houses and buildings of Pittsfield, her hometown. In the dream, a recurring one since childhood, she would put her head down, sprint ahead, and leap, only to fall heavily to the ground. Again and again she would repeat the maneuver until at last, after numerous tumbles and bruises, she would hover just a bit before the painful fall. Finally, after increasing periods just above the ground, pulling through the air like a frog through water, she would suddenly gain altitude and fly. It was a glorious experience when she made it to the clouds, but thanks to the disrupted, bizarre sleep patterns associated with her job, the occasions when her soaring reached such an altitude were few and far between.

''lo?'

'Patty Moriarity?'

'Yes?'

The LED on her bedside clock read 6:00, not that early, but she had been riveted to the computer screen in her office until nearly two, researching serial killers.

'Sorry to have woken you.'

'No, no, I was just getting up.'

The woman chuckled.

'I always say that, too. Patty, it's Kristine Zurowski from the academy. Remember me?'

'Of course.' Patty instantly conjured up the image of a pleasant, dark-haired woman, who, like herself, was in her early thirties. The similarities between the two of them hardly ended there. Kristine was also intelligent, extremely intense, and as committed as Patty to making it to detective in the state police. The two of them each finished close to the top of their class, and, within a shorter time than any of the other graduates, Patty had made detective. Not long after that, she heard that Kristine had, too. 'Everything all right with you?'

'I'm absolutely exhausted all the time,' Kristine said, 'if that's what you mean by "all right." My husband has a photo of me pinned to the pillow so he can remember what I look like.'

'Believe me, if I had a husband, he'd have a photo pinned up, too. It's like be careful what you wish for. So, what's up?'

'You know I'm attached to the Norfolk barracks.'

Norfolk County was south of Middlesex, Patty's unit.

'I had heard that, yes.'

'Well, I'm calling you from a crime scene in Dover. A man named Cyrill Davenport was in his Cadillac when it blew up in the driveway of his mansion. The bomb squad says someone wired his car. He is – *was* – the CEO of Unity Comprehensive Health.'

Patty sucked in a jet of air. Davenport would be the third managed-care executive in the area to be murdered in the last eight weeks. The first, Ben Morales, was shot – *executed* would be a more appropriate word – outside his home in Lexington. One bullet, mid-forehead, fired by a .357 of some sort. No witnesses. Patty was the investigating officer initially assigned to head the investigation. It was her third murder case, but the first in which the killer wasn't immediately known.

The second managed-care executive, Marcia Rising, had been gunned down in the secured parking lot of her guarded HMO office building, also in Middlesex County – this time with a nine-millimeter. Once again there were no witnesses. The similarities between the two deaths brought greatly increased interest and concern all the way up the state police chain of command, from Patty's immediate boss, Detective Lieutenant Jack Court, through the detective captain, the major, and finally to Colonel Cal Carver, and Carver's right-hand man, Lieutenant Colonel Tommy Moriarity, Patty's father.

Immediately following the Rising murder, with Tommy Moriarity's tacit blessing, Wayne Brasco, a long-time detective and close *compadre* of Lieutenant Court in the Good Ol' Boy Club, was assigned to take over for Patty and oversee the investigation. Patty would continue to work with him, but Brasco, in every sense of the term, would be The Man. While Patty was displeased with what she saw as an undeserved demotion, she was even more pained by the selection of Brasco, for whom she had no respect as a cop and whom she had already warned more than once to stop calling her Sweet-cakes, Babe, and the like.

The phone tucked between her chin and shoulder, Patty was already out of bed snatching clothes from her bureau and closet.

'Kristine, it's great of you to call me so quickly. I'll get in touch with Wayne Brasco, my partner on this one, and we'll be out there in just a little while. I guess you know this case is number three.'

'I do, but don't bother calling Brasco.'

'Why not?'

'Because he's already here. Apparently someone from Norfolk called him, because he's been here almost from the beginning, glad-handing the guys like this was some sort of frat party and ignoring every part of me except for my breasts. A couple of minutes ago, he jokingly let slip that you were also on the Middlesex cases with him – something about your being assigned to work with him as a favor to your father.'

'That's absurd.'

'You don't have to tell me. I was with you at the academy.'

'Thanks. I'm really upset that Brasco didn't call me.'

'The man's a cartoon. I don't know how you put up with him. He's like something from the fifties.'

In a tribute to her flexibility and fitness, Patty had brushed out her hair (cut short since a druggie seized a fistful of the longer version during an arrest), pulled on underwear, socks, a pair of slacks, and a dark blouse, buttoned it up and tucked it in all without dislodging the phone.

'Tell me something,' she asked as she slid on her belt, tightened it, and finished things off with a navy blue sweater vest. 'Have you guys found an envelope yet?'

'Not that I know of, but mostly it's been the lab people so far. We'll get our shot in a little while.'

'I'll be out as soon as I can.'

'Great.'

'And, Kristine, thanks again.'

'I just hope I'm nearby to see Brasco's face when you show up.'

'You may have to pull my fist out of it first.'

'Now, *that* would be my pleasure.'

Lost in thoughts of the managed-care murders and the disdain of Wayne Brasco, Patty was half a block past Serenity Lane before she realized she had missed the turn. No surprise. Driving was an instant hypnotic for her, and after just a few minutes on the road she was invariably lost in something – classical or country music or, more often, a case. She swung her three-year-old Camaro, a rally-red Z28, into a tight U, then paused by the curb to compose herself and take in a few more seconds of Beethoven's Sixth.

Breathe in ... breathe out.

The exercise failed to lessen the stabbing pain caused by her nails digging into her palms. There was nothing to be gained by making a scene here with Brasco, she cautioned herself. Some kind of response to his snub was most definitely called for, but timing was everything. She just had to watch for the right moment and seize it.

A young uniformed policeman, stationed halfway down Serenity Lane, checked Patty's ID, told her she was driving a really neat car, then motioned her past. The crime scene, cordoned off by yellow police tape and several sawhorses, was dramatic. Two fire engines, half a dozen cruisers, vans from the bomb squad and forensics, and an ambulance were still parked on the street. Beyond them, a dozen or so people – local cops, detectives, and crime-scene investigators – watched and waited as the laboratory people finished their work. Well off to Patty's right, Kristine Zurowski and another officer were ascending the front walk to a Greek-revival-style mansion that Patty found repugnantly ostentatious. Ahead of her was a more tasteful but no less vast colonial with all of the windows shattered. The pungent smells of explosive and fuel still permeated the air.

Welcome to the Davenports'.

Patty flashed her shield at one more inquiring officer, then ducked beneath the yellow tape. The front yard was illuminated by hazy morning light plus a series of spots. In addition to the burned and twisted metal of Cyrill Davenport's car, Patty could make out significant segments of the man himself, including an elbow and nearly intact head. She stared skyward for half a minute before she was composed and ready to make her way across to Detective Lieutenant Wayne Brasco.

Brasco, a thick, stubby, unlit cigar clenched in his teeth, was chatting with two other men, still waiting for the green light to begin their work. He was a bull-necked specimen with a slightly simian face, a perpetual five-o'clock shadow, and hairy, tattooed forearms. A fog of cologne and cigar invariably hung around him, occasionally augmented by beer. While there were those who, out of earshot, derided Brasco's intelligence, Patty knew better than to under-estimate his street smarts or his shrewdness. He wore a wedding ring and as far as she knew had a wife, but that didn't stop him from boasting of the 'deals' he had made with the 'chicks' he had arrested.

A shadow of surprise crossed Brasco's face as she approached, dispelled almost immediately by a broad grin.

'Hey, if it isn't my gal Friday. Guys, meet the legendary Patty Moriarity, Tommy's kid.'

Patty shook hands with the men from Norfolk, Corbin and Brown, both of whom seemed at first glance to be more enlightened than her partner.

'Thanks for calling me, Wayne,' she said.

He shrugged matter-of-factly and said, 'I was going to.'

'Bomb squad say anything yet?'

'Nope, but what can they say? The dude was blown to smithereens, and it wasn't an accident. Ba-da-bing, ba-da-boom. Case closed.'

Brasco laughed at his own attempt at flip humor. Patty was pleased when neither of the other two officers joined in.

'Well, for those of us not as knowledgeable about explosives as you are,' she said acidly, 'there may be one or two things we can learn.'

Had Brasco ever bothered to spend time talking with her, or even looking through her file, he might have learned that through taking several courses, Patty was making herself something of an expert on ordnance and explosives.

'Well, that's one of them coming over here right now,' Brasco replied, an irritated edge appearing in his voice. 'You can ask your-self.'

A baby-faced officer who could easily have passed for Opie on *The Andy Griffith Show* approached the quartet and was introduced to Patty by Corbin as Chipper Dawes.

'Well, we're all done,' Dawes said.

'Thanks,' the Norfolk detective replied. 'You'll get us a report as soon as possible?'

'No problem.'

'So what do you think?' Patty asked. 'Semtex?'

Dawes looked at her with surprise and undisguised respect.

'As a matter of fact, yes,' he said. 'We're fairly certain of that. Probably wrapped around the drive shaft, just behind the transmission.'

'So what's this Semtex all about?' Brown asked, angling his rotund body, purposefully or not, so that Brasco actually had to step to his left and forward to insert himself back in the ring of conversation.

'The terrorist's friend, we call it,' Dawes explained. 'Plastique. Similar to C-4. It can be molded into almost any shape and worked into almost any space. Forty pounds or less flattened the American embassy in Kenya.'

Patty sensed Brasco's discomfort and bore in.

'The IRA is supposed to have more than three tons of the stuff. With a little knowledge, it's a cinch to make. Have you found the detonator?'

'No. I'm going to stick around for a while longer to look, but I have my doubts we will.'

'So,' Patty continued, now on a roll, 'if the Semtex was wrapped around the drive shaft, the detonator was possibly some sort of centrifugal fuse that went off when it reached enough RPMs.'

'You're exactly right, Sergeant,' Dawes said. 'Two weights come together and form a contact that sends a small electrical impulse to the blasting cap, and ka-boom. There are other ways the Semtex could have been detonated, but this is what we think at the moment.'

Lost in thought, Patty toed the ground and glanced down. A charred lump – probably a portion of a leg with bone protruding out – lay on the lawn just a few feet away. At that instant, two lab people scurried over, labeled it, marked the location on a chart, and dropped it into a large plastic evidence Baggie.

'Chipper,' she asked, 'do you think this could possibly have been the work of an amateur – someone who's just angry at managed-care executives because of something a managed-care company did that hurt them or maybe killed a loved one?'

'Not really,' Dawes replied. 'Whoever did this knew what they were doing. It may not look it, but blowing up a car in a driveway without substantially damaging the house twenty feet away is not easy.'

'This woman's a keeper,' Corbin said. He was an imposingly tall and muscular black man with dark, intelligent eyes, and Patty wondered what life would have been like had someone like him been assigned to her case. 'You'd best stick pretty close to her, Wayne. She'll make you look smart.'

Brasco merely shrugged. His eyes were flint. Even in the dim light Patty could see him flush. She felt like a guerrilla, making quick, annoying strikes at the enemy. *Next time maybe you'll call me.*

'There's more evidence this guy was a pro,' Brown added. 'I interviewed Davenport's wife. She didn't see or hear anything before the explosion, but she also admits to having had a good deal to drink last night – and from the looks of her, I would bet most nights before that. However, she insists that her husband's Cadillac was in the garage and the electronic door was closed. That means someone had to get the door open without disturbing anyone, then get through the security system of the car and get it out onto the driveway, then set the explosive.'

'So maybe whoever wanted revenge hired a pro,' Dawes ventured, excited to be one of the gang of detectives.

'Or maybe he was a pro to begin with,' Patty tried, testing the notion out on herself as much as the others. 'You know, some HMO doctor or managed-care company just happened to do something to upset the wrong person – a professional killer.' She surveyed the scene again, then thanked Dawes and turned to the Norfolk men, pointedly ignoring Brasco, who looked something like the loser in a round of musical chairs. 'Lieutenant Corbin,' she said, 'we need to get inside the garage.'

'The three of us were already there briefly before you arrived. As soon as the crime-scene people are done, we'll be opening the door.'

'We can wait if you insist, but I'd rather not. Lieutenant, as you know, this is the third death in what is almost certainly the work of a serial killer.'

'Yes, I'm well aware of that.'

'Well, did Wayne tell you about the letters?'

'The what?'

One glance at Brasco told Patty she had struck another nerve. If the killer had once again left alphabet letters about, as he had in the first two cases, Brasco clearly wanted to be the one to discover them. Immediately, he inserted himself between her and the Norfolk detectives.

'Yes, Patty, thanks for bringing it up,' he said confidently, clearing the insincerity from his throat. 'I was waiting to get clearance from Lieutenant Court to tell you two about the letters when Patty arrived. He hasn't called back yet, but I assume Jack won't have any problem with sharing the information with you.'

'That'd be nice of him,' Corbin said, with thinly disguised sarcasm.

'We've kept this information internal in case we needed it,' Brasco went on.

'We understand.'

'Well, in each of the other cases, the killer has left a calling card – two, in fact. Each of the first two victims had an envelope alongside them. The first one contained the letters *E* and *R*, and the second one the letters *R* and *T*. Both envelopes and all the letters were clean. Obviously, the killer couldn't put an envelope in the car he was about to blow up, so I strongly suspect something is in the garage.'

You wouldn't suspect your knees were bare if you had forgotten your pants, Patty thought savagely.

'What about the garage?'

The man behind the query, tall and straight, looking as distinguished as any diplomat, wore the full uniform of a lieutenant colonel, complete with a multitiered rainbow of decorations above his left breast. At the sight of him, Brasco stiffened. Corbin extended his hand.

'Colonel,' he said.

'Roosevelt,' Tommy Moriarity replied. 'Good to see you again. It's been a while since that forensics conference in Boston.'

Corbin introduced Brown to the second in command of the state police force.

Patty hesitated, gauging the situation to determine the greeting the man would like from her. Finally, she reached out and took his hand in both of hers.

'Hi, Colonel,' she said. 'I'm glad to see you.'

At six-three, Moriarity was nearly a head taller than his daughter. For the briefest moment it looked to Patty as if he was going to bend down to embrace her, or kiss her on the cheek. Then he simply smiled the creased, weathered smile she loved so much, and returned the greeting.

'You know Wayne Brasco?' she asked.

'Of course. Your wife and family okay?'

'Yes, sir.'

'Margo, isn't it?'

Patty knew her father might have only met Brasco's wife once, possibly years ago. She wasn't the least surprised that he remembered her – he remembered everyone.

'Yes, sir, Margo. She's doing great.'

'So?'

Although the question was directed more or less to the group, Brasco was not about to pass up the opportunity to impress the colonel.

'So, it's another managed-care executive,' he said. 'The other two looked like professional hits. So does this one. Probably Semtex, we're guessing. I just told Corbin and Brown here about the alphabet letters we found with the other two victims. It's my guess there must be letters in the garage.'

Patty stifled a groan.

'Roosevelt,' Moriarity said, 'do you think you could check with the crime-scene people and get us permission to take a look in there?'

'No problem.'

Moments later, the detective returned and indicated that so long as they were careful, they could enter the garage through the kitchen of the house. Just leave the garage door alone until someone could determine how it might have been opened and closed by the killer without the electronic code and without anyone knowing. Stepping around and between grisly remnants of Cyrill Davenport, they entered the house through the front door.

Using a handkerchief, Patty gently opened the door from the rear hallway to the garage. Then she extracted a slim, powerful flashlight from her purse, located the light switch, and flicked it on with a pen.

It took just three minutes of searching before Tommy Moriarity said, 'Well, Lieutenant, it looks as if you are absolutely right.'

He indicated a heavy metal rake, tines propped up against the back wall. Impaled on the tine at each end of the row was a three-inch white square that looked as if it was cut from a file card. Meticulously, artistically printed on one card was the block letter *B*, and on the other, an *E*. Careful to touch nothing, the four of them peered at the finding as Patty further illuminated it with her light.

'*E, R, R, T, B, E,*' she said softly.

'Heartbeat?' Corbin offered.

'Possible,' Patty replied. 'Maybe it's parts of several words in a quote.'

They searched the garage for another five minutes, but found nothing unusual or out of place. Back outside on the driveway, Moriarity encouraged Corbin and Brasco to keep him informed and to contact him if there was anything he could help them with, including passage around any bureaucratic roadblocks to their investigation. Then he motioned Patty to a spot on the lawn where the two of them could talk unheard.

'You okay?' he asked.

'Good enough. You?'

With friends, Patty often referred to herself as *the son my father wishes he had had.* Her wonderful older brother, Tom, a wilderness guide and expert fly-fisherman, was often unemployed but always busy advocating for various environmental causes. He was also openly gay and exceedingly happy – except for those infrequent times he spent with their father.

'Soon,' Patty's brother would say every time he ventured east from Oregon. 'Soon the guy's going to figure it all out. What a force he'll be then.'

Moriarity scuffed at the ground with the toe of his spit-polished shoe.

'I'm doing all right. I miss your mother, that's for sure.'

It had been two years since Ruth Moriarity lost a heroic battle with ovarian cancer – two years during which Tommy seemed to have aged a dozen.

'Yeah,' Patty said, risking a squeeze of her colonel's hand. 'I miss her, too.'

Moriarity seemed to sag for a moment, then just as quickly pulled himself up ramrod straight.

'So, how are you doing on these cases?' he asked.

Patty shook her head.

'We're working like hell on them, but nothing so far. My bet is it's either a disillusioned, disgruntled physician or the relative of someone who died because of managed-care negligence. Our hope is that sometime soon the killer will feel the need to get his message across to the public more stridently, and move closer and closer to being out in the open. Then maybe we can get a hook into him.'

'You still upset about Brasco taking your place in charge of this case?'

'Nope. I'm fine, Dad.'

'Good. I'm glad you understand why the change was made. Brasco's been around a good while. I imagine you'll learn a lot from him.'

'I've learned a lot already.'

'I heard he's got a cryptographer and a psychologist on the case.'

'That he does.'

Patty narrowly avoided choking on the words. Even before the murder of Marcia Rising, she was concerned that the letters found beside Ben Morales's body might be the start of something and had both the code-breaker and profiler at work. In one of his first acts after taking over as head of the investigations, Brasco had sent out a memo to all the higher-ups summing up the department's efforts to date on the two managed-care killings. In it, he unabashedly took full credit for bringing both specialists on board.

If Tommy Moriarity picked up on the venom in his daughter's voice, he hid it well.

'So,' he said, 'you're still happy you became a cop?'

Tommy's dream for his daughter centered around at least law school, and at most the Presidency. He didn't speak to her for two months after learning she had taken the state police exam without consulting him.

He's the perfect father, she often said to friends, *so long as you do what he wants.* 'I'm very happy being a cop,' she said now.

'I hear good things about you from Lieutenant Court.'

He can't stand me, Dad, or any other woman detective, for that matter. He and his pal Brasco are absolute Neanderthals. If a male version of me had handled this case exactly the same way I had, believe me, he'd still be running it.

'I'm pleased to hear that,' she said.

Tommy shifted uncomfortably. This wasn't going to be the moment he suddenly blurted out how proud he was of her and what she had become, or how sorry he was for not insisting she be left in charge of the managed-care murders. If anything, Patty suspected he was embarrassed at how much pressure had been brought to bear on him to not protest her demotion to Brasco's second fiddle. At some level, she thought, he had to be proud that she had chosen to follow in his footsteps. But then again, maybe not.

'So,' he said, 'we're still on for our dinner a week from Friday?'

Without ever really discussing it, they had gone from eating together twice a week following the death of Ruth Moriarity to every other.

'My place, same time,' Patty said with forced cheer.

'Well ... good luck with this case. Call me if I can be of any help.'

He gave her a wooden hug, turned, and headed off across the lawn, stepping to his left to avoid what looked like a piece of Cyrill Davenport.

Chapter 5

The Boston chapter of the Hippocrates Society had been meeting on the third Thursday of each month since its inception fourteen years ago. Initially, the three founders of the chapter met at the home of one or another of them. Soon, driven by a steady increase in membership, they moved to a conference room at Harvard Medical School. Now, for nearly four years, meetings had been held in the amphitheater of the Massachusetts Medical Society – a spectacular modern structure located in a Waltham office park, featuring a massive four-story glass atrium at the main entrance, which opened onto terraced gardens and a bamboo forest.

The avowed goal of the Hippocrates Society was to recapture the practice of medicine from the capricious and viselike grip of the managed-care industry. Begun originally in San Francisco, the Society now had chapters in Chicago, Philadelphia, New York, and Houston, as well as its most rapidly expanding member, Boston. It was named for the fourth-century BC Greek physician, who was now widely recognized as the father of medicine. Hippocrates held the then-heretical belief that illness had a physical and rational explanation and did not represent possession of the body by evil spirits. He also preached the natural healing properties of rest, a good diet, fresh air, and cleanliness, and wrote the Oath of Medical Ethics taken today at most medical-school graduations.

Will arrived at the medical society with fifteen minutes to spare before the seven P.M. start. He had spent the last hour with John Doe, who had, over the past forty-eight hours, made the transition from near-hopeless physical disaster to medical miracle. Following his remarkable surgery there had been a rocky period during which his coma remained dense, his temperature once reached 106 degrees, and his systolic blood pressure persisted below 80 despite the most vigorous treatment.

To make matters worse, the shock and hypothermia had caused his kidneys to shut down, producing no urine output at all. Will brought in specialists from cardiology, neurology, and nephrology – the kidney experts. He and his residents delicately monitored dozens of body chemicals, working under the dangling sword of non-functioning kidneys, which meant that toxins couldn't be cleared from John Doe's body. In addition, without kidneys, the blood level of administered medications was a challenge to control and could, in fact, have easily become a source of lethal complications.

Hour after hour, the man's life hung by the thinnest of threads. Suddenly, twenty hours after Will had stepped back from the operating table and stripped off his gloves signaling the end of the surgery, a single magnificent drop of urine appeared in John Doe's catheter ... then, a minute later, there was another. Kidney function was returning, and from a treatment standpoint, anything was now possible. Will, the nurses, the residents, and the nephrologist toasted the event in the nurses' lounge with coffee and stale doughnuts.

Just three hours ago, nearly two days after he was left for dead in an alley, the man remarkably and progressively regained consciousness. All at once John Doe had a real name – Jack Langley – and a life. He was a salesman from Des Moines, Iowa, and father of three, and had been incapacitated by sudden, severe abdominal pain. He was down on one knee when he was attacked by three men. Fortunately, it appeared that Langley wasn't conscious for most of the ensuing beating. Now, hardly out of the woods but certainly improving, Langley was filling the nurses in on the details of his life even as they were bringing him up to speed on his close brush with mortality.

Will was pleased to find that most of the medical society amphitheater's 140 state-of-the-art conference seats were occupied. As he stepped into the hall, he was immediately surrounded by colleagues wanting some sort of update on the latest in the managed-care killings. As head of publicity and public relations for the Boston chapter for the past two years, Will had expected to be contacted by the press if not the police, but so far nothing.

An eager OB named Runyon, clearly more interested in what he had to say than in any grisly headlines, captured the conversation.

'So, get this one, Will. Twenty-three-year-old woman develops severe abdominal cramping. It's the holiday weekend, so she gets called by the HMO on-call doc, who phones in a scrip for indigestion.

43

The office is closed for the weekend, so no arrangements are made for follow-up. She is worse by morning and calls again and gets another doc who calls in a different prescription, insinuating that last night's doc doesn't know what in the hell he's doing.'

'Tubal pregnancy,' Will said, anxious to speak with Tom Lemm, the Society president.

Runyon looked crestfallen at having the tag line of his tale preempted.

'Exactly,' he said, speaking to those nearby, as Will had headed off. 'She bled out on the way to an ER – as in *died*. Can you believe it?'

Will spotted Lemm, a family practitioner in his fifties, on the far side of the hall. By the time he reached the man, he had been regaled by a surgeon, whose name he didn't know, with the story of a woman whose HMO told her to wait awhile to have her thyroid biopsy repeated because the evidence of cancer from the first set of seven painful needle biopsies was inconclusive. Three months later, her husband was transferred to another state and assigned coverage with a different HMO. When the woman's cancer suddenly began rapidly growing, the new HMO refused to pay for treatment, claiming it was a preexisting condition.

'Hey, Will,' Lemm called out as he approached, 'this may be our largest gathering yet.'

He motioned to the crowd, and Will noticed as he followed the gesture that his partner, Susan Hollister, had just entered and was casting about for a seat.

Thanks for showing up, Suze. I owe you one.

'I've got a couple of cases, Tom. Do you think they're appropriate given this latest murder?'

'Are they funny?'

'That depends.'

'On what?'

'On whether you mean funny, ha ha, or funny, all of a sudden I can't see out of my right eye.'

'Which are these?'

'A little of both.'

'Well, you're on the agenda. There's more tension than usual from what's going on, but I don't see any reason to withhold an anecdote or two. Tonight it'll be right after we finish discussing the status of the class-action suit. After your report, we'll decide what we're going to do about the big debate against Boyd Halliday next week.'

'What do you mean?'

'I spoke to him an hour ago. He says it would send the wrong message to the public and the killer if he called off the debate.'

The debate, billed as a forum, had been organized by the Wellness Project, a respected independent consumer health-care coalition, and was scheduled for venerable Faneuil Hall in downtown Boston. Halliday, the powerful and dynamic CEO of Excelsius Health, was to be matched up against Jeremy Purcell, a world-renowned surgeon, Harvard professor, philosopher, and former president of the Hippocrates Society. Thanks in large measure to Will's efforts, publicity for the forum, which was titled *Managed Care: Boon or Boondoggle*, had been extensive, and a sellout was anticipated. Of course, the managed-care murders had only heightened interest in the event.

'How does Jeremy feel about it?' Will asked.

'I'm surprised you haven't heard,' Lemm said. 'Jeremy's had a fairly large coronary. He had emergency bypass surgery at White Memorial.'

'And?'

'He's reasonably stable now, but he won't be ready for next week. We have to decide what we're going to do.'

'Halliday's a force,' Will said, in what he knew was something of an understatement.

'He is that. Listen, I've got to get this show on the road. Don't worry about your stories. If people want to laugh they'll laugh. I think one of the big reasons we're getting more members at every meeting is you and your stories.'

'I don't make them up, I just read them.'

'That's the point. They're real.'

'Okay, I'll do my best.'

'Will, you're doing great things for this organization, and don't think we don't appreciate it.'

'Well, garsh, thanks, Mickey,' Will said in his highly tuned Goofy imitation – the only one in his repertoire.

Lemm, a lean six-footer, shambled up to the podium and silenced the crowd with a few taps on the microphone.

'Three nurses die in an accident and are spirited up to the pearly gates,' he began, without any introductory remarks. 'Saint Peter is there and asks each one, "Who are you, and why should you be allowed to walk through these gates?" "I was a nurse in a private doctor's office for forty-five years," the first responds. "I instructed patients on how to take their medicines; I gave out lollipops to the children – sugar-free, of course." "Go right in," Saint Pete says.

'The second nurse walks up. Same question from Saint Pete. "I was a nurse in a hospice," she says, "and for many years I soothed dying people's fears of crossing over to the other side, and made the transition a peaceful and enlightening one." "Please go right in," Pete says again. "Milk and cookies are on the right." The third nurse comes forward. Again, Pete asks about her qualifications for admission. "I did case reviews for a managed-care company," she says. Pete checks his massive golden book. "Ah yes," he says, "I have you right here." He swings open the gate, and as she starts in, he adds, "But we've only got you scheduled for a three-day stay" '

Laughter from the assembled was enthusiastic, even though Will suspected that most had heard the joke before. Lemm was right. These men and women needed to laugh. Their profession, in many cases their dream, was under constant attack, and the AMA, the organization they had counted on to man the battlements, had mounted a feeble defense. The well-oiled machine of the managed-care industry had cut through the various medical specialties like a thresher.

It probably wasn't totally fair to draw the analogy between the way managed care overwhelmed the practice of medicine one specialty at a time (giving concessions to the ophthalmologists at the expense of the GPs, then suddenly regulating the ophthalmologists) and the way Hitler swept through Europe a country at a time, but Will was hardly the first physician to see it that way. There was a remarkable, intensely moving Holocaust memorial near Quincy Market in Boston. At the entrance was a quote from a Lutheran pastor named Martin Niemöller.

**In Germany they came first for the
Communists, and I didn't speak up – because
I wasn't a Communist.
Then they came for the Jews, and I didn't
speak up – because I wasn't a Jew.
Then they came for the trade unionists, and I didn't
speak up – because I wasn't a trade unionist.
Then they came for the Catholics, and I didn't
speak up – because I was a Protestant.
Then they came for me – and by this time
there was no one left to speak up.**

'Let's begin this meeting as we do all our meetings with a reading of the roll – physicians who have notified us they are leaving patient care or retiring from medicine prematurely. Their specific reasons vary, but the themes behind them do not. These physicians can no longer handle the paperwork, frustration, and inconvenience to their patients, if not actual danger, of corporate medicine.'

The reading of the roll, consisting of as many as twenty names each month, was, as always, painful. Along with most of the names was a short statement of the reasons this fifty-one-year-old family practitioner or that forty-eight-year-old obstetrician decided to look elsewhere for the emotionally fulfilling, economically rewarding life that they at one time felt was worth the years of sacrifice, exhaustion, and escalating financial outlay demanded by medical school and residency.

This month, three of the nine names on the roll were well known to Will. One of them had been a clinical instructor of his in med school. *Half of all physicians recently polled*, he was thinking glumly and angrily, *had said that given the chance, they would not do it over...*

After the reading of the roll, Lemm called on the Society's legal committee, which reviewed in detail the status of a class-action suit being brought against several of the largest HMOs by the Hippocrates Society in conjunction with a number of state medical associations and some individual physicians. The case, which had been plodding forward for almost five years but was now gaining some momentum, charged the HMOs with extortion and with violating the federal Racketeer Influenced and Corrupt Organizations Act.

Other legal actions from around the country were also reviewed, including a lawsuit in California accusing the health plans of interfering with physicians' ability to make independent medical decisions. The plans threatened physicians with economic loss, the suit was charging, in an effort to deter them from fulfilling their duty owed their patients and encourage them to place unreasonable and often unsafe restrictions on the level of medical services that might be delivered to their patients.

The legal team's presentation was interrupted a number of times by applause. In the analogies to the Nazi takeover of Europe, the lawyers and physicians of the legal team were the resistance – sniping at the enemy, disrupting them wherever possible. When they had finished their presentation, there was an almost palpable drop in energy throughout the hall.

47

'So,' Lemm announced, perhaps sensing the same thing, 'before we do new business, let's hear from our illustrious publicity and public relations chairman, Will Grant. What do you have for us tonight, Will?'

There was a smattering of applause as Will took over the microphone. He had been painfully shy as a child, and as an adult had never been that comfortable speaking in public. But over time he had managed to convince himself that looking or sounding like a fool wasn't that big a deal. After two years, reporting to the Society each month held no great stress – especially when he had material such as he did tonight.

'Before I present a couple of cases,' he began, 'I want to say that advance ticket sales for our forum with Boyd Halliday of Excelsius Health are brisk, and we already may have sold out Faneuil Hall. When I'm finished, Tom has some announcements to make regarding that event, which is going to be held despite the recent managed-care murders.

'As many of you know, my writing is about as dynamic as a snail derby. Thankfully, our committee has Randy Harrington, who continues regularly to submit wonderful letters to the editor and op-ed pieces to both papers as well as some suburban publications. This past month two of them have been published, one in the *Globe*. I hope you've had the chance to read them. If not, they are on our web site. Randy, could you take a bow?'

Harrington, a slightly built pediatrician with a pediatrician's penchant for colorful bow ties, did as he was asked.

'Will Grant is a much better writer than he would have any of us believe,' Harrington said after the applause had quieted, 'especially for a surgeon.'

'Roughly translated,' Will replied, 'that means I know several words with more than one syllable and own at least five books that don't require crayons.'

Tom Lemm laughed loudest of all.

'So,' Will went on, 'as you know, your crack publicity and public relations committee members are constantly casting about for stories we might submit to the papers or at least present to you all. Tonight I have two of them in which our friendly neighborhood HMOs combine medicine and mathematics to give the best possible care to their constituents.

'A Newton psychiatrist writes: *I admitted a twelve-year-old boy from orthopedics to our inpatient adolescent unit. He had bilateral*

48

ankle fractures sustained after jumping off the peak of the roof of his family's garage. It was no challenge to diagnose the boy with major depressive illness and to conclude that his leap was a bonafide suicide attempt. I contacted the medical director of his HMO and requested a two-week hospitalization to do intensive family work in an attempt to provide him with a safer home environment, to initiate antidepressant medication, and to monitor his pain meds since one fracture needed to be repaired with an open reduction. I presented the case, including the mental-status exam, which was positive for a profoundly depressed mood, constricted affect, suicidal ideation, substance abuse, feelings of hopelessness and worthlessness, and sleep and appetite disturbances.

'Now, tell me again, the HMO medical gatekeeper asked, how high was the building he jumped off?

'What has that got to do with anything? This kid is hell-bent on killing himself. He needs at least fourteen days in the hospital.

'I'll ask you again – how high was the garage?

'Two stories, I said. What difference does it make?

'If it really was two stories, he said, I'll give you two days of initial authorization.

'Two days?!! So if it was three stories I'd get three days?

'Two days is what I can give you. You can call back after that and request approval for more, but I can't guarantee you'll get them.

'If this were your son, I'm sure your response would be different, I said. But, then again, he'd probably be dead by now, you Janus-faced bastard.

'The gatekeeper hung up on me. Eventually I got a total of six days for the kid. In the lobby the day he was discharged, I heard his father call him a little jerk. The next day I submitted my resignation from the hospital and started looking for a nonclinical job. Thank you, managed care.'

The ending, tragic though it was, brought sustained applause. The members' exuberance was born purely of frustration. Every one of them had encountered similar, logic-defying bureaucratic stone-walling of the way they wished to practice medicine.

'You had to have made this up,' someone cried out.

Will shook his head.

'I don't have that kind of imagination,' he said. 'These are real stories from real people. Okay, one more math-and-medicine case, this one a quickie from a surgeon in Worcester. Patient comes to see her with bleeding, horribly painful hemorrhoids. The guy's done everything his family doc asked him to – soaks, suppositories, stool softeners, rubber donut. Finally, sleepless, in constant pain, bleeding through a pad, and unable to sit at work, he comes in for surgery. The surgeon dutifully calls for the HMO's preapproval and is stunned to have the young voice on the phone ask how large the hemorrhoids are. Clearly the lad is parroting questions off a computer screen, the surgeon writes. What difference does it make how large or small they are, she asks, THEY'RE KILLING HIM!!! Just say you'll pay for this man's care and let me fix him up. Ma'am, I'm afraid I can't do that, the kid says. I need to know the size of the hemorrhoids before I can approve payment for the surgery. Okay, okay, okay, says the surgeon – on the faculty at the medical school, incidentally – the guy's hemorrhoids are roughly the size of Nebraska. The lad making medical decisions for his HMO over the phone thinks for a few seconds, fills in the blank on his screen, then approves the procedure.'

The laughter this time was heartfelt, but also a bit edgy. Having medicine practiced over the telephone by HMO MDs or, even worse, non-MDs was a constant sore point for most of the Hippocrates Society members.

'That's it until next month,' Will said. 'Back to you, Tom.'

Lemm returned to the podium and silenced those who were still buzzing over Will's cases.

'One last piece of business,' he said. 'As many of you know, Jeremy Purcell, who was to champion our cause at next week's forum, has had emergency bypass surgery. He's reasonably stable at White Memorial but has been absolutely forbidden to participate in the debate. We can't back out of the deal, so we need to select someone who can face up to Boyd Halliday. Jeremy has promised to make his notes and slides available and to spend time coaching whomever we choose. As a last resort, I will do this, but you all know as well as I do that I am a plodder – a behind-the-scene type of guy. I'll help, and even sit beside our champion, but we really need someone with more panache than I have, someone with just the right balance of intellect, passion, and humor.'

Will, focused approvingly on Lemm's words more than on the man himself, suddenly realized that the Society's president was staring directly over at him. Before he could react, an internist from Springfield had waved his hand and shouted out, 'I nominate Will Grant!'

'Second!' a dozen voices rang out.

'Third!' someone yelled.

'Fourth!'

Lemm waved the members to quiet down.

'Will,' he said earnestly, 'I know you must be feeling like you've been set up. Well, I am here to assure you that you have.' Laughter. 'Calm down! Hush up, please, all of you. I'm sorry, Will. I apologize for making light of this. And seriously, it was Jeremy who suggested you as his replacement just yesterday, and the executive committee agreed. I know there's not much time for preparation, but we will help you in any way we can, and if you want me, I'll be right up there on the stage beside you as your aide-de-camp.'

There was absolute silence throughout the auditorium.

Will sighed. He knew he desperately did not want to publicly debate the flamboyant president of Excelsius Health. He also knew that he couldn't say no to the Society.

'I've been humiliated and utterly degraded before,' he said without leaving his seat. 'I suppose that means I'm well prepared for an encounter with Boyd Halliday.'

'Will ... Will ... Will ... Will,' someone began chanting, as if they were ringside at a prizefight. One hundred and forty joined in.

'Will ... Will ... Will ... Will.'

'There being no further business,' Lemm shouted out over the din, 'I'll see you all at Faneuil Hall. Nice job, all. Meeting adjourned.'

Of all the dumb things, Will thought, as he drove out through the largely deserted parking lot. *You are no more equipped to match up with Boyd Halliday than you are to bat against Pedro Martinez.* He pulled off to the side of the road, set his palm pilot on the wheel, and called up Tom Lemm's cell phone number. Lemm would just have to do it. Before he could dial, his own cell began ringing.

'Dr. Grant?' a woman's voice asked.

'Yes.'

'This is Ellie Newell. I work in the comptroller's office at the hospital. Mr. Davidson is my boss. I called him about this, and he called Mr. Brodsky. Apparently, Mr. Brodsky told him you would want to hear what's just happened.'

Seth Brodsky was the longtime CFO of Fredrickston General.

'What's this about?' Will asked.

'It's about your patient, John Doe, in the ICU.'

'He's not John Doe anymore. He just woke up and told us his name. It's Langley, Jack Langley from Des Moines, Iowa.'

'Yes, I know,' Ellie said. 'I just spoke to his wife.'

'You did?' Will had called Marybeth Langley just a few hours before.

'I also spoke with an officer at Midwest Industrial Care, the HMO that covers the Langley family.'

'And?'

'Dr. Grant, correct me if I'm wrong, but it seems Mr. Langley is still facing a long hospitalization.'

'If there are no serious setbacks, he is. The man was essentially dead when he was brought in. It's a miracle he's alive at all. I would guess ten more days. Maybe even two weeks.'

'His bill already – counting, among other factors, the cost of the ER, the OR, the surgical team, the recovery room, the ICU, and a number of consultants – is in excess of forty-five thousand dollars.'

'I'm not surprised.'

'Well, Midwest Industrial has flatly refused to pay anything and will not pay for any subsequent care.'

'That's ridiculous. What reason did they give?'

Ellie Newell hesitated.

'Well,' she said, 'the insurance company has a strict policy regarding all surgery. No coverage unless the procedure is preapproved by them or approved within twenty-four hours.'

'But the man was in a coma!'

'I know.'

'How can they do this?'

'Mr. Davidson told me that you of all doctors wouldn't even bother asking that question – that you'd already know the answer.'

Will felt himself deflate.

'You know, Mr. Davidson is absolutely right,' he said. 'He's absolutely right. Thanks for calling me.'

Will ended the call, then called Tom Lemm.

'Tom, it's Will.'

'Hey, I hope you're not upset with me for the way I railroaded you back there. Desperate situations call for desperate measures.'

'No problem,' Will replied. 'I was just calling to see if we could get together tomorrow. We've got a lot to do before next week.'

Chapter 6

Marybeth Langley was a petite, energetic woman with a sweet face and manner. For the week since Will's call, she had been spending nights in a small B&B in downtown Fredrickston and days at the bedside of her husband, Jack. Despite the persistent refusal of their HMO to pay for any of Jack's surgery, consultations, or hospitalization, she and her husband had decided to remain at FGH and under Will's care until it was medically appropriate for him to return to Iowa. Finally, that time had arrived.

It was mid-afternoon on a chilly, gray Thursday, the day of the Faneuil Hall managed-care forum. Will had repaired an electrician's painful hernia in the morning, then worked his way through a reduced office schedule. He wanted to leave at least an hour for a final review of the mass of notes and articles he had accumulated regarding the shortcomings of managed care – especially Jeremy Purcell's insights and strategies. Throughout college and medical school, Will never took an exam that he felt truly ready for, but never had he felt as ill-prepared for anything as he did for this debate. Saying yes to Tom Lemm and the Hippocrates Society was certainly noble enough, but it was evolving into one of the dumbest, most impetuous things he had ever done. He reminded himself for the hundredth time that he could only do what he could do, and then turned his attention to discharging his prize patient. The titanic struggle the two of them had endured together had forged a friendship that went well beyond the usual doctor–patient relationship.

'So, Jack,' Will said, 'it looks like this is it.'

'Looks like.'

Langley had proven to be a bright, well-read man – a laconic Midwesterner with a subtle sense of humor, who listened to country-western music almost around the clock and loved his job selling heavy machinery, although his life's dream had once been to become a veterinarian. The pictures of and by Langley's kids had been taken down and packed. Nurse's discharge instructions had been checked over by Will, then given. Langley, dressed in chinos and a loose-

53

fitting Kansas City Royals sweatshirt, was seated in a wheelchair, the required mode of transportation for discharge.

For nearly a minute, nothing was spoken. Will, distracted momentarily from the impending forum, was trying to remember when he had ever felt so good about a case. Jack Langley was alternating between projecting what it would be like to hold his kids again and wondering when he would be able to return to work.

Marybeth, deeply religious, was processing her overwhelming gratitude for the droll, soft-spoken, surprisingly unassuming man who had saved her husband's life, and thanking God that there were men and women in the world who could do what he had done for their family. She knew very little of him except that he was divorced and had two children, and that her husband, in his understated Midwestern way, absolutely adored him. Silently, she prayed that life was treating him well. Earlier in the day Will had quite casually mentioned that he had arranged for himself and all of the consultants to rub their charges off the massive balance sheet she and Jack were facing. She took a wad of tissues from her purse and dabbed at the corners of her eyes.

'So,' Will said finally, 'you'll keep in touch?'

'Of course.'

'And you'll have your doctor call me straight off if there are any problems?'

'I don't expect there'll be any – not any medical ones, anyway.'

Will sensed a fullness building in his throat. He had never had that much reserve about crying in public, but this just wasn't a time he wanted to.

'I heard some interesting news last night,' Marybeth said, as if sensing Will's predicament. 'I was talking to my cousin Peggy. She lives in a suburb of Des Moines. She was telling her friend Claire about what was happening to us with the HMO refusing to pay and all. Well, it turns out Claire used to work as a claims adjuster for that same HMO. She says that she and the others who worked her job were instructed by the company to reject one out of every ten claims out of hand. Don't even bother to come up with a reason, just reject it. It seems the company had tried this approach to saving money and found that only thirty percent of the rejected claims were ever contested by the doctors. They just didn't have the time or resources to battle over such things.'

'Lord. I'd like to say I'm surprised and stunned, but I'm not. In many instances, the cost involved in disputing an HMO decision makes it not worth it. I'll make sure our hospital isn't one of the seventy percent in this case, but I hope you're planning on fighting this, too.'

'My cousin Pam's husband is a big-time attorney in Des Moines,' Marybeth said, 'as well as being one of the most obnoxious people on the planet. I've already spoken to him. He says he specializes in making people wish they had never crossed paths with him.'

'That's quite a specialty. Well, Jack,' he said, taking the man's hand in his, 'you've been one hell of a patient. I don't throw around the term *hero* very frequently, but you are certainly one of mine.'

'And you're certainly one of ours,' Marybeth said. Not waiting for a handshake, she threw her arms around Will's neck. 'Thank you, Doctor,' she whispered in his ear. 'Thank you for saving my husband's life.'

Dr. Jeremy Purcell hadn't been nearly as much help as Will had expected. For one thing, some pneumonia and a urinary-tract infection from the catheter were keeping him down. For another, his notes, while impressive in volume and scope, were not that well organized or easy to read. With Tom Lemm's help, they had put together a reasonable, albeit dry, presentation. They even had a PowerPoint production of sorts, although it would never win any prizes for flair.

Anxious to get in some final rehearsal, Will hurried back to the office, where he had left the carton full of notes, articles, and slides in preparation for the trip into Boston. He was Custer, riding off to inspect the troops, only this time he knew what Little Bighorn held in store.

Fredrickston Surgical Associates occupied most of the second floor of the Medical Arts Building. The airy central waiting area was half full. On a Thursday, they would be Susan's and Gordo's patients. Will felt relieved knowing that none of them was his. He still had an hour or so to review before making the thirty-five-mile drive into Boston.

'We're all excited about tonight, Dr. Grant,' the receptionist said.

'Are you coming, Mimi?'

'Once we knew you were going to be part of it, my husband and I tried getting tickets, but there are none. It's a sellout.'

'You might be just as well off staying home together and watching professional wrestling. The guy Halliday who will be representing managed care has been preparing for months. I've had a week.'

'Oh, Dr. Grant, you'll do great.'

'I wish I had your confidence.'

'Just tell them all what goes on around here with all the paperwork and delayed payments and grumpy patients.'

'I may do that.'

'Excuse me, Dr. Grant?'

A trim, attractive Asian woman approached him from one of the seats to his right. Her ebony hair, cut in a pageboy, was very appealing.

'Yes?'

'Dr. Grant, there's no reason you should remember me, but there's no reason I would ever forget you.'

'I'm embarrassed I don't re –'

'Please don't be. My name is Grace Davis. That's my husband, Mark, over there.'

Will glanced over at an athletic-looking man in his early forties – business or perhaps law was his guess. He also caught sight of the ornate grandfather clock that Jim Katz had lent the practice. In forty-eight minutes he had to be on the road.

'I'm sorry,' he said, 'I'm still not able to –'

'My maiden name was Peng. Grace Peng. For more than a year I was a regular at the –'

'Oh my God! Grace! I don't believe this.'

Excitedly, Will held her by the arms and studied her face. It was most definitely Grace Peng, but it wasn't. The Grace Peng he knew was a woeful, down-and-out alcoholic who was a regular patron of the Open Hearth a decade ago. She was a woman of intelligence and potential, whom he and everybody else around the Hearth was drawn to and wanted to help. But sooner or later, her anger and virulent drinking drove them all away. More than one of the volunteers and staff – perhaps Will included – predicted a premature and possibly violent death for the woman.

'Gosh, but you look wonderful. How long has it been?'

'More than ten years since I saw you and also since I had my last drink.'

Inadvertently, Will glanced at the clock again. Forty minutes.

'It sure looks as if you have a tale to tell,' he said.

'I'm so sorry. You're in a rush. I didn't mean to hold you up.'

'No! Well, I mean yes. I have a speech to give tonight in Boston. I'm a little nervous about it.'

The transformation in the woman was absolutely astounding. She was always filthy and disheveled – more so even than most of the

56

Open Hearth patrons. To the best of Will's memory, Grace had gone off to yet another treatment center and had never been heard from at the Hearth again. If, as she said, it had been more than ten years ago, the twins were about to arrive and he was hustling about trying to hook up with a practice. His involvement with the place he had helped found fell off for a couple of years.

'I had no idea you were working here,' she said.

'Well, who are you here to see?'

'Dr. Hollister.'

'For?'

'I was referred to her by the clinic where I had my mammogram. They're suspicious of cancer.'

'I'm sorry to hear that. Well, I certainly hope that's not the case.'

'I'm afraid it is. My husband has my mammograms. It's not that big, but even I can see it.'

Thirty-five minutes.

'Dr. Hollister is one of my partners. You'll really like her.'

'Now I don't want her to be my doctor.'

'Why? You said you haven't even met her.'

'I want you, Dr. Grant. If I had known you were here, I would have insisted they refer me to you.'

'But –'

'I'm sorry. I know you're in a hurry. I'll just cancel this appointment and reschedule with you. We can talk then.'

'Grace, we make it a point in our practice not to switch patients.'

'I'm sure Dr. Hollister will understand when I tell her that I wouldn't be alive if it weren't for you.'

Thirty minutes.

Will sighed inwardly. 'Why don't you and your husband come into my office,' he said.

'There is so much about me and my upbringing and my life that I would never let you or anyone else at the soup kitchen know,' Grace said as Will held her mammograms up to the window. As she predicted, the cancer was quite easily discernible – a marble-size density in the upper outer quadrant of her left breast. If the adjacent lymph nodes were cancer free, the lumpectomy to remove it would be quite routine. 'You and some of the others at the soup kitchen were incredibly kind and nonjudgmental,' she went on, 'but you were the only one who really pushed through my anger and denial to talk with me. Even when I was filthy and acting abominably, you kept trying. Then one night you told me that it was horribly difficult for you to see

57

so many patients who wanted to live but had terminal illness, then to have to come to the soup kitchen and see me systematically killing myself. You gave me the name of a priest. Do you remember?'

'Father Charlie,' Will said wistfully. 'I remember now. He was a patient of mine, sober in AA for many years.'

'And he was dying of cancer. You knew that when you sent me to him. He talked to me for a long time, then he arranged for me to go to a special treatment center. He never would tell me how it got paid for. I certainly didn't have any money. I was there for nine months, during which time I had almost no contact with the outside world. While I was there, I got a letter Father Charlie had written to me just before he passed away, telling me how proud he was of me.'

'He was a wonderful man.'

'I went back to school in L.A. Eventually I got a master's degree in social work and married Mark. It's no surprise that I specialize in addictions. Last year Mark took a job as the head of the English department at Maplewood Academy, and we moved back here.'

'Now this,' Will said, gesturing to the mammogram.

'Now this,' Grace echoed wistfully, but without rancor.

'And I can't talk you out of wanting to change from Dr. Hollister to me?'

'Absolutely not, unless you're not on Steadfast Health's list of approved providers.'

'I am.'

'Dr. Grant,' Mark Davis said, 'take it from me. When Grace makes up her mind like this, there's no sense even *trying* to argue with her.'

'Okay, okay, you guys wait here. I'll see what I can do.'

As he left his office, Will stepped around the carton of material he had planned to review.

Well, he thought, *it's a good thing no one ever died of humiliation.*

If Will expected Susan Hollister to give up her patient without discussion, he was mistaken. The two of them had clashed occasionally over treatment philosophy or a surgical approach, but even those conflicts were short-lived.

'Will, why didn't you just tell this Mrs. Davis that we simply don't do things like this in our practice?' Susan asked. 'You know as well as I do how many times when we're covering for one another, a patient decides she likes me better than you because I'm a woman, or Gordo better than me because the patient's Scottish, or you better than Gordo because you're not overweight. If we aren't firm about not doing this sort of thing, there will be nothing but chaos

58

and discord.'

A confrontation with Susan on this of all nights was the last thing Will wanted or needed. In no more than ten minutes he had to leave for Boston.

'I thought that because Grace had never met you,' he tried, 'and had a history with me, we might make an exception.'

Susan was clearly exasperated.

'I don't think so. This woman was referred to me, and I feel as if I should take care of her.'

Will checked his watch.

'Susan, I can't believe I'm stuck in the middle like this. Listen, why don't you come over and talk to her. I only have a few minutes before I have to head into the city, and I'd like to get this resolved. The poor woman has breast cancer. It seems the least we can do in this situation is to let her choose someone she's known for ten years to operate on her.'

Susan glared at him for a moment, then visibly softened.

'I'm sorry, Will,' she said. 'You're absolutely right. My nose was just out of joint. This isn't the typical case I was talking about. You two do have a history. Go tell your Grace Davis that it's fine for you to take care of her. I'll even assist in doing the procedure if you need me.'

Will felt a flood of relief.

'Thanks, Suze. In case you couldn't guess, at this moment, my mind is on other things than who does this breast biopsy.'

'I understand. I'll see you in Boston. And, Will, relax about tonight. I'm sure you'll knock 'em dead.'

Chapter 7

Faneuil Hall had been a gathering place for the artists and intelligentsia of Boston for more than 250 years. Over that time, its grasshopper weathervane, still perched atop the building's cupola, had become a symbol of 'The Hub,' a city characterized by liberal thinking and more than 140 colleges and universities. Samuel Adams and other patriots once spoke beneath its roof, rallying the colonists to strike for independence from the British. None of the building's history was lost on Will as he parked in a nearby garage, entered the first-floor market area, showed his ID to the guard blocking the stairway, and ascended to the second-floor meeting hall through a metal detector.

There were still nearly forty-five minutes to go before he and Boyd Halliday were scheduled to square off. A sign at the foot of the stairs, adjacent to the metal detector, announced that, for security reasons, ticketed guests only would be admitted beginning thirty minutes before the forum. Two managed-care executives shot to death, a third killed by a bomb. Speculation on the killer's identity and motive was rampant, with most guesses leaning toward a disgruntled HMO patient or patient's relative. There was some pressure from law enforcement to postpone the forum or to cancel it altogether, but in the end, it was felt that the second floor at Faneuil Hall was small enough for private security and the police to cover, and that the public was sick of bending to terrorist threats of any kind.

The meeting hall was inspiring – an elegant seventy-six-foot square featuring a thirty-foot-high ceiling and walls adorned with portraits of George Washington, Samuel and John Adams, and Daniel Webster, among others. Doric columns supported a three-tiered balcony running along the sides and back of the hall. Four hundred wooden folding chairs had been set out in neat rows. All would soon be filled. At the front of the hall was a stage and on it a draped dais with five name placards – *Boyd Halliday, Excelsius Health; Marshall Gold, Excelsius Health; Roselyn Morton, Wellness Project; Thomas Lemm, MD, Hippocrates Society; Willard Grant, MD, Hippocrates Society.*

Willard!

Could the forum possibly be off to a worse start, Will wondered. First, matters surrounding Grace Peng had eliminated his rehearsal time, now Willard. Will disliked the name as much today as he had the first time he was teased about it. He disliked it as much as he hated beets. He disliked it enough to have insisted that the shortened version be on all his diplomas and certifications, and had not changed it legally only because he had never gotten around to it.

'Why not William?' he asked as his mother was cleaning him up from yet another losing fight.

'Too common,' was her stock answer.

Then, when Will was eight, *Willard*, the story of a social misfit who raised rats to be killers, hit the movie houses. Three years of being called Ratboy honed his temper and fighting skills, and cemented his feelings.

Willard.

'So, I think we're ready, yes?'

Will spun to the voice. Tom Lemm appeared calm enough. He was, as usual, conservatively dressed – dark suit, solid brown bow tie.

'Ready as we're going to be.'

'I checked the PowerPoint stuff. It looks pretty darn good if I do say so.'

'PowerPoint always looks good. What we have is pretty dry, Tom.'

'Facts, not anecdotes. That's what Jeremy said would win the day for us. I thought we agreed on that.'

'I suppose we did. Tell me something, how did they know my name was Willard?'

'No idea. Not from me, that's for sure. You've always been Will to me. Why, is there a problem?'

'No. No problem. Who's Marshall Gold?'

'Halliday's business manager and right-hand man – sort of a data nerd, I think. I just met him for the first time.'

'I've never even met Halliday in person.'

'Well, thar she blows,' Lemm said, indicating a pair of men just to their left. 'Let's get the intros over with.'

Marshall Gold, late forties, close-cropped gray-black hair, gold wire-rimmed glasses, met them first and shook Will's hand firmly.

'I'm pleased to meet you, Dr. Grant,' he said, perhaps maintaining his grip for an extra instant. 'You have the reputation as quite an excellent surgeon. We're happy to have you on our panel of provider physicians.'

'Thanks. Is that your job, the provider panel?'

'Along with the other duties that go along with being Mr. Halliday's personal assistant. I understand you two haven't met each other yet. We should take care of that right now.'

Will had seen some photos of the Excelsius Health CEO, but none of them conveyed the force of the man. He was slightly taller than Will, perhaps six-one, with dense, pure white hair, the weathered face of an outdoorsman, and eyes so intensely gray that Will wondered if he was wearing some sort of tinted contacts.

'So, Dr. Grant,' he said, impaling Will with those eyes. 'After years of sniping at us in the press, you finally get the chance at an all-out frontal assault.'

Will was immediately en garde.

61

'I hadn't intended any sort of assault, Mr. Halliday, just a dissemination of the facts as I know them.'

'Yes, of course, facts. That will be refreshing.'

That did it. Halliday had only one chance to make a first impression, and as far as Will was concerned he had used his poorly. They were enemies and would remain so until the man did something incredibly admirable.

'I had been led to believe that this evening was going to be a civil discussion of the issues,' Will said, feeling the heat in his face that used to follow being called Willard.

Halliday's smile held no warmth.

'Dr. Grant, you are publicity director of an organization that is trying to hurt my company, if not put it out of business altogether. I intend to be civil with you only as it suits my purposes.'

'Well, well, well, I see that we've all gotten acquainted with one another,' Roselyn Morton gushed as she approached the four combatants.

She was a lusty woman, straight out of the society pages, meticulously coifed and wearing a form-fitting designer dress that aesthetically could have been a size larger, or even two. The four men introduced themselves and shook her hand, although it was clear to Will that she and Halliday had some prior connection.

Morton took several minutes to review the format of the evening, which she said was to be a brisk, issue-oriented presentation and discussion surrounding managed care. There was to be a fifteen-minute opening from each side, followed by ten minutes each spent addressing the points made by the other. Next there would be five questions for each team chosen by a Wellness Project committee from audience submissions, with a strict two-minute limit on the answers.

'If I tell either of you that time is up, I would like you to stop immediately,' she said. 'Mr. Gold and Dr. Lemm may speak at any time, but the minutes they take will be counted against your side. Lastly, there will be five minutes for each team for summation. The side that goes first at the beginning will go last here. If all goes well, we'll be done in an hour and twenty minutes. Questions?'

'Who goes first?' Will asked.

Roselyn Morton looked over at Halliday.

'Oh, I'm sorry, Dr. Grant,' Halliday said. 'I was asked about this a couple of weeks ago, and said it was perfectly all right with me if your side went first.'

'Did Dr. Purcell know that?'

'I assume so.'

'Well, he didn't say anything to me about it.'

'Gentlemen, gentlemen,' Morton pleaded, 'supposing we simply flip a coin. Winner goes first. Dr. Grant?'

'Heads,' Will said, certain only that if Halliday wanted him to go first, there must be some disadvantage for him to do so.

'Heads it is,' Morton sang out.

From a spot beside the stage, Will and Tom Lemm watched the sellout crowd assemble. There were uniformed security people patrolling the main floor and up in the balcony, and Will knew there were police scattered about in street clothes as well. Reporters and cameramen filled the back of the hall.

'So, Will, what's your take on Boyd Halliday?' Lemm asked.

'Clearly not a man who enjoys coming in second.'

'Do you?'

'I hope I don't disappoint you, Tom, but my finish-first-at-all-costs phase caused me nothing but trouble and pain. Most of the time now I'm more than satisfied with just competing and trying my best, regardless of whether I win or not. In fact, except for in the OR, I think winning is often vastly overrated. Christ, is that the governor?'

'This is big stuff, Will.'

'Tell me again why I'm the one with the dueling pistol and you're the second?'

'Because I'm dull and I can't stand to lose. Listen, don't worry. You'll handle this guy fine.'

Jim Katz and his wife, Julia, entered with Gordo and his wife, Kristin. Behind them came Susan, who was unaccompanied but looked less drab and bookish than usual in a tweed wool suit. Cameron was the first to spot Will and pointed him out to the others, who smiled and waved. Then he left the group to give Will a bear hug.

'No kilt?' Will asked.

'Knowing your curiosity about what lies beneath, I dinna want to distract you. Are you ready for battle, Braveheart?'

'Gordo, the truth is this all sounded better when I said I'd do it than it does right now.'

'I can't believe it. The lad is cool as kelp in the operating room, and here he is shaking in his boots.'

'I can't help it if I'm allergic to humiliation.'

'Well, you better be entertaining. I told Kristin this was our night out for the month.'

'Hey, easy does it. I can't handle any more pressure.'

'Well, then, make us proud.'

'I'll try.'

'What's this Willard thing?'

'A misprint.'

Roselyn Morton's opening remarks were neutral enough, although at one point she did aver that excesses in the former system of fee-for-service health care gave birth to the need for major health-care reform, a conclusion that Will felt was debatable.

Wait! Will wanted to scream as he heard his introduction beginning. *Wait, I'm not ready yet! I'm not ready yet! And for God's sake, please don't call me –*

'Dr. Willard Grant.'

To polite applause, Will took the stack of notes he and Lemm had prepared, which included pages with the PowerPoint slides printed on them, and woodenly approached the podium. Clearly, he appreciated now, it would have been better to go second. With no idea what approach Halliday was planning to take, he would have to stick to the script he and Lemm had put together.

'It has been well over twenty years,' he began, 'since the onset of myriad attempts to reform the fee-for-service delivery of medical care that many physicians grew up with. The current incarnation, an alphabet soup of various forms of managed health care, has pitted physicians and patients alike against insurance companies, physicians against other physicians, and even physicians against patients. There are lawsuits upon lawsuits, skyrocketing physician dissatisfaction, rampant early retirement, and an unprecedented malpractice crisis.

'Many managed-care programs feature coverage called capitation, in which primary-care physicians are paid a set amount to deliver care to a patient for a year. Any lab tests, X-rays, and specialist consultations are paid for from that up-front money. What remains at the end of a year is what the physician gets to use to pay the expenses of his practice and feed his family. The initial amount paid is hardly large, and primary-care physicians know they are in essence being paid to cut corners. If a doctor goes over the budget in his evaluation and treatment, the excess is his responsibility.'

Will glanced briefly at the audience for anyone nodding in sympathy and understanding with his points. If there were such people out there, he missed them. A few already seemed asleep. With the help of the PowerPoint tables and charts, Will illustrated that there are more uninsured now than there were before health-care reform began – more than forty million. He spoke of the more than 350,000 patients refused care in hospital emergency rooms last year because they couldn't pay. He showed graphs comparing the per-patient cost in the U.S. versus countries with national health insurance, such as Canada and Great Britain. Careful to omit the three who had recently been murdered, Will listed the astronomical salaries and stock holdings of the top ten managed-care executives in New England. He was just halfway through his initial presentation when Roselyn Morton announced that he had one minute left.

Surprised and flustered, Will tried to sift through his notes to those facts he felt would have the most impact. What he succeeded instead in doing was to shove most of the sheets over the edge of the podium, where they floated to the floor like mutant leaves. For the first time since he began his presentation there was a reaction from the audience – a collective gasp, peppered with some sympathetic whispers and some not-so-sympathetic laughter. For a frozen moment, Will stood there, uncertain whether to go for his notes or to try and ad lib one or two final points. Instead, with a mumbled thanks, he scooped up the sheets and returned to his seat.

'You did great,' Lemm whispered.

'Did you like that little touch at the end? Inspired, I think.'

'Who hasn't dropped something in their life?'

'I'm sure they're all thinking that very thing, Tom, and not something like, *He's a surgeon?*'

Boyd Halliday, smiling, strutted up to the microphone, his white hair glistening beneath the elegant chandelier.

'Rumor has it,' he began, 'that the President is going to create a new cabinet post to oversee managed health care. However, Congress has insisted that the secretary he appoints will only be allowed to hold office for three days.'

Will groaned. Two seconds and the man had already won over the audience with self-deprecating humor. A minute later, Halliday switched on a film, possibly done by an Oscar winner, which made managed care seem responsible for everything that was good about America and American medicine. Where Will's data was presented in PowerPoint, with a character occasionally moving aimlessly on the screen, Halliday's film, *Together We Can Make a Difference*, used Disney-level animation and a score that had some in the audience tapping their feet. Where Will presented columns of statistics,

Halliday showed smiling children and scrubbed Midwesterners, each relating a heartwarming account of how their managed-care company came to the rescue during their darkest hour. What statistics he did present had to do with unchanged maternal/child health despite strict HMO limitations on their hospital stay together, and patient satisfaction that exceeded surveys done when fee-for-service was the way to go.

Halliday's final minutes were spent looking at cost savings for various medical conditions since the managed-care revolution. By the time he had finished, Will doubted there was a soul in the hall who wasn't a believer in the man's cause. Both Will and Lemm took notes for the rebuttal period, but there was so much flash and so little substance in Halliday's presentation that it was hard to find any point on which they could gain much purchase.

You want to do this part? Will wrote on the legal pad before them.

You're doing fine, Lemm wrote back. *Just relax a little bit, and you will succeed.*

If Will succeeded at anything over the minutes that followed, it was at not embarrassing himself any further. Rather than attempt to refute the glossy-but-vacuous picture painted by Halliday, he completed his factual presentation and added some of the data they had not included on the PowerPoint program. He felt a bit more animated, but the audience still seemed lost to his point of view.

Before taking over the microphone, Halliday held a prolonged, whispered conversation with Marshall Gold. For a moment, Will thought Gold might take over as a gesture of fairness to their thoroughly beaten opponent, but it was Halliday who again stepped to the mike. This time, the CEO of Excelsius Health took him on point by point in a structured, mechanical defense of the positions of managed care. Round two was much less of a defeat for Will and the Society than round one had been, but it was a defeat nonetheless. It had to have been bookish Marshall Gold who had so quickly and effectively organized Halliday's rebuttal phase, and Will found himself grudgingly admiring the man.

The questions submitted by the audience and chosen by the Wellness Project panel were all softballs, which both Will and Halliday handled without a hitch, though also without doing any significant damage to the other. Will rated round three as a tie, but weighted it significantly below the first two in terms of impact. Time had just about run out.

Halliday's summation was a nifty, professionally done PowerPoint show that made the one Will had presented look at best unimaginative.

Efficiency and cost-cutting are not the least bit incompatible with compassionate health care...

While HMOs may at times not have an extensive choice of physicians, patients can rest assured that those we do select have been carefully screened not only for ability, but for a history of psychiatric, drug, or alcohol problems...

Statistics have shown that our restrictions on length of hospitalizations have not compromised surgical outcome in the least...

Statistics also show no change in morbidity or mortality even though we are paying surgeons less than they earned per case under fee-for-service....

Smug son of a bitch, Lemm wrote on the yellow pad.

He has reason to be, was Will's reply.

'Well, here are the notes for your concluding statement, Will,' Lemm whispered, handing over a stack of five-by-seven cards, some of which Jeremy Purcell had prepared. 'I think this'll be pretty good.'

Halliday concluded his remarks and returned to his seat accompanied by generous, appreciative applause. Will remained in his seat for several seconds after his name was called out. The night was nearly over, and in truth, from what he could tell, he hadn't accomplished a damn thing. It wasn't as if he had mortally wounded himself or the Hippocrates Society and its goals, but he certainly hadn't helped to promote them, either. He carried the file cards to the podium, then took a few more seconds to scan the crowd. It was, he realized, the first time he had made any real contact with them.

Yes, of course, facts, Halliday had said. *That will be refreshing.... Dr. Grant, I intend to be civil with you only as it suits my purposes...*

Suddenly, with barely a hint from inside himself that he was going to do it, Will took the stack of note cards and set them aside. Then he lifted the microphone from its stand and carried it to the side of the podium.

'Mr. Halliday has spoken a great deal tonight about statistics,' he began, with no clear idea where he was headed. 'I took biostatistics in medical school. I was hardly a legend in the course, but I did pass. One thing I learned was that well-designed, truly meaningful, unflawed clinical studies are about as rare as ... as a day without dozens and dozens of conflicts between physicians of every specialty and the insurance companies charged with deciding what they can and cannot do for their patients, and how much they will be paid for doing it. Put another way, if you happen to be the person being shipped from one ER to another because your HMO doesn't perceive your illness to be life-threatening, statistics that say you'll make it through your crisis without dying don't mean a hell of a lot.

'In addition to biostatistics, I also took a course entitled "The Art and Practice of Medicine." That one I did do quite well in. Basically, what we learned about in the art and practice of medicine was people – not the kind of actors we saw in that movie, scrubbed and healthy and happy, but people who are sick ... or injured ... or confused – real people often at the very crossroads of their lives. People like Roy, a ten-year-old boy hospitalized by his pediatrician for profound malnutrition. Fifty-four pounds he weighed. It took an extensive, delicate evaluation, but finally the diagnosis of anorexia was made – an unusual though not unheard-of occurrence in a boy of this age. Tube feedings and intensive family therapy helped the pediatrician and psychiatrist and nurses to save his life. Imagine if this was your child and he had died. Imagine the devastation to the survivors. But doctors doing what they had studied and trained to do kept that nightmare from happening. The point? Well, through a clerical mistake, Roy's discharge diagnosis was listed as anorexia, not malnutrition. Same boy, same illness, same miraculous outcome, different word. Alas, whereas the family's HMO would have paid for the life-saving hospitalization if the diagnosis was written as malnutrition, the bureaucrats who decide such things adamantly and forever refused to pay for anorexia – a diagnosis they considered psychiatric, and therefore not covered by the family's plan.

'Recently, Karen, a registered nurse in a hospital not far from here, with fifteen years of unblemished service, committed a fatal medication error. An investigation concluded that she was exhausted and harried because corporate cost-cutting had left her floor woefully short of registered nurses, and she had been picking up extra shifts and performing extra duties on those shifts. Do you think she or the family of the dead patient want to hear about statistics and dollars saved by substituting LPNs and aides for RNs?'

There was no movement at all among the hundreds in the audience. No sound. Will cleared his throat, then took a sip of water. Seated in the center of the fourth row, Gordon Cameron made eye contact and almost imperceptibly nodded. Will plunged ahead, feeling like a halfback who had broken through the line and was now running free in the open field.

'Last week a fifty-three-year-old loving, caring internist by the name of Mark White was chastised and threatened by a non-MD managed-care official for ordering excessive diagnostic tests on his patients. That call was the final straw for this physician, who had never been sued, who did volunteer work at a free clinic, who was a past chief of medicine at his hospital, and whose filled-to-over-flowing practice was as totally devoted to him as he was to it. He spoke briefly to his staff and to the patients in his waiting room. Then he put on his coat and left ... Quit ... Just like that ... Good-bye, Dr. White.

'A survey by the *Western Journal of Medicine* recently reported that the average primary-care physician spends forty minutes a day dealing with managed-care hassles, mostly around referral and prescription issues. Since there are around one hundred thirty-seven thousand primary-care docs with managed-care contracts, that translates into more than twenty-one million hours of patient-physician interaction lost to those hassles. Using the average three visits per patient per year, and an overly generous twenty minutes per visit, more than twenty-one million patients could have had access to a primary-care physician during the time those docs are now spending on managed-care issues.'

Will paused to let the notion sink in. He still had no clear idea how he was going to wrap things up, but he sensed that desperation had led him to the path he should have been traveling all evening – that medicine must be, at its core, always and ever, about each individual patient. He caught movement out of the corner of his eye, and initially thought that either Roselyn Morton was coming over to give him the hook or Boyd Halliday was about to turn the forum into a free-for-all. Instead, Tom Lemm approached and handed him a typed sheet.

'I think this might be just what you need,' he whispered.

Will scanned the paragraph and immediately understood.

'So, where does this leave us?' he asked the crowd. 'Fee-for-service has been deemed too expensive, and managed care is too, well, managed. Under the one system, lots of doctors were felt to be making too much money. Under the other, managed-care executives are pocketing tens if not hundreds of millions, while searching daily for ways to further cut services and payments, as well as ways to weed out from their coverage those who are most in need of proper health care – the old, the infirm, and the poor. In Europe and Canada, nationalized health care has been at least as successful as the system we have in place. If nothing else, all of the citizens of those countries have access to care. Whether it is their system, or a hybrid of theirs with our own, changes are needed and needed desperately.

'I want to close with this note that we received at the Hippocrates Society and that my trusted cohort Dr. Tom Lemm just produced for me. It's from a man who works in an auto-body shop north of Boston – one of those regular guys I was talking about. I seriously doubt we'll ever be seeing Vic Kozlowski in any promotional videos. He doesn't suffer from a dramatic, life-threatening illness. But believe me, Vic has something to say to all of us gathered here tonight. So here he is, in his own words.'

For emphasis more than any physical need, Will cleared his throat again and took another sip of water.

'I don't think it's really appropriate for my doctor to do, Vic writes, *but every time I visit him he tells me about how the HMOs are dictating every move he makes and ruining his practice. Then he tells me he shouldn't even be saying such things because he might get in trouble. It makes me so sad. He is a wonderful doctor, but he's scared to speak up against the HMOs.*

'It's bad for me, too. I can't get an antibiotic that I need because it's not on the HMO-approved formulary, but the ones that are in there either don't work or make me so sick they don't stay in my body. So, if I do what's best for me and get the medication that works, the payment is more than fifty dollars. Well, I don't have to tell you that to a family of four with one income, that is a hard chunk.

'We already pay sky-high rates, and they keep rising while our copays keep rising as well. The bottom line is I feel I might as well be uninsured. The doctor doesn't make me feel confident and the circle is never-ending. The patient is the butt of the whole thing. I truly believe that America is helpless. I am so nervous every time I get sick. This probably seems totally trivial to you, but believe me, most of the patients in this country feel the same way I do. Thanks for reading this.'

Will walked back around the podium and replaced the microphone. 'And on behalf of myself, Dr. Lemm, and the Hippocrates Society, thank you all for caring enough to attend tonight.'

The huskiness in his voice was as surprising as it was un-intentional.

Several silent seconds passed. Then the applause began, building like the sound of a river churning downstream toward a falls. Then, with Gordo leading the way, slamming his huge hands together, most of the crowd rose, cheering out loud. Thoroughly drained, Will nodded sheepishly and returned to his seat. Still the clamor continued. Roselyn Morton took the microphone and thanked the audience and participants, but it was doubtful anyone heard through the noise. The forum was over. Will sat for a time until he felt reasonably confident his legs would hold him, then descended the steps to the main floor, where he was mobbed. Gordo, Jim, and their wives hugged him. Susan squeezed him tightly and whispered something about his making the whole profession proud. Several members of the Society pumped his hand and said no one had ever done so much for their cause so quickly.

As the crowd began to disperse, Will's attention was drawn to a woman standing off to the side, wearing tight-fitting jeans cinched with a heavy-buckled belt, a tan silk blouse, and a black vest. Her face was fascinating – vibrant and intelligent – with scattered freckles across the bridge of her nose and wide, emerald eyes that seemed possessed of their own light. For a time, she just stood there, eyeing him curiously until the last of the well-wishers had departed. Then, her gaze still fixed on him, she approached and handed him a business card.

'Please give me a call,' she said, punctuating the request with the tiniest wink.

Before he could speak a word, she turned and was gone. Her jeans highlighted an athletic, totally appealing behind. She moved with confidence and perhaps even a bit of swagger. Will watched until she had disappeared down the stairs. The vacuum she created in front of him was immediately filled by a few lingering fans, each anxious to tell him how his spontaneity and emotional sincerity had snatched victory from the jaws of defeat. When at last he was alone, the woman's face still dominating his thoughts, he took a look at her card.

Patricia Moriarity
Detective Sergeant
Massachusetts State Police

71

Chapter 8

Patty woke from a troubled sleep at ten after three. Her dream this time – what she remembered of it – featured multiple burned and bloodied body parts interspersed with varying images of Dr. Willard Grant. The two homicides she had handled before the managed-care murders were exercises in police and crime-scene procedure, not in detective work. In the first, the victim had taken out a restraining order against her violent boyfriend, and half an hour after she had returned from court he kicked in her door and stabbed her twenty-five times. The second, a lover's quarrel between two gay men, had ended in a single impetuous gunshot to the heart.

The shooting death of Ben Morales, CEO of Premier Care, was the first murder she had been assigned where the suspect wasn't ready-made. Now, that one case had grown to three, and no one doubted that a serial killer was at work. On paper, she was still part of the team from Middlesex working the case, but thanks to Wayne Brasco, she was justifiably feeling more and more like an outsider. Meetings were being held that did not include her and were called nothing more than impromptu discussions when she found out. Consultants were being called in without her knowing about them. The profiler she had originally lined up – a young, talented woman – had been replaced by a more experienced, though in her mind far less capable, man.

Tired of having her ideas demeaned and brushed off, Patty had decided on her own and on her own time to attend the Faneuil Hall debate. It just seemed to her like a charged setting where something might possibly happen. And something had, only not at all what she had expected. Wrapped in the darkness of her room, she sat on the edge of her bed and wondered about Grant and why he was occupying so much of her thoughts.

There was no question he appealed to her. His looks were hardly classic Hollywood, but she had never been attracted to square jaws and dimpled chins. His face was narrow and angular, almost gaunt, but there was a gentle vulnerability to it that brought her images of the man curled up on a couch, glasses perched on the tip of his nose, reading by a winter fire. It was his eyes, though, that affected her the most – wide and dark brown, enveloped by shadows of strain and fatigue, yet still bright and intelligent. This was not a simple man, she decided after just a few minutes of watching him at the podium. This was a man who felt things deeply, who had honest humility, and who also, she suspected, had a past that included some significant pain.

Patty shuffled to the couch in her living room and sipped some decaf cinnamon tea before attempting to read herself back to sleep – first with an Agatha Christie she had read at least once before, then with some Emily Dickinson poetry. By four-thirty, her angry thoughts of Wayne Brasco and her pleasant ones of Willard Grant were scrambled with the frustration surrounding three violent deaths and nearly eight weeks of fruitless investigation. Sleep, at least for this night, was over. She tied a terry-cloth robe tightly about her waist, padded into the guest bedroom, which doubled as her at-home study, and switched on her desk lamp, the base of which was a remarkable Northwest Eskimo carving of a polar bear. The lamp had been a gift from her brother, Tommy, in honor of her graduation from the police academy.

Willard Grant. She knew precious little of the man. It would be fun to learn more. She rotated some residual stiffness from her shoulders, then switched on her PC, called up her favorite search engine, and typed in the name. Surprisingly, a seventy-five-page list of Web sites that contained the name popped up, encompassing 717 separate items. Intrigued, Patty began to scroll down the pages. After just a few minutes she was ready to give up. There were a few sites involving a Reverend Willard Grant in historical documents dating back before the Revolutionary War, but all of the rest, it seemed, pertained to a rock/jazz fusion band that took its name from the intersection where their first recording studio was located.

Grinning at the image of herself poring through countless Web listings at four in the morning, searching for a man to whom she had spoken all of five words, Patty highlighted page 33, which, for no particular reason, she considered her lucky number. The page was filled with more band sites, most of them in German.

Enough! she thought. *He wasn't wearing a ring, but that doesn't mean he isn't married. Go for a run. Do some push-ups. E-mail some friends. But stop this teenage –*

Patty stared at an item near the bottom of the page. It was from the Ashford *Sentinel* – the police log from May 27, four years ago.

Domestic disturbance, 94 Martin Road. Dr. Willard Grant taken into custody for arguing with responding officers. No charges filed.

There was no more information.

Taken into custody. No charges filed.

'What was that all about?' she muttered.

The best scenario she could concoct was that Grant's wife or else a neighbor, or perhaps even one of their children, had called the cops because of a noisy argument. When the officers arrived, Grant refused to calm down or perhaps to leave the house for the night in order to defuse the situation. He was eventually removed by the officers, by force, and then calmed down quickly enough so that no charges were filed. Maybe the responding officers even knew him. Maybe he did some medical work for them or their families. Cops and docs – especially surgeons and ER docs – tended to share the bond of full moons and early-morning crazies.

Just as quickly as that, Patty's romantic fantasies were gone, replaced by thoughts that were much more serious and sinister – thoughts of a father of two with a bullet in his forehead, and a company CEO, shot through the throat, and finally, a meticulous suburbanite, blown to bits in his driveway. The issues Willard Grant had discussed at Faneuil Hall didn't exactly qualify as a motive, but there could certainly be more going on. Add an anger-management problem to the man's passionate dislike for HMOs, and something well might be brewing.

In twenty minutes Patty had showered and dressed and was speeding through the early morning toward Salem along largely deserted streets. The Middlesex state police detectives unit was one floor below the district attorney's office, located in a small shopping mall near the center of town. Patty used her security code to enter, left the overhead lights off, and switched on the desk lamp in her cubicle. Her desktop, while somewhat cluttered, was still neater than any of the men's except for Lieutenant Court, who was at times fastidious to a fault. She had a single poster on the wall, sent by her brother, which looked amazingly like a mullioned window looking out on the Cascade Mountains. She had added a rod and set of paisley curtains, tied back to complete the illusion.

Sensing she was on to something, Patty settled in front of her computer and logged in. In moments she would be linked over space and time to the Criminal Justice Information System, an almost

74

inconceivable amount of data on criminals, as well as on everyday citizens with no police record at all. She was about to become something of an expert on one Dr. Willard Grant. Her first stop was the Registry of Motor Vehicles.

Discovery number one was that Willard Grant used the name Will on his driver's license, which Patty sensed might already be a violation of state law. He had two citations in five years, both for speeding, both paid. His current address was in Wolf Hollow, a modestly upscale condominium development in Frederickston. Backtracking, Patty found a Maxine Grant still living at the Martin Road address in Ashford. Since the domestic-disturbance incident four years ago, Will Grant was either separated or divorced. A quick check of Fredrickston records showed a divorce two years ago. Two children, Daniel and Jessica, both the same age. An adoption, perhaps, but more likely twins. Patty wondered where the children were the night their parents argued and Will Grant was hauled off by the Ashford police.

Seated in the pleasing quiet of the office, Patty logged on to a second site, the WMS – Warrant Management System. It took only a short while to learn that Grant had no outstanding arrest warrants against him. Patty sensed that in spite of herself, she felt strangely relieved at the news. Still, there was the aftermath of the disturbance in Ashford.

With several choices available to her, Patty next logged on to the Board of Probation site. The BOP recorded every court action in the state and was in the process of merging with the data banks of all other state boards of probation, as well. CORI, the Criminal Offenders' Records Information segment of the BOP, was her first stop. Willard Grant (Ashford address) lit up immediately in the form of a three-month restraining order, taken out by Maxine Grant the day after the incident reported in the Ashford newspaper. Patty opened a spiral-bound pad and noted the information. She had intervened in enough domestic-violence cases to find them totally abhorrent, and that was even before her grisly first homicide case. What little warmth she still held for Grant vanished, replaced by heightened interest in him as a suspect in a string of murders that until now had no suspects.

A few minutes later, that interest expanded like a party balloon.

She had searched through the Interstate Identification Index (III) and the NCIC – the National Crime Information Center – without adding anything to what she already knew, and was about to call it quits when she decided to visit one last site – the Criminal History

System Board. The CHSB, located in Chelsea, just north of Boston, was manned twenty-four/seven and contained a vast data bank, overlapping some of the others but also including information on lawbreakers who either hadn't yet made it onto other sites or had been overlooked for one reason or another.

Willard Grant was forty-one. Teaming up with the night officer on duty, a young-sounding man who introduced himself as Matthew MacDonald, Patty searched through the CHSB for Will or Willard Grant, beginning with the year he turned seventeen. When she reached twenty-one, Will Grant again lit up. It was an arrest at the University of Massachusetts in Amherst for leading a sit-in at the office of the dean. Public service and two years' probation.

There was no mention of the cause for which the sit-in was held, but the zealous action against a perceived social injustice fit well with the man who, twenty years later, was active in the Hippocrates Society and vehemently opposed managed care.

'There's more,' MacDonald said from his desk, twenty miles south and east of where Patty was seated. 'In addition to being booked for illegally blocking the egress and entrance of a public building, Grant was charged with shoving a security guard. It doesn't look as if that charge led to a court appearance, but I can't be sure. There are still holes in some of these reports.'

Patty's spiral pad was filling up.

Just three years later, there was more – another arrest, this time for assaulting a fellow med student at some sort of book burning.

'Book burning?' Patty asked.

'That's what it says here,' MacDonald replied. 'The other student's name was Streeter – Owen Streeter. Apparently, no official charges were filed.' Patty was recording the information when MacDonald said, 'Wait, this is interesting.'

'What?'

'Will Grant was picked up as a suspect in the bombing of a lab at the medical school. Same year.'

'Arrested?'

'I don't think so, but the Amherst police were impressed enough to put him in the data bank.'

'I wonder why?'

For a few seconds, MacDonald was silent.

'I think I know,' he said slowly.

'Go on.'

'There was someone in the lab at the time of the explosion – a janitor, it says here. He was killed.'

MURDER!!!

Patty wrote the word across the center of a blank page in her notebook, then added drops of blood coming off the legs of the *M* and *Rs*. She noted the date and for the time being ended her conversation with MacDonald, but not before extracting his promise to keep searching the intervening years for more on Grant and to call her if anything additional turned up. Her shift was about to begin, and even before this latest turn of events, she was behind in her paperwork. Still, strongly sensing that this was no dead end, she was unwilling to put matters on hold. Using the Net, she jotted down the names and URLs of the newspapers in Amherst, as well as the nearby towns and cities, including Northampton and Springfield. Before she could make her way into those newspapers' back issues, the door to the office opened. It took just a few seconds to recognize the voices of two men as Jack Court and Wayne Brasco.

'I don't care if she did embarrass you in front of the Norfolk guys, Wayne, there's no way I can take her any further off the case unless she fucks up.'

The overhead fluorescents flickered on. Patty's cubicle was farthest from the door – just a few paces from Court's office. Brasco's was just inside the door.

'I could work better with Sonnenblick or even Tomasetti,' he said.

'You don't have to work with her, Wayne, just put up with her. Throw her a crumb here and there. Show her how real detectives handle a murder investigation. The moment she steps out of line, she's off the case.'

Patty heard Brasco grunt as he settled in front of his desk, then Court's footsteps as he headed down the row of detectives' cubicles toward her. He stopped when he realized she was at her desk, the nonplussed expression on his hawklike face clearly stating that he was calculating how much, if anything, she had heard.

'Morning, Patty,' he said.

'Lieutenant.'

Patty slid her arm over the notebook to cover up the macabre rendering of the word *MURDER*.

There was an unpleasant pause before Patty's CO favored her with one of his most engaging, yet insincere, smiles.

'We'll be meeting in the conference room at eight,' he said. 'Carry on.'

The moment she heard the exchange between the two men, Patty conducted and resolved the internal dialogue surrounding whether or not to share her information and suspicions regarding Will Grant. She returned Court's nod and remained motionless until she heard the door to his office close. Then she slipped the spiral notebook off her desk and into her shoulder bag.

Chapter 9

Impassioned Plea Helps Doc
Lambaste Managed Care

Four hundred of the city's best and brightest, including Governor John A. Fromson, sat in stunned silence at Faneuil Hall last night as Fredrickston surgeon Willard Grant emotionally and effectively chastised managed-care companies for placing profits before patients and before physicians...

The article was the headliner in Section B of the *Globe* – the City Section. There were two copies of the paper on Will's desk when he arrived at the office, along with two copies of the article itself, neatly cut out by the Associates' dauntless receptionist, Mimi. There was also a copy of the *Herald*, which contained an article saying essentially the same thing, albeit in many fewer words.

Will had begun his day as usual by making rounds at the hospital, where nearly everyone seemed already to have heard about the forum and his unofficial victory over Boyd Halliday. Several people – two nurses, a lab tech, and a ward secretary – buttonholed him to share their own angry managed-care stories. Two others felt the need to tell him how pleased they were with the care *their* HMOs were providing for their families. Even his patients seemed to have heard some version of the debate.

Will persistently denied doing anything special, but in truth he was puffed over the turnabout he had been able to effect in the encounter with Halliday. He was not, however, at all pleased that the Willard cat had been let out of the bag. Even his office staff was surprised and amused that he was not a William. It didn't help that the classic horror flick that had initially caused his dubbing as Ratboy had not too long ago been remade, and to generally favorable reviews, as well. As he flipped through a dozen excited e-mails, mostly from Hippocrates Society colleagues, Will wondered if he had ever even bothered telling the twins his true given name. Most likely, he acknowledged, even if he hadn't, Maxine had found a way.

In addition to the article, Mimi had dutifully left a copy of the day's appointment schedule on his desk. Patient visits, sandwiched about the removal of a large fatty tumor from a woman's back, were light. This was exactly the mellow, stress-free day he would have prescribed for himself after an evening that hadn't ended until nearly two in the morning.

He was scanning the list of patients when he remembered the card Detective Sergeant Patricia Moriarity had given him, along with the request that he call her. He had little doubt she wanted to speak to him about the managed-care murders. Others in the Hippocrates Society had already been questioned. He took the card from his wallet and studied it absently as he thought about the woman. In all likelihood there had been a shoulder holster and pistol under her vest. Except for the one time a friend had dragged him to a firing range, he had never even held a real handgun. Patricia Moriarity lived by one. He gave a moment's thought to calling her, then wedged the card alongside his desk blotter, protruding out as a reminder. This just wasn't the time he wanted to be grilled about serial killings and his views on managed care.

'Dr. Grant, it's Mimi. Could you come out here, please?'

Will did as the intercom requested and found Grace Peng – Grace Davis, he remembered – seated alone in an otherwise empty waiting room. He was struck, as he had been yesterday, with the remarkable transformation in the woman, who had essentially been a bag lady not that many years before.

'Do you have a moment to speak with me?' she asked, quite obviously agitated and distressed.

'Sure, come in to my office.'

She settled into one of the two walnut-stained, Danish modern chairs that Jim Katz's interior-decorator wife had chosen for each of the offices.

'My insurance company is Steadfast Health,' she said.

'I've done some business with them.'

Will hadn't actually had all that much contact with the company, but he had operated on a number of patients whom they covered. From what he recalled, Steadfast Health was smaller than most of the

HMOs, and for the most part more civil.

'Well, they are refusing to allow you to do my surgery.'

'When did they say that?' he asked, wondering if somehow last night's forum and the resulting publicity could have already had some undesirable fallout.

'Yesterday. Just in case there was some clause or other like the one they have requiring preapproval for everything, I called them shortly after we got home from here to inform them about the change we wanted from Dr. Hollister to you. The woman who answered the phone checked around and then called me back to say they have a contract with Excelsius Health that includes the requirement that the referral surgeon is the only one allowed to operate on Steadfast Health patients.'

Will was stunned. Was this yet another managed-care game?

'What do you mean contract?' he asked. 'What's Excelsius Health got to do with this?'

'From what I was told when my primary-care doctor scheduled my mammogram, Steadfast Health is too small to have cancer centers the way Excelsius Health does, so their patients are X-rayed at the Excelsius mammography clinics, and if they need it, they're treated at the Excelsius cancer centers. Then, I guess, Steadfast Health reimburses them somehow.'

'Well, this is just crazy,' Will said. 'I'm on the provider panels for both Steadfast Health and Excelsius.' Even though, he chose not to add, Excelsius had tried several times in the past to have him removed from their provider list for various technicalities, including failure to get a form in on time.

'No matter what,' Grace said, 'my husband and I have decided that we want you to do my biopsy, even if we have to pay for it ourselves. We have some money saved and –'

'Stop right there. This is absolute nonsense. You aren't going to have to pay for this yourselves.'

The oversize manila folder with Grace's mammograms in it was still propped against his desk from the previous evening. It was ironic and somewhat amusing that he had completely missed the Excelsius Health label in the upper left corner. Briefly, he scanned the films once more. The cancer was as he remembered – not huge but, in truth, indisputable. Biopsying the lesion would be technically simple, as would be its removal, provided there were no local lymph nodes with cancer in them. If the cancer had spread to the nodes – a part of the system draining foreign matter from the body – a meeting with the oncologist would be worth having to decide whether removing the lump or the upper outer quadrant of the breast would be statistically the best way to go.

Charles Newcomber was the radiologist who had read the mammogram, dictated his reading, and subsequently referred his patient to Susan. Emphasizing his title to the Excelsius Cancer Center operator, Will had no problem getting patched through to the man, who had a rather high-pitched voice and a fairly pronounced British accent.

'Dr. Newcomber,' Will said after introducing himself, 'I'm here with a Mrs. Grace Davis, who had a set of mammograms that you correctly read as showing probable cancer.'

'Well, I'm certainly relieved at being deemed correct about such a thing.'

'Oops. I'm sorry, Doctor. I hope you know that's not what I meant. I really do apologize.' Will expected the man to say something that would help ease his discomfiture, but there was only silence from the radiologist. 'I ... um ... the problem I'm calling about is that you referred Mrs. Davis to Dr. Susan Hollister, who is one of my partners.'

'Yes?'

'Well, it turns out that Mrs. Davis and I have a history together that goes back more than ten years.'

'How sweet,' Newcomber said.

Will sensed his neck redden, but held his tongue in check. Newcomber was part of the Excelsius Health family. It was quite possible he was aware of the forum and its aftermath. Perhaps he had even been there.

'Dr. Newcomber, Mrs. Davis is here with me right now. She would like me to perform her surgery. I have spoken with Dr. Hollister, and she has no problem with the change.'

'I'm afraid that isn't possible.'

'What?'

'Dr. Grand, first of all, this cancer center has an approved list of consultants from which we select a surgeon based on our patients' hometown and any sexual preference. Dr. Hollister is on that list. You, sir, are not. Secondly, I have made it a point to personally get to know any surgeon to whom I make a referral. I don't know you at all. If Mrs. Davis has a problem with that, I suggest she make an appointment to come in and share her concerns with me.'

Will could barely speak.

'Dr. Newcomber,' he managed, 'who is your supervisor?'

81

'*I* am the supervisor, sir,' came the acid reply.

'Well, you're not the boss!' Will shot. 'And my name's Grant, not Grand.'

He slammed the receiver down.

A call to information gave him the number of the headquarters of Excelsius Health. He and Boyd Halliday had mixed it up yesterday, and Will was more than ready for another go.

'There's no way they're going to get away with this,' he muttered as much to himself as to Grace.

'Excelsius Health, the leader in cost-effective, comprehensive health care. How may I direct your call?'

'This is Dr. Grant. Mr. Halliday's office, please.'

'One moment.'

'Boyd Halliday's office. May I help you?'

'This is Dr. Will Grant. May I speak with Mr. Halliday, please?'

'Dr. Willard Grant? From last evening?'

'That's right.'

'Um ... just a moment, please.'

For nearly two minutes, Will sat with the phone pressed to his ear, listening to a Spanish flamenco guitar piece and looking across at Grace. Her transformation, while certainly remarkable, was not the only one of its kind he had encountered. Over his years as a physician and as a volunteer at the Open Hearth, he had known a number of alcoholics and drug addicts who had failed at rehab again and again, only to suddenly get it and become straight and sober forces for good in their own lives and the lives of many others. His own dentist had survived a horrible stretch of drinking, during which he was hospitalized more than two dozen times in a ten-year period. Now, twenty years into recovery, the man was something of a saint, practicing his craft with wonderful skill, while helping countless men and women in and out of his profession to face their demons and prevail.

'Dr. Grant?'

'Yes.'

'Marshall Gold here. Mr. Halliday is at an all-day conference. Is there anything I can do to help you?'

The time spent on hold had done nothing to help Will calm down. Barely pausing to breathe, he recounted the situation with Grace Davis and his disturbing conversation with Charles Newcomber.

'I am on the provider panel for both Steadfast Health and Excelsius,' he railed, 'and so there is absolutely no reason to prevent me from caring for this woman –'

'Dr. Grant –'

'I promise you, if Boyd Halliday doesn't intercede in this case and set matters straight, he'd better be watching the news and reading the papers, because I won't hesitate to bring Grace Davis to them and –'

'Dr. Grant,' Gold repeated calmly.

'What?'

'We're sorry for the confusion. We have no problem honoring Mrs. Davis's request to switch to you for her surgeon.'

'You don't?'

'No, sir.'

'But Newcomber –'

'The arrangement we have with Steadfast Health has, from time to time, generated some confusion. I'm sorry that you, of all physicians, on the day after the Faneuil Hall forum, of all days, have been caught up in it. Hopefully, in the very near future, Steadfast Health and Excelsius will be merging, and such misunderstandings will be eliminated altogether.'

The freight train of Will's anger screeched to an immediate halt.

'You can speak for Halliday on this matter?'

'As I said, you are not the first physician to be caught up in this sort of situation. So long as you are a provider on our panel, which I most certainly know you are, you have been screened in depth by our credentialing committee and have been deemed to be a quality physician.'

'I ... well ... thank you, Mr. Gold. Thank you very much. Mrs. Davis will be very pleased to hear that.'

'Is there anything else?'

'No. No, I guess not.'

'Dr. Grant, I assure you, we are not the soulless, money-grubbing monsters you have worked so hard to portray us as.'

'Maybe you're not,' Will replied distantly. He set the receiver down softly.

'So, I guess you're my surgeon,' Grace said.

'I guess I am. I don't know why I'm sitting here feeling like a jerk when I didn't even do anything but stick up for our rights. The company made the offensive call, then the company took it away. It's as simple as that.'

'It's as simple as that, except that you have passion for your profession and your patients and don't want to have that stolen away from you.' She stood and set copies of the morning's *Globe* and *Herald* on his desk. 'I'll make an appointment for you to examine me and speak to me and my husband about what's in store for us, and also to schedule the biopsy. With any luck, you'll get to help save my life a second time. I'm not sure I subscribe to this one, but an ancient Chinese belief is that if you save someone's life, you are responsible for that person and what she does with the rest of her life, having presumably cheated the fates out of an intended victim. If that's really true, I would wager you have quite a number of souls on your plate.'

Before he could respond, she reached across the desk, briefly took his hand in hers, and was gone, leaving the faintest scent of something springlike swirling in the air.

Will checked the morning's schedule once again. He still had ten precious minutes to review lab reports and dictations and to sign the stack of payment requisitions for those companies who refused to allow a rubber stamp, proxy, or any signature other than his in black ink. Two minutes into the ten, his private, direct line – the line reserved for family, close friends, and other physicians – began ringing.

'Dr. Grant?'

The voice was tinny – mechanical and robotic – the sort of distorted, disembodied, computer-generated voice that telemarketers were using more and more to announce that you had just been chosen to receive three free days and two free nights at one of Orlando's newest resorts, or to ask you to call for the absolute lowest mortgage rates possible, even if you have been refused credit in the past. Only this call had come in on a number that none but the most dogged, resourceful telemarketing firm could ever have obtained. Will resisted the impulse simply to hang up.

'Who is this?' he asked.

'Is this Dr. Grant?' the totally creepy voice asked again.

'It is. Now, who is this? What do you want?'

'You did well last night, Dr. Grant. Very well.'

'Use your regular voice or I'm hanging up,' Will managed, though with less force than he had intended.

'All in good time. We are very proud of you, Doctor. Very proud. These companies have got to be made to pay for all those they have killed.'

Will sank back in his chair, stunned at the notion that this might be the one who had recently murdered three people. However, within just a second or two, his surgeon's mentality kicked in and was demanding action. He snatched up a pen and wrote the caller's words down as closely as he could remember.

'Are you responsible for the killings?' he asked, searching his thoughts for any other action he should be taking. Aside from staying focused and prolonging the conversation as long as possible, he could think of nothing. Along the margin of the paper, he wrote:

> *?Man?*
> *?Woman?*
> *Halting speech?... On purpose?*
> *We ... not I*
> *We ... not I*
> *Several times ...*

'This is war,' the voice said. 'In war people die. These corporations earn millions off the blood of the innocent. You implied as much last night. Now you are one of us. You are our brother in this war – a fellow soldier. If you need us, we will be there for you. If we need you, we expect your cooperation. Top drawer of your desk – back left corner. We are counting on you to deliver the message that we are engaged in a holy war to avenge the innocent.'

There was a click and, an instant later, a dial tone.

Will continued writing furiously until he was certain that most of the chilling diatribe was on paper. Finally, he scanned the transcript. His handwriting was deplorable under the best of circumstances and would have been the butt of office jokes had not Gordo Cameron's been even worse. Carefully, he reprinted those words that were particularly illegible. Then, his palms unpleasantly damp, he pulled open the top drawer of his desk and peered down at the contents. In the back left, on top of the usual mélange of letters, articles, notepads, photographs, prescription pads, paper clips, writing implements, and scattered surgical instruments, was a plain white business-size envelope with the flap tucked in, not sealed. Inside were two pieces of white index cards, each three inches square. A *C* was printed on one with some kind of marker. An *N* was printed on the other. Aware that he had done the wrong thing by touching the envelope at all, Will carefully replaced the letters and set the envelope back where it was in his desk.

Then, with an unpleasant gnawing in his gut, he slid Patricia Moriarity's business card to the center of his blotter and called.

Chapter 10

Six minutes after Will ended his conversation with Patricia Moriarity, two uniformed state policemen, sirens blaring, arrived at the Fredrickston Medical Arts Building and began the process of sealing it off. There were at least a dozen different practices of varying specialties in the building, in addition to a pharmacy, an optician, and a bagel store. Will knew that for at least the rest of the morning, there would be massive inconvenience for all of them.

Susan was doing a case in the hospital, and Jim Katz had the day off. But Gordo had arrived in his office while Will was speaking with Grace Davis. Now he was stuck there, and not at all pleased about it. Arms folded, his bulk threatening to overwhelm his desk chair, he stroked his beard and gaped over at Will in disbelief.

'Willy, now tell me again,' he said, 'just what are ye doin' consorting with a murderer?'

'Hey, you've got it backward, Gordo. It's him ... or her ... or them ... or it – I couldn't even tell, for chrissakes – that's consorting with *me*. Because of the things I said at the forum last night, the bastard has decided that I'm a kindred spirit of his – a brother in the war against managed care is how he put it. In fact, I had this feeling while I was listening to him that he might have actually been there last night.'

'That gives me the willies – or maybe out of deference to you I should say the creeps. How could they have gotten into this building and then into your office?'

'I was hoping you might be able to come up with a theory to explain that.'

'Well, given the crack security company that watches over this place, my guess is an entire terrorist cell could be operating here every night without being noticed.'

'You might be right. Think we ought to try and get in touch with Jim?'

'I can't imagine something like this happening and him not wanting to know about it. In case you hadn't noticed, he's a wee bit of a control freak.'

'I'll have Mimi try and find him.'

At that instant the receptionist called in over the intercom. 'Dr. Cameron, would you tell Dr. Grant that Detective Moriarity is out here looking for him?'

'Consider it done, lass. Do us a favor and see if ye can locate Dr. Katz.'

Her expression businesslike, Patricia Moriarity shook Will's hand, then motioned him over to the corner of the waiting room farthest from the receptionist. She was wearing a black hip-length leather jacket over dark slacks and a light blue sweater. Will couldn't help but notice that the only ring she wore was on the third finger of her right hand.

'Dr. Grant, the crime-scene people will be here any moment to go over your office. Is there a place we can speak in private?'

'We have two empty physician's offices. Either one would be fine.'

'You choose.'

Will led her to Susan's consultation room, which was on the side of the suite directly opposite Gordo's. The size and setup of the room were nearly identical to Will's, but the modern art on the wall and extra touches Susan had added to the basic decor – curtains with a repeating Parisian street scene and a small reading table by the bookshelf – made it quite distinctively hers. Moriarity pulled one of the patients' chairs away from the desk and motioned Will to the other. Then she flipped open a notepad and slid a government-issue pen from the wire.

'Dr. Grant,' she began, with no pleasantries or even a mention that they had met just twelve hours before, 'what on earth were you thinking when you pulled that envelope out of your desk and opened it before calling me?'

Will took a few seconds to stabilize himself.

'I ... I think I was so bewildered and frightened by the call that I wasn't really thinking straight.'

'And there was nothing about the caller's voice that you recognized?'

'It was totally mechanical. In fact, whoever it was might have been typing the words into a computer that then read them over the phone.'

'That technology is available.'

Even when she was writing, Patty kept her eyes on Grant. Despite what she had learned of the man – his temper, his history of violence, his suspected though apparently never documented association with an explosion that had killed a man – he had a vulnerability and sensitivity about him that seemed real. She reminded herself that if sociopaths had a major, it was gentleness and genuineness – just ask those who knew charming Ted Bundy or John Wayne Gacy, who dressed as a clown to entertain hospitalized children. As far as she was concerned, until proven otherwise, this man was a suspect in three violent murders.

Will forced himself to remain calm as Moriarity grilled him about his whereabouts at the time each of the three managed-care executives was killed. He expected the questions – even without a phone call like the one he had just received, others in the Hippocrates Society had been interviewed – but not the icy, disbelieving tone in which they were delivered. Even with the help of his calendar, the firmest alibi he could come up with was that on the nights of two of the murders – Morales and Rising – he was on call in the hospital. Of course, he was forced to admit, with his pager he could just as easily have been outside the hospital as in. If there was an emergency requiring his immediate presence, there might have been a problem, but in most situations he could have bought some time by giving instructions to the nurses and the resident on duty. The morning of Cyrill Davenport's execution, he was at home, trying as usual when he wasn't on call to catch up on lost sleep.

After writing down his responses, Moriarity again took him step by step through the minutes preceding, during, and following the eerie call. She was clinical if not cold, and even the most innocent attempt on his part to inject anything light or personal was immediately stonewalled. It did not take long before the fact that she had the sort of scrubbed, earthy good looks that most appealed to him was lost in the chill of her interrogation and in the realization that she did not believe his only connection to the murderer was through the phone call.

'Dr. Grant, tell me again why you think there is more than one killer?' she asked.

Will consulted his notes and read off each time the words *we* or *us* were spoken by the caller.

'You have no idea how the killer could have gotten your private, inside line?'

'None at all. It's not like it's the combination to Fort Knox, though. People do have the number.'

'And you have no idea how the killer or someone associated with the killer could have gotten into your office?'

'The maintenance people in this building probably make eight-fifty an hour. It wouldn't take much to get one of them to put the envelope in my desk. Hell, with what I earn, it wouldn't take much to bribe *me* into doing it.'

'There's nothing funny about this, Dr. Grant.'

'And there's nothing funny about you insinuating that I might have murdered three people,' he snapped back.

'Did you?'

'No. Why would I call you about a phone call that never happened and put that envelope in my desk?'

'Crazy is its own definition, Doctor. Sooner or later, most serial killers need attention, and many of them also need to prove that they are smarter than we are. That's when games like claiming you received a call from the killer begin.'

'I'm not crazy and I didn't kill anyone. Should I have a lawyer here?'

'If you want one.'

At that moment, Wayne Brasco appeared at the doorway, looking like he just rode into Dodge. He was wearing jeans with a wide, hand-tooled belt, cinched with a massive silver horseshoe buckle, a suede jacket, and alligator cowboy boots. He glared first at Patty, then at Will.

'Why didn't you call me about this?' he snapped, gesturing to the office in general.

Jesus. Patty felt herself flush at being rebuked in front of someone, let alone a suspect.

'You were out of the office when I got the call from Dr. Grant here about the alphabet letters. I felt we needed to get right down here, so I called the crime-lab people and I told Tomasetti to get ahold of you. Didn't he?'

Patty flashed on the notes in her shoulder bag dealing with Will Grant's past. Originally, she had decided to keep the information to herself until she could investigate the charges in more detail and see if there was anything else on the man between the explosion in the lab at medical school and the restraining order taken out against him by his wife. Now, with the phone call and the envelope, whether real or concocted by Grant himself, things had changed. The longer she held information back from Brasco, the worse it was going to be for her.

'This Grant?' Brasco growled, pointedly ignoring her question about Tomasetti.

Patty groaned inaudibly and introduced the two men.

'Lieutenant Brasco is in charge of the investigation of the

managed-care murders,' she explained, disgusted with herself for trying to mollify the jerk at all.

Brasco made no attempt to shake hands.

'So, what's this all about?' he asked Will.

'I ... um ... I've been interviewing him,' Patty said evenly.

'So now I'll interview him. That's what officers in charge are supposed to do.'

Will looked over at Patty, embarrassed for her. He wasn't the most socially aware being on the planet, but he certainly knew a boor when he saw one.

'I ... need to speak with you first, Wayne.'

'So, speak.'

'In private?'

They left Will in Susan Hollister's office and found a spot in the waiting room out of earshot from the crime-scene people and the two uniformed officers who were keeping the office staff from getting in anyone's way. Patty considered beginning on the offensive by demanding that Brasco apologize for his behavior in front of Will Grant and also by reminding him of his failure to call her from Cyrill Davenport's place. Instead, she propped herself against the wall, extracted her notes, and ran through them. She could tell from Brasco's hardly subtle expression that she should have brought up her research at their team meeting with Lieutenant Court. Brasco was a pigheaded brute, but he was hardly stupid.

Stick a fork in Patty, folks, it looks like she's done, she was thinking.

'So,' Brasco said when she had finished, 'let me get this straight. You uncovered this guy with a recurrent history of violence, connection to a murder committed by some sort of social-action group, and current active membership in another social-action group that just happens to hate HMOs, and you didn't feel this information was relevant enough to share with the rest of us.'

'I ... um ... wanted to dig into things a little deeper before – well, yes, yes, that's exactly what happened.'

Brasco raised his hands in a 'suit yourself' gesture.

'I'll take over interrogating this suspect from here,' he said.

'Mind if I listen in?'

'I think you've done enough for one day. Why don't you interview the staff? We can discuss this whole business with Jack later on.'

'You're in charge,' Patty said.

'You're damn right I am,' Brasco replied.

★ ★ ★

ERRTBECN

Deflated by this latest round with Wayne Brasco, Patty mulled over the two new letters as she gathered her things and prepared to leave the offices of Fredrickston Surgical Associates. They had to be part of a multiple-word message – a saying? ... a place? ... a company name? She was the last of the investigating crew remaining, but she was reluctant to go, sensing that her involvement in the managed-care murders might soon be over.

You can only do what you can do, sister, she reminded herself. *You can only do what you can do.* The world was full of Wayne Brascos and Jack Courts. If she was going to make it, she would have to learn how to deal with them. *Well, the hell with them,* she thought, heading for the door. *If they want me off this case, they're going to have to pry me off.*

'Sergeant?'

Will Grant stood just a few feet behind her.

'Yes?'

'Do you have a couple of minutes?'

In addition to the stack of reports she had to write covering the past few hours, there was a session scheduled at the office with Lieutenant Court and the other principals in the managed-care case.

'I'm in a bit of a rush. Perhaps –'

'It's very important.'

'Something you didn't tell Detective Brasco?'

'Something I *chose* not to tell him.'

The vulnerability in his eyes made her uneasy. She reminded herself again about the ingratiating charm of sociopaths.

'I suppose I can listen. You know, we're wary of people who try and drive a wedge between members of an investigating team. We call it splitting.'

'Forgive me for saying it,' Will replied, 'but it didn't seem to me as if Lieutenant Brasco was treating you as a teammate.'

'Is your office empty?'

Will settled in behind his desk. Patty took the chair directly across from him.

'That was a very frightening session I had with your teammate,' Will began. 'I would bet that he's not a legend on the force for his subtlety.'

'He has other strengths.'

'He thinks I killed those people.'

91

'Did you?'

'I *fix* people. I play with my twins every chance I get, and I work at a soup kitchen that I helped start, and when people are broken or hurting, I fix them.'

'That's reassuring to hear,' Patty said, realizing that, at some level, it was.

'Lieutenant Brasco came in armed with a number of items from my past. I don't like the man at all, but I have to admit he did an amazing amount of homework in a very short time.'

'And?'

'He didn't do enough.'

'Did you tell him?'

'He was so aggressive that I was afraid to say a word to him about myself without having a lawyer. And I can't even afford to get the squeaky brakes on my car looked at, let alone hire a lawyer.'

'You may have to.'

'I sure hope not. That's why I wanted to speak to you.'

'You should have spoken to Lieutenant Brasco.'

'Do you know about the information he had about me?'

'Yes, I ... I know about it.'

'The restraining order my wife took out on me?'

'Yes.'

Will withdrew a file from the bottom drawer of his desk.

'I admit I have a bit of a temper,' he said, 'but Maxine, my ex, makes me look like a puppy. She's capable of going off like a volcano. The night our neighbor called the police, she had gone absolutely berserk for almost no reason. She threw a pot and a vase through the window, but wouldn't admit to doing it. In fact, when the police came, she insisted that *I* did it. At the officer's insistence, she requested the restraining order. Neither the police nor the court wanted to hear my side of the story.' He passed the file over. 'The day after Maxine filed the restraining order, she had it rescinded. Our marriage counselor insisted on it, because Maxine told her the truth. In case I ever needed it, which I haven't, two of our closest friends wrote notarized letters stating that they had been present at times when Max went off at me almost as violently as she did that night. Fortunately, she has never blown up like that against the kids. In fact, they say she's done much better at controlling her temper since her lover moved in with her.'

Patty scanned the documents, which were impressive. She knew that in the case of restraining orders, the police and courts invariably sided with the wife until matters could be sorted out. Generally speaking, the policy was as it should be, but there were still times when husbands were penalized unjustly.

'There were other issues, as well,' she said, sensing some thawing of her feelings toward the man, as well as some guilt that it was she who had failed to dig deeper before passing over the information about him to Brasco. 'An arrest in college for assaulting a police officer.'

'We were protesting the firing of a black faculty member,' Will said wearily. 'The man I shoved was campus police. He wouldn't stop prodding us with his nightstick. He pushed me, I pushed back. He got his feet tangled up and fell. There were like a hundred witnesses. Eventually, when the truth came out, *he* was put on probation.' He produced another file from his desk, this one considerably thicker than the other, labeled *Medical License Renewals*. 'I put this stuff together because, when we apply for a medical license or renewal, the form asks about arrests.'

In addition to documentation of the incident outside the dean's office, there was extensive material dealing with a fight in medical school that resulted in Will's arrest and subsequent exoneration.

'The guy was psychotic,' Will explained. 'He was also tougher than I was, and he beat the snot out of me. Six months later he got expelled for cheating and repeated acts of violence.'

'You seem to bring out the worst in people.'

'I guess you might say that, but thankfully, there are those who would disagree with you.'

'One more thing,' Patty said. 'The lab.'

Will rolled his eyes in frustration.

'Brasco almost took my head off over that, but it was like the moment he saw my name and the word *murder* together in some computer search, he stopped looking.'

Patty used the tip of her tongue to moisten her lips, which had become unpleasantly dry.

'Go on,' she said.

'I was a social activist all the way through school. Heck, I would be more of one now, too, if I had the chance. In med school we formed an organization for protest, mostly against the pharmaceutical industry for giving medical equipment to impoverished students with their company logo on it. We named our group after a comic book – the Justice League – but we never really did much because we were just too busy trying to survive med school. Shortly after the lab explosion, some unnamed source told a reporter that it was us.'

'But it wasn't.'

'No,' he said, 'it wasn't. The newspaper chose to shoot first and ask questions later, just like your Lieutenant Brasco.'

It wasn't Brasco, it was me.

'Did they ever find out who did it?'

'A Ph.D. who had been booted out of the lab because of doctoring some research results and costing them a big grant. It was in the papers. I don't have the article, but I'll bet it wouldn't be hard to find.'

'I'll bet it wouldn't,' Patty said glumly.

'Pardon?'

'Nothing,' she said. 'I mumble sometimes. So, do I get to keep all this to show Lieutenant Brasco?'

'I'll make copies and send them to you. I have your card.'

'Make the copies and just hang on to them,' Patty said. 'If, as you say, the killer really has adopted you to be his public voice, we'll be seeing each other again very soon.'

'I'd like that very much,' Will said.

For the first time, there was a glint of mischief in his eyes.

For the first time, Patty didn't avert hers.

Chapter 11

If you didn't do anything, then you don't have anything to worry about.

Will wondered how many times he had heard that maxim from his parents, or how many times he had used it on his own kids.

If you didn't do anything, you don't have anything to worry about.

Well, he hadn't done anything other than pick up the receiver, so why was he feeling so worried? The answer to that question was, of course, that three wealthy, powerful corporate executives had been murdered, and the police were under intense pressure to arrest someone. Motive, opportunity, method. Delightful Lieutenant Brasco had latched on to him like a mastiff on a bone, hitting over and over on the fact that Will scored high on two of the three suspect requirements. And as for the third, the mastiff was quick to point out, anyone could pull a trigger, and almost anyone could go online for a few hours and learn how to blow someone up.

'Why don't you just save us all some time and hassle and tell us you did it so we can reassure the public and get you some much-needed help?'

'Why would I go out of my way to plant those alphabet cards in my desk?'

'Don't make me answer that, Dr. Grant.'

At the end of the morning, after Will had shared his documentation with Patty Moriarity, it seemed to him as if she might be a small port in the gathering storm. But even if she did believe he was being used by the killer, it was doubtful she had much clout. Brasco didn't seem to care much about how she felt one way or the other.

To no one's surprise, Will was on call again both for the group and as backup for the ER. The evening was pleasantly hectic. A code 99 at eleven had the emergency physician backed up, so Will waded in, suturing both the winner and loser of a tavern brawl, evaluating a woman with belly pain, and even stabilizing a child with a febrile seizure until the pediatrician arrived. The busy pace helped keep his mind from drifting too much to the chilly electronic voice and the notion of what it must take to cold-bloodedly kill a person, let alone three.

Patty had told him the significance of the two letters in the envelope and had disclosed the other six after extracting the promise that he would share the information with no one. At various breaks in the evening, he tried playing around with the eight letters, but nothing leapt out at him that made any sense.

At two o'clock, suddenly drained, he made his way up to the surgical on-call room and dropped face-first onto the bed. When the jangling phone shattered a bizarre, X-rated dream featuring a scantily clad, green-eyed brunette with a shoulder holster, he had been deeply asleep for three uninterrupted hours. Remarkable. The switchboard operator apologetically reminded him that he had asked for a five-fifteen wake-up call. Just before he tarnished his reputation by calling her insane, he remembered his eight-o'clock case.

If it was possible to call anyone with cancer of the pancreas lucky, Kurt Goshtigian qualified. In general, by the time pancreatic cancer caused any symptoms, it was too late for anything except con-dolences and maybe some palliative chemotherapy. But Goshtigian's tumor had been diagnosed by accident on a CT scan done after a beam swung loose on the construction site where he was working and struck him in the lower chest. There was nothing more than a deep bruise from the impact of the beam, but an incidental finding, still well contained in the portion of the pancreas referred to as the head, was a cancer. Now, a week later, Will was about to cure that cancer through the surgical approach known as a Whipple procedure.

He showered, dressed in a fresh set of scrubs, and paid his customary early-morning visit to the ER lounge for coffee, OJ, and a doughnut with the soon-departing night-shift crew. He was surprised to find Gordo there, powdered sugar still flecked in his beard like Christmas snow. He was regaling the nurses with one of his trademark jokes – the one dealing with Ian MacGregor, seated at his usual spot at the bar, deeply and morosely in his cups and, of course, speaking in the heaviest of brogues.

' "... See that pier out there," MacGregor says, "I built that pier. So, do they call me MacGregor-the-Pier-Builder? Noooo! And that shed over there. I built that, too. Do they call me MacGregor-the-Shed-Builder? Noooo! And ... and that stone wall out there? I set every single one of them stones in place myself. So am I known as MacGregor-the-Stone-Setter? Noooo! But fuck one lousy goat ..." '

Will joined in the laughter. Even though he had heard the joke enough to qualify as an expert on it, Cameron's delivery was hilarious enough to make it fresh every time.

'Gordo, what are you doing here at this ungodly hour?'

'Kristin's snoring woke me up. She swears it was me waking us both up, in addition to the neighbors and a bunch of them in the cemetery down the street, but I know better. Since the powers that be are about to put me on probation for not getting my discharge summaries dictated, and since I'm going to be spending twenty or thirty hours assisting you with that Whipple, I thought I would come on in and get caught up.'

'Kristin's like a hundred and fifteen pounds,' Will told the crew. 'Somehow, I can't imagine her snoring any louder than a sparrow if she ever even snores at all. My money's on the Scotsman here. Did you guys save me my jelly stick?'

'We practically had to pry it out of Dr. Cameron's hands with a crowbar,' a nurse said, 'but there it is.'

'Hey, Gordo, you know jelly stick's my lucky doughnut. I can't start a big case like this Whipple without having had one.'

'Mea culpa,' Cameron said, 'but excuse me for pointing out that it's the poor slob you're operating on that needs the luck.'

'Good point.'

Will knew he wasn't kidding himself about the jelly stick. For as long as he could remember, he had been a creature of lucky maneuvers and talismans, of lucky shirts and rituals. Although his superstitions didn't run so deep as to paralyze him or even alter his life very much, he did cling to certain routines and clothing when playing poker with his friends in their monthly game or when preparing to do a case in the OR.

After fifteen minutes of small talk, and another Scottish joke, Cameron headed off to the dictation carrels in the record room and Will made his way to the medical library. The Whipple he was about to perform on Kurt Goshtigian was among the most complicated of surgical procedures. Developed in the thirties, the technique was necessitated because the pancreas is anatomically not clearly separated from the GI structures surrounding it – the gallbladder, the duodenum segment of the small intestine, the bile duct, and often the stomach, as well. After the cancerous head of the pancreas and parts of the other organs were removed, the remaining portions would be sutured back to the small intestine to restore continuity and function. Gordo's sarcastic reference to Will's painstaking, time-consuming technique in the OR notwithstanding, if things went well, the operation would take four to six hours, and the result would be a cure.

Will had performed or first assisted on fifteen or so Whipples over the years – certainly enough to feel confident about the procedure. Still, the technique and anatomy were complex and variable enough to warrant reviewing them before stepping into the arena. It was crucial before beginning the Whipple to examine the area thoroughly using a laparoscope in order to be as convinced as possible that there was no cancer outside the head of the pancreas. Evidence that the disease had spread to local organs or the inner wall of the abdomen would mean that it was essentially incurable and would strongly if not absolutely mitigate against a procedure as extensive as this one.

After forty minutes of review and actually performing the operation in his mind, Will felt energized and ready. He called the twins to wish them a good day and to review the plans for the rest of their weekend together. Then he made rounds on his three hospitalized patients and finally headed up to the OR suite in the east wing of the second floor.

Thanks to a huge gift from a grateful family's trust, the surgeons' dressing room, like the ORs, was state-of-the-art – plushly carpeted with three private showers and a steam room. Following a routine from which he seldom if ever varied, Will left his wallet and watch on the shelf of his locker, laced up his red Converse Chuck Taylors left foot first, pulled disposable shoe covers over them right foot first, tied on a hair cover, then a mask, and finally slipped on the glasses and magnifying loupes he only used in the OR. Next, for five minutes he sat, eyes closed, breathing deeply and slowly, making no real attempt at clearing extraneous thoughts from his mind, but willing himself to relax and thanking God for the opportunity and skill to be a surgeon. By the time he was ready to enter the scrub room, he was experiencing a most pleasant calmness and euphoria. They were sensations he had come to expect, although this one was even more intense than what he was accustomed to.

Kurt Goshtigian was just being wheeled up to the OR when Will entered the scrub room. Gordo, already scrubbed and gowned, was on the other side of the glass OR door, along with a surgical resident who would do the prep and drape on Goshtigian's abdomen. Will hurried past the scrub sinks and out of the narrow room and caught up with his patient's stretcher, actually bumping into it, just as it reached the OR. Goshtigian was a solid, weathered fifty-four-year-old with tattoos on his muscular forearms and over his deltoids. His coarse black hair was graying, and his silver stubble suggested he hadn't shaved for a couple of days. Will pulled his mask down and apologized to the man for bashing into him.

'I'm pretty sure I've never done that before,' he said, wondering if maybe he shouldn't have broken his routine by rushing out of the scrub room.

Goshtigian, dry-mouthed and groggy from the pre-op meds, smiled up weakly and patted Will on the arm.

'You're just excited about getting to muck around with my innards,' he said.

'We're going to get that cancer out of you, Kurt, and you're going to be as good as goo.'

'You mean new.'

'Pardon?'

'You said *goo* when you mean *new*.'

Will had no idea what the man was talking about. Probably the pre-op meds, he decided.

'Yes,' he said. 'Well, if you're ready, I'm going to go scrub in. My partner Dr. Cameron is there in waiting for you. I'll be in soon.'

Will replaced his mask and headed back into the scrub area. The wonderfully pleasant sense of well-being and connection to his world had, if anything, grown more intense. He was halfway through a four-

98

minute scrub when he realized that he had broken his routine again, this time by taking the hexachlorophene-impregnated brush to his right arm and hand before his left. *Strange. No big deal, but strange just the same.* When he backed out through the scrub-room door and then into the OR, Kurt Goshtigian's abdomen was already washed, shaved, prepped with an antiinfective, and covered with sterile drapes. Carrie Patel, the best anesthesiologist on the staff, was in the process of putting him to sleep. With a nurse's help, Will slipped into a gown, had it tied behind him, then drove his hands one at a time into latex gloves, taking pains to do the left hand first. As usual, Gordo was talking almost nonstop.

'So, lad, are ye all boned up on the Whipple? The man's first name was Allen, you know. Allen Whipple. Now, there's a piece of trivia for you...'

Beneath his mask, Will smiled at his partner, even though he realized he wasn't picking up everything Gordo was rambling on about. It was always good to work with him in the OR. For one thing, he was skilled and quick as a surgeon and intuitive as an assistant, and for another, his demeanor kept the team loose and upbeat, even through the most grueling cases.

The initial laparoscopic evaluation went smoothly and showed what Will had prayed it would – no evidence for spread of cancer into the organs adjacent to the pancreas. Throughout the procedure, though, Will sensed a very mild fuzziness to his thinking, and he also noticed that, on and off, especially with fine movements, his hands shook ever so slightly. *Low blood sugar?* he wondered. He had eaten as usual, so the possibility seemed remote. *A virus of some sort?* No symptoms to go along with the mild light-headedness. In fact, on the whole, he still felt upbeat and positive.

'Ready, everyone? Well, okay. Number-ten blade, please, Beth.'

'Again, please?' the scrub nurse asked.

Will felt a spark of irritation.

'I called for a ten, a number-ten blade.'

There was more of an edge to his voice than he had intended. The nurse in turn, glaring at him from above her mask, slapped the blade into his palm with more force than usual for her. Across the table from Will, Cameron immediately reacted to the rocky start.

'Okay, Willy,' he said, 'a-cutting we shall go.'

The incision Will made, though quite large, was precisely the length he had planned. After bleeders were clamped and cauterized, he sliced open the peritoneal membrane, exposing the structures beneath. So far so good, except that Will was beginning to sense things weren't good at all. He was feeling nauseated now, and his light-headedness was more constant. For the first time, he wondered if he was going to be able to continue with the operation.

Using large clamps and retractors, he and Cameron pulled the margins of the incision wide apart. The intestines, arrayed just beneath where the peritoneum had been, were moved aside with damp towels, exposing the blood-tinged structures of the operative field, glistening under the harsh saucer lights overhead.

Will's mouth now felt desert dry. He peered down at the organs – pancreas, stomach, liver, gallbladder – and at the arteries, veins, nerves, and ducts servicing each one. In his mind, he had mapped out almost every second of this procedure. Now he couldn't remember where he was to start.

'Everything okay, there, Willy?' Cameron asked.

Will glanced up at him from over his mask.

'I ... all of a sudden ... I'm not feeling so good.'

'You need a basin? ... Need to step away?'

'Huh?'

'Will, look over at me. Kara, take those glasses off him. Let me see his eyes....'

'I'm ... okay ... just... need ... moment to...'

Will felt the light-headedness intensify and a profound dizziness set in as well. His knees became rubbery, and his vision began to darken. He tried to speak, but only guttural sounds emerged from beneath his mask. Clutching at the sterile drape, he lurched to one side, then pitched forward heavily, landing face-down in the gaping incision.

Chapter 12

The inestimable blackness was pierced by sound – garbled voices captured by Will's gradually increasing consciousness. Next came the ghastly sensation of choking – a tube the size of a redwood, clogging his throat.

Will tried to move his arms but met immediate resistance at the wrists. From his earliest days as a med student in the hospital, he had watched patients be intubated and put on a ventilator – some comatose, some semiconscious – and wondered what it could possibly have felt like. He had even asked some of them after they were on the way to recovery and had concluded that the degree of helplessness, pain, and horror of the situation was a function purely of how much medication they had received. From time to time, especially with emphysema cases, the relief of being able to get in enough air made the breathing tube tolerable. But mostly, the discomfort was quite frightening, especially in the initial hours, before there was any chance to learn to cope.

Will knew he would never again have to ask a patient about the sensation.

He thrust his tongue against the hard rubber airway that had been slipped into his mouth next to the tube and then taped in place to keep him from biting down. Awareness was rapidly returning, along with swirling memories of becoming sick, terribly sick, in the OR. He must have stopped breathing, or come damn close. The fact that the discomfort and panic seemed manageable suggested he was being medicated. Was this the first time he had been awake? With no little effort, he forced his eyelids apart. Even before his focus sharpened, he knew that he was in the ICU. The fluorescent lights over him were midday bright. Across the cubicle, two nurses were talking.

Was it a stroke? he wondered. Is that what had happened to him? A cerebral hemorrhage of some sort? Methodically, he tested his hands and arms, then his feet and legs. No problem moving anything.

The incision! He had gotten horribly dizzy and toppled over into the incision. He could envision the blood and the coils of intestine as he pitched downward toward them. But there the images stopped.

How long had he been out? What happened to his patient?

He opened his eyes wider. As his consciousness grew, so did the suffocating discomfort in his throat. He also became aware of another unpleasant sensation – the desperate need to pee. *Easy, easy*, he told himself. There was no way he could have been unconscious on a respirator in the ICU and not have had a catheter inserted to drain his bladder. *Easy*. The pressure and urgency was almost as dreadful as the tube. He had never been a hospitalized patient before. Now he wondered if he had been sympathetic enough with those who were.

The nurses were two whom he knew well, Anne Hajjar and Donna Lee. He banged the back of his hand against the guardrail.

Donna rushed over, clearly pleased to see him awake. Sharp features and close-cut blond hair, she was a new wife in her late thirties and a hardened veteran of the ICU wars. Like the other unit nurses, she called all but the most unapproachable physicians by their first name.

'Will, hi there, it's Donna. Welcome to the land of the living.'

Will nodded that he understood.

'Are you in any pain?'

He twisted his hand and pointed toward the tube.

'Ken Millstein is taking care of you. Your blood gases are looking pretty good, so maybe he'll be able to pull that tube out after all the labs are back. Meanwhile we can keep you medicated.'

Will shook his head. *No. No medication. I can handle this ... just not too long.*

'Okay, but you sort of woke up a little while ago and started tearing at the tube. That's why we medicated you and put those restraints on.'

I understand.

'Go after the tube again like that and we'll have to beat you with a stick. Do you know what happened to you?'

No.

'Apparently, you had a seizure of some sort while you were doing a case. You immediately lost consciousness, and then a few minutes later you stopped breathing altogether. You were rushed down to the ER, and they put the tube in there. Your EKG is normal, so it doesn't look like a coronary, and your chest X-ray doesn't show any sign of aspiration. Is there anything you need right now?'

Will wriggled the fingers on both hands and pointed back at the restraints.

'Anne?'

Anne Hajjar, willowy, brown-eyed, and eternally lighthearted, materialized at the opposite side of the bed from Donna and squeezed Will's hand. Of all the nurses in the hospital, she was his favorite.

'Hey, big boy, we're glad you're coming around,' she said. 'We were a little worried when they dragged you in here.'

'He wants the restraints off,' Donna said. 'I told him if he pulled that tube out it would not go well for him.'

'I suspect it would be the last thing that shape he ever pulled,' Anne said, undoing the Velcro cuff and strap on her side.

As soon as the restraints were removed, Will brought his hands together and pretended to be writing on an imaginary pad. Donna left and quickly returned with a stack of progress-note paper on a clipboard and a Bic pen. At that moment, internist Ken Millstein moved in next to Anne. He was a slight, Harvard-trained doc about Will's age, but half a foot shorter, with a rapidly receding hairline and a penchant for baggy suits. He and Will and their wives had been friends from their earliest days at Fredrickston General, and the Millsteins had been one of the very few couples who hadn't found it necessary to side with one or the other of them after the divorce.

'Eventful day,' Millstein said.

I guess, Will wrote. *How long have I been here?*

'Two hours, give or take. You had us worried for a while there.'

How is my patient?

'Gordon is still in the OR with him. I think he called Jim Katz in to help finish the procedure. Apparently you got a ten from the Russian judge for that dive you took.'

Very funny.

'Any idea what could have happened? Because I sure don't.'

None. I have never passed out before.

'Will, you didn't just pass out. You stopped breathing. Your blood pressure was heading south when Steve Edelstein in the ER decided to go ahead and intubate you.'

Good man.

'Any medical history we should know about?'

Asthma as a child.

'Meds?'

None.

'Feel okay now?'

Groggy.

'No surprise there.' Millstein checked Will's pupils, then examined his heart and lungs. 'I'll tell you what,' he said. 'I've run so many labs that your HMO is probably going to put a bounty on my head. As soon as I have most of them back, I'll get anesthesia in here and we'll pull that tube.'

How about the catheter?

'First the tube. Sorry. You want the nurses to give you something?'

Just a little, Will wrote this time.

'Five of morphine, Donna. Repeat it as needed.'

Thanks.

'Just bear with us, my friend,' Millstein said. 'We're going to get to the bottom of this.'

With the help of the intravenous morphine, Will drifted in and out of a comfortable haze. At times he dreamed – a high-speed auto chase, a green-faced judge sentencing him to prison for something, swimming in perfectly blue Caribbean water alongside a woman who looked vaguely like Patty Moriarity. At one point, in the middle of a disturbing vignette in which his hands were about to be chopped off by someone, he awoke to see Gordo Cameron looming over him.

'Greetings, lad,' he said. 'You sure gave me and the gang in the OR one hell of a fright there. I'm glad you're coming around.'

How'd you do with the case?

'He should make it through the next few hours, but that's all I can say at the moment. Jim came to the rescue and assisted. We had to repair a couple of torn vessels, then we went ahead and did the Whipple. He lost a fair amount of blood and dropped his pressure a couple of times.'

Did I tear the vessels?

'Your head hit the incision like a bloody meteor. Some vessels were bound to rupture. But, really, it was manageable. Once we got the bleeding controlled, we irrigated everything like crazy. There's bound to be infection, but that's what we have antibiotics and infectious-disease specialists for. Plus you just don't look like someone with a lot of devil germs on his face. What on earth do you think happened?'

No idea.

'Well, don't use up your energy writing. We can talk after that tube comes out. Who's takin' care of you?'

Millstein.

'Good man, Millstein. A little scrawny by my standards, but sharp. Well, lad, I'm going to head on over to the recovery room to check on our boy.'

Thanks, Gordo.

'Just don't ever do that again. My poor knickers had to be permanently retired.'

Donna Lee appeared and pulled Cameron aside, beyond Will's field of vision.

'I don't believe it!' Will heard Cameron say. 'I don't –'

Will envisioned the nurse stopping Cameron short with a finger to her lips. He banged on the bed rail to get her attention.

What's up?

'Nothing.' Donna's tone was icy. 'Dr. Millstein will be up to speak with you.'

Tube very uncomfortable ... could I have a little medication until he arrives?

'He'll be here before long. Just close your eyes and relax until he gets here. And don't touch that tube.'

The woman was gone before Will could write anything further. What could she have said that Gordo didn't believe? Why was she refusing even a small amount of medication to help him deal with the tube? Why the sudden coldness? He shifted his position in bed and tried as best he could to ignore the discomfort in his throat and bladder.

For a time he lay there, trying to divert himself with thoughts of Kurt Goshtigian. He had a decent enough patient-physician relationship with the man, but their history was not a long one. Even if Goshtigian fully recovered from his Whipple procedure, a lawyer could certainly make a good case for Will having caused the need for additional surgery and powerful, potentially life-threatening antibiotics, as well as prolonged time under anesthesia. Still, no judge or jury could find him negligent when clearly some medical problem beyond his control or knowledge had caused the incident in the OR. Will took pride in the fact that despite a high-risk specialty, he had never yet been sued, but he hardly took the fact for granted. As a surgeon, the specter of a malpractice action was always hovering not far away.

Even without medication, Will began to drift off. Images of the OR floated about for a time, then gave way to a comforting darkness. Everything was going to be okay, he told himself. The diagnostic tests he would undergo over the days and weeks ahead would show no brain tumor, no vascular anomaly within his skull, no hemorrhage, and no irregular cardiac rhythm. The incident would be written off as a simple faint, caused by a virus, fatigue, dehydration, or factors never to be determined. Such a faint was known technically as vasovagal syncope, the sort of physiologic reaction that commonly accompanied stresses such as horrible news or a grisly sight. In such instances a sudden, powerful discharge of electricity along the large vagus nerve caused rapid dilation of the veins in the abdomen and legs and marked pooling of blood in those vessels. The resultant drop in blood pressure produced an instantaneous loss of consciousness. Fainting was the brain's effort to protect its critical circulation by 'insisting' that the body lie down.

Vasovagal syncope, Will thought, as sleep enfolded him. *Yes, that's it. That's what they're going to conclude.*

'Will?'

Ken Millstein stood by Will's left hand. Standing beside Millstein,

Anne Hajjar looked down at Will with the stony impassivity of a sphinx. On the right side of the bed was anesthesiologist Ramon Bustamante, also looking grim.

Will opened his eyes and managed a weak thumbs-up, to which neither the nurse nor the physicians reacted.

Something's wrong, he thought. *Something's ...*

'Will, Dr. Bustamante's here to remove the tube; after that we'll talk.'

The Philippine anesthesiologist moved forward and used a syringe to deflate the balloon cuff that held the tube in place below Will's vocal cords. The inflated cuff also prevented him from aspirating his stomach contents into his lungs.

'Mrs. Hajjar, you have the backup tube ready?' Bustamante asked.

'Right here.'

'You tested the balloon?'

'Yes.'

'Suction?'

'Ready.'

'Okay, then, Doctor,' the anesthesiologist ordered unemotionally. 'Cough when I say so ... and ... now!'

Will coughed feebly and the redwood tree instantly vanished from his throat. He sputtered and gagged as the nurse suctioned his mouth and throat with a hard plastic tube. Then, eyes tearing, he sagged back against the pillow, sucking in drafts of sweet air. Bustamante listened to his chest, assured himself that neither lung had collapsed, then turned and left without a word. Anne Hajjar slipped oxygen prongs into Will's nostrils, did a blood-pressure check, nodded to Millstein that it was satisfactory, and quickly followed the anesthesiologist out of the cubicle.

For fifteen seconds, Millstein just stood there looking down at Will.

'Feel able to talk?' he asked.

Will cleared his throat as forcefully as he could manage.

'Sure,' he rasped, nearly overcome now by apprehension.

'Okay. I've gotten most of the lab work back, including a comprehensive panel I requested for drugs of abuse.'

'That would be negative.'

'Well, you can say so, Will, but it wasn't.'

Will felt his heart sink.

'That's impossible.'

'You lit up for fentanyl, Will. Big time.'

Fentanyl – one of the most powerful of all narcotics. It was used as a painkiller via a time-release patch and in an IV to put patients to sleep in the OR before they were intubated. It was highly addictive and too often an instrument of death in those anesthesiologists who chose to experiment with it by sequentially pushing up the dose they injected into themselves.

'I tell you, that's impossible. I've never taken any painkillers stronger than Tylenol.'

'Two different samples,' Millstein said. 'Fentanyl confirmed in both of them by emergency gas chromatography and mass spectrophotometry. Large amounts were in your blood when you passed out, Will. There is absolutely no doubt in anyone's mind about that.'

Will found the bed control and raised himself upright.

'This is absolutely insane! I didn't take anything.'

'I don't see how that can be true,' Millstein said evenly. 'I can try and help you, Will, but only if you tell the truth.'

The chilliness of the nurses and the anesthesiologist was certainly explained. Fear and anger tightened the muscles at the base of Will's skull. A jet of bile rose in his throat.

'You've known me for years, Ken. You've got to believe me.'

Millstein shook his head slowly.

'I don't know what to make of this, Will. I've learned to repeat abnormal tests that don't fit, and that's just what I did here. But if I don't trust our lab when a test is repeated with the same results, I might as well pack up and find another profession.'

'It wasn't my blood,' Will said desperately.

Again Millstein shook his head. Will could see now the deep sadness in his eyes.

'We ran a urine, too. Straight from your catheter. Chain-of-custody handling. No breaks in the chain. It was positive, too. *Strongly* positive, I might add, and you know how rapidly fentanyl is cleared from the body. Will, with all that's involved, this is way beyond me. I've reported everything to Sid Silverman, and he's called the police. They'll be here shortly if they're not here already.'

'Jesus,' Will said. Silverman, the president of the hospital, was in bed with several managed-care companies and had been openly critical of the Hippocrates Society and Will in particular. 'I'm in no shape to deal with fucking Silverman or the police. Let me out of here, dammit! I'll sign out AMA! Bring me the form.'

He leaned forward, then just as quickly fell back as a spear of pain thrust itself through one eye and out the back of his skull.

107

'Easy, Will.'

'No! I'm out of here!'

Mindless of the IV lines and catheter, Will battled through the headache, grabbed the side rails, and pulled himself forward again, scrambling toward the foot of the bed.

'Hands!' Millstein cried out, restraining him with surprising strength.

In seconds, the room was full of uniformed bodies, each trying to hold him down. A hand clutching a filled syringe moved into Will's sight. Helplessly, he watched as the needle was slipped into a port of his IV and the syringe emptied.

Moments later, a gentle, pleasant wave washed over him and he sank back into a dark, welcoming sea.

Chapter 13

'You've got to be kidding, Sergeant.'

Benois Beane, seated in a well-worn leather easy chair in his office, stared across at Patty, shaking his head in utter disbelief.

'It's the truth. His body was loaded with a very powerful narcotic – one that doctors, but not most other people, would have easy access to.'

From the moment they first shook hands, Patty liked the Open Hearth director. There was an engaging openness to him and an appealing wisdom in his face that she guessed was born of hard times. She had phoned him and driven over to the soup kitchen after a stop in the ICU at Fredrickston General.

Shortly after she had been raked over the coals by Wayne Brasco and Jack Court for withholding the information about Will Grant from them, a call from her father alerted her to the latest bizarre twist in the managed-care case – the drug overdose of their only suspect. Sitting in on the tense meeting with Court and Brasco had been Sean Digby, a young, eager detective who had come on board about six months after Patty and been immediately accepted by the guys. This was the first time Digby had attended one of their skull sessions on this case, and Patty had no trouble figuring out why. He was clearly being groomed to take her place should she falter any more, and calling him in like this was a strident warning that she was skating on thin ice.

Unwilling to make any moves without clearing them with both Brasco and Court, she called the two men together and asked permission to go out and check on the situation at Fredrickston General. Their response was predictable.

'So, what is this?' Brasco exclaimed. 'You called us in to tell us you want to go out and check on a guy in a coma? What's next? You'll call a meeting if you want to blow your nose?'

'You know, Patty,' Court added, 'you've got to show more independence in this thing. You don't have to check with us for everything you learn or do – just the important things.'

No surprise. She was damned if she involved the two of them and utterly damned if she didn't. Was it that she was a woman? That she was her father's daughter? That she had a master's degree in criminal justice? That she had an independent streak? Probably all of the above and none of the above. And there was nothing she could do about it, absolutely nothing, except put one foot in front of the other and take the path that felt right. Quitting was not an option.

Will was still sedated when Patty arrived at the ICU. The nurses she spoke with seemed shocked about what had happened in the OR and what had subsequently been discovered in his blood and urine, but they were also disappointed and angry. Will Grant certainly wasn't the first physician they had grown to love and respect who turned out to have a hidden problem with alcohol or drugs, but he was the first one to have unveiled his shortcoming in such a spectacular way.

'Must have just gone for a little more of a thrill and overshot,' Anne Hajjar said with a matter-of-factness that seemed blatantly forced.

Patty did learn that absolutely none of the staff saw this one coming. If Will Grant had any faults as a doc, they were that he cared too much, often hurt too deeply when things didn't go well, and spent way too much time in the hospital. Otherwise, as a physician and as a man, he was the total package.

'Before this happened,' Hajjar said, 'we all thought Dr. Grant was the catch of the year, even though it seemed he never left the hospital long enough to date.'

'I expect he'll have a good bit of free time now,' Donna Lee added. 'I just hope he uses it to get some help.'

More confused about Will Grant than ever, Patty had left the hospital and driven over to keep her appointment with Benois Beane, whom she tracked down after discovering Will had won an unsung hero award from the Boston Celtics for the work he did at the Open Hearth. Following her session with Will in his office, it was easy for her to believe he had no involvement in the managed-care slayings. Now, however, there could be no way around the fact that he had taken a potent narcotic and then attempted to perform surgery.

Would the real Will Grant please stand up?

'Sergeant Moriarity,' Benois Beane was saying, 'we have twenty-eight people who work here and a couple of hundred who volunteer regularly and probably know Will Grant. I'd wager not one of them would believe he knowingly took drugs and went into the OR.'

Let alone killed three people, Patty almost added, but didn't.

'I just don't get it, then,' she said. 'The drug was in his blood. That's a given.'

'I don't care. If it was in his body, someone put it there.'

'Tell me how.'

'I can't, but I can sort of prove he doesn't take narcotics.'

'Go on.'

'A few months ago, maybe three, one of our regulars, Sophie Rennet, died after a long battle with cancer. Will was her surgeon and did his best, but the cancer had gone too far from the start. It just so happened that one night when Will was working here, Sophie's family called to say that she had passed on. Will and I both went over to her place to pay our respects and for Will to pronounce her dead so the mortuary could come and get her. As we were leaving, her son handed us a box containing her medications, saying he hoped maybe someone else could use them. Inside were bottles and bottles and vials and vials of narcotics – all kinds of narcotics. Once we got back here, Will took a hammer to each of the vials and flushed the pills down the toilet. I saw him do it.'

'But he could have just as easily told you he was taking the medicine back to his office.'

'Exactly. I have known a lot of addicts in my day, a *lot* of addicts, and not one of them would have thrown away such a stash. I would think that's got to prove something.'

Patty thought of several rebuttals to Beane's logic, but she knew in her heart that none of them carried much clout.

'Are you sure he's awake?'

'It doesn't matter. He's got to wake up sometime.'

Hospital president Sid Silverman's distinctive tenor worked its way into the darkness. The other voice, irritated and sardonic, was Donna Lee's. The veteran nurse and Silverman, once an endocrinologist on the staff of FGH, had known each other for years. Now they had something else in common – a clear distaste for one Will Grant. Will tested his arms and legs and found that the wrist restraints were back in place. *Shit.*

'I just came from the recovery room,' Silverman was saying. 'The guy looks bad, real bad. His blood pressure won't stay up. There's talk about bringing him back into the OR to open him up again and see if something's bleeding.'

'That's terrible,' Donna said.

'You're damn right it is. If he doesn't make it, his family could end up owning this place.'

'I doubt they'd want it. Well, go on in there. We haven't given him anything for a while, so he should be pretty light.'

Will kept his eyes closed but sensed Silverman approaching his bed. He pictured the man glaring down at him, his paunch stretching the vest of his trademark three-piece suit.

'Welcome to the ICU, Sid,' he said keeping his eyes shut for a few more seconds, then slowly opening them. 'I don't suppose it matters to you, but I didn't take any fentanyl.'

'It was in your blood and in your urine,' Silverman said flatly. 'Do you have any explanation that I can give to the executive committee when they meet in an hour?'

'I didn't take anything. Listen, can you crank me up halfway? I don't like lying flat like this. I feel like I'm on a slab getting ready to be sacrificed.'

Silverman hesitated, then raised the head of the bed.

'And while you're at it, Sid, could you please tell the nurses to take these restraints off? I'm not going to cause any trouble. Promise.'

'I'll send the nurses in when I'm finished,' Silverman said. 'I asked if you had any explanation for how the fentanyl got into your body.'

'Maybe someone put it in my breakfast. Everyone knows I have OJ and a jelly stick on the days when I operate. Maybe someone injected it in there.'

'Maybe. You're also going to have to explain how two unopened vials of the stuff got into your locked locker in the surgeons' lounge.'

'That's absurd.'

'The locker was opened and there was the fentanyl, wrapped in a washcloth.'

'The same person who poisoned me put them there. Can't you see that? And, Sid, not that I have anything to hide, but you had no right to open my locker without my permission.'

'I didn't open it, Will. The police did. They got a warrant very quickly. Your locker and your office, and maybe your condo as well.'

'Jesus. Sid, can't you see that this is all a setup? Someone's doing this to me. Someone who knows me pretty damn well or has made it their business to learn about me.'

'Like the evil managed-care companies?'

'Don't be snide. I haven't the strength or the inclination to deal with it right now.'

'Okay, then, here's the situation. I'm recommending to the executive committee that you be suspended from the staff immediately until this matter can be resolved. I actually have the authority to do this myself, but I want their support.'

'Why don't you just ask me to take a week's leave or something? I promise I won't work until I get clearance from the executive committee. Besides, don't suspensions have to be reported to the Board of Registration?'

'Any change in privileges gets reported. Will, you should use the time off to check yourself into a treatment center someplace. Get in touch with the physician-health people at the medical society and have them recommend a good one.'

Will sensed himself about to blow. Fists balled, he forced his hands upward until the broad restraints cut into his wrists.

'I didn't take anything,' he said through nearly clenched teeth. 'I have never taken anything, and I'm not going to any goddamn treatment center.'

'Suit yourself,' Silverman said, his stubby fingers wrapped around the bed rail. 'You're going to have a day after you're discharged from here to get your strength back, then twenty-four hours to wrap up your dictations and any other business here. After that, until you're convicted or cleared of drug charges, I don't want you near this hospital. I'm sorry, Will. I had hoped you'd be more forthcoming.' He turned and strode to the doorway, then turned back. 'Our PR people are together right now working on damage control, but there's no way we can keep this from becoming a media circus as soon as the press gets word of what happened. And believe me, they *will* hear about it. I'd suggest you notify Maxine so she can prepare your children. I would also give your malpractice carrier a call so they can keep on top of things.'

112

Silverman left, and a few minutes later Anne Hajjar came in and removed Will's restraints.

'Dr. Millstein will be up in a little while,' she said.

'I want to sign out.'

'Please wait and speak with him.'

'It won't matter. He can discharge me or I'll sign out AMA. I didn't take any drugs and I want out of here.'

'Dr. Grant, please. Just don't do anything crazy until Ken gets here. We have a security guard right outside.'

'I won't cause any trouble. Anne, you've known me for years. Do you think I'm someone who would take drugs and then go into the operating room to do a complicated case?'

'I only know what I hear,' she said. 'I hope it turns out you didn't, but I admit it sounds like you did. By the way, your wife called from the lobby. She's on her way up.'

It's ex-wife, Will wanted to say, but didn't bother.

Maxine, stylishly dressed as always, today in a floral print silk blouse, navy blazer, and gray slacks, knocked on the doorway and nodded gravely to the nurse as they passed.

'You all right?' she asked.

'Physically I'm fine. How'd you know I was here?'

'Gordon called and told me, then a few minutes after that, Karen Millstein called.'

'I could win the Nobel Prize and news wouldn't travel any faster.'

'In case you don't know it, you didn't win the Nobel Prize.'

'I didn't take any drugs, either.'

'Gordon said it was in your blood and urine.'

'I didn't take any drugs.'

Will wondered how many times he would say the phrase over the hours, days, and weeks ahead.

'I thought you'd been acting strange lately.'

'You came to tell me I've been acting strange?'

'I came to see if you're all right.'

'I'm not all right. I didn't take any fentanyl and nobody believes that.'

'You passed out in the operating room and then stopped breathing and then had the drug in your blood and urine. What are people supposed to think?'

'I didn't take any drugs. Sid Silverman was just here. I'm about to be suspended from the staff.'

'What else could they do?'

'He says the media is going to be all over this. We've got to try our best to protect the kids. Maybe you should go away for a week until the firestorm blows past.'

'Maybe we will. Listen, Will, Mark and I talked and decided that until this business is resolved, I'm going to limit your visitation with the twins – no visits for the next week, then once a week in the playroom or yard at our place, three hours maximum, supervised. That is, provided your psychiatrist says it's safe.'

'I don't see a psychiatrist.'

'You will now.'

'That's ridiculous. You can't do that.'

'Can and will. Don't make me go to court for a restraining order. Besides, if our situations were reversed, you know you'd do the same thing.'

Will sank back and stared at the ceiling. This wasn't the time or place to battle Maxine, especially when he was totally outgunned. He lived for his medical practice and time with his children. Now, in a matter of just a few hours, he had lost both.

Who? Why? How?

For the first time, the questions took center stage in his mind.

Was the managed-care killer somehow involved? If so, to what end? He was supposed to be the ally of the movement. Why would they want to destroy him?

'Will? Are you listening to me? I asked if you thought you might be sued for this.'

'How should I know?' he replied, still staring overhead. 'If I'm sued, I'm sued. That's why I have malpractice.'

'Excuse me, sir,' Maxine said, 'but if you're sued for this, you *don't* have malpractice. Have you forgotten?'

The clause! In fact, he *had* forgotten. In an effort to stem the bleeding from malpractice premiums that were going through the roof, Fredrickston Surgical Associates had decided to switch their coverage to PSF – Physicians Security Fund – a small physician-owned company based in Indiana. Among several clauses designed to keep premiums down was one omitting coverage for any incident involving the use of alcohol or other mind-altering drugs. It was not surprising that Maxine knew the details of his malpractice insurance better than he did. She was a businesswoman, and an avaricious one at that. If he were wiped out by a claim, which as of this moment seemed exceedingly possible, her finances would take a significant hit.

'I'm sorry,' he said, 'but I just can't get worked up about that right now.'

'But it's true.'

'Yes, I suspect it's true.'

'Damn you, Will. Don't you ever think of anyone but yourself?'

Wolf Hollow Condominiums was a well-maintained, middle-class development situated a few miles outside the city. Will's unit, a two-bedroom, two-and-a-half-bath town house, was in the block farthest from the clubhouse and outdoor pool, thus bringing its cost down from absolutely prohibitive for him to merely unaffordable. Still, the kids enjoyed the pool and the game room, and had actually made some friends there. It would be hard to one day have to tell them that the place had become the property of Kurt Goshtigian or his heirs.

It was nearly eight when Will arrived home, having signed out against medical advice. Ken Millstein simply refused to authorize an early discharge for someone who had spent a large portion of the day on a vent due to a massive drug overdose and respiratory arrest. If nothing else, he insisted on a psych evaluation to determine whether or not Will was a danger to himself or anyone else. Ultimately, Will relented, and a colorless shrink named Yvonne Sands took more than an hour to determine that he was, in fact, mentally able to go home. Still, Millstein made him sign the AMA papers.

As Sid Silverman had predicted, the executive committee voted unanimously to suspend him from the hospital staff until his situation could be resolved. It seemed like only a matter of time before the Board of Registration suspended him, as well. Was there any way his disability insurance would pay anything without insisting he admit that he was an addict? Maybe he could claim a severe, paralytic depression and simply crawl into bed for a year or two. At the moment, such a diagnosis would not be stretching the truth very far. Will pulled into his parking space, grateful that no reporters or cameramen were lurking about, but he knew it was just a matter of time before they descended on 10-108 Wolf Hollow Drive, hungering for any sort of information about him and his life.

Compared to the house in Ashford, the condo was quite modest. Even so, Will liked the hardwood floors and the view of the woods out back, and bit by bit, as the bookshelves filled and art – framed prints or the twins' masterpieces – began to fill the walls, the place had become home. There was no evidence inside that the police had been there yet. Feeling numb and detached from his life, Will brewed a pot of tea, then sank onto the couch in the small den.

Who? Why? How? After a few minutes, the three burning questions were joined by a fourth: *What now?* He wanted to fight back – *needed* to fight back – but he knew things were only going to get worse. A lawyer? Probably that was the place to begin. He really didn't know any who handled this sort of thing. Thanks to the no-drug clause, there was no chance his malpractice company would provide one, and the incompetent weasel who had handled his divorce would probably succeed in getting him the gas chamber. What sort of retainers did lawyers charge these days, anyhow? At a recent Society meeting he had heard of one insisting on $50,000 up front. Was that possible?

The divorce and ongoing settlement payments had hit his finances hard, as had increasingly restrictive managed-care policies. He had maybe ten thousand in the bank, fifty or so in his retirement fund, and perhaps thirty that he could wring out of the condo. Not much to show for seven years in surgical practice. Jim Katz knew a lot of well-placed people. Maybe he or one of the other two partners could recommend someone.

Will sipped at his tea and stared across at the dark screen of the TV.

Shit. What in the hell had just happened to his life?

The doorbell had rung several times before he became aware of it. *Let the circus begin,* he thought. The guest bathroom overlooked the parking lot. Rather than answer the door, he went upstairs, carefully opened that bathroom window, and peered down. Patty Moriarity, alone, paced back and forth across the front stoop. Faced with the vast emptiness of his condo and, in fact, his world, a visit even from her was welcome.

'I'll be right there,' he called down.

'The Fredrickston PD called and told us what happened,' she said when he opened the door. 'I checked with the ICU at the hospital and they told me you were about to sign yourself out. So I decided to see if I could catch up with you here.'

He motioned her into the living room. She was wearing black jeans and the leather jacket he had now come to associate with her, and aside from maybe a little lipstick, wore no makeup. There was no gun that he could see, but he imagined a shoulder holster or a pistol strapped to her ankle.

'It's locked in the car,' she said before he could ask.

'Just wondered.'

Keeping her jacket on, she settled in at one end of the burgundy sofa Gordo had given him for his then-new place, while he took the recliner the people at the Open Hearth had chipped in to buy for him.

'So,' she said, 'it sounds like you've had a time of it since we last spoke.'

'Calling it the day from hell wouldn't do it justice.'

'I haven't spoken to the DA yet, but the FPD guys tell me there's a chance you'll be arrested soon for the drugs they found in your locker. I suppose there's a chance the DA could go for an attempted-manslaughter charge if the guy makes it, and maybe manslaughter if he doesn't.'

'That's great, just great. Sergeant Moriarity, I didn't take any drugs. Someone did this to me.'

'The killer?'

'I have no idea. Why would he do something like that? He said I was going to be his buddy from now on – his spokesman.'

'You don't take drugs of any kind?'

'I smoked dope from time to time in college and med school. That's it. Now I don't even take Tylenol.'

'Any idea how the drug got into you?'

'If I hadn't passed out the way I did, I'd blame someone in the lab putting it in my specimens. I'm superstitious and I have a few rituals that a lot of people know about. Maybe someone put the drug in my juice at breakfast, or the doughnut I like to eat.'

'What kind is that?'

Will felt color rush to his cheeks.

'Jelly stick.'

'I'm a glazed-cruller person myself, but those Krispy Kremes are starting to win me over. Dr. Grant, the people in your hospital have a great deal of respect for you. They've told me you're one of the best. Same goes for the people at the Open Hearth. I just came from speaking with Benois Beane. You're like a god to some of them.'

'That's nice to hear. So you believe me about the drugs?'

'At the moment I don't know what to believe. You see, everyone I talked to says you're a great surgeon and a terrific person but you work too hard – longer hours than anyone they've ever known. A couple of them don't know how you do it. Now, all of a sudden, a serial murderer is calling you on your private line, you almost kill a man when you pass out in the operating room, and you're found to be loaded with narcotics. Don't you think it seems possible, even likely, that you are coming apart from all the hours you spend working?'

'That's ridiculous.'

117

'Maybe it is. Maybe it isn't. What are you going to do now?'

'Find a lawyer, I guess. I don't intend to hand over my life without a goddamn good fight.'

The words were there, but they were belied by the dazed, vulnerable look in his eyes.

'I'm glad to hear that,' she said.

'You just don't expect this kind of stuff when you sign up.'

'Maybe not, but it's all there in the fine print that nobody ever reads.'

For a time, Patty gazed across the room at nothing in particular. How much she wanted to believe him – that he didn't create the mysterious phone call as a means of setting up a public platform for his views on managed care; that he didn't accidentally overdose on a powerful narcotic; that he would never even consider killing anyone. She wanted to believe him because, at the moment, she needed him. Her first major case, and she was being shoved out the door. Unless she came up with something, and quick, she would be back to chasing down shoplifters full-time.

What would Tommy Moriarity think if he knew she was contemplating joining forces with their chief suspect in a series of vicious murders? ... What were all those women thinking the moment they opened the door to let in charming, handsome, vulnerable Ted Bundy? ... How much denial was she in about her attraction to this man?

'Dr. Grant,' she suddenly heard herself saying, 'I need your help.'

'At the moment I can't believe anyone needs my help for anything,' he said.

'Your career is on the line if you can't prove you're innocent of taking any drugs. Well, mine is on the line unless I get a break in this managed-care case, and soon. The truth is, it's the first one of any consequence that I've gotten since I joined the force. A lot of people, including your friend Brasco, think that the only reason I'm still on the case is because my father is second in command of the state police.'

'How can I help?' Will asked.

'First, I want permission to tap your phones – here, your cell, even the one in your office.'

'If you think you need to.'

'For a while you won't have much privacy.'

'When the media gets ahold of what happened this morning, I don't suspect I'll have much privacy anyway. Besides, if you've been investigating my life you must have learned that outside the hospital, my kids, and the soup kitchen, I don't really have one. It's been months since my last date.'

Good!

'I'll give you my home number and my cell. If the killer calls, day or night, I need you to contact me immediately. If you have any ideas about who could be doing this or why, I need you to call me. If you can connect anyone to this drug business, anyone at all, that's important, too. I'll even take any theories that might come to you.'

'I suppose I could do that.'

'One last thing. I would really appreciate it if you didn't tell anyone we have this arrangement.'

'I wondered about that, given that I'm still a suspect.'

'To Brasco you are, but I've pretty much decided to believe you – at least for the moment.'

As Patty spoke the words, the reality of what she was doing hit.

Unprofessional, amateurish, and downright dangerous, her father would say. *You don't go into a man's home without another officer nearby, if not right in the room with you – especially when that man is a suspect in your murder investigation. Jesus, girl, what were you thinking?*

'I ... I've got to go,' she said, standing abruptly. 'Here are forms for the wiretaps. Sign them in front of a notary and get them to me at the address on my card. I'll let myself out.'

'Wait, you don't have to go. Stay for just a little while. Maybe we could brainstorm.'

Somewhere in the midst of Will's second sentence, she closed the door behind her.

Patty knew that in addition to her own vulnerability and feelings of isolation, she had just blatantly gone against policy and procedure because of the admiration and attraction that were building inside her for Will. Angry with herself and more than a little embarrassed, she hurried to the Camaro. She was unlocking her door when a photographer stepped out from between two parked cars and snapped off three quick shots.

'Hey!' a female reporter called from somewhere behind the man. 'How about an interview?'

'Go screw yourself!' Patty shouted back.

The stench of burning rubber filled the car as she screeched out of Wolf Hollow Parking Lot 10.

Chapter 14

Nowhere to go. Nothing to do.

With the abruptness of a racing car hitting a wall, every aspect of time had changed for Will. Just six days ago, hours had passed like minutes. With surgical consults to visit, notes to dictate, patients to see, cases to do in the OR, exercise to squeeze in, and evenings and weekends with the kids to arrange for, to say nothing of the mundane aspects of running his life and continuing his work at the Open Hearth, he had wistfully prayed for just an extra couple of hours each day, just an extra day or two each month. Now, the days that had followed the unfathomable events at Fredrickston Hospital had seemed interminable.

It was ten in the morning when the phone rang for the first time that day. After waking at six, Will had scrambled a trio of eggs and served them to himself with a toasted bagel and some OJ. He had rinsed what few dishes there were, put them in the washer, and failed on his third attempt to get into a Michael Crichton novel, usually a sure thing for him. Finally, he had taken a tube of caulk to the bathroom off the kitchen to tack down a small block of tiles that had been loose for at least a year. It was a good bet that Michelangelo didn't work more meticulously on the Sistine Chapel ceiling.

Nowhere to go. Nothing to do.

Over the past six days, caller ID and the bathroom window overlooking the parking lot and front stoop had become his staunchest allies. Initially, the reporters had been merciless in their attempts to get at him. Only in the past two days had their calls and visits begun to die away. Now, expecting yet another BLOCKED on the display, he checked the ID on the phone in the kitchen. AUGUST MICELLI, 617-483-5300. Will snatched up the receiver.

'This is Dr. Grant.'

'Dr. Grant, this is Gladys from Attorney Micelli's office speaking. I know your appointment isn't for three more weeks, and this is short notice, but we've had a cancellation for noon today, and Mr. Micelli thought you might want to come in.'

'I can be there,' Will said, hearing a small jet of enthusiasm in his voice for the first time since that moment in the OR.

'However,' the woman added, 'he asked me to tell you not to get your hopes up and to remind you that he really just takes the cases of people *suing* doctors, not the doctors who are being sued.'

'I understand.'

'You know where the office is?'

'Park Street in Boston. Right down the street from the State House.'

'We'll see you at noon.'

The recommendation to try August Micelli, MD, LLD, had come from Susan Hollister, who did not know the man well but did know that his intelligence was respected by physicians, even though the nature of his law practice was reviled. It was while Will was turning his practice over to her that Susan had suggested he might call the man, who was widely advertised as 'the Law Doctor.' The patients Susan inherited from Will included Grace Peng Davis, on whom she had operated the following day, and several others whose surgery needed doing.

After being turned down for legal support by his malpractice carrier as expected, Will had tried two attorneys – one local and one in Boston. Emotionally and intellectually, he failed to connect with either, and the retainers and fees each demanded would have virtually broken him even before the game of saving his professional, personal, and financial lives began. Visions of running out of money and lawyer at the same time had sent him trudging back to the sanctuary of his condo. When he returned from the disappointing session with the second of the attorneys, there was a letter from a third firm waiting in his mailbox. However, rather than offering him representation at an exorbitant fee, this attorney was announcing that he and his firm had been retained by Kurt Goshtigian and his family to institute a malpractice claim against him. After two extra trips to the OR, it appeared that the man was going to make it, but his debility would be profound, if not permanent.

Will was dressing for the trip into Boston when the front doorbell sounded. He scurried over to the bathroom-window observation post. Beneath him, a husky black man in a business suit stood motionless by the front door. Not a reporter, Will guessed; the man was simply too well dressed. He discarded salesman as a possibility for the same reason and decided to open the window.

'Yes?' he called down.

The man squinted upward at him.

'Dr. Willard Grant?'

'Yes.'

'My name's Sam Rogers. I'm an investigator with the Board of Registration in Medicine. May I come in for just a moment, please? I have a letter I need to hand-deliver to you.'

Will knew even before he opened the door what the official-looking envelope contained. Still, Rogers explained it to him.

'This is a summary suspension of your privilege to practice medicine in this state of Massachusetts. It has been issued because of the suspension recently ordered by Fredrickston Hospital. It is effective immediately and may be appealed through channels established by the board. Do you have any questions?'

Without bothering to read the letter, Will tossed it onto a pile of junk mail and unopened bills on the coffee table. Somewhere in the mound of mail was another letter – one he *had* read. It was from Tom Lemm, unofficially requesting that he remove himself from his very important and sensitive position with the Hippocrates Society until his pending matter with the hospital could be satisfactorily resolved.

'Are you here to investigate what was done to me?' Will asked Rogers.

'No, sir. I may well be investigating your case sometime in the future, but for the moment my assignment is to deliver this letter and explain its contents.'

'Thanks,' Will said with no emotion whatsoever. 'As far as I'm concerned you've done your job and done it well.'

'In that case,' Rogers said, 'if you wouldn't mind signing off on that right here...'

Will would have been the first to admit that he had never been on anyone's best-drivers list. His reflexes were sharp, and that certainly helped, but even under the best of circumstances his thoughts were constantly wandering, as was, all too often, his car. Although he had never been involved in anything more destructive than a minor fender bender, he sometimes wondered if there were accidents he would never know about for which he had been responsible.

This morning, traffic was light, and the drive into Boston was less grueling and perilous than usual. Susan had told Will little of Augie Micelli except that he had once been on some sort of board or community-service organization with her and that he had been treated poorly by the Board of Registration in Medicine and the medical community. Micelli's response to both had been to get a law degree and subsequent notoriety as the Law Doctor – highly promoted in the press and on billboards as the place to go for justice against physicians responsible for bad outcomes. It was Susan's hope that the similarities in the ways Micelli and Will had been treated might lead him to agree to get involved in Will's case. It was a long shot, but in this mounting gale, even the smallest landing field would be welcome.

As Will turned off the Mass Pike and headed into the Back Bay, he found himself thinking of Patty Moriarity. Since her visit to Wolf Hollow Drive, she had not been among the hordes who had tried to reach him by phone or through simply showing up on his doorstep. He assumed the wiretap on his phone was in place and still functioning, but he had no way of knowing if her position as an investigator on the case was surviving.

He gave passing thought to reaching out to her, but nothing she had said or done during her odd visit had encouraged such familiarity, and her abrupt departure had accomplished just the opposite. He expected to reconnect with her if he ever received another call from the murderer, but so far nothing. Maybe he simply wasn't good enough for the serial killer anymore.

He left the Jeep in a lot off Tremont that was more expensive than some surgical procedures and walked along the Boston Common to Park. Although the street itself was elegant, the Law Doctor's office was not. Located on the third-floor alley side of a four-story brownstone, it consisted of a small, eclectically furnished waiting room, off which was an entrance from the dimly lit hallway and one other door, presumably to Micelli's inner sanctum. The oriental carpet was threadbare in spots, and the two framed prints on the wall – a farm scene perhaps by one of the Dutch masters, and a courtroom depiction that might have been offered as a premium for subscribing to a law magazine – had little to do with each other. A bottle-blonde woman in her late forties peered up from behind her granny glasses as he entered, and smiled kindly.

'Dr. Grant?' she asked in what he could immediately tell was a dense Boston accent.

'Yes.'

'I'm Gladys. Please fill out this registration form. Bring it in with you when you go. Mr. Micelli's on the phone right now, but it shouldn't be too long.'

'I'm in no hurry,' Will replied, in the understatement of the day.

The form, clearly meant for someone who was hoping to sue a doctor, contained only a few lines of demographic questions that Will could answer. He finished it in less than a minute and slipped it into his thin black leather briefcase, which contained copies of the lab reports from the hospital that Susan had obtained for him, as well as of the letters of suspension from Sid Silverman and the Chairman of the Board of Registration in Medicine. In addition, there was the letter from the multipartnered law firm in Worcester that told him he was being sued for malpractice. That letter included paragraphs taken directly from some law boilerplate, describing the legal basis for Kurt Goshtigian's action against him.

Please consider this letter, together with the attached complaint, incorporated herein, to constitute a written demand for relief on behalf of your former patient Kurt S. Goshtigian. We intend to file a lawsuit following the expiration of fourteen (14) days from the mailing of this demand.

It is our contention that through your negligence and use of mind-altering drugs at the time of Mr. Goshtigian's cancer surgery, you have caused infection, excess bleeding, extended operating-room time, substitution of principal surgeons, additional surgery, and additional medication. In addition, your negligence has caused unnecessary pain and suffering for Mr. Goshtigian and his family. Please provide your medical malpractice and personal-liability carriers with the enclosed documents and have their attorneys send us notice of representation. The amount of damages to be demanded will depend on Mr. Goshtigian's survival from your malpractice and his condition at the time of discharge and subsequent to that time, but in no case will it be less than fifty (50) million dollars.

Fifteen minutes passed during which Gladys answered four calls, each, it seemed, from a potential new client. Just as Will was beginning to get restless, the door to Micelli's office opened and a thick-waisted, broad-shouldered man emerged, who had probably been an athlete at one time, although clearly not anymore. He had dense gray-black hair and olive skin and was wearing a light-blue sport shirt open at the collar, with no jacket. He could have easily played one of Don Vito's bodyguards in *The Godfather*, except for his eyes, which

Will did not appreciate until the two of them had shaken hands and he had settled down on the hard-backed chair beside Micelli's desk. They were very dark, with an intriguing forcefulness and intelligence. But in those first moments together, Will saw something else as well – the sadness and ennui of a man who didn't care about much.

'Drink?' Micelli asked, heading over to a sideboard with three crystal decanters labeled SCOTCH, WHISKEY, and RUM, half a dozen glasses, and a brass ice bucket. 'It's past noon.'

'No thanks, Dr. Micelli.'

'For chrissakes, don't call me that. Augie'll do fine; Mr. Micelli if you have a need to be formal, but please, no "Doctor." '

He splashed two fingers from the SCOTCH decanter into a Waterford tumbler, added an ice cube, and took a gulp before heading over to his chair. There was a law degree from Suffolk on the wall behind his desk alongside a medical degree from Harvard, but no other certifications or, for that matter, pictures of any kind. One wall was a floor-to-ceiling bookshelf filled with carefully aligned sets of legal tomes that appeared as if they had never been read. The window to Will's left looked out on the side of a building. The wall behind him included the door to the waiting room and a small fireplace, neatly painted, with three logs decoratively and probably permanently arranged. The Law Doctor. With all the advertising, Will had conjured up visions of a massive medico-legal mill with lawyers scurrying from exquisitely appointed offices into mahogany-paneled conference rooms and libraries.

'You look a little dismayed,' Micelli said. 'Not what you had expected?'

'No. I ... I mean yes. I mean not exactly. All those ads...'

'And worth every penny, too. Malpractice cases come in here by the barrel. Just listen to that phone ringing. Most of them are frivolous, ridiculous, or simply nasty and vindictive. But a certain percent of them have some merit, and once in a while the ol' amputated-the-wrong-leg or plucked-out-the-wrong-kidney mother lode comes hobbling in. But you see, Dr. Grant, I don't actually do the cases. In fact, I don't do any cases at all, so I don't need much help and I don't need much space.' He drained what remained in his glass and immediately restocked it. 'I bring the cases in, evaluate them from a medical standpoint, and either ship them off to one of the firms that can actually do something with them or send them on their way to pursue their complaint if they want, but not with me.'

'And you get a finder's fee from the firms you refer to?'

'Sometimes a really big one, plus as many dinners at swanky restaurants as I care to accept. They all want to be my friend.'

'Isn't that fee splitting?'

'By any definition of the term I would say so, yes.'

'And isn't that illegal?'

'In medicine it's illegal. You can't refer a patient to a specialist and then get a kickback from that specialist. In law it's considered good, sound business.'

Will sighed and stared out the window, as uncertain whether he wanted to continue this session as Micelli probably was. Finally, he shrugged and asked if the lawyer wanted to hear why he had come.

'You go ahead with your story if you want to,' Micelli replied, 'but as Gladys told you, the only help I might be is to give you the names of some firms to call. Our motto here is if it takes work, we don't want it.'

He managed a thin smile, but there was nothing cheerful in the way he said the words. Will may have been a surgeon, but he could recognize depression when he saw it, and probably alcoholism, too. *Thank you, Susan Hollister.*

'I think I'm going to go,' he said.

'Suit yourself.'

'You know, my partner Susan Hollister said you have had some trouble of your own.'

'Plenty of it.'

'And she said because of that you might have some sympathy with what's happening to me.'

'I might. That doesn't mean I can be of any help.'

'Well,' Will said, 'exactly what is it that happened to you?'

Micelli eyed him for a moment, then drained his tumbler. It was as if the question was one nobody had ever asked.

'I killed my son,' he said simply.

Will stifled any knee-jerk response.

'Go on,' he said.

'You sure?'

Will nodded.

'Okay. Remember, you asked for it. I was an internist with all the right medical pedigrees, very full of myself,' Micelli said in a near monotone, virtually devoid of the emotion inherent in the terrible account. 'My then wife and son and I were in Utah, set to go on a camping trip into some pretty remote country. Ryan had a little fever and a stuffy nose. His mother wanted to cancel the hike. I told her he

126

was nine and she was being overprotective. I even checked him over so she would be reassured. A little red throat was all. So off we went.'

Will could see the shattering end of the story already and wanted to spare both of them any unnecessary anguish.

'Meningitis,' he said.

Impressed, Micelli nodded.

'Two days out with no radio. I raced back for help, but by the time the helicopter reached them, he was gone. Just like that.'

'I'm very sorry. That's so sad.'

'So was what happened afterward. A few months later I went into what they called a paranoid depression. No history of prior mental illness. Scared the hell out of my wife, my neighbors, and a lot of people at my hospital. I was about the only one around who thought I was normal. Rather than get me help, or ask my wife to get me hospitalized, my hospital panicked and suspended me. After that I was hospitalized and properly diagnosed and treated. The paranoia and crazy behavior went away almost immediately and has stayed away. But by then the Board of Registration had suspended me, as well, until they could investigate why I had been kicked out of my hospital.'

Once again, Will could see what was coming, and again stepped into the account.

'Then,' he said, 'because you had your license suspended, the managed-care companies dropped you from their provider panels.'

'Exactly. It was a cookie-cutter response by the board and by them, without so much as an investigation or a hearing. So even though the board eventually reinstated my license, most of the companies held to their decision. Once worth suspending, always worth suspending. There was no way I could practice – at least no way I could practice and get paid for it. Well, no matter now. I make ten times more doing this than I ever did being an internist – and work a fraction of the hours. Too bad, though, because I actually liked doing it, and I was pretty damn good at it, too.'

'I'll bet you were, Augie,' Will said. 'Listen, I'm sorry for all you've been through. I really am. But I hope you can take some pride in the way you've managed to deal with all that's happened without going down for the count. I don't think I could have handled something happening to one of my kids that bravely even if I *didn't* believe I was responsible.'

Without a word, Micelli made his way to the sideboard and poured a third drink, this one more substantial than the other two.

'So,' he said, taking a gulp, then clumsily wiping his mouth on the back of his hand, 'it's your turn now. Assume I know everything about you that the newspapers and TV can tell me.'

Clearly, Augie Micelli was now under the influence, although not strikingly so. Will debated if there was any percentage in staying. Even if he decided to leave and renew his attempts to connect with a lawyer who fit his requirements of being talented, empathetic, and reasonably affordable, he knew that the trip into Boston had been worth it. Whether he and Augie ever saw each other again or not, he still owed Susan thanks. According to the story Augie had shared, the man was hardly as responsible for his son's tragic death as he seemed to want to believe. Still, the boy was dead.

Will's external world was crumbling, that was all too true, but Dan and Jess were healthy, wonderful kids. And even if he hit rock bottom and lost everything else, he would still be their father and they his children. Even if the only purchase he had on the sheer wall up from this nightmare was them, he would still have a firm hold from which he could start the climb. His heart ached for Augie and the terrible emptiness he had to deal with each day, but it no longer ached for himself.

'You know what,' he said finally, 'if you know that much about me and my situation, then you really are already in a position to know whether or not you can be of any help to me.'

'I can tell you right now that I can't. This just isn't the sort of thing I do.'

'I can see that. Listen, here are copies of some letters I brought for you to review. I'll leave them with you anyway, just in case you can think of someone who might want to work with me. One of the letters is from a law firm that is representing my former patient. Because of a clause in my group's malpractice policy, I don't have any coverage for what's happened. Fortunately, even though they'll get everything I have if I'm found at fault, it won't be much. All the information you need to reach me is on that sheet I filled out.'

'I'm sorry I can't be of any help to you,' Micelli said.

'I'm sorry about your son,' Will replied.

For twenty minutes after the door closed, Augie Micelli sat, staring unseeing out the window, feet on his desk, rising once only to replenish the scotch and ice in his glass. Losing Ryan would always be the worst thing that had ever happened to him – far beyond the subsequent financial losses and breakup of his marriage. But this was the first time he could remember speaking with anyone about the pain of losing his practice. Unlike what he was doing now, practicing medicine had never been about the money.

He opened his desk drawer and set a silver-framed photo from it on his desk – one of Ryan smiling down from the limb of a massive, ancient oak.

He drained his glass. Drinking like this had been really stupid. He had made a deal with himself not to do it around clients anymore, and now he had broken that agreement. He swallowed what remained in his glass.

What in the hell difference does it make? In fact, what difference does anything make? Guilty or not, Will Grant has gotten himself into this mess. He can damn well get himself out. If he needs to, he can just go to law school or become a grocer or do landscaping or ... or...

Micelli stood suddenly and hurled his tumbler into the fireplace. The shattering glass had Gladys in his office in seconds.

'Are you all right?'

'I'm fine, fine. Sorry about the glass. I'll clean it up myself. Meanwhile, could you please get me Gil Murray in the Middlesex County DA's office? Tell him it's about the Will Grant case.'

Chapter 15

'I miss you, Daddy.'

'I miss you, too, sport. We'll see each other next week. Meanwhile, just keep oiling that new glove and then, with the ball in the pocket, tie it up like I showed you with one of those heavy rubber bands we bought.'

'O-okay.'

'Danny, it's okay to cry if you want to, but please know that I'm all right and everything's going to be fine. It's just going to take a little time. The things that have been said and written about me aren't true, and before long everyone will know that. Okay?'

'Okay. Sean's mother won't let him come over here to play any-more.'

'I'm so sorry. That must make you very sad.'

'Only a little. Sean's a jerk most of the time, and he wasn't my best friend anyway.'

'Just the same, it's got to be hard for you.'

'We know you didn't do anything wrong.'

'And that's all that matters to me. Now, I'll see you both next week, and before too long everything will be back to normal. Got that?'

'Got it.'

'You're a brick.'

'You're a wall.'

'You're iron.'

'You're steel.'

'Your ... nose is running.'

'Da-ad.'

Will said good-bye and set the receiver down slowly.

'You bastards,' he muttered, at once sickened and furious at the pain that the twins were experiencing. 'You fucking bastards.'

Augie Micelli's story had been a heavy dose of perspective for him, but the reality of his situation was still overwhelming and, it seemed at the moment, virtually hopeless. Whoever had set out to destroy him had done a masterful job. He was a rag doll, hung out to dry and swinging helplessly in the breeze. Even worse, aside from a few friends like Benois Beane, he was alone in the certainty of his innocence. There was no grass-roots crusade mounting, no letter-writing campaign, no pass-it-on e-mails. Even his partners and a number of his friends seemed to have stepped back and taken a wait-and-see position.

You can only do what you can do, he reminded himself for the thousandth time. *You can only do what you can do.*

He was sifting aimlessly through the mound of mail on the coffee table when the phone began ringing. The caller ID read simply ERROR. Will hesitated. Then, both curious and prepared to hang up, he picked up the handset.

'Hello?'

'Hello, Will Grant,' the electronically distorted voice said. 'Your life has certainly been quite eventful since we last spoke.'

Will wondered if Patty was on top of this. She hadn't given him any instructions in terms of whether or not he needed to keep the killer on the line for any specific length of time, like the cops in the movies always tried to do. In fact, she hadn't even told him whether the tap on his line was done at his phone, at the line outside, or at the phone company. *Stay calm but sound upset*, he told himself. *Calm but upset.*

'I don't want you to call me anymore,' he pleaded. 'Give yourself up and I'll see to it you get the best therapist around. You're sick. You need help.'

'*I* need help? Goodness, but those are strong words from a man who has done what the papers and TV say you've done. Face-first into a patient's incision. That sort of publicity isn't good for our cause, Dr. Grant. Not good at all. We have no place in this crusade for drug addicts.'

'I'm not one of you, and I'm not a drug addict.'

'Oh, but you are. These managed-care companies are your enemy just as they are ours. I read where you are claiming to have been set up.'

'I was.'

'Well, if not one of the managed-care companies you exposed at Faneuil Hall, then who? Was it Halliday? Because if it was, he could and should be moved up the list, say to tonight.'

'Stop it! Please, you've got to stop this insanity!'

'Funny, that's precisely what we begged our mother's so-called caregivers. You've got to stop her insanity, we told them.'

A mental-health patient! This is all about a mental-health patient. Will flashed on the many instances he had encountered over the years of managed-care companies refusing detox or even counseling for alcoholics and cutting short hospitalizations for psychiatric cases, even though there was concern that the patient was or might be suicidal. Of all the patients the industry had shortchanged since its rise to power, those with mental illness headed the list.

'Did your mother kill herself?' he asked. 'Is that what's behind all this?'

'When you have proven yourself reliable, Dr. Grant, we will increase your level of responsibility and knowledge. In the meantime, if you have any information as to who might have set you up, or you need to contact us for any reason, any reason at all, simply place a personal ad in the *Herald* containing the phrase *In war there are casualties*. We will contact you. Meanwhile, I suggest that you stay safely indoors tonight. The piper's on the loose and he must be paid. Good day, Dr. Grant.'

'Wait!...'

The tension had become almost unbearable around the state police in general and among the Middlesex detectives in particular. It had been over a week since the managed-care killer had been heard from – a week that coincided with Will Grant's bizarre drug overdose in the OR. Spurred on by what he and Jack Court considered Patty's reckless and potentially disastrous solo visit to the apartment of their only suspect, Brasco was keeping the pressure on her with a constant barrage of callous remarks and a string of time-consuming ticky-tack assignments related to their case, the latest of which was reinterviewing the security people in the Fredrickston Medical Arts Building. Meanwhile, there had been no letup in the day-to-day business of robberies, assaults, drug deals, and various other demonstrations of man's inhumanity to his fellow man and to society. The result, from the CO down to the rawest rookie, was stress.

The afternoon was heavily overcast and more humid than any early spring day had the right to be. It was ten after three when Patty swung the Camaro into her spot and made her way through the sparsely patronized mall to her office. There was yet another meeting scheduled with Court to review the lack of progress on their biggest, most visible case. In order to appease Brasco, Patty had not only interviewed those security people on duty the night before and the day of the killer's intrusion into Will's office, but she had tracked down all the personnel who had covered the company for the past month. Not surprisingly, she had come away with nothing except the hassling she was about to get for being late to Court's meeting.

She punched in her code on the security pad, waved to veteran Brian Tomasetti, who was building a pyramid of magnetic balls on the top of a Dunkin' Donuts carton, and hurried past Brasco's empty cubicle. She paused at the door to her own space long enough to toss her jacket onto the back of her chair, and was just about to race off when she saw the light flashing on her voice mail. Even before she keyed in her password, she knew it was trouble. Three messages. The first was prefaced by Gil Kinchley at the phone company – the man who had turned the court order she had obtained into a wiretap.

'Well, Sergeant Moriarity,' he said, 'I think this is what you've been waiting for.'

Barely breathing, she sank into her chair, the receiver pressed against her ear, and listened to the eerie exchange between Will and the killer.

'It's Gil again,' the second message said. 'Our people say he – if it even *is* a he – was probably using a call diverter, more likely two. It's like call forwarding, only it doesn't go through us. The technology is readily available in any spy store. The equipment is well made, very effective, and makes a call almost impossible to trace. Ring me if you need anything. We'll keep on this.'

The third message was from Will.

'Patty, it's Will. I hope you got that. Call and let me know what you think and what I'm supposed to do. I tried keeping him on the phone as long as I could.'

Wayne Brasco appeared at the doorway, startling her.

'Sergeant, are you going to join the rest of us at the meeting you're already late for, or are you going to exercise a woman's prerogative to talk on the phone no matter what?'

'I think you'd better bring Lieutenant Court in here,' she said, ignoring the remark.

'Tell me again,' Court said after he, Patty, and three other detectives had listened to the message on speaker for the second time. 'When did the call come in?'

Patty knew this was coming. She also knew she deserved it.

'Two hours ago.'

'But you just picked the message up now?'

'I had meant to forward it to my cell phone, but I was racing around so much I forgot.'

Ask that gorilla next to you why I was racing around so much.

'So we've lost two hours.'

We wouldn't have had this tap at all if I hadn't gone out and gotten it! she wanted to scream.

'There's still time,' she said.

'To do what?' This time it was Brasco.

'He's going to kill tonight.'

'A brilliant deduction, Mrs. Holmes.'

Patty stood and glared at Brasco.

'Back to my office, everyone!' Court snapped, intercepting any escalation in the hostilities. He waited until the others had gone past him, then stepped in front of Patty. 'Moriarity, we're having enough trouble without losing two hours like this,' he said.

'I understand. I'll be more careful from now on.'

'And another thing.'

'Yes?'

'What's going on with this guy Grant that he's calling you Patty?'

'I ... um ... I don't know.'

She had never been much of a liar, and it was clear from her CO's expression that he wasn't buying her denial.

'You just be careful,' he said. 'Be damn careful.'

Without waiting for a response, Court turned and headed back to his office. Patty snatched her briefcase from the floor and followed.

'All right,' Court said when the team had settled back in his office, 'thoughts?'

'I still think Grant's dirty in this,' Brasco said. 'I think he's playing us like a violin. His big screwup was overdosing on that drug. Now it's damage control for him – using someone from that damn Society of his to make it seem like he isn't involved in these killings.'

'Patty?'

'I think the call strongly suggests Grant is innocent, but at the moment that doesn't matter. What does matter is that the call also implies someone is going to get killed tonight.'

'So?'

Patty withdrew a manila file folder from her briefcase and opened it.

'Well, believe it or not, there are ninety-seven managed-care or health-insurance companies of one kind or another headquartered in Massachusetts alone – HMOs, PPOs, MCOs – alphabet soup. Most of them are within thirty miles of Boston. There are another twelve in New Hampshire and a few more in Vermont and Maine. If we limit ourselves to this state and eliminate the three companies where someone's already been killed – and I'm not at all sure we should do that – we have ninety-four companies to contact and warn. I have a list of them here with phone numbers and a contact person, usually the membership or PR coordinator.'

There was silence while the group waited for a reaction from Court. Patty sensed that the last thing he wanted to do was to find any merit in her suggestion, but she also knew contacting the CEOs of the companies was the thing to do.

Finally, Court inhaled deeply and exhaled slowly.

'Okay, we have enough people here to make these calls over the next hour or two. Might as well include the companies that have already had someone murdered. What do we tell them – just for all their executives to be careful?'

'Don't go walking around alone,' Patty said. 'Bring a guard along when they walk to their car. Keep their personal cars out in the open, not in their garage where someone can work an explosive into place without being seen.'

'Is it worth notifying the TV and radio stations?'

'I don't know. The killer must suspect that Will Grant's phone is tapped, otherwise he wouldn't take the sort of precautions he has. But if we go public, we remove any doubt. I hate to put the guy in harm's way.'

'I say go with it,' Brasco blustered. 'Grant's a damn drug addict. Almost killed his patient. The execs who have been murdered were all upstanding citizens. They all were big into charitable causes.'

'So is Will Grant,' Patty snapped. 'He started the Open Hearth soup kitchen in Fredrickston when he was a medical student, and he still volunteers there.'

'That doesn't change anything, and neither does your grandstanding here. You just conveniently neglected to mention that list you're holding is one *I* told you to put together.'

'You know, Brasco, I've just about had it with you, you sexist –'

'Enough!' Jack Court slammed his fist on his desk. 'Moriarity, divide up those phone numbers. I'm warning you, you and Wayne better find a way to work together on this thing, or one of you is going to go. And I'm warning you about something else, too. Keep your personal life separate from your work.'

Forcing Court's warning to the back of her mind, Patty made the twenty or so calls she had been assigned. The effort to alert all of the managed-care CEOs in the state seemed akin to trying to stop an elephant with a pop gun, but at least they would have done what they could do. The best they could hope for was that the killer's dramatic proclamation about the piper being on the loose and needing to be paid was his way of keeping the police off balance – one of the I'm Smarter Than You Are ego games that ultimately led to the capture or death of so many like him.

Now there was nothing more to do but sit down and analyze the tape that had been made of the killer's call. Not surprisingly, Brasco had again managed to maneuver her out of the loop by suggesting that he and Court meet with the new profiler to pore over the recording. Patty was assigned to contact the cryptographer and, even though there were no new alphabet clues, to go over the letters they did have in light of the new information on the tape. She had a different idea, but it wasn't one she wanted to discuss with her CO.

She wasn't surprised when she called Will to find him at home and anxious for company. He was openly relieved to hear that, in her mind at least, any lingering doubt about his not being connected to the killings was gone. What she didn't share with him, but grudgingly acknowledged to herself, was that for days she had been looking for the opportunity to see him again.

It was almost seven by the time she pulled into a parking space marked GUEST, not far from Will's condo. On the drive over, she listened to Yo-Yo Ma's contemplative score from *Crouching Tiger, Hidden Dragon*. Spurred on by the horrible events of Will's week, she found herself trying to rank some of the worst things that had ever happened to her. Certainly, her mother's illness and death headed the list, and there were some tragedies over the years that had befallen her friends. But most of the rest, dating back to middle school, it seemed, centered about bad choices she had made in men, including last year's follies with Jerry Parkhurst, a wildly attractive and successful mergers-and-acquisitions attorney, who lived in a stunning waterfront apartment in Charlestown.

Parkhurst seemed like a potential keeper – a match for a lifetime – until after they had finally slept together following their fourth or fifth date, when he almost casually mentioned that in addition to his penthouse bachelor pad, he also had a sixteen-room mansion in Newton, where he lived 'unhappily' with his wife and two children. That was a bad one, and would have been even more painful if she had actually fallen in love with him. But with images of the vivid imprint of her hand on the side of his face, and some tincture of time, the sleaze had become a relatively distant memory. In terms of pain, it was certainly nothing compared to what Will was going through now.

With Jerry Parkhurst strutting through her brain like Harold Hill in *The Music Man*, Patty rang Will's bell.

'Be right down,' Will called from the window above.

Dressed in rumpled chinos, a light-blue button-down, white socks, and slightly worn Nikes, he looked every bit like a man who had lost his medical license, was facing criminal drug and manslaughter charges, and was being harassed by a serial killer.

'You okay?' she asked.

Will made no attempt to mask his discouragement.

'I can handle everything that's happening to me,' he said, 'but people aren't being kind to my kids. That I can't handle. Forgive me for saying it, but I really want to kill some of them.'

'I don't think I'd do very well at dealing with that, either.'

Patty accepted the offer of a Diet Coke, set her tape recorder on the coffee table, and motioned that it was okay for Will to sit on the couch where they both could have access to the control buttons. The distance between them was the same as when he was on the recliner, but

136

she knew there was something more to the sensation of having him sitting there. In her head, Jerry Parkhurst and Jack Court were engaged in some sort of heated discussion that she decided not to try to overhear.

'Let's start by listening to the whole conversation with no interruptions,' she suggested. 'Then we'll play it again and again if necessary until we both feel we've squeezed every ounce of juice from it.'

It was the fifth time Patty had listened to the eerie exchange. While the gender of the caller was electronically obscured, the cadence and choice of words made her almost certain it was a man.

'Do you think he's going to kill someone tonight?' Will asked as she clicked off the tape and rewound it for another pass.

'I'm hoping, praying, he's just jerking our chain,' she replied. 'Toying with us.'

'He doesn't seem like the toying type to me.'

'Why do you say that?'

'I don't know – maybe because this is a vendetta – anger but with a point to be made, and maybe a demand somewhere down the road. This person – *these people* if you believe all those references to *we* – is avenging the loss of someone they loved.'

'I see your point, but what about the letters? Aren't they some sort of game?'

'I don't know. Dramatic effect, maybe. Maybe the killer expected the press would glom on to the letter thing right away, and the publicity and speculation would go through the roof. *People*, the *National Enquirer*, *Larry King* – the works.'

'You think they're going to spell the mother's name?'

'That would be my first guess if it didn't seem so obvious and didn't point directly at the killer.'

'Well, I hope you're wrong about him being totally serious, Will. Because if this guy kills again, he gets two for one.'

'Explain.'

'My CO has made it clear that unless we produce a break, and soon, the team on this case is going to be revamped. He neglected to say, "Starting with Moriarity," but he didn't have to.'

'In that case, let's listen to that tape again,' Will said. 'The guy keeps saying "us." Let's see if we can convince ourselves once and for all that there are more than one of them. Then maybe we can get a pen and some paper and see if we can come up with any other hints.'

'I really appreciate your help with this,' Patty said, 'especially with all you're going through yourself.'

'I need to get my mind off my own stuff.'

Without either of them orchestrating things, Patty slid a few inches closer, and Will gently lowered his arm down around her waist. She hesitated, then set her head on his shoulder. For a time, neither of them moved.

'Do you think we're just making our bad situations worse?' she asked.

Will stroked her hair.

'Not from where I'm sitting,' he said.

Chapter 16

'Careful there, Jennifer. Handle that suction with care and never, ever forget, that's brain you're suckin' on.'

'Yes, sir,' the med student said grimly.

To keep the nervous tremor in her hands at bay, she braced them against the patient's skull.

Standing across the table in OR 4 of Boston's prestigious White Memorial Hospital, Richard Leaf noted the protective maneuver and smiled beneath his mask. The kid, a Harvard senior, was bright and witty and had a better than decent body. Now he could see that she was resourceful, as well. The potential for something interesting was very much there. He could tell from the way she had been looking at him on morning rounds since she started her neurosurgical rotation. He had Tuesday free next week and his wife had a board meeting scheduled at some society foundation or other. Maybe something could be set up for then. Tonight, though, he had another fish to fry – a fish by the name of Kristin O'Neill. His mouth grew dry at the prospect.

'Be gentle, there, Jen. That's it. That's it. You're doing great. We're almost done.'

It had been a tricky piece of surgery, but the patient's cancer, a low-grade malignant astrocytoma, was gone. In all likelihood it would be cured after a course of radiation and chemo.

The legend grows, Leaf was thinking. *The legend grows.*

'Take over, Jeff,' Leaf said to his resident. 'Let Jennifer help as much with the closure as you feel comfortable with. You've all done a terrific job. Thank you. Thank you all very much.'

He stepped back from the table to allow the resident to take his place, then dramatically stripped off his gown and gloves and strode out of the OR, reveling in the gazes he knew were fixed on him.

Leaf was as talented a surgeon as he was flamboyant, and as handsome as he was talented. From his earliest days of awareness in grammar school, he knew he was special. Through his years as class president and all-state athlete, he had come to know that he was destined to do great things. Now, at forty-five, wealthy by most people's standards and world renowned for his skill as a neurosurgeon, his remarkable life was becoming even more so.

Hub Health Care, the HMO he and three other physicians had started just six years ago, was on the verge of making a public offering. The moment the stock went public, Richard Leaf would instantly go from wealthy to rich. Hub Health's money people were estimating that, for starters, each of the founders would increase his net worth by thirty to forty million – and that was a lowball projection.

Leaf showered. Then, breathing deeply just to keep himself in check over what his life held in store, he entered the busy main corridor of the hospital and headed for his office. Just two days ago, in about this very spot, he was leaving the OR when he literally collided with the library cart being pushed by Kristin O'Neill. Nothing – not the ugly salmon-colored volunteer's jacket, not her conservative skirt and loose-fitting blouse, not the barrettes with which she controlled her reddish-blond hair, not her wire-rimmed glasses – could negate her natural beauty. As she presented herself, there were some who might pass her by without even noticing how rarely fine her features were, how sensual her movements, or how incredibly full her breasts, especially compared to her narrow waist. But that group would certainly not include Richard Leaf.

She was in her twenties and wore no wedding ring – no jewelry of any kind, in fact; not that adornment was needed on this woman. By the time they had laughed over the incident and had spoken a bit, she had accepted Richard's invitation to coffee. His fantasies at that moment would have put a July Fourth fireworks display to shame. Over coffee he learned that she was home in Boston helping to care for her invalid mother while taking some time from a Hollywood acting career that was about to break through. The idea for her to do some volunteer work at the hospital had come from her mother, who had been a salmon-coated information lady for years before her diabetes and kidney failure made it impossible to continue.

By the time he had handed a twenty to the waitress for their six-dollar bill and waved off receiving any change, a rendezvous had been set at the Scandinavian Motor Inn south of the city. With Kristin's gaze threatening to set his white coat on fire, Leaf went through information to call the manager of the hotel and book a room.

'It sounds like you do this often,' she said, her expression suggesting she might be even more intrigued if that were true.

'No way,' Leaf lied, unwilling to take any chances. 'Taking out people's brain tumors is my style. It just so happens that Maury Gross, the manager, is a former patient of mine. A few years ago he had a tumor the size of a golf ball. Couldn't walk. Had trouble speaking. Now he runs and does the Sunday *Times* crossword in ink.'

'It must be really wonderful to be able to cure someone of cancer,' she sighed.

Eyes closed, Leaf stretched out on the king-size bed in room 181 of the Scandinavian Motor Inn and imagined what it would be like to see Kristin O'Neill ease open the door and step inside. The woman was perfect in every respect – and an actress to boot. It would be really something to have slept with her and then to have her become a big star. She had the looks, so it certainly seemed possible. He checked the time and then took the painkiller-and-tranquilizer combination that experience had taught would keep him from coming too soon.

The room was candlelit in exactly the way it had been for the other trysts he had arranged there. Champagne was chilling in a silver ice bucket on the desk. Velvety-voiced Morgana King was singing 'A Taste of Honey' on his CD player. On the bureau, sandalwood incense was smoldering alongside an envelope containing a couple of tabs of ecstasy, just in case Kristin wanted it at some point. He surely didn't need anything, even ecstasy. Of all the women he had ever slept with, this one was possibly the hottest. His marriage wasn't in any trouble, and Cindy was certainly decent enough in bed, but she wasn't nearly enough. John Kennedy had been quoted as saying that he got a terrible headache unless he had a woman every other day – or maybe it was every third? No matter. Kennedy was a remarkable, powerful man, and so was Richard Leaf. And for Kennedy, even Jackie wasn't enough.

Leaf slipped his hand down his boxer briefs and gently massaged himself while he waited. Time passed, during which he thought about the night ahead but also reflected on the incredibly rapid rise of Hub Health. Exclusion was the key, he had told his partners when they were first starting out – careful screening of applicants and their lab work, and rejection for any reason of those likely to cost Hub significant sums in the short or long haul. *Preexisting condition* was their watchword. The finance people had told him that Hub stock absolutely couldn't miss, and he was going to have a bundle of it.

At precisely the time they had agreed upon, there was a light knock on the door. Leaf's lingering fear that the young beauty might not show instantly evaporated.

'Come in, it's open,' he said, trying for a cadence and tone of voice that was something of a cross between Bill Clinton and Sting.

The door swung open. A man slipped into the room and closed the door quickly behind him. He was wearing a black motorcycle jacket and a baseball cap with the brim pulled low enough to obscure his eyes, and he was carrying a small orange pillow.

Leaf, hardened against panic by years in the neurosurgical OR and convinced that, whatever the situation, money could cure it, glared at the intruder.

'What the fuck is this? Where's Kristin?'

'Kristin is back where I found her, turning tricks for rich, horny men like you.'

'So what is this, some sort of shakedown? How much do you want? Take what's in my wallet, then get the fuck out of here.'

'What this is, you self-centered jerk, is payback time.'

'Wait ... do I know you?'

The man merely shook his head.

'You do now,' he said. 'That's for sure, and I don't think you'll ever forget me.'

Calmly, he withdrew a pistol from his waistband and jammed it into the pillow.

'No! Please, wait. I can pay you anything – anything y–'

The three rapid shots, from eight feet, were deadly accurate. Heart, throat, forehead – straight up the line.

Leaf saw the hole materialize in the pillow and felt the scalding heat of the shots as they entered his body. But slumped back against the bloody pillow, his head twisted grotesquely to one side, he never saw the man extract a plain white business envelope and carefully set it beneath the palm of his right hand.

141

Chapter 17

EXCELSIUS HEALTH CANCER CENTER

Cancer. The word, while carved into the granite archway identically to the other three words, and highlighted in gold like the others, stood out as if the others did not exist. In spite of herself, Grace Peng Davis paused on the sidewalk and stared up at the letters through a raw drizzle.

Sticks and stones can break my bones, but names can never hurt me. Well, she thought viciously, *this one can.*

It was Grace's first day of chemotherapy for the cancerous nodule that Susan Hollister had removed from her breast. Dr. Max D'Antonio, the oncologist, had assured her that there was really no rush to begin the treatments, but both she and her husband wanted the tumor out and gone and any remaining vagabond cells blasted with poison as soon as was possible. IV Adriamycin and Cytoxan every three weeks, Dr. D'Antonio had told them – two drugs that were toxic to every cell in the body, but more so to those that were rapid multipliers, especially cancer cells. In between visits to the clinic, she would be taking oral medication, as well.

> God grant me the serenity to accept the
> things I cannot change,
> Courage to change the things I can,
> And the wisdom to know the difference.

Grace had been exposed to the Serenity Prayer at her first AA meeting more than a decade ago but had never paid it more than lip service until, with Dr. Will Grant's help, she finally connected with people who helped her get honest with herself about her alcoholism. Now, although her life was in remarkable order, it wasn't unusual for her to recite the prayer to herself every ten minutes when she needed to get through difficult situations.

God grant me the serenity ...

Mark Davis took his wife's arm and guided her into the building.

'You're doing great,' he whispered.

They both knew how fearful she was and always had been of doctors and hospitals. And although the cancer center was a glittering, modern outpatient clinic, with comfortable furniture and dazzling artwork on the walls, it was more of a hospital than she would ever care to see.

Only Mark would ever fully appreciate how anxious she had been about having her surgery done by a doctor she didn't even know. It was such a blessing that day to have run into Dr. Grant the way they did, and later such a terrible blow to learn that his license had been suspended because of drugs. But Dr. Hollister had helped soften the blow by being kind and patient with both Grace and Mark, and best of all, she unabashedly supported Dr. Grant's claim that he was innocent.

The receptionist, a prim young Hispanic woman with *Carla* on her name tag, greeted her warmly, then handed her a clipboard with some forms attached.

'I already filled these out,' Grace said, 'when I came here to meet Dr. D'Antonio.'

'Oh, I remember who you are,' the woman said, 'but these aren't our registration forms. They have to do with transferring your insurance from Steadfast Health to Excelsius Health.'

'Transferring my insurance?'

'I guess you hadn't heard. Excelsius has taken over your insurance company. We were told that the change has been in the works for a long time, and that Steadfast Health had sent out a mailing.'

'We had heard there might be a change when we were initially sent here for Grace's mammogram,' Mark said, 'but we had no idea Steadfast Health had actually been taken over already, and we certainly didn't get a mailing. You didn't know anything about this, Grace, did you? ... Grace?'

'Huh? ... Oh, no. No, I didn't know Steadfast Health had actually been taken over already. We had heard there might be a change.'

Grace, battling a sudden wave of anxiety, was unaware that she had used her husband's exact words. At three that morning she had been awakened by a similar episode of panic, but after half an hour or so, she was able to fall back to sleep.

God grant me the serenity to accept the things I cannot change ...

She tried to ignore the perspiration in her groin and soaking into her dress beneath her arms. No big deal, she told herself. Dr. D'Antonio had given her medication to help her relax for her treatment. Phyllis, her AA sponsor, had assured her that taking the sedation was definitely the right thing to do. If this was as bad as her anxiety was going to get, she could handle it. Nobody told her getting chemotherapy was going to be pleasant.

'Well, that's what we've been informed,' Carla was saying cheerfully. 'As of today, Steadfast Health is part of Excelsius. We have lots of Steadfast Health clients here. All of them are being given the choice of switching to Excelsius or changing to another company. If you choose to go to another company, your chemotherapy will be turned over to whatever doctor your new HMO allows you to select.'

'Thank you,' Mark said.

They retreated to seats in the waiting area and filled in the form authorizing the transfer of their coverage to Excelsius.

'Good thing we checked into this last week,' Mark said. 'I would have hated to have to change doctors ... Hon, are you all right? You don't look good.'

'I'm fine, fine. Just a little apprehensive.'

'You should tell the doctor.'

'He already told me to expect this first day to be frightening.'

'I still think –'

'Mark, please! I know you mean well, but I just want to get this over with. Besides, they have a nurse practitioner in there or nearby while the drugs are going in. There's absolutely nothing to worry about.'

Her husband, generally not at all demonstrative about his feelings, merely nodded that he understood and, after an appropriate pause, looked at his watch.

'You go ahead to work,' Grace said. 'Phyllis will be here later on to take me home and fix dinner. I'm fine, honey, really. Don't worry. Here, gimme a kiss for luck. Not one of those pecks on the lips; I want the wet, juicy kind you're so good at. Mmmmm. Now, be gone. The students need you. I'll call you when I get home.'

Grace watched as her husband hesitated at the doorway, then left for his office. Of all the unmerited gifts made possible by her sobriety, he was by far the greatest. She returned the clipboard to the receptionist. The worst thing about all this, she was thinking, was that she wasn't the least bit sick when this whole nightmare started. Logically, she was grateful for the early detection of her cancer and the fact that the tumor was small and there was no evidence for spread. But emotionally, all she could think about was that she was feeling fine when she was called into the radiologist's office for the

144

bad news. No symptoms whatsover. How could anyone improve upon no symptoms?

'I know you're feeling fine,' the radiologist, Dr. Newcomber, had said, 'but trust me and this X-ray here, you're not.'

Grace scanned the waiting area. *Who are all these people?* she wondered. *What're their stories? How had they reacted the first time they heard the word* cancer *applied to them?*

'Grace Davis.'

The sound of her name startled her. It was Judi, the nurse she had met during her orientation to chemotherapy. They had sat together in a small, windowless room while the woman outlined all of the effects and side effects of treatment. It had not been a heartening conversation. She had started with hair loss, the most dreaded and expected side effect of the drugs. There was no doubt, she said, that Grace would lose her hair. It would probably occur about two weeks after her first treatment. Most women got their hair cut very short before it happened, but, even so, she should be aware that the short hairs would be annoying when they fell out, getting in her mouth and nose.

It would have been okay if the nurse had stopped at hair loss. But there was a litany of side effects to review. Nausea was of course a major topic. Grace would be given an arsenal of drugs to help alleviate that symptom. Judi had patiently reviewed each pill and its potential side effect.

'Ativan works quite well for anxiety but will make you drowsy. Vicodin is good to take if you have pain, but it is addicting if you take it more often than prescribed, and it may make you constipated.'

It seemed like there was a potential side effect for every part of Grace's body. Her fingernails might become discolored and break easily. Urinating could burn and bowel movements would be painful. Finally Grace just looked up from the myriad of papers Judi had given her.

'Tell me there is at least one upside, please; tell me that my skin will never look lovelier or it will make my eyes shine brightly.'

Judi responded with a weak, ironic smile. No, there was no upside. At best, Grace could anticipate four months of malaise and an assortment of disrupting discomforts.

'Oh I forgot,' Judi had added, 'you'll be extremely sun-sensitive for a while after your therapy.'

So much for the celebratory getaway with Mark to Aruba after all this was over. Maybe Greenland.

Finally, after Judi had pushed back in her chair, her arms folded, her expression indicating that the number of times she had done this might be getting to her, Grace had screwed up her courage to ask the big question.

'How will you and Dr. D'Antonio know that this is working?'

'What?' replied Judi, as if Grace had asked the single most stupid question in the world.

'The chemotherapy – how will you know that it works, that I am getting the expected result?'

'Well, there is no way of knowing. We can certainly tell that it *hasn't* worked if you get a bone, liver, or brain metastasis. But we will never know with absolute certainly if it *has* worked. From a statistical standpoint, we draw the line at five years, but of course there are some patients who do get a recurrence after that.'

Great.

With memories of that first meeting with the nurse roiling in her brain, Grace followed her into the treatment area. The place abounded with plaques and posters with pithy life-affirming sayings. There were even stuffed dolls carrying placards that read things like: *Live large, love hard, laugh often.* On every surface there were pamphlets and brochures for a myriad of services. Advertisements for cute hats you could buy online, notices of support groups, including one that showed how to do makeup and scarf tying so you could *look your loveliest during this difficult period of your life.*

There were also notifications of various financial-aid plans for treatments for patients without insurance – low-interest loans for up to $200,000. Grace said a silent thank you to Steadfast Health or Excelsius Health or whoever they were today. She couldn't imagine going through this hell and having to worry about how to pay for it. She had seen the statements of benefits for the tests and surgery to date, and they exceeded the value of their Saab. She was sure these next four months would approach the cost of their house.

In addition to the literature, there were huge baskets of hard candies in every room.

'You might want a couple of these,' Judi said. 'The taste of chemo can be pretty awful.'

'I thought it was intravenous.'

'Oh it is, but your bloodstream carries the medicine throughout your body, including the nerves in your mouth and nose. You can taste it from the inside.'

They entered the expansive treatment room. Toward one end was a long, cherry-paneled nurses' station. In front of it was a horseshoe of eight leatherette recliner chairs. Each had an IV pole and a side chair for a guest. There was a bank of TVs above the nurses' station so that patients could try to divert themselves during treatment.

Grace gazed around the room. All but two of the recliners were occupied. In one lay a woman sound asleep under a blanket, the IV tube twisting to accommodate her position. Her bandanna had slipped off her head, revealing tufts of brown-gray hair scattered around an otherwise bald pate. Her pretty gold hoop earrings contrasted sharply with the grayish cast of her skin.

Feeling nauseous even before the treatment began, Grace followed Judi to her designated recliner. How hale and hearty she must look in comparison to the other women here. She still had her hair. Her skin, one of her best attributes, still had its unblemished glow.

By the next time I come, I'll look like them, she thought.

She managed a sad smile at the sudden notion that the room looked like some kind of weird day spa in reverse – a place that took beautiful women and made them tired, bald hags.

'Spa Toxique,' she thought, and then realized she had said the words out loud.

'Don't think of it that way,' Judi said, as if she had heard versions of the dark humor before. 'Think of the medicine as Pac-Man hunting through your body, munching all the evil cells.'

Judi donned her latex gloves and asked Grace if she was ready. 'First, I am going to insert this needle into the port Dr. Hollister implanted during surgery.'

The port was right below Grace's right collarbone. She could feel it just under her skin.

'Take a deep breath.'

Grace inhaled and clutched the arms of the recliner as Judi passed the needle through her skin and into her upper chest. Surprisingly, it didn't hurt as much as she had anticipated.

'Now we're going to draw some blood through this tube to see what your cell counts are. Today is really a formality and a baseline because we're pretty sure your red and white blood cells and platelets are all present in healthy numbers. But as you go through your chemo, your counts will drop considerably. We can't start a treatment if the counts are too low. In fact, sometimes you may need medication to bring them up. Otherwise there's a danger of bleeding or infection or severe anemia.'

Great.

Once the tests were done Judi returned with the drugs – some form

147

of steroid, and one to make her drowsy. Next was a large syringe filled with what looked like cherry Kool-Aid but was, in fact, the cellular poison Adriamycin. In spite of herself, Grace watched the liquid pass into her chest. From within her bloodstream, Grace could smell and taste the powerful medication – a sharp, almost musty odor, reminiscent of some sort of cheese ... a taste like ... like what?

'Just close your eyes and relax,' Judi said.

... to accept the things I cannot change ...

With the help of the sedative and the Serenity Prayer, she began dozing off, cloaked in the conviction that soon this theater-of-the-absurd production would end and she would find herself back in her life.

... Courage to change the things I can ... Relax ... And the wisdom to know the difference ... Relax ... Relax...

The dream she drifted into was at first pleasant ... the lake ... two young girls playing together at the water's edge ... she and her sister, Charlotte ... their mother, arms folded, back to them, standing on top of the water, gazing off at nothing in particular ... their father, shoulder against a tree, eyes narrowed, watching, watching ... Did he know already what he was going to do to his girls? ... Had he already started? ... The dream became a strange, drug-aided montage of images in which Grace was both a participant and an observer, totally aware she was dreaming, yet completely immersed in the scenes.

When the itching first began, it was as if it were happening to the Grace in the dream. She wondered if somehow, seeing her father like this, watching her, watching Charlotte, knowing what he had done to them, was causing the uncomfortable sensation. The itching increased and now was joined by a burning sensation ... her arms, her belly, her face. Along with the girl in her dream, Grace began to scratch.

Over just minutes, the itching grew more intense and the burning more disturbing. The dream blurred, then faded altogether. Grace opened her eyes and raised her arm. Her fingers were swollen and stiff. Crimson welts with irregular, pale margins interlocked with one another like a jigsaw puzzle, until they virtually covered all the skin on the arm. Her belly, too, was covered, and her other arm. *Hives*, she thought, remembering something similar from when she was a teen. Similar, but not nearly as bad. *Hives.* The burning, especially on her face, was becoming quite frightening. Something else was becoming frightening, too – she was beginning to have trouble breathing, a tight sensation in her chest that made it hard to draw air in.

'Hello! Help me, please,' she called out. Her voice was harsh and cracked, and not nearly as forceful as she expected it to be. 'Help me...'

Her lips felt badly swollen – swollen and on fire. The breathing problem was rapidly getting worse. She needed to sit up to get air in. Needed to sit up ... needed to sit up ...

Now there were footsteps ... then voices.

'Oh my God! Grace, can you hear me?' Judi's voice. 'Nod if you can hear me. Get a stretcher out here and get her to the examining room!'

'There's not much room in there.'

'Just get the stretcher! Run that saline wide open. Grace, you've got to lie back. Get oxygen on her, a mask. Five liters or more. Tell Carla to call nine-one-one. Get an ambulance here! Also tell her to call Dr. D'Antonio. Tell him she's having an anaphylactic reaction ... We need the crash cart *stat*! Epinephrine, zero-point-five. Draw it up. I'll give it. Also Benadryl twenty-five IV. Make it fifty!'

'She's hardly moving any air!'

'Get a blood-pressure cuff on her! Quick. Here, help me lift her onto the stretcher. Jesus. Carla, did you make those calls?'

'She's not moving any air. I can't get a BP.'

'Epi is in. Get her into the corridor by the examining room. We need the crash cart. Jesus, this has never happened here ... absolutely never! Grace, can you hear me? Squeeze my hand if you can hear me.'

'No BP.'

'Carla, are they coming?'

Grace's panic had exploded. It was as if someone had pulled a broad piece of tape tightly across her nose and mouth. No matter how hard she sucked, air just wasn't getting in. She struggled against the hands that held her, struggled to sit up. She clawed at the oxygen mask. She pounded her fists on the bed. Finally, exhausted, she sank back, still trying with all her strength to get in even a tiny bit of air.

'I'm going to try and intubate her.'

'Have you done it before?'

'In Advanced Life Support class. Never in an emergency like this. What else can I do?'

Grace felt her head being tilted back. A metallic rod was being jammed into the back of her throat.

'Everything's swollen back there. I can't make out any landmark. Dammit, where's the rescue squad?'

Help me, please! ... God, grant me ... grant me ...

Grace knew she hadn't said the words – knew she couldn't. She felt herself stop struggling. She felt herself stop trying to suck in air. Overhead, the lights dimmed. Her panic lessened. The words of the nurses became garbled and distant.

A veil of darkness settled over her, accompanied by a growling, low-pitched drone.

The droning sound grew softer.

Softer.

Finally, there was silence.

Chapter 18

Spurred by an unseasonably cold, rainy spring, near record numbers of meals were being served at the Open Hearth Kitchen almost every night. For Will, the place had always been an island in his often furiously paced life. Tonight, he knew, asking for any kind of significant diversion from the place was probably asking too much. Last night, as he sat in his apartment with Patty Moriarity, someone had walked into a motel room on the South Shore and fired three lethal shots into one of the leading neurosurgeons in the country – a man who just happened to be one of the partners in an expanding, highly successful HMO. Victim number four. Four out of... out of how many? Even worse, the killer had made the point of calling Will essentially to announce that he was going to do it.

'Hey, you. You gonna just stand there staring into the flames, or are you gonna stir that pasta?'

Benois Beane, his gentle face crinkled in a trademark grin, stood, hands on hips, just a few feet away.

'Hey, Beano. Sorry. In case you couldn't tell, I'm a little distracted. Here, look, all stirred.'

'You do that very well. We'll have to see about bringing in more surgeons on pasta night. It's hard going for you, huh?'

'Yeah, you might say that. Beano, what's been happening to my life is absolutely insane. I want to fight, but there's nothing to push against. I want to lash out, but there's nothing even to hit. I don't know who framed me, I don't know why, I don't know what to do about it. And as if that craziness wasn't enough, this frigging killer thinks I'm his spiritual brother, joined at the ideological hip by our mutual hatred for HMOs.'

'I heard about that brain surgeon.'

'What you may not have heard was that the murderer called me ahead of time to proclaim his intention to kill another one of our enemies. "The piper's on the loose and he must be paid," he said.'

'Lord. The cops been any help?'

Will conjured up images of last evening's embryonic connection with Patty, but couldn't even manage a smile. For nearly an hour the two of them had sat together on his couch, his arm around her, her head resting on his shoulder. Neither of them was willing to speak or break the mood in any way. Will sensed that their bond was forged as much by exhaustion and frustration as by their attraction to each other, and he was determined not to read too much into the moment. Still, they were together, touching. Then suddenly, having spoken barely a word, Patty had stood, kissed him first on the cheek, then briefly on the mouth, mumbled an apology, and left. Just like that.

'They seem to be doing the best they can, Beano,' Will said, 'but the guy is good. He knows handguns, he knows explosives, he knows surveillance electronics. He studies his victims and finds ways to get at them without any witnesses.'

'And why is he doing this?'

'He only shares things with me a bit at a time. It's like a game. But from what he's let me in on so far, someone close to him – his mother, it appears – was killed by what he perceives was managed-care policy. I'm guessing she was discharged prematurely from an ER or a psych ward and went ahead and killed herself.'

'She wouldn't be the first. I've lost two clients whom we couldn't get into a detox because of refusal by their HMO.' Beane donned a padded mitt and helped pour a mountain of spaghetti into a giant colander. 'Well,' he said, 'I don't want to make things any worse for you, but there is something I need to talk to you about.' He turned to a gangly teenager who was moving dishes out to the serving area. 'Arielle, can you take over for Will, please? Get some help emptying those two other pots into this strainer, rinse the pasta, then fill up two of the deep serving pans.'

'Glad to.'

Beane put his arm around Will's shoulder and guided him to his office.

'I'm not sure whether or not you know it, Will, but after Grace

Davis ran into you at your office, she and her husband, Mark, began coming in here to volunteer. Three times so far, I think. Maybe four. Coming back completed a circle for her. I was seriously considering hiring her part-time to help out our counseling staff, as soon as her chemotherapy was over. Although she was before my time when she used to be a client here, her story and the way she carries herself now certainly impressed me.'

'Me, too. I felt terrible having to tell her I couldn't do her surgery, and even worse having to tell her why.' Beane's grave expression brought a sudden chill. 'Is she all right?' Will asked.

'Her husband called just a little while ago. She had an allergic reaction during her first dose of chemotherapy.' He pulled a pink telephone-message pad sheet from his pocket and read the words. 'He said it was shock. Ana-fil-ack-tic shock.'

Will felt ill. Anaphylactic shock was the most fearsome of allergic reactions. Massive histamine release causing hives, precipitous blood-pressure drop due to widespread pooling of blood in dilated vessels, and airway obstruction due to swelling of the membranes in the throat and bronchial tubes. It was a terrifying medical emergency that was often fatal.

'Did she die?' he managed, dreading the answer.

'According to her husband, almost. One of the rescue-squad people performed an emergency tracheotomy in the cancer clinic. She's in intensive care at your hospital. I'm not sure whether or not she's regained consciousness.'

'Thanks for telling me. I can call the unit for information.'

'Are you going to go over there?'

Will pictured Sid Silverman, puffed with anger, insisting that he not set foot in the hospital. There was no legal order to back up the demand, but Will had seen no reason to make his situation worse by putting Silverman to the test. Now there was one.

'In the morning,' he said. 'I'll go in and see how she's doing first thing in the morning.'

Given the choice this night between table cleanup, which was his usual job, and staying behind the counter to serve, Will chose the latter. He was in no shape for much contact with the public. Gina, the full-time staff person in charge of scheduling and deploying volunteers, put him on salads. The line of clients, a number of whom still had their own home but could afford neither food nor fuel, seemed endless. Will recalled the early days when the Open

Hearth was more of a food pantry than a kitchen, and marveled at the energy of the place. Tonight, four paid staff were working alongside fifteen or so volunteers, ranging from ten years old to seventy. It was a good bet that none of those volunteers knew Will was one of the founders, and that was certainly the way he wanted it. What he didn't want, however, was the notion that before long, without a medical license, he and the twins might end up in the line on the other side of the counter.

I'm sorry, Doctor, but you're a little overqualified for our Burger King trainee program...

'Hey, there, mister, am I allowed two salads if I pass on the spaghetti and meatballs?'

Patty eyed him from over the food-protection hood. She had on her worn leather jacket and a floppy black and red leather cap that looked perfect on her.

'I would hate to offend the memory of my sainted mother,' he said. 'That spaghetti sauce is her recipe.'

'No it's not.'

'You're right. It's not. My sainted mother had trouble boiling water. But she really would have loved that sauce.'

'I still think I'll pass,' she said, 'although I no longer have to be as light on my feet as I was when I was chasing after a certain serial killer.'

'They took you off the case?'

'To all intents and purposes they did, yes.'

'Shit. I'm sorry.' Will glanced at the line, which was starting to build up, and passed across two plastic bowls of salad. 'Dressings are over there,' he said. 'I highly recommend the ranch and highly don't recommend the diet Italian. Finish your salad, give me fifteen minutes, and we can blow this joint.'

'I have all the time in the world,' she said.

Along with the hospital and a remarkable antique-car museum, Will considered Steele's Pond to be among the best things about Fredrickston. Tucked in the woods just west of the city, two miles around, Steele's had paddleboats, a popcorn cart, and a hot-dog stand in the summer, and picture-book skating in the winter. The air, scrubbed by an afternoon of rain, was crisp and clean – perfect for a walk, Patty said. She followed him to the small parking area at the south end of the pond, locked the Camaro, and walked with him to the water's edge. After a few silent minutes staring at the dark, still surface, she slipped her arm in his and let him guide her to the rutted dirt track that circumnavigated the pond.

'So,' she began, 'sorry I left the way I did last night. My brain was threatening to explode with all that was going on inside it.'

'No problem. I enjoyed spending what time we did together.'

'Me, too. Was it okay for you to desert your post at the salad station? People were still coming in.'

'I've always been the last choice to be stationed at salads. Maybe it's the hand–eye coordination required there. The trainee they replaced me with is already twice as good as I was. Benois Beane, the director, was relieved to see me go.'

'Having spoken with Benois about you, I'll bet he's never relieved to see you go. It's really an amazing place. You must be so proud of what you started.'

'Thanks. It wasn't just me, but you're right, I am. There's no way the little group of us all those years ago could possibly have envisioned what it was going to become.'

'In a way, it made me sad. So much poverty. I kept thinking that maybe someday it won't be needed.'

'Wouldn't that be something? Of course, such a world would require a few consecutive federal administrations that actually cared about educating the kids, and making sure they have jobs waiting for them when they finish school, and giving them reasons not to take drugs.'

'It's all about having hope,' Patty said.

'It's all about hope. So, you're off the case?'

'Yup. The killing last night was the last straw. My CO felt a reorganization was called for. So in the beginning it was my case, and now I'm off it altogether even though I really haven't done anything wrong, except maybe have two X chromosomes. Actually, I have my CO's permission to stay available to Wayne Brasco, just in case he can't read my writing on any of the three or four feet of reports, notes, and documents I've got to turn over to him tomorrow. Not that Brasco would be interested in *anything* I've generated.'

'You okay about this?'

'I don't know. Maybe. Maybe it's for the best. The thing I feel worst about is my father. He never wanted me to be a cop in the first place. I really wanted to be part of the team that nails this guy.'

'It's hard. You're playing the killer's game by the killer's rules, and he's damn good at it.'

'I guess. I'm not good at dealing with failure, but I also know this

154

isn't some sort of contest. The blood all over that motel-room bed was quite real, and even though he was a philandering jerk, I feel awful about that surgeon. From what I can tell, he actually knew from our warning that there was potential danger last night, but apparently, seducing yet another trophy was more important to him than staying alive.'

'Do you think a woman killed him?'

'It's certainly possible. If it was a man, Dr. Richard Leaf must have been one surprised puppy.'

They became aware of movement to their right and left a moment before three youths, two white, one black, stepped from behind trees on either side of the path. Two of them were built like football linemen. The third, considerably smaller, was wearing a Celtics' jacket and a Red Sox cap. He stepped forward to confront them, his hands twitching excitedly at his sides. He had acne-scarred skin and emitted a dense aroma of marijuana. Had Will been alone, he would have spun around and taken off, but none of the three had a weapon that he could see, and Patty showed no inclination to run. Instead, she continued holding gently on to his arm. At one moment she tilted her head just enough to touch his shoulder. He could sense absolutely no tension in her.

'Well, well,' the teen said, 'it appears we have visitors to our toll area. We hope you are prepared to pay.'

'What do you want?' Patty asked firmly.

'Well, that wicked hat of yours for starters, right, guys?'

'Right you are, dude.'

'And for seconds, oh ... um ... let me see ... how about ... your wallets.'

'Yeah, their wallets. Hey, good idea, dude. Good idea.'

Patty slipped her arm free of Will's. She pinched her cap by the bill, took it off, and wearily wiped imaginary sweat off her forehead with the back of her hand. Then she set the cap back in place.

'Actually, *dude*, it's a terrible idea,' she said. 'I have two other things you might want to see, *dude*, before we give you this cap and our wallets. Wanna guess what they are? Huh, *dude*? Wanna guess?' She grinned at him most menacingly. 'Well, first there's my badge, and second, perhaps a source of even more concern to you assholes, is my gun.'

She slipped her hand inside her jacket, but the silent vote had already been taken. In unison, the three youths whirled and bolted off into the woods. Patty watched them go, then slipped her hand back inside Will's arm.

'Let's see,' she said, 'where were we?'

'Why didn't you bust them?' he asked.

'And ruin a perfectly lovely romantic walk? I don't think so. There are plenty of punks like those around, but evenings with a handsome, funny doctor are pretty tough to come by.'

'Is your gun really in there?'

'It was, before I locked it in the trunk of my car. I try not to be packing when I take romantic walks.'

'Me, too,' Will said. 'Besides, the two big ones were all blubber. I could have handled them if I had to.'

'I know. I've read all about your temper, remember? They'll never know how lucky they were. Now, where were we?'

He turned and, cradling her face between his hands, set his mouth on hers and rested it there until her lips parted. Their second kiss, with Will bracing his back against the trunk of a sprawling chestnut tree, lasted a minute or more.

'Now do you see why I let them go?' Patty whispered.

'"I see," said the blind man as he picked up his hammer and saw.'

'Ugh.'

'And I promise not to report you for dereliction of duty.'

Will put his arm around her, and for a time they just walked.

'You thinking about the case?' he asked finally.

'I guess there were reasons they demoted me to being Brasco's assistant after it became apparent these were serial killings. But I haven't done anything to deserve being dropped from the team. They needed a scapegoat.'

'Is there anything you can do about it? Can your father intervene?'

'I doubt he would, but I don't want him to anyway. This is my gig.'

'I understand.'

'I'm not going to give up, though – especially as long as you're our main connection to the killer. I'll keep at it on my own time if I have to.'

'Any way I can help?'

'Just keep letting me vent. Will, I've looked at these murders from every angle I could think of, but I still can't get past the feeling that there's something I'm missing, or something I haven't done.'

'Maybe it's in those letters.'

'Maybe.'

'Speaking of which –'

'*M* and *N*,' she said, 'tucked neatly beneath the hand that had removed countless brain tumors by day and, from what we've learned so far, stroked countless women's bottoms by night. I don't know why, but try as I might, I'm having trouble warming up to the guy.'

'That's okay. He's having trouble warming up at all. *M* and *N*, huh? Do you think after we finish here we could go back to my place and use my set to play a little homicide Scrabble?'

'Triple word. Double letter. *I* before *E* except after *C*.'

'Precisely. Okay, Sergeant, here's the way this all shakes down for me. This is a family of killers at work, not just one. I mean family as in brothers and sisters – at least one of each, maybe more. I feel almost certain of it. The guy who's calling me said "us" over and over. It looks to me like some managed-care company just tried to cut corners with the wrong patient, and now it's backfired on them all. Given their policies, it was only a matter of time before someone went postal on them. These killers are furious over the death of their mother, and they won't stop until everyone everyplace knows what happened to her.'

'Then why haven't they just gone right to the press?'

'In time they probably will. But at the moment, even though they're smart and professional, they're also insane and arrogant and imbued with a bitter, angry sense of irony. I think they want to involve me because having a doctor on their side validates what they're doing. They're grooming me to be their spokesman, just as I was for the Hippocrates Society.'

'But now you've fallen from grace.'

'Big time. I think if I don't set things straight and get back to work soon, they're going to lose interest in me. They've chosen me to present their case to the public, and unless I can get out from under the charges against me, they'll have nothing. They're either going to demand I find out who did this to me and get myself back on the staff at the hospital, or –'

'Or decide you're not worth the energy and maybe pay you a little visit with a couple more letters.'

RTERBECNMN

A phrase? A name? A clue?

With the Scrabble board on the coffee table by the couch, Patty and Will took turns arranging and rearranging the tiles.

'Look,' she said. '*E TEMB R.*'

'September!'

'Or November, or December – even October if he's holding back a couple of Os.'

Will shuffled around the remaining tiles, searching for the suggestion of a word, then shrugged and shook his head.

'The mother's birthday?'

'Maybe. What about *remember*?'

Patty spelled out *REMEBR*, then lined up the *T, C, N,* and *N.*

'Remember somebody.'

'That may be it. If it is, it's not nearly as obscure as I would have guessed.'

'Whatever it is, there still seem to be a lot of missing letters.'

'That's a frightening thought.'

'We – I mean, *they* have a cryptographer working on the letters. There are ten of them now. He should be able to come up with some serious possibilities.'

'Here's some more,' Will said. 'Let's see you solve *this* puzzle.'

He placed tiles spelling *KI S ME* across a triple word.

'Let's see now...'

Patty used the *K* and put *AN DO* beneath it. She slid her hands behind Will's neck and drew him close.

'I never really liked Scrabble before,' he said.

'That's because you never played it with me.'

At that instant, the phone began ringing. Once ... twice ...

'It's him!'

Three times ... four ...

Reluctantly, Will pulled away and hit the speaker button on his phone.

'Yes?'

Anticipating the frightening electronic voice, he squeezed Patty's hand.

'Will Grant? Micelli here. Augie Micelli.'

Patty and Will sagged in unison.

'Hey, this is a surprise,' Will said.

'Believe me, it is to me, too. Listen, I sure as hell hope you've been staying in shape during your time off, because you've got a long, tough road ahead of you. I've decided to take your case and do whatever I can to help you out of the mess you're in.'

Will listened for the slurring that would suggest Micelli was in his cups, but the Law Doctor sounded sharp and focused.

'That's wonderful,' he said.

'I'm assuming you didn't take any fentanyl. If you're lying to me about that, we're not going to be friends anymore.'

'I didn't take anything.'

'Good. That part of things is settled. I spoke to a pal of mine in the DA's office. They're still of a mind to prosecute you for attempted manslaughter or something, but I don't think it will take much of a breakthrough on our part for them to change their position.'

'Let's get to it, then.'

'The first thing we've got to do is somehow get them to back off and give us some time and space. Then we've got to get your license and staff privileges restored. We're not going to take this lying down.'

'Just show me where to push,' Will said.

'Our first, second, and third priorities are to figure out how a drug got into your body when you never took it. After we know *how*, we can start working on *who* and *why*. Put your thinking cap on and give me a call. I'll be in the office after eight tomorrow.'

'Should I ask why you've decided to do this?'

'No,' Micelli replied sharply, '*I* should be asking why I decided to do this.'

Will listened to the dial tone for a few seconds, then shut off the speaker.

'Hey,' Patty said, 'that's great. You've got yourself a lawyer.'

'I'll bet he's very together when he's sober.'

'Well, hopefully dealing with you will help give him religion as far as that goes. Now you've got a team on your side – him and me.'

'That's some team.'

'Your new barrister did make one small error, though.'

'He did?'

'Yes.' She pushed him onto his back and settled gently on top of him. 'He said we weren't going to take this lying down.'

Chapter 19

It was just after eleven when Will entered the busy lobby of Fredrickston General Hospital. From what he could recall, not even his first visit back home after the separation from Maxine felt this strange. Less than two weeks ago he had entered the hospital as a widely respected surgeon prepared to perform a difficult case. By that day's end, he had been vilified as a narcotic addict, signed himself out of the intensive-care unit against medical advice, and gone home with a warning from the hospital president not to return to the place until the allegations against him had been resolved. Now, here he was back at FGH again but, like the Monopoly square, just visiting.

Balanced against the uneasy tension of his return to the hospital were the feelings and sensations lingering from the night just past. He and Patty had made exquisite love, then slept and loved again, and finally dozed off until almost dawn. She was at once caring and patient, sensual and passionate. She was witty and quick, gentle and edgy, absolutely cynical yet surprisingly naive and vulnerable. And physically she was as pleasing, comfortable, and imaginative as he would ever need a woman to be.

Although Mark Davis was the one who had picked eleven as the time to meet at the ICU, Will knew the hour was about as good for him as it could be. Morning rounds were over for most of the docs, and many of those who weren't in the OR were back in their offices. In addition to his partners, he certainly had friends on the staff whom he wouldn't mind running into, but the majority he would be just as happy avoiding. Even with the favorable hour, his return to the corridors of FGH wasn't pleasant. By the time he reached the unit, he had passed four physicians and three nurses. Although prior to the incident, he was cordial enough with all of them, none greeted him with any warmth or tried to extend their brief encounter into a conversation, and one of the docs pointedly ignored him. Will wasn't surprised.

Over the years, beginning with a truncated med-school course on alcoholism and other addictions, he had been to half a dozen or more AA meetings. From the patterns of the stories shared at the meetings and the scientific studies discussed in the courses, he had no doubt that alcoholism, like addiction to other drugs, was a medical illness – a psychological, genetic, and biochemical disease, as opposed to the moral issue so many made it out to be. Unfortunately, many other caregivers did not share that opinion. Doctors and nurses caught in the nightmare of drug and alcohol dependence too often found themselves deprived in their colleagues' minds of the right to be ill and the chance to recover, simply because they were health-care professionals and should have known better. The pervasive prejudice made Will terribly sad even before he himself became a victim of it.

Mark Davis, wearing a gray turtleneck and tweed sport coat, was waiting just outside the door to the unit. He was an angular, intense man, who sounded over the phone this morning as if he were still reserving judgment as to whether Will had or had not gone into the operating room stoned on narcotics.

'They just brought her back from getting an X-ray and they're washing her up right now,' he said. 'The nurse said it would be twenty minutes.'

'Fine. Do you know who her nurse is?'

'Anne something.'

'Hajjar. She's excellent, one of the very best.'

'That's good to know. Visiting Grace like this is very kind of you. We don't have much family, and her mother is too frail to make the trip up from New York.'

'Nonsense. We do go back quite a ways. What she went through yesterday must have been absolutely terrifying. I'm anxious to see her and also to translate medicalspeak if you need me to. Mark, listen, there are a couple of things I'd like to do around the hospital while I have the chance. Why don't I meet you back here in twenty minutes?'

'Is this connected in any way with what you are going through?'

Will studied the teacher's expression and saw only concern. 'As a matter of fact, it is, yes. I'm going to retrace some of my steps from that morning, to see if I can figure out who could have done this to me – and how.'

'I hope you find whatever it is you're searching for,' Mark said. 'You mean a great deal to Grace, and so you also mean a great deal to me.'

Will headed off, pausing for a moment to glance back at the fine man whom once filthy, intoxicated, angry Grace Peng would one day meet, beguile, and marry.

You never know, he thought, as much regarding his current plight as the one Grace had dealt with by finally letting go of her fears and immersing herself in recovery. *You stay in the game when the going's tough because you never know how it's going to come out.*

In the hopes that something, anything, would connect, Will headed back to the on-call room to re-create physically and in his mind the few hours between falling asleep that morning and stepping into the operating room. The idea of doing this had been his new attorney's.

'We've got to start somewhere,' Micelli had said when Will called and agreed to pay a modest retainer to seal their relationship, 'and I suggest the beginning. For the time being, I can handle the cops and the courts, but sooner or later, preferably sooner, we've got to come up with some answers. Before you tell me anything more, retrace your steps and cement every movement of that morning in your mind. We'll talk later in the day.'

Ignoring the whispers and the stares, Will went to the surgical on-call room and unlocked the door using the keypad. It had been just after two when he went there for the first time that early morning. He then slept uninterrupted until the wake-up call he had put in for at five-fifteen. Could he have been called out of the room for something and simply not remembered? Impossible. Could he somehow have been drugged earlier in the night and then injected with fentanyl while he slept? Not impossible, but far out, and the powerful narcotic, rapidly absorbed, would have had to be in a time-release form – a mode of delivery that existed only in a skin patch. Being both superstitious and a creature of habit, it was not difficult to retrace his movements and actions from that morning.

When he reached the staff lounge in the ER, two of the nurses actually went out of their way to come in and ask how he was doing – bright spots in an otherwise gray homecoming. He fought back the urge to plug in the 'I didn't willingly take any drugs' tape and simply thanked them for being nonjudgmental. One of the women, a mother of two in her early thirties named Bobbi Hamill, checked the calendar and confirmed that the day he was drugged was her day to bring in the customary dozen doughnuts. Will and she had been quite friendly over the years, and there was no way he could imagine her purposely trying to ruin him. But then again, there was no way he could imagine *anyone* purposely trying to ruin him. The coffee they drank every morning in the ER was from a pot prepared in the room and replenished by whoever finished off the dregs. Neither of the nurses could remember someone pouring a cup for Will.

The OJ they drank came in individual cartons. Will wondered to himself whether someone might have injected one of those cartons with fentanyl, then set it aside until it was the right moment to hand it to him. The possibility didn't seem that ridiculous, but he had no recollection at all of who had passed the carton over to him. Finally, he used Bobbi's memory and the staffing chart from that day to make a list of all those who were or might have been in the room. The only person who stood out at all was Gordo.

Gordo.

As Will retraced the path he would have taken from the ER to the surgeons' lounge, he wondered about the man who had been his partner and friend for so many years. He wouldn't be the first to work closely with someone and even see him socially but not really know him. Everyone had a dark side. He tried to dismiss the possibility that Gordo was the one, but couldn't. Somebody had done this to him. That much was certain.

The lounge was deserted. Will opened his locker using a key. Empty. No surprise there. His stuff – soap, shampoo, deodorant, watch, journals, change of socks and underwear – was undoubtedly packed in an evidence box at the Fredrickston police station. Mentally, he retraced the steps he would have followed when dressing for the OR. Nothing unusual. The hair covers, shoe covers, and paper masks were all in boxes by the door to the scrub room. Gordo was already in the OR when Will was dressing. Could he have tampered with a paper mask or hair cover knowing that Will was likely to be the next person to take one? Again, far out but remotely possible.

With several scenarios playing in his brain, each one of them seriously flawed, Will headed back to the ICU. Anne Hajjar, the nurse he had felt closest to over the years, was standing just inside the glass doors.

'Welcome back,' she said. 'We've been worried about you.'

Another kindness. Will's battered faith began, ever so slowly, to return.

'It's been hell,' he said, 'but I'm still out there turning over stones to find out how this could have happened to me.'

'You just make sure you're okay as far as drugs go,' she said, her almond eyes fixed on him, 'because if you're not, if you're fooling yourself, nothing will be okay.'

'I appreciate that,' Will said, and he did. 'Grace Davis's husband around?'

'He's in with her.'

'She okay?'

'She's alive. Given what she went through, that's okay. The kid who did the trach had never done one before.'

'What a brave thing to do.'

'You said it. He had a horrible decision to make and went with what he believed. We've done everything we can to make sure Grace and her husband understand that. Unfortunately, while he definitely saved her life, the guy made a bit of a mess of things. The ENT people are going to have to repair the damage to her trachea. But before they can do that, she's aspirated some blood and now has a bit of a pneumonia.'

'Just make sure she gets you taking care of her until she's out of here.'

'That's very kind. No problem. I'll stay close to her. Speaking of getting out of here, it looks as if your patient Kurt Goshtigian is going to make it.'

'You know what?' Will said. 'I've been so wrapped up in my own deal that I completely forgot to check on him. Of course, that may also have something to do with the fact that he and his family are suing me for like a gazillion dollars.'

'Maybe they'll back off once he's home. He really has had a tough go of it. I lost the pool when he made it through last Sunday. His family's in there with him now, so you may want to steer clear of room one.'

'Thanks for the warning.'

'I think you'll remember the room Grace is in,' Anne said with a wry grin. 'It was yours.'

Will paused at the doorway to Grace's cubicle and tried to imagine what he looked like when he was transferred there from the ER on a vent. Grace looked surprisingly good. She was pale and extremely weak, but awake and alert, communicating with her husband by hand signals, some carefully mouthed words, and the clipboard and blank progress notepaper Will knew only too well. She had oxygen running into her lungs through the tracheotomy that had saved her life. On the wall to the right side of the room, her latest chest X-rays were displayed on an illuminated view box – two views, one shot from her back through her front and one taken from side to side. At a brief glance, Will could easily make out the fluffy white density in her left lung that represented the pneumonia he had been told about.

'Greetings,' he said.

Grace managed a weak smile and a wave. In addition to her pallor, her respirations were slightly rapid and shallower than normal. So long as her condition remained like this, the ICU was exactly the place she should be.

You OK? she wrote.

'Define *okay*. I feel as though I've been hit by an invisible bus. I'm trying to fight back at whoever nearly killed me, but nobody seems to notice. How about you?'

Grace made a so-so sign.

'She seems a little more worn out than she was earlier this morning,' her husband observed. 'Maybe they shouldn't have taken her down to radiology for those X-rays.'

'We wheel patients down there if we can because they're better quality than the films done by the portable machine,' Will replied. 'Here's one of the reasons she's not feeling better, this white stuff right back here. A pneumonia.'

He pointed to the area on himself. At that moment, another finding in the films caught his eye. There was a small density inside the wall of Grace's right chest, just below her third rib, perfectly round and much whiter even than the bone, which suggested that the object was metallic. The lateral view confirmed the object's presence and located it toward the front and fairly deep. Almost certainly, it was a BB.

'Look at this,' he said.

Grace smiled.

BB, she wrote. *Brother shot me.*

'How old were you?'

12.

'On purpose?'

Who knows?

'I never even knew about this,' Mark said. 'My wife, shot. What a mysterious, exotic woman you are, Grace. Having met the man, though, I don't have to stretch my imagination too far to see him doing it and it not be an accident.'

Grace waved him off, but her expression suggested she agreed.

'Did your parents take you to a doctor?' Will asked.

Grace nodded.

'I imagine he said trying to get it out was more trouble than it was worth, and that it would either work itself out or stay there for the rest of your life.'

Another nod.

'Obviously, he was right, because there it is.'

There it is, she wrote.

'And there it will stay.'

Keep your spirits up.

'I appreciate that. Listen, don't worry about me. Somehow I'll come out of this okay. And don't worry about what's going to happen with your chemo.'

I know.

'There are alternatives. Right now you should just concern yourself with getting better. Well, I think I should leave you to rest.'

Thanx.

'I'm just grateful you made it. What a thing to go through.'

You, too.

Will smiled, kissed her on the cheek, shook Mark's hand, and turned toward the door.

'Dr. Grant?' Mark said.

Will turned back. Mark had moved closer to the X-ray view boxes and was peering at Grace's films.

'Yes?'

'If this BB is here on her chest films, then wouldn't you expect it to be on her mammograms, as well?'

'Some of the views, yes, of course.'

'Well, it wasn't there.'

'Pardon?'

'It wasn't there.'

'Are you sure?'

'As you can probably tell, Dr. Grant, I am a very meticulous man – not obnoxious about it, I hope, but I am a stickler for details. There was no BB on Grace's breast films – not any of them. Did you see it there, hon?'

She shook her head tentatively.

Never thought about it, she wrote.

Will tried to remember the distinctive density in Grace Davis's mammograms, but he couldn't. It would only have been on a couple of the views – perhaps two or three out of ten – but from what he could tell, it definitely should have been on some. He did sense that, just as with these films, had there been a BB on the mammograms he would not only have noticed but commented on it. Instantly, a meteor shower of questions flashed across his mind. Could the camera angles of the mammograms possibly have cut out the BB? Possible but not likely. Could he, Grace, *and* Mark Davis all have missed the BB in the other set of films? Again, possible but not likely. Did he ever read the radiologist's dictated report? Doubtful. There wasn't any question about the cancer that was there, so what the radiologist had to say really didn't matter to him. Could Grace's mammograms have been accidentally switched with another woman's? Ugh. The possibility was sickening but not really feasible, because the cancer in the X-ray had been biopsied and confirmed by a pathologist.

Nevertheless, it appeared quite possible that some sort of mix-up had occurred.

Over two decades of working in hospitals, Will had encountered almost every imaginable permutation of error. Working under enorm-ous time pressures, with massive volumes of patients and procedures, handicapped by human frailties, imperfections, miscommunications, and personality disorders, to say nothing of fatigue, mechanical failure, and the vagaries of biology, caregivers made mistakes. Many of those mistakes passed by totally unnoticed or caused no in-convenience of any great magnitude. Some of them altered lives, and some either devastated lives or, sadly, ended them.

Will knew he had enough problems of his own to work out without trying to track down the source of this odd conflict. Still, he also knew there was no way he wouldn't do it.

'Guys, listen,' he said, 'I don't have a good explanation for this, but I'm sure there is one – at least I *think* there is one. I'll check with someone in radiology here, and then I'll speak to the person at the cancer center who did those mammograms.'

It was only then that he recalled his unpleasant encounter over the phone with radiologist Charles Newcomber. That time he had gone over Newcomber's head and prevailed, but it would be a pleasure to put the pompous prig on the hot seat once again.

'Please keep us posted,' Mark said.

'Oh, don't worry,' Will replied, knowing that this time the en-counter with Newcomber would occur in person, and that this time he would have the hospital X-rays tucked under his arm. 'I will.'

Alone in his office, Augie Micelli sipped on a brandy, stared across the room at a spider plying its trade in the corner, and scratched boxes around words on a yellow legal pad – his way since college of working through problems. From the portable CD player on the floor by his desk, Gene Ammons's soulful tenor sax was playing 'Willow Weep for Me.' A drug addict, Ammons was known as Jug, perhaps for the way he drank, Micelli thought fondly, or maybe for the stretches he did in the jug before, at forty-nine, he died.

Although Micelli had been there at his desk for several hours with a drink close at hand, he was still far more sober than not. There was significant work to do, so he had been treading the delicate line between maintaining a clear head and keeping the shakes in check. It was a case that, when all was said and done, might not even pay the electric bill. But if Will Grant was telling the truth, if he had been framed and was now being purged from medicine much as Micelli, himself, had been, taking the case had been the right thing to do. Now the trick was seeing to it that Grant never made it anywhere near a courtroom, and that meant figuring out how he could have been railroaded so smoothly.

Spread out across the desk and on the floor around him were articles, xeroxed book pages, and printouts from the Internet, all dealing with the narcotic fentanyl. Usual dose; onset of action; route of administration; duration of action; pharmacologic effects; side effects; symptoms of overdose; chemical formula; metabolites. Gene Ammons had moved on to 'I Remember You,' Micelli's favorite on the album, which was to say the one that made him feel most blue.

'Not good,' he muttered as he considered the case, 'not good at all.'

The only explanation that fit all the facts was that Will Grant was both an addict and a liar. Micelli bounced the eraser of his pencil on an article dealing with the pharmacokinetics of sufentanil, ten times more powerful than fentanyl, eight hundred times more powerful than morphine, and of carfentanil, which was nearly fifteen times more powerful even than that. He found himself thinking about a statement from one of his law-school professors, and wrote it in block letters at the bottom of the yellow sheet.

IF YOUR BELIEFS DON'T FIT WITH THE FACTS, THEN JUST POUND THE HELL OUT OF THE FACTS UNTIL THEY DO.

He snatched up the phone and dialed. Will Grant answered on the first ring.

'Okay, Doctor,' Micelli said, making a series of boxes around the words, 'take me through that day again.'

Chapter 20

Embarrassed, angry, frustrated, humiliated, impotent. Patty couldn't remember ever having felt more uncomfortable. For more than two months her life had been consumed by the need to find a killer and bring him – or her – down. Now, to all intents, her part in the case was over. She would be helping to keep the day-to-day operations of her unit moving along while Wayne Brasco would be working with Sean Digby, who had come on board well after she did, and a veteran detective named Brooks, who had transferred to Middlesex from Hampden just a month ago.

'Look at it this way,' Jack Court had tried to explain to her, 'with me tied up with this case along with the others, you're going to be like running this place. Brooks is too new to have that responsibility, and Digby is too green. The rest of them aren't nearly as competent as you are.'

Bullshit!

In some ways, it felt as if she was leaving the force altogether. She sat at her desk, grateful that the phone hadn't rung and that no one had felt the need to stop in and talk to her. Set in neat piles on the floor around her were the tangible products of countless hours of work and thought about the managed-care killer – stacks of documents, computer printouts, interviews, newspaper clippings, photographs, and transcripts.

It wasn't right, she was thinking as she identified each of the piles with a carefully printed sheet and bound them with heavy rubber bands. There was some sort of commission or ACLU lawyer someplace who would be more than happy to take up her banner and prove in court that she was being removed from her case without just cause. But then, even if she could find such a champion, her career on the force would be over. It was lose–lose for her all the way around. If she could just hang in and get past this disappointment and embarrassment, there would be other times for her to prove herself. In fact, although she wasn't about to tell Court or Brasco, she wasn't totally certain she was going to let go of this case yet.

169

Even thoughts of Will and the night just past weren't enough to give her flagging spirits much of a boost. He was a bright, caring, terrific guy – totally genuine and very attractive. Making love with him was great while it was happening, but she knew, as she suspected he did, too, that both of them were stressed, vulnerable, and needy. The passion, spontaneity, and chemistry between them were real, and she had absolutely no regrets, but she suspected Will would agree that they would probably have been better off to have waited.

Stacked on top of one another, the piles of exhaustive work reached two feet or more. Reluctantly, Patty hauled them down to Court's office. As far as she could tell, neither the lieutenant nor Brasco had looked at much of what she had amassed to this point, and there wasn't much chance they would now. The two men were sniggering about something, but stopped abruptly when she arrived and didn't bother to explain what it was.

'All right, Pat,' Court said with fake cheer, 'let's get this over and get you onto a couple of new cases.'

'I thought maybe we could take a few minutes and I could explain how all this is organized,' she said. 'I have these areas cross-referenced. Here's the key I put together for that.'

She passed over three sheets, single spaced – the product of hours of work. Brasco favored her with a disinterested grin and set the sheets down on the stack, where they would likely remain for eternity. Court, perhaps sensing an impending escalation in tension, cleared his throat.

'So, Pat,' he said, 'is there anything else you feel we should know before we get on with business?'

'Well, yes, as a matter of fact there is.'

'Okay, then, go on.'

Could Court have possibly been more patronizing? Brasco clearly had one use and one use only for women, but the lieutenant had a bright social worker wife and two daughters. Surely his disregard for her couldn't just be that she was female.

'Thanks,' she said. 'I just want you to know that something feels off to me about this whole thing. I keep sensing that the real object of this guy's anger isn't the managed-care executives, it's us – I mean the police.'

Brasco raised his hands in bewilderment.

'Sergeant, maybe it's because I don't have a master's degree like you do, but that theory of yours just went right over my head. What's to question? This whack-job's mother croaks because of something a managed-care company does to her – maybe a premature hospital discharge, maybe refusal to have her evaluated in an emergency ward. They do such things all the time, only this time the lady dies and her kid just happens to be a professional killer – or else he becomes a damn good one in a big hurry. He sets out to right the wrong of her death, while at the same time humiliating the HMOs and terrifying their executives.'

'An arrogant, egomaniac son of a bitch,' Court added. 'Just like all the others who go around killing to make a point.'

'I know that's what the profiler is telling us,' Patty said, 'and that may be the whole deal, but –'

'But what?' Brasco demanded, his voice up an octave or so.

'It just seems too neat, that's all. Why would he just tell us it's about his mother the way that he did?'

'Because that's what it's all about!' Brasco exclaimed. 'He's insane over losing her. Now we even know her name.' Brasco was mindless of the glare from Court.

Patty felt as if she had been slapped.

'What are you talking about?'

'The letters,' Brasco replied, now clearly into his braggadocio too deeply to back out. 'After that neurosurgeon bought it, I went over all the letters with the cryptographer. It only took us a couple of hours. The *M* and *N* were the key. According to him there's a ninety percent chance the killer's spelling *Remember Clementine*.'

'The mother's name is Clementine?'

'That's right. So now all we have to do is scan the databases of all the hospitals and also the medical examiner's office, looking for the death of a woman named Clementine. Meanwhile, we're going to –'

'Wayne, listen,' Court cut in, 'if you haven't any further questions for Pat, perhaps it's best to just let her get on with her work.'

Patty had already caught on that Brasco was supposed to shut up about whatever it was they were planning to do. It took somewhat longer for him to come to that conclusion.

'Huh? Oh, yeah, sure,' he said. 'Listen, thanks for all the paperwork, doll. We'll keep you posted.'

Patty willed herself not to burst into tears and also not to leap on Brasco and claw off his face. At the moment, there wasn't a damn thing she could do except to find a safe, quiet place to lick her wounds. If Brasco caught the killer, good for him. But she decided for certain at that moment, one way or another, he was going to have competition.

'You got it,' she said.

Head high, she made a military about-face and left Court's office, taking pains to close the door softly behind her.

'Wayne, what in the hell were you thinking,' Court said as soon as it was clear Patty wasn't going to return. 'I thought we decided she was out. If she's out, then just let her go. I agree with you that trapping the killer through that drug-addicted doctor is the way to go. But sharing anything with her can only mess things up. She's screwing the guy, for chrissakes.'

Jack Court slid the black-and-white eight-by-ten photo from an envelope on his desk. Patty and Will were locked in an embrace just inside the open door of his condo.

'A work of art,' Brasco said.

'It's a good thing the guy who took this owed you a favor.'

Brasco puffed out his chest like a pigeon.

'Sometimes it's better to have a little bargaining session with a perp than to bust him or, even better, her.'

'Keep your methods to yourself, Wayne.'

'As you can see, they work. O'Gary'd been set up in the bushes opposite Grant's place off and on for days. This wasn't exactly what he was looking for, but he's photographed Ms. Moriarity before, and there she was at five A.M. this morning, all bleary-eyed and sexed out. Given the high profiles of Grant and the managed-care killings, he felt it might have made it all the way to the front page.'

'I'm glad you were able to dissuade him. I have much better uses for this photo.'

'Like payback for a certain colonel.'

'Tommy Moriarity bad-mouthed me out of a promotion I deserved. When we bust the managed-care killer, I don't want his frigging daughter snagging the headlines. Now, with this photo, there's not a damn thing Moriarity will do about my taking her off the team.'

'After we get this jerk,' Brasco said, 'maybe we should have a little talk with Tough Tommy about a couple of promotions.'

'Maybe we should,' Court said. 'Maybe we should at that. So, are we all set with the VDS people?'

'Just about. Later today, they tell me. Believe me, this is the way to go.'

'And they assure you they can do this?'

'That's what they say.'

'Good enough. Stay on them. So long as they don't screw things up, we're all set for tonight. Meanwhile, we'll keep up the search for

Clementine.' Court examined the photo once more. 'Cozy little scene, this.'

'I can't believe Iceberg Patty's caved in like this. I suspect Tommy'll do just about anything to protect his little darling from the fallout. I'll tell you something else, too: Whether it's drugs or aiding and abetting, or both, Will Grant is dirty. He's going all the way down with this, and if we're lucky, she's going to fall with him.'

With her mood as gray as the afternoon sky, Patty took Route 128 north to Lexington. She had Beethoven's darkly heroic Third Symphony, the *Eroica*, playing at almost top volume. Given the disillusionment and the politics of deception that surrounded the piece, it was the perfect choice for the day. This was the masterpiece Beethoven had originally planned to publish as the Bonaparte Symphony when, in 1804, Napoleon turned his back on democracy and the people and crowned himself Emperor of France. In a Beethoven biography she had read not long ago, it was written that, upon hearing of the tyrant's action, the composer ripped the title page from the score.

Patty knew that Jack Court bore some resentment toward her. Until this latest session, though, she never realized how much. Wayne Brasco and he were always tight, but his behavior today was unconscionable – risky, too, given that Tommy Moriarity could easily quash any advancement for him should he learn about the way his daughter had been treated. Well, she wasn't going to tell her father anything, but neither was she going to slink off the case on which she had worked so diligently. Brasco, with all the intuition of a mollusk, seemed to be following a script written by the killer. Find Clementine, get the names of her children, and arrest the suckers. It was as simple as that. And maybe it was, too. But Patty's intuition would not stop crying out that something wasn't right.

Resting on the seat beside her was a printout with the names and addresses of the four executives that some individual or group had murdered. Assumptions are the detective's greatest nemeses, her father had once told her class at the academy. When a case isn't going well, clear your mind of all assumptions and force yourself to go back to the beginning. Patty hadn't been able to get hold of the widower of Marcia Rising, but Ben Morales's widow was waiting to meet with her, as was Cyrill Davenport's. Richard Leaf's distraught widow had agreed to be interviewed again, but only if absolutely necessary. Patty had decided to leave her for last.

Morales, murdered with a single shot to the head, was victim number one. He was a young, vibrant leader, active in civic affairs, who seemed, on paper at least, to be a man of compassion and character, able to handle wealth and power without making many enemies. It was the descriptions of him by his friends and coworkers that troubled Patty most as her investigation progressed. Marcia Rising, though respected by many, seemed to have been avaricious and ambitious to a fault. Cyrill Davenport was a reserved, methodical, money-making machine, who at times showed open disdain for his alcoholic wife. And Richard Leaf was, from what Patty had learned about him, a megalomaniacal, womanizing egoist, who believed he was above most of society's laws. None of the three would have been a poster child for the managed-care industry, and it was easy to see how the killer might have chosen any of them to be the first victim – but not Ben Morales.

The Morales home, on a quiet, unostentatious street, had a well-groomed front lawn that today featured a bicycle with training wheels lying on its side. Patty had met both of Morales's young daughters and felt as ill today thinking about what life held in store for them as she had during that initial investigation. Morales's wife, Wendy, opened the front door before Patty had reached it. She was a trim, fair-skinned blonde who seemed to have aged years in the two months since her husband's death. She served Patty some tea and willingly answered her questions.

'Does the name Clementine mean anything at all to you?'

'Nothing.'

'How about Marcia Rising?'

'Still no bells. After you called and asked about her, I looked for her name when I cleaned out Ben's desk at work, then again when I went through his study upstairs. There was nothing.'

Wendy was maintaining her composure, but Patty could see the inestimable pain in her eyes.

'Are you all right to do this?' Patty asked.

'There really is nothing left for me from all this except to help find Ben's killer.'

'I appreciate that. Okay, how about Dr. Richard Leaf?'

'The latest victim. From what I read in the paper this morning and heard on the news, he's not a man I would care to know.'

'Me, either.'

'I don't think I've ever read his name or heard Ben mention him, but I didn't look through all the boxes again after Ben was – after he was killed.'

'Are those boxes still here?'

'Upstairs. It's fine with me if you want to look through them.'

'I do. How about Cyrill Davenport?'

Wendy shook her head.

'The truth is, I was crying a lot going through Ben's things, and I don't think my concentration was really all that good.'

'I understand.'

'If you don't mind working in his study, I can set you up there. Our nanny is away, but I'll do my best to keep the girls out of your hair.'

'They won't bother me.'

'I still can't believe this, I just can't. Civic organizations loved him; business organizations honored him.' Her eyes moistened. 'Do you know much about him?'

'What you told me when I first was investigating his – his death, and also from interviews I did at his business.'

'He was born in absolute poverty in Mexico.'

'I do know that.'

'And do you know that his company's worth more than doubled in each of the five years he was the CEO?'

'He sounds like quite a guy.'

As Patty trudged up the carpeted stairs, she suddenly felt a consuming fatigue take hold. This whole investigation had felt like one step forward, two steps back. Now, here she was, all the way back to the beginning.

'Here you go,' Wendy said, gesturing to the carpeted floor in a richly paneled study.

Patty looked inside the room and deflated even more. There were five good-size cartons piled with files and papers that looked as if they had been tossed in randomly. Reflexively, she assessed the situation. Time to completely examine the material: hours. Chances of coming up with anything significant: zero or close to it. End of assessment.

Later, Wendy. I think I'll come back another time to do this.

The words were midway from her brain to her lips when she heard her voice saying, 'Thanks. If I need anything, I'll yell.'

Cursing herself for not simply backing off and letting Brasco make a fool or a hero of himself, she settled into Ben Morales's soft leather high-backed chair and began. An hour passed with one carton done and most of a second. Outside, the afternoon light had begun to fade. Morales's papers were mostly dry and technical and gave little feel for the man who had guided Premier Care to a very solid place in a fiercely competitive industry.

Near the bottom of the second carton, thick with bound legal documents and loose sheets, was a cardboard file pocket with the word *Merger* written in pencil in the upper right corner of one side. Her curiosity suddenly yanked from the doldrums, Patty dumped the contents of the file onto Morales's empty desktop and started with the first sheet, a memo to Morales written in a flourished hand on plain white typing paper. It was dated six months ago.

Dear Ben,

I was very pleased to hear from you and to learn that, although you have reservations, you are at least willing to allow us to present the benefits to all of us from bringing our companies together. Responses from the others we have polled have been quite encouraging, but I feel that the inclusion of Premier Care would be the boost that really gets the project rolling. Ultimately, I feel certain a merger would be to the good of all. Let's meet in the next week or two to share our feelings on this matter. After that, if we are in agreement, we can involve the lawyers and bankers and begin to tinker with possible formulas for stock disbursal.

Warmest regards,
Boyd

Boyd! It had to be Boyd Halliday. The Faneuil Hall debate where Patty had first laid eyes on Will and Boyd Halliday seemed eons ago. Will had come across that night as earnest, intelligent, humorous, and self-effacing; Halliday as brilliant, intense, droll, and urbane. The fact that Patty had a long-standing personal bias against the profit-motivated HMOs probably affected her overall negative impression of Halliday, although Will's unassuming good looks may have had something to do with that, as well.

The legal reports seemed to be repeated attempts on the part of several different merger-and-acquisition experts to devise a formula for assigning stock and power to at least seven managed-care companies, all of them located in the Northeast. In addition to Premier Health, Cyrill Davenport's Unity Comprehensive Health was on the list. However, the companies headed by Marcia Rising and Dr. Richard Leaf were not. Aside from the original memo, there did not seem to be any further direct contact between Halliday and Morales.

176

A merger, Patty thought as she set the last of the documents aside. *Now, what's that all about?* Had it ever actually happened? Was it still on the table? Where did Ben Morales stand on the possibility? Were the other victims' companies involved?

Suddenly energized, she inspected the contents of the final cartons in much less time than the first two, then called and firmed up an appointment with Gloria Davenport.

When Patty finally came downstairs, Wendy Morales was preparing macaroni and cheese in the kitchen.

'Find anything helpful?' Wendy asked.

'Maybe. Did you know anything about a merger or proposed merger between Premier Health and some other companies?'

'No, but that's not possible. Ben would never allow it.'

'Why?'

'This company was his life. He had wonderful plans for it. Someday he hoped to use it as a vehicle for bringing health-care coverage to those who couldn't afford it. He would sooner have lost his arm than his company.'

'Do you mind if I borrow those cartons for a while? I'd like to go through them again. I promise to return everything very soon.'

'No problem. Just a minute and I'll help you carry them down. You can't stop right in the middle of preparing Kraft Macaroni and Cheese, you know. I add a little ketchup and some sour cream. That's how my mother used to make it for me.'

'Sounds delicious,' Patty said. 'For me it's always been chunks of hot dogs.'

After the last of the cartons was loaded into the Camaro, Wendy shuffled back to the house, head down. If Patty needed a reason to keep pounding away at the managed-care murders, there she was. She waited until Ben Morales's widow had closed the door, then took the Beethoven out of the CD player and replaced it with Willie Nelson's 'If You've Got the Money (I've Got the Time).'

A merger, she thought again as she pulled away. *Is that a piece of the puzzle, or is that the puzzle?*

Chapter 21

The mammography unit of the Excelsius Health Cancer Center was beautifully appointed, with richly paneled walls and warm, inviting furnishings. Given the unpleasant exchange that had taken place with Charles Newcomber over the surgical referral for Grace Peng Davis, Will decided that a frontal assault on the man was the way to go rather than trying to call and set up an appointment.

Shortly after Will left home for the drive to the cancer center, Augie Micelli called his cell phone and insisted that he pull off to the side of the road.

'Okay, now,' the attorney said, 'give it to me once more. I want to hear your account of the day you passed out in the OR – inch-by-inch, moment-by-moment. I want everything.'

'I just spent a while this morning retracing every move I could remember.'

'Okay, tell me about that, too. There's a hole in this someplace and we've got to find it.'

The Law Doctor sounded vibrant, focused, and energized – a completely different man from the one Will had watched get progressively drunk during their first meeting. Sounding very much like a courtroom barrister, he guided Will through his account with carefully phrased, incisive questions designed to coax out information without being leading. When he was satisfied Will had nothing further to add, Micelli shared what he had learned about the pharmacology of fentanyl. It was an astounding amount of information – far more than Will had ever possessed.

'Has learning all that helped in any way?' Will asked.

'Not yet, but knowledge isn't represented as a torch for nothing. Assuming you are telling the truth, and I choose to make that assumption, we are searching for an explanation of an event that defies explanation.'

'I understand.'

'I'm behind you all the way on this, Grant,' he said, 'but I sure could use some sort of a story that makes sense about how that stuff could have gotten into your body.'

'I have a whole bunch of stories that make absolutely *no* sense,' Will replied. 'Will that help?'

'Keep trying. And remember, it doesn't have to be right, it just has to be plausible.'

Finally, with the promise to stay in touch at least twice a day, Will hung up and pulled off the soft shoulder, back onto the road. With his understanding of both law and medicine, Micelli was going to be a godsend. As Will headed off, he almost immediately became lost in yet another conundrum – the strange finding of the BB in Grace's chest that did not appear in her mammogram. As with the fentanyl, no explanation made sense, but there was a reality that simply could not be ignored.

The scenario that he kept coming back to was that Grace was a rather thin woman, though broad across the shoulders. Perhaps somehow the angles of the X-ray camera in taking her breast films simply missed the BB. Not very likely but, as the Law Doctor said, plausible – certainly a possibility worth reviewing with Newcomber and also with one of the radiologists at FGH. In fact, Will decided as he pulled up to the clinic, he was going to get a second opinion no matter what. The trick would be getting back into the hospital again without being spotted by Sid Silverman or one of his security people and tossed out onto the street like a barfly. He had made it once. Making it a second time might be asking too much.

Will's plan to get to Charles Newcomber was simple – act as if he knew what he was doing and not use his real name. Before leaving for the mammography unit he had called in as Dr. Davidson, hoping to review some films with Dr. Newcomber. He was assured by the operator that the doctor was, in fact, in his office and currently on the phone. Will entered the building carrying an X-ray envelope containing films of his left ankle, taken several years ago after he twisted it in a pickup basketball game.

Remember, he told himself, *look confident, keep moving.*

The crowded waiting room was just what he needed. Two women were queued up in front of a silver-haired receptionist, who was manning the counter alone and seemed frazzled. Seven or eight others, most of whom had someone with them, filled many of the chairs. Will surveyed the room quickly as he strode toward the reception desk. There was only one corridor off the waiting area – Newcomber's office had to be down there someplace.

179

'Dr. Davidson,' he said, smiling and holding up the envelope of films as he marched confidently past the receptionist and down the corridor. For several uncomfortable seconds he expected her to call him back and demand more information, but self-assuredness and the title 'Doctor' won the moment. To his left, a sign directed patients to the dressing and X-ray rooms. To his right were a series of offices. The doors to each of them were closed except for the one farthest away, which faced the corridor. A discreet plaque fixed to the wall beside it read *Dr. Newcomber*. Seated inside, behind his desk, dictating into a handset, was an unimposing, rotund, ruddy-faced man with a mop of pure white hair. Will was still approaching the door when he realized that what looked like a full head of hair was actually a silver monk's fringe topped by one of the worst hairpieces he had ever seen.

He was at the doorway before Charles Newcomber glanced up. The radiologist's expression was one of interest as he scanned Will up and down.

'Looking for someone?' he asked, his voice soft and high-pitched, his tone somewhat inviting.

'Dr. Newcomber.'

'You found him.'

Newcomber continued his appraisal. Will stepped into the room and gently closed the door behind him.

'Dr. Newcomber, I'm Dr. Will Grant.'

The radiologist's color drained. He placed the handset on the desk.

'I thought you were in prison. What do you want?'

'To come in and speak with you.'

'I'm busy and you're a drug addict. Get out.'

Will took a small step forward.

'It's about Grace Davis,' he said, 'the woman I called you about a while ago who wanted to switch surgeons.'

'I don't talk about my patients.'

'You read a cancer in her mammogram and she had the tumor removed and diagnosed by pathology, but I don't think it was her X-rays you read.'

'That's crazy.'

Newcomber had picked up a pencil and begun fidgeting with it nervously.

'She's had a BB in her chest wall since she was a child,' Will went on. 'It's there in the chest X-ray that was done this morning but not in her mammograms – at least not that her husband or I remember.'

'That's ridiculous. I'm sure you just missed it. Probably stoned on something. Now, get out.'

The man's discomfort was almost palpable. Will took another step toward him. He was now five feet or so from the desk and reminding himself not to lose his cool or do anything stupid.

'Let's just look at her films together,' he said.

'You have a notarized release?'

'I'm a doctor, for goodness sake. Don't you want to know if there's been some sort of mistake?'

'I don't make mistakes. Now, get out or I'll call security.'

'I didn't come here looking for trouble,' Will said, feeling his frustration and his temperature beginning to rise. 'Just get the films and let's look at them together.'

'No!'

The pencil snapped in two. Newcomber's face was radish red. He was on his feet now, his hands gripping the edge of his massive desk. Will decided to press on. Either the man was going to break down or he was going to go ballistic and let something slip to explain why he was reacting so excessively. Certain he was in command of the situation, Will made the slightest move forward again. The moments that followed were a blur. Newcomber suddenly yanked open the right-hand drawer of the desk, jammed his hand in, and came out with a snub-nosed revolver clutched in his stubby fingers. Hand quivering, he aimed it at the center of Will's chest.

Will had never had a gun pointed at him for any reason. He froze, his mind frantically sorting out the possibilities available to him. There was no way to tell how close Newcomber was to pulling the trigger, but the amalgam of fear and fury in his expression said that a shooting, accidental or purposeful, could happen any moment. Will raised his hands and took a step back toward the door.

'Easy, Charles,' he said. 'Easy. Don't do anything you'll regret.'

'Now, get out!'

His eyes still fixed on the portly radiologist, Will backed away. Without looking, he reached behind him, grasped the knob, and opened the door. He could now whirl and dive into the hall, but if the man began spraying shots, one or more of them was bound to hit.

'I didn't come here to cause you any trouble,' he heard himself saying.

Newcomber said nothing. The revolver drifted slightly to the right, away from Will's chest. The man's tension seemed as if it might have lessened just a bit.

Will risked pressing on. 'Listen, Charles, whatever is going on with you, maybe I can help. I'm a really good doctor. I'm sure you are, too. We only want what's best for our patient. That woman Grace Peng Davis is very special. She was once a hopeless alcoholic – a real fringe player in life, an outcast. Then she got sober and pulled herself out of the gutter. Yesterday she almost died from her first chemo treatment. Now therapy for her cancer is going to be a problem. She doesn't deserve this. Charles, we're doctors. If there's something the matter with all this, we need to help her.'

'Get out,' Newcomber rasped, now clearly hyperventilating. 'Get out or I swear I'll kill you.'

'Call me,' Will said. 'Wolf Hollow Drive in Fredrickston. I'm in the book. Please call and we can talk.'

He backed through the door, half expecting to see flame suddenly spit from the muzzle. Finally he pulled the door closed, turned, and hurried down the hall.

Charles Newcomer sank back into his chair, sweat accumulating beneath his toupee, soaking through his shirt, and glistening across his forehead and upper lip. More than a minute passed before he loosened his grip on the revolver. Finally, some of his composure regained, he lifted the phone and dialed. An answering machine took his call. There was no greeting, only a beep.

'Listen,' he said, 'Will Grant was just here. He knows something's wrong with Grace Davis's mammogram. You told me she was the last one. You promised me no one would ever know. Well, Grant's suspicious. He's going to keep poking around. I can handle him, but I'm going to destroy the films – all of them. I want the rest of the money you owe me, I want the videos, and I want out.'

He slammed the receiver down.

'You promised,' he muttered, removing a printout list from his desk drawer, folding it in thirds, and slipping it into the pocket of his sports coat. 'The money, the video, and a ticket out of here. You promised.'

Chapter 22

For the second time in six hours, Will entered the hospital from which he had been professionally and physically suspended. This time, though, the security guard in the lobby merely looked at him and nodded. He was expected. The phone in his condo was actually ringing when he arrived home, shaken and bewildered from the bizarre encounter with Charles Newcomber. As with every call now, Will lifted the receiver expecting to hear the killer's unsettling electronic voice.

'Grant?'

'Yes.'

'It's Sid Silverman.'

Sid, listen, Will came close to blurting out. *I'm really sorry I came into the hospital this morning. I had to see a patient of mine.*

'What's up?' he managed instead.

'We need you to come into the hospital for a meeting. Three o'clock.'

'What's this about?'

'I'd rather everyone learned about this at the same time, but I can tell you that just a little while ago, your friend the serial killer called Jim Katz.'

'But why would he –'

'Sears Conference Room, third floor, three o'clock.'

'Okay, okay, I'll be there. Should I bring my lawyer?'

'You can do what you want, but you won't need one.'

'Sid, I trust you so much that I won't bring one,' Will replied, with syrupy sarcasm.

What now? Will wondered as he entered through the lobby and headed downstairs to radiology. *What can the psycho possibly do to me now that he or someone else hasn't already done?* Surely the killer couldn't have selected Jim Katz as Will's replacement. Katz was a political conservative, who had nothing to do with the Society, and in fact was on the board of one of the managed-care companies. He was independently wealthy and was just playing out the string in his surgical practice because he loved the hard-earned stature and universal respect he enjoyed throughout the hospital. In fact, Will, Gordo, and Susan often wondered if Katz would be one of those whose health collapsed shortly after his retirement or who took to drinking for lack of anything stimulating to do.

It was two-thirty, and always the multitasker, Will had taken advantage of his free pass into FGH by making an appointment to review Grace's chest X-rays with Rick Pizzi, the radiologist on duty. Disappointed that there was no message from Patty waiting for him at the condo, he had called from a pay phone and spoken briefly with her.

'That was a really nice night, thanks,' was the extent of her comment on their lovemaking.

'For me, too,' he'd replied, wanting to say much more.

Patty, having spent much of her day on the case to which she was no longer assigned, was behind in chasing after those cases to which she was, including the wounding of a shopkeeper during a holdup. There wasn't time for more than the brief exchange of reports of her interview with the widow of Ben Morales and his encounter with Charles Newcomber.

'Let's talk later if we can,' she said, 'but with the shooting they just set on my plate and this next interview, I think I'll be working most of the night.'

The too-brief conversation had left Will with an aching emptiness in his chest. He left for the hospital reminding himself that over the past fifteen years, Maxine was the extent of his serious involvement with women. That hardly qualified him as an expert.

Radiology was, as usual, busy. Rounding a corner, Will nearly collided with Gordon Cameron. The Scotsman was a spectacular vision in a boldly striped dress shirt, paisley tie, and deep burgundy trousers, held up by a pair of broad plaid suspenders. Each of the colors seemed to clash with every one of the others, as well as with his thick, red-orange beard.

'Will, me boy, you're off a couple of floors! We're meetin' in the conference room on three.'

For years, any contact with Cameron raised Will's spirits. Today, though, he had to hold his niggling concern about the man in check. It was hard to look directly at him without demanding to know if he was the one who had somehow managed to poison him with fentanyl.

'Gordo, you have really cloaked yourself in sartorial splendor this day,' Will said. 'You are positively intimidating. If Braveheart had dressed this way, I believe he'd still be charging through the heather, slicing off heads, and mooning the British.'

'Trust me, lad, you don't know the half of it. The hard part of pulling this outfit together was finding a set where the suspenders and thong matched.'

'Ouch! So, do you know what this meeting is about?'

'Just that it has to do with Jim and you. Listen, Will, I need to tell you that I'm really sorry I haven't been in better touch. Things have been so hectic around here without you that I haven't called to see how you were doing.'

'Nonsense. I've been far too busy living the high life to make time for anyone.'

'Well, it may not seem it, but I have been thinking about you.'

'Duly noted and appreciated.'

'Thanks. Now, what are you doing down here in the bowels of the hospital?'

'I've run into an interesting problem with a film. Rick Pizzi's going to go over it with me.'

'The only suspended doctor in the history of the hospital who manages to run into an interesting problem with a film. Now, that's what I call devotion to the profession. Want company in there? We can't start this meeting without you anyway.'

'Come along.'

Pizzi, stocky and higher strung than most radiologists, had come to FGH at almost the same time as Will. However, their career paths, at least from an economic standpoint, then quickly diverged. Radiology, without much patient contact, wasn't a specialty Will would have chosen, but it certainly had things to recommend it. An avid pilot, Pizzi now owned a pressurized Cessna, as well as a snazzy fishing boat and a Porsche. He also was still in his first marriage and spent most of his infrequent on-call nights asleep at home.

Two sets of Grace's chest X-rays, taken a day apart, were in place in four panels of the ten that filled the wall behind Pizzi's desk.

'So,' he asked, 'were you able to get ahold of Mrs. Davis's mammograms?'

'Not yet. They're at the mammography center of her HMO. I will, though, I can promise you that.'

'And you feel certain there was nothing like this in any of the views?'

'As you may have heard, Rick, I've been under a little stress lately,

185

so I'm not going to claim to be one hundred percent certain about anything. But I did look at the mammograms carefully when Mrs. Davis first came to my office, and I never noticed anything like this. Her husband doesn't remember seeing anything in her films, either. He's a teacher, not a doc, but he claims to have an unusually sharp eye for details. The question is,' Will said, 'is it possible for every one of the views of a standard mammogram series to miss this?'

Pizzi considered the question, then shook his head.

'I don't believe so,' he said. 'Depending on technique, it would be present in three standard views, maybe four.'

'And if it wasn't?'

Rick Pizzi's expression darkened.

'Then,' he said, 'I would have to adopt the position that the mammograms weren't hers.'

'Mammograms that weren't hers. Mother of God, Will, what have you gotten yourself into?' Cameron asked as they trudged up four stories from the basement.

'This time.'

'Pardon?'

'You mean what have I gotten myself into *this time*. This is the woman who almost died from an anaphylactic reaction to her first dose of chemotherapy.'

'I heard about this case. The rescue-squad paramedic did a trach on her, yes?'

'Exactly. Saved her life from all I can tell.'

'Fascinating.'

'Actually, she's a patient of our practice. Susan did the biopsy and excision.'

'So the woman really has breast cancer.'

'*Had*, I hope. The cancer was about two and a half centimeters, but the sentinel lymph node Susan took was negative. The thing is, the cancer that was removed might not be the one depicted on her mammogram.'

Cameron stopped after three floors to catch his breath.

'Tsk, tsk, Gordo,' Will said, 'too many doughnuts, not enough treadmill.'

He was pleased with the doughnut reference even though it had been unintentional.

'Ach, laddie, you couldn't be more wrong. It's nothing I do wrong, it's just my hereditary, familial, inherited, genetic bronchitis. It acts

186

up every year on precisely this day. There, it's already better. So,' he went on as they headed up the last flight, 'let me get this straight. The radiologist mixed up her films with someone else's, but that person happened to have a cancer in the same quadrant of the same breast as our patient.'

'I think that about sums it up.'

'That's one lucky radiologist.'

'I should say.'

Cameron paused outside the Sears Conference Room.

'So what do you make of it all?' he asked.

'Don't know. But I do know I'm not done thinking about it.'

Or about whether you're the one.

The chairs in the conference room, which were normally set up in rows, were stacked along the walls, except for those dozen or so that were spaced around a large cherry-wood table. Hospital president Sid Silverman was seated on the far side, flanked by cardiologist Dr. Hans Gehringer and an attractive, conservatively dressed brunette who just had to be a lawyer. Silverman inadvertently caught Will's gaze and nodded a weak greeting, his expression that of a man about to be sick. To Gehringer's left were Susan Hollister and Jim Katz. Cameron took the chair between Katz and Patty's nemesis, Wayne Brasco.

Occupying the two seats to Brasco's left were bookend women in business suits – also attorneys, Will guessed. He suspected they might be connected with the Board of Registration in Medicine. He hesitated briefly, then took the middle of the three remaining empty chairs. There was no sense in even trying not to stand out in this group.

Apparently it had been decided that Silverman was going to run the show.

'Well, thank you all for coming on such short notice,' he began. 'I assure you we are confronting an emergency of the highest order and that every one of us needs to be here.'

He then asked for introductions around the table.

'Hans Gehringer, medical chief of staff here at FGH.'

'I'm Susan Hollister, a surgeon in the same practice as Will Grant. I am also a supporter and long-standing friend of his.'

'James Katz, also a member of the practice and the reason for this meeting.'

'Gordon Cameron. What Susan said goes double for me. I know Will Grant is a good man and a great surgeon, and I feel we should do whatever we can to help him get through this mess.'

187

'Detective Lieutenant Wayne Brasco, Massachusetts State Police. I've been directing the team assigned to the managed-care killings. We expect to bring this criminal to justice, and quickly.' He looked directly at Will. 'His reign of terror and death will be brought to an end one way or the other.'

Will's dislike for the man, already fully formed, mushroomed. Brasco was arrogant, self-serving, and violent – a man to be feared. It was no wonder Patty had had such a difficult time with him.

As he suspected, the two women to his right were both from the Board of Registration in Medicine. One, Jane Weiss, introduced herself as the chief counsel, and the other, Diana Emspak, was the head of the investigation and enforcement unit – process server Sam Rogers's boss, Will supposed.

'I'm Will Grant,' he said when it was his turn. 'I never willingly took any drugs. I haven't done anything wrong. I have never wanted to be anything other than a good doctor. I understand your needs to protect the patients of this hospital and the people of the state, but terrible action has been taken against me without consideration of the lack of any corroborating behavior in my past.'

'We appreciate your feelings,' Silverman said, his tone patronizing and insincere enough to knot the muscles in Will's neck.

At that moment, Tom Lemm, the president of the Hippocrates Society, entered the room, wearing a navy sports coat and perfectly knotted iridescent blue bow tie. It seemed that Lemm took too long searching for a seat before he realized that both of the two available chairs were next to Will. He settled into one, shook Will's hand uncomfortably, and accepted Silverman's introduction.

'Dr. Lemm, we appreciate your being able to get here on such short notice. I know it was a long drive for you. Jill?'

'I'm Jill Leary,' the dark-haired woman on Silverman's right said, 'chief counsel for the hospital.'

Silverman cleared his throat for transition.

'We are here because of something that has happened involving Dr. Grant and Dr. Katz and, indirectly, all the rest of us. Dr. Katz?'

Katz straightened some notes on the table in front of him. It was only then that Will realized the man did not look at all well. He was pale, almost ashen, and there was a slight tremor in his hands as well as the faintest tic at one corner of his mouth. Katz coughed, swept an errant wisp of thinning hair from his forehead, and poured a glass of ice water.

'At eight o'clock this morning,' he began, 'a call came for me at

188

home on a line that is unlisted. The voice was electronically altered in the way Dr. Grant has described. Initially I thought it was a crank call of some kind, but after a few words I had no doubt it was the killer. I was in my study at the time and had a pad of paper close at hand, so I wrote down what he – what *it* – had to say and typed my notes out immediately afterward. I believe my recording of the incident is quite accurate. If I may:

'*Dr. Katz, listen to me and listen to me carefully. I will not repeat myself. Dr. Willard Grant is being treated poorly by those who do not understand what a martyr he is in the struggle to avenge the harm brought down on so many by those companies that control health care. In all likelihood, framing him for drugs was the work of one of those companies – retribution for his victory over them at Faneuil Hall perhaps, or more likely because we have chosen him to speak for us as he has done so eloquently for the Society. He should not be suspended from his hospital and his profession. Rather, he should be honored. You have been chosen to right the wrongs that have been done to this man, a leader in the war against managed care.*

'*Dr. Willard Grant's reputation is crucial to our mission. He must be quickly restored to the practice of medicine, to the staff of your hospital, and to his position within the Hippocrates Society, or punishment will be meted out, and you, Dr. James Katz, will be the recipient. This is no idle threat. We hope you know by this time that we are very good at what we do, and very determined to have our point driven home about the dangers of managed care. You have seven days from this noon to use your influence to see to it that our demands come to pass. In the top right drawer of your desk at work are two envelopes – one is for you, and one for Dr. Grant.*

'*We have chosen Dr. Grant to present our views and grievances to the public. For him to do so effectively, the stain currently on his reputation as a physician must be removed. We want you to see to it that Dr. Grant is in the position to state our position publicly as we have written it for him. You are either with us on this, Dr. Katz, or you are against us. There is no middle ground. I hope for your sake that is clear.*'

Katz actually sloshed water from his glass trying to raise it to his lips. Even though the years had taken some toll on the man, he still was a skillful surgeon who lived his life with quiet dignity. Will ached to see him in such a state. Even though he had predicted to Patty that the killers might make some effort to restore his decimated credibility, he was stunned at the cruelty of their threat. It was quite apparent that the others were, too.

'Nice friends you have there, Dr. Grant,' Silverman said. 'Detective Brasco?'

'One second, Doctor.'

Brasco pulled out his cell phone, made a call, and spoke in hushed tones, nodding his head importantly.

'As long as you're done with the envelopes, why don't you bring them right over,' he said, raising his voice loudly enough for all in the room to hear. 'Third-floor conference room at the hospital.' He grinned in an odd, smug way. 'No, the *L* doesn't surprise me at all. Not at all.'

An *L*. Jim Katz's death sentence had arrived in an envelope in the form of the letter *L,* undoubtedly block printed on white cardboard. Brasco's expression at that moment was as subtle as a wrecking ball. The *L* didn't surprise him in the least. *Why not?* It had to be that he knew something, Will thought. It had to be that he and the cryptographer had solved the killer's puzzle.

'Sorry,' Brasco said, setting his cell phone aside. 'Where were we? Ah, yes, we were starting to debate the merits of giving in to the demands of a serial killer. I would like to say here and now that our position, like that of the President, is that we don't bargain with terrorists.'

The knot in Will's neck muscles tightened once again. Brasco was a cowboy – an explosive with a minuscule fuse.

'Well, Lieutenant,' Silverman said, clearly appalled by Brasco's insensitivity toward Jim Katz, 'I would say you've made your position quite clear. However, I would like the rest of you to feel free to tell us what you can and would be willing to do to protect Dr. Katz, who has done so much for our hospital and community. Miss Leary?' He nodded to the hospital attorney.

'Since we first learned of the nature of the killer's demands,' Leary said, 'we have been discussing how far we might be able to go in reinstating Dr. Grant, at least temporarily. There is some precedent in our hospital, albeit from a number of years ago, for lifting a physician's suspension while the claims against him are being investigated. Our medical staff executive committee is willing to consider the possibility out of deference to Dr. Katz, but they would insist on a psychiatric evaluation of Dr. Grant as soon as possible by a therapist chosen by us or the Board of Registration in Medicine. They would also very much like some other sort of mitigating evidence relative to the allegations of drug use, which Dr. Grant has so staunchly denied.

They have requested at least some notarized affidavits from respected members of the medical or civic community attesting to his moral character, and they would prefer something more concrete and substantial – hard evidence that at least suggested Dr. Grant's innocence.'

'Ms. Weiss,' Silverman said to the board's attorney, 'is there any chance the board would agree to stay Dr. Grant's suspension pending an investigation of the allegations against him?'

Weiss, dark and studious, held a brief, whispered exchange with the other board attorney.

'Ordinarily, I would say no,' she replied. 'The board exists to protect the public. We take a very harsh position in disciplining physicians when there has been patient harm, as in this case, or in many instances even the possibility of patient harm. However, there are most certainly extenuating circumstances here. Dr. Katz, I was informed that you actually served as one of the members of our board.'

'That was a few years ago, but yes,' Katz said, still quite gloomy. 'Governor Wilcox appointed me. I served for two years.'

'You have a fine reputation throughout our office.'

'Thank you.'

Again the board attorneys whispered to each other.

'Given the severity of what happened with Dr. Grant in the OR, we can't make any promises,' Weiss said finally. 'But if your executive committee approves his reinstatement, it is possible the board would follow suit. Dr. Grant, have there been any new developments in your efforts to determine what happened to you?'

'Theories,' Will said, taking pains not to look in Gordon Cameron's direction, 'but nothing firm yet.'

'And you do agree to get an evaluation by a psychiatrist certified in addiction medicine?'

'Absolutely.'

'And some letters attesting to your personal character?'

'I'll do my best.'

'The more, the better.'

'No problem.'

Weiss turned to Katz.

'Dr. Katz, Attorney Emspak and I are both terribly disturbed by what is happening to you. We will do everything we can to help ensure that no harm comes to you.'

'I very much appreciate that,' Katz said, 'just as I appreciate that

191

there are no guarantees at this point.'

'Dr. Lemm?' Silverman asked.

'Our organization has a great deal of respect for Dr. Grant and the work he has done both as a surgeon and as a member of the Hippocrates Society. We are looking for any valid excuse to reinstate him. However, as I'm sure you all know, his is a very high-profile case. It sounds as if all three of our agencies – the hospital, the board, and the Society – will be out on a very thin public-relations limb, as the press is almost certain to latch on to this.

'I think we should have a carefully crafted and well-coordinated explanation as to why we have changed our position on this case. Perhaps, in the absence of anything other than a supportive psychiatric evaluation and some letters of support, we can allude to other elements of Dr. Grant's case that have come to light without being specific. I am sure that I speak for the Society when I say that what it seems we need to do is to give Detective Brasco and his people enough time to catch this killer, while at the same time protecting Dr. Katz in any way we can.'

Silverman allowed multiple conversations to hold sway for a time, then turned to Will.

'Dr. Grant, I would ask that you redouble your efforts to save us from the public-relations volcano that is certain to erupt the moment it is learned that our organizations have reinstated you – *if*, in fact, we do. The killer has given us one week to reverse the suspensions. I suggest we meet here again at this time the day after tomorrow. By then we'll know from Dr. Grant if any other information has been unearthed regarding his claims of innocence and from the board if you have found an addiction specialist to evaluate him. Hopefully we'll be in a position to vote and, if we decide to proceed, to begin preparing whatever explanation we need for the press.'

'Good,' said Weiss. 'Dr. Grant, do you have any problem doing your part?'

'I'll be happy to pay the independent evaluator and to try and come up with some theory or evidence you all can use with the press. Before I promise anything else, I'd like to see what the killer is insisting that I say to the media, but of course I would do anything I could to protect Dr. Katz.'

At that moment, as if on cue, there was a knock on the door. Brasco leapt to open it and returned with two manila folders. He glanced at one – apparently the one that held the letter *L* – kept it, and tossed the other in front of Will.

'I admire your nobility, Dr. Silverman,' Brasco said, returning to his chair, 'and yours, Dr. Lemm, and also the good ladies of the Board of Medicine, but I would have to say that in my opinion you are choosing a path that could backfire in a big-time way if this man goes out and gets himself overdosed again. Personally, I feel we can supply enough protection for Dr. Katz until we put this psycho away for good. Believe me, Doctor, we've protected witnesses against larger threats than this one.'

'Excuse me, Detective Brasco,' Will said, 'but I think you are underestimating these people. They are predators – vicious, brilliant, and remorseless. Just look at the way they've killed. Having dealt with them already, I can only say that in my opinion, if they want Dr. Katz dead, they will find a way.'

'That's only because you're probably one of them, you friggin' junkie!' Brasco snapped with startling abruptness. 'You're just trying to save your own hide.' He stood, sending his chair hurtling backward. 'Well, let me tell you something. This whole discussion is unnecessary, because before your week is up, we'll have nailed the bastard. You all can do whatever you want, but let me tell you one more time: We don't make deals with terrorists, and we also don't make deals with junkies!'

Before anyone else could say a word, Brasco whirled and stormed out of the room.

Chapter 23

For several minutes, those remaining in the Sears Conference Room sat in stunned, motionless silence. Finally, Sid Silverman stood, adjusted his vest, and gathered his papers together.

'The day after tomorrow, then,' he said, as if Brasco's outburst was too outrageous even to acknowledge. 'Dr. Grant, please be sure Attorney Weiss has a way of getting ahold of you.'

'Here're my cell phone and home numbers,' Will said, passing them over to her. 'I ... I know this situation isn't easy for any of you. Jim, I just want you to know that I am horribly sorry for what this monster is putting you through. Julia, too. If you all decide to go along with the killer's demands and reinstate me, I promise to keep a very low profile and not cause any problems. I doubt Lieutenant Brasco will be back here for our next meeting, but *I* will. Hopefully, before too much longer, you'll all know what I know, namely that I'm not guilty of anything.'

The meeting ended without fanfare. Drained, Will remained in his place as the others left the room. Jim Katz, still pale and shaken, hurried out without so much as a glance at Will. Of the others, only Susan and Gordo made eye contact with him.

Will felt sad about this latest turn in his insane saga, but he also felt, in some strange way, vindicated. From the moment the fentanyl was detected in his blood, he had been a pariah in the hospital, among his colleagues, and in the press. Now, thanks to a murderer – a multiple murderer – the Society, the hospital, and the Board of Registration in Medicine were begging him to give them a reason, any reason, to restore his medical license, position within the Society, and hospital privileges. If he was being selfish in the face of Jim Katz's anguish, so be it. No one could fully understand what he had been through, or how desperately he wanted his life back. He wanted to belong, to be challenged again. He wanted his children not to be ostracized from their playmates. He wanted to matter in the world that had mattered so much to him. He wanted to be a doctor again.

Was that so wrong?

It was quite possible that even letters of support from Benois Beane and Susan and Gordo and Jim, and maybe a couple of the docs who hadn't turned away from him, would not be enough to convince the attorneys from the hospital and the board, but for the moment that was all he could think of to do.

Susan.

Will was gathering his notes together when he realized he had intended to speak with her after the meeting about the BB in Grace's films, radiologist Rick Pizzi's opinion, and the strange, violent reaction of the man who had referred Grace to her in the first place. He stuffed the papers in his briefcase and was just pushing back from the table when Sid Silverman returned to the room. His moon face was more flushed than usual.

'I thought I'd find you still here,' he said.

'I was just fixin' to leave.'

'I came back to see to it that you do.'

'What?'

'You're still suspended from here.'

'So?'

194

'So, I want you out of this hospital until – when and *if* – we restore your privileges to work here. Personally, Grant, I think you're dirty. I think you took that drug, and I think that somehow you're more involved with this killer than you would let anyone believe. If it weren't that Jim Katz's life is at stake, I would have leapt up to support Brasco's position in a heartbeat. And if something happens to Katz, I hope you're prepared to live with it. Now, get out of here.'

Having issued the order, rather than leave, Silverman stepped back against the wall and waited, his arms folded against his chest as tightly as his anatomy would allow.

Will wanted so desperately to charge across the room and punch the hospital president senseless. *Stupid, insensitive bastard.* In what he hoped was exasperatingly slow motion, Will stood up and made a pretext of repacking his briefcase. It was then he realized his cell phone was ringing. Gesturing *what can you do?* to Silverman, he answered it.

'Grant, Micelli here,' the lawyer rasped. 'You someplace you can talk?'

'I can talk, Augie.'

The longer you have to stand around and wait, Sid, the happier it makes me.

'Grant, listen. As I told you earlier, I've been studying the pharmacology of fentanyl and thinking about how this could have happened to you.'

'And?'

'The drug had to be inside your shoes – those red sneakers you wear every time you operate! It's the only explanation that makes any sense other than that you're a liar, and I've chosen not to consider that possibility anymore. The drug – probably a lot of it – was soaked into the insoles of your OR shoes and allowed to dry there. Then, your own sweat reconstituted it and you absorbed it through your feet, just as if your socks were giant fentanyl patches. We have to find those shoes, Grant. Any idea where they could be?'

Stunned, Will sank down into the chair, the cell phone pressed tightly against his ear. *Was it possible?* Micelli was crazy. There was no way he was right this time. Still, Will was well known for the red Chuck Taylor All Stars he invariably wore in the OR. He decided to hang on to the possibility, at least for the moment. Like Micelli had said, they were long on facts and way short on explanations.

'I have no idea where they can be now,' Will said. 'The ER nurses put everyone's clothes into a labeled plastic bag. I never got them back. Maybe the police have them.'

'They don't. I checked.'

'I can check with the nurses in the ICU.'

'No! *We've* got to find them, but we need a cop there with us when we do. A cop or someone from the DA's office. And also someone in authority at your hospital. So, for God's sake, don't go looking for them, because if you luck out and actually find them, you've ruined everything. We'll need a tight chain of custody. Listen, I know someone in the DA's office who owes me a favor. Maybe he'll come. Meanwhile, see if you can get someone from your hospital to meet us in the lobby there at, say, eight tonight. Call me if you can't pull that off.'

'I'll do my best. I know a state police detective I might be able to get.'

'Terrific. For this search, the more witnesses the merrier. It's the shoes, pal! It's always the shoes!'

Will slipped the phone back in his briefcase and turned dramatically to Silverman.

'We need to talk, Sid,' he said.

Sid Silverman flatly refused to represent the hospital in the search for Will's OR shoes. Instead, he led Will to attorney Jill Leary's office, stayed long enough to ensure she would be available at eight, and left with another warning that when his business with Leary was finished, Will was to wait outside the hospital until Micelli's group convened in the lobby. Learning that the infamous Law Doctor was representing Will did nothing to brighten Silverman's day.

'I thought Micelli just sued doctors,' he said.

'He's making an exception in my case.'

'Why?'

'I think it's because he believes I could be innocent, Sid.'

'Well, I don't.'

'You know what I think? I think Micelli's right. I think the shoes are how I was poisoned. And I think you're frightened to death that you might be wrong about me and wrong in the way you've treated me. And when we find out that he's right, and you're wrong, I want my staff privileges back on the spot. And you know what else I want, Sid? I want you never to speak *to* me or *about* me again.'

It took most of half an hour for Will to bring Jill Leary up to speed on the pharmacology of fentanyl and on the evolution of his relationship with Augie Micelli. Given her outwardly severe demeanor, she

196

was surprisingly kind and, from what he could tell, nonjudgmental. Still, he felt distracted and rushed his account wherever he could. He hadn't yet had the opportunity to call Patty and invite her to meet them at the hospital, and he also needed to track down Susan to see if something could be set up involving the two of them and Charles Newcomber.

'Tell me something,' Leary said. 'If what your lawyer believes happened is actually what did, don't you think that whoever is responsible would have gone out of their way to locate your OR shoes and dispose of them?'

It was a good question – a very good question, in fact. Will took some time to think his answer through.

'I guess it's possible they did just that,' he said finally. 'But if the police don't have my clothes from that day, and they're not in the ICU and not in the ER, then either a clothing bag with my name on it was thrown away accidentally, or someone took it. And since I can't imagine housekeeping just chucking a patient's belongings' bag away without giving it to a nurse, we would have to deal with the likelihood that whoever poisoned me got rid of it.'

'I suppose at first blush I can buy that logic,' the lawyer said, her smile genuine and warm. 'Well, it's my night to make dinner for my husband and kid, so I'd better run. I'll see if I can poke any holes in your theory on the way home, and I'll see you back here tonight at eight.'

'Terrific.'

'And, Dr. Grant?'

'Yes.'

'I'm sorry this is happening to you.'

Using a hospital phone, Will tried Patty at home and on her car phone. They had agreed that so long as his home, his cell, and his office phones were tapped, they would try to avoid talking on them. When they did connect through one of those phones, it would be strictly business. Use of the word *danger* meant that Will would call her car phone from someplace safe.

When Will arrived at the office of Fredrickston Surgical Associates, Susan was seeing the last of her patients. It had been more than a week since he had been there, and the staff greeted him with edgy warmth. It was, he knew, a natural reaction. The more time that passed without his exoneration, the more doubt that accrued.

'Doin' fine,' he said to the receptionist before she even asked. 'Not to worry. I'm doin' fine.'

He failed to reach Patty again, this time using the phone in Gordo's office. Then he sat at his uncharacteristically ordered desk, bending and unbending a paper clip as he tried to remember what normal felt like. What would life be like now if he had simply said no when Tom Lemm and the rest of the Society had so skillfully maneuvered him into the Faneuil Hall debate?

'Hey, big fella, I heered you wuz waitin' fer me.'

Susan sidled into Will's office and took the chair opposite him. She was unpretentiously elegant in an ankle-length skirt with a bright African print and a beige silk blouse. Her sorrel hair was, as usual, pulled back in a tight bun.

'Thanks for sticking up for me at that session today,' Will said.

'I wish that fop Silverman had given me the chance to say more. I'm sure this has been hell for you.'

'I'm ready to have it be over, that's for sure. Maybe tonight.'

'What do you mean?'

Will recounted the call from Micelli and the search that was to commence at eight.

'You're welcome to come along, Suze.'

'If I thought it would make any difference, I would. I hope you know that, even though, believe it or not, I am being taken to the Bruce Springsteen concert tonight.'

For emphasis, she bit on her lower lip and played a few notes on an imaginary guitar.

'I didn't know you were into The Boss.'

'Let me put it this way – everyone I know is excited that I'm going, so I am, too.'

'You'll love him.'

'Anything's possible. Hey, before I forget, what's going on with Grace Davis and her X-ray?'

'That's actually what I wanted to see you about.'

'Grace's husband told me she had a BB in her chest that wasn't in her mammograms.'

'Exactly. She was shot by her brother when she was a kid.'

'You saw the mammograms?'

'I did that day you agreed to let me take over her case. I can't be sure the BB wasn't there, but it seems unlikely I would have missed it. Yesterday I went to see Dr. Newcomber, the mammographer at the Excelsius Health Cancer Center.'

'He's an odd little duck.'

198

'You've met him?'

'A couple of times. I think he's gay, but other than that I have no read on him.'

'Well, what I think happened is that he read her films correctly, then mistakenly put someone else's films in her jacket. I just didn't notice that the name on the jacket and the name on the films were different.'

'Someone who also had a left upper outer-quadrant cancer?'

'I guess. It's the only explanation I can come up with.'

'If that's the case, I must have missed the name difference, too. I studied those films before I did her surgery.'

'It's possible. The name on the film isn't something we go out of our way to check.'

'I suppose.' Susan's nonplussed expression made it clear she was searching for other explanations. 'So, what happened when you went to see Newcomber?'

'Are you ready for this? When I asked to review Grace's films with him, he got really frightened. He was gripping the edge of his desk so tightly I thought it was going to splinter. Then he said he needed a notarized release from Grace to show me anything. Then, when I said that was a ridiculous demand to make to a fellow physician, without any warning he reached in his desk drawer and pulled a gun on me.'

'A what?'

'A snub-nosed revolver. He threatened to shoot me if I didn't get out, and it seemed he was just panicked enough to do it. His face was flaming red and his hand was shaking. I half expected to see smoke coming out of his ears.'

'If he had done that to me, he wouldn't have had to bother pulling the trigger, because I would have just died on the spot. So, what do you want to do?'

'I want to see him again, this time with you in tow and clutching a notarized release from Grace Davis. And if he makes a move for that right-hand desk drawer, I'm going to launch myself over his desk, rip off that god-awful hairpiece of his, and ram it down his throat.'

'Goodness. The dark side of Will Grant.'

'Believe me, there is one. No one's ever pointed a gun at *me*, either.'

'Should I call and make an appointment with him?'

'The cancer center's not that far away from here. I favor just showing up. Maybe I'll sort of hang back in the corridor until you're through the door of his office, then I'll slide in behind you.'

'Nine A.M. okay?'

'Fine. I'll meet you here and we can drive over together.'

'And the notarized release?'

'Jill Leary, that hospital attorney, will be here tonight when we look for the shoes. If she can't or won't do it, I'll figure out something.'

'I hope this search works out for you, Will. I'm sick of people getting angry at me because you're not here to take care of them and they have to settle for me.'

'That's nonsense. Just keep your fingers crossed tonight while you're at the Fleet Center screaming for Springsteen.'

Susan stood and held up four sets of crossed fingers.

'Just practicing,' she said. 'Hey, one more thing, could you give me the names of a couple of Springsteen's songs? In case you couldn't guess, I really don't know much about him except that he's a hunk.'

'"I'm On Fire," "Born to Run," and "Badlands" – all theme songs of mine at the moment. For that information, I want a T-shirt.'

'See you in the morning, Doc. If my date's impressed with those titles, you get your shirt.'

Chapter 24

'Detective Kristine Zurowski, please. Tell her it's Detective Moriarity calling.'

Her phone on hands-off, Patty was mired in traffic halfway to Serenity Lane in Dover. The cartons she had taken from Ben Morales's study rested on the backseat of the Camaro. Although she hadn't made it through all of Morales's papers, what she had read and learned from Wendy Morales had her head spinning. Morales had blocked a merger attempt by Boyd Halliday and Excelsius Health. Not long after that, he was murdered. Now it was time to see if she had stumbled onto a pattern. One memo, nearly lost within reams of paper, suggested that the new corporation, which would include Morales's Premier Care, would also include Cyrill Davenport's Unity Comprehensive Health.

'Hey, Patty, are you okay?'

'I'm fine, Kristine.'

'Someone just told me you got taken off the big case.'

'The rumor mill is really cranking. You heard about it almost as soon as I did.'

'That thug Brasco?'

'He had some help from our CO, but yes. They thought some new blood was needed.'

'Blood with Y chromosomes?'

'Possibly. No, make that *probably*.'

'You should file a complaint.'

'Maybe someday. Right now I'm complaining the only way I know how, by staying on the case without their knowing it.'

'Yea, Patty.'

'Thanks. So, Kristine, have you guys made any progress?'

'Nada. The going theory is that these are vengeance killings, but what else is new? We have the alphabet letters, but no one's been able to crack them yet. We hear HQ is putting together a task force to centralize all information. I thought you might actually be involved in that.'

'Only by not being on it. Listen, as far as the letters go, I can make you a hero. Brasco and the cryptographer have come up with *Remember Clementine*. The code-breaker is ninety-something percent certain that's it. They think Clementine might be the name of the killer's mother.'

'You believe that?'

'I don't know. Maybe. The killer sure as hell wants us to believe that, so I'm at least a *little* skeptical.'

'Clementine,' Kristine mused. 'You know anyone named Clementine?'

'Only the one who is lost and gone forever.'

'Dreadful sorry. It does sound a little bogus to me.'

'See what I mean? I'm going to ignore Clementine for the time being and keep heading in this direction.'

'You need a buddy?'

'Do yourself and your career a favor and steer clear of me for the time being. If I can ever get out of this one-twenty-eight traffic, I'm on my way over right now to speak with Gloria Davenport. That's actually why I'm calling you.'

'She know you're coming?'

'Yes. I wanted to clear my visiting her with you first, though, being as she's in your bailiwick.'

'Consider it cleared, especially after giving me Remember

Clementine.'

'I also want to know anything you've got on her.'

'You think she's got something to do with her husband being blown up?'

'No, but you may be closer than you realize.'

'Well, we've interviewed her twice. The first time she was intoxicated, and the second time she was merely drunk. She handles her booze impressively well, though, I'll give that to her. And she puts up a pretty good front. No one here including me is suspicious of her except for the fact that she is, as of the explosion, one wealthy woman.'

'How wealthy?'

'You saw where they live. I don't know how much the stock she's about to inherit is worth, but I can tell you that as of this moment the company is privately owned, and I must believe that a good chunk of those tens of tens of millions once possessed by her husband now belong to her.'

'Interesting.'

'Listen, you'll keep me up to speed?'

'If I know it, you'll know it.'

It was nearing six when Patty pulled up the driveway of 3 Serenity Lane. Cocktail time. As she approached the front door, she was thinking, at least in part, of how good a gentle gin and tonic with a wedge of lime would taste, provided she could put her feet up on something at the same time.

The massive colonial showed no sign of the carnage and wreckage that had so recently occurred there – a testimony to the power of money. Gloria Davenport, whom Patty never saw when she was last at Serenity Lane, answered the door herself, although Patty caught a glimpse of a maid scurrying past in the background. The mental image she had formed of a fiftyish, overly rouged bottle blonde wasn't that far from the truth, but in some ways, perhaps with the help of surgery, Gloria had managed to retain a good deal of femininity in her figure and bearing, as well as her neck, face, and especially her eyes, which were a very soft blue. She didn't have a drink in her hand, but Patty could tell one had been there not that long ago.

'Why, you're lovely,' Gloria said, extending her hand and welcoming Patty into a home that was at once elegant and comfortable. 'I thought police detectives who looked like you were only found on TV or in the movies.'

'Thank you. I don't think the people I arrest pay much attention to my looks.'

The sitting room to which Patty was led featured matched satin love seats that might have been centuries old and an array of other antiques. A filled ice bucket and glasses were on the coffee table along with some mints and a half-empty glass of something amber. Patty commented on the room and the house, and confirmed her notion that, in fact, the love seats were Louis Quatorze.

'I know better than to expect you to be drinking while on duty,' Gloria said, after establishing that Patty should address her by her first name, 'unless you're one of those tragic, tortured detectives whose character development they try to compress in the interest of a two-hour movie by simply making them alcoholic.'

'I drink,' Patty said. 'Sometimes more than I should. At the moment, though, I have a lot on my mind, and I've found that alcohol often makes me not as sharp as I could be. You should certainly go ahead if you wish.'

'And I shall. Well, aren't you a breath of fresh air. You investigate murders, you know antiques, you give your hostess permission to drink, and, most important of all, you say Louis Quatorze with a decent French accent.'

'Thank you again. My father barely made it past high school, so he pushed education on me and my brother. He used to say that every single day we managed to stay in school translated into ten thousand people in the world we wouldn't have to take B.S. from in our lives.'

Gloria's raspy laugh was robust and genuine.

'That's a very wise observation.'

'Possibly so, but at the moment, with about six years less formal education than I have, he's my boss.'

Gloria laughed again. If she was in any way intoxicated, Kristine was right: She handled the state well. As if speaking to that point, she refilled her glass and added two ice cubes.

'Gloria, I know you've been interviewed more than once regarding your husband's murder,' Patty said.

'That would be correct.'

'So I'm sure you know that his is just one of what looks like a string of serial killings – four of them now – apparently related to someone trying to avenge the death of a friend or relative.'

'The mother of the killer, one of the policemen told me.'

'We have reason to believe there is more than one killer – possibly a brother and sister.'

'Why would you believe that?'

'The killer has been funneling information piecemeal to us through a physician he keeps calling – a physician with a very public position against managed care. It's as if he, or they, have chosen the doctor to be their press secretary – someone whose own stature more or less validates them.'

'Someone from the Hippocrates Society?'

Patty looked up at the woman, impressed.

'As a matter of fact, yes. So, you know about the Society.'

'Not all that much, but everyone in our industry knows about them. They've become quite a thorn in our side over recent years.'

Our industry. Before this visit, Patty had formed the impression of Gloria Davenport as some sort of dilettante, uninterested in anything other than drinking and finding ways to spend her husband's money. Forming impressions of people on too little information was a habit she resolved, once again, to break.

'Gloria, you say *our* industry. Were you very involved in your husband's business?'

'I'm not surprised that you are the first policeperson to ask me that question. The rest of them seem content to believe that I am nothing more than a chronically besotted spouse who was lucky enough to marry a health-care baron, and now even luckier to inherit all his money.'

'But that's not true?'

'Well, maybe the besotted part is. I don't blame Cyrill totally for my drinking, but I will say that he was ... how should I put it ... difficult. Do you know much about OCD, obsessive-compulsive disorder?'

'Some.'

'Well, Cyrill has – *had* it. Unfortunately, he was the only one close to him who didn't know it. And for as long as I knew him, chief among the things he was obsessive and compulsive about was making money.'

'Pardon me for saying so, but it seems like he did a good job of it.'

'I suppose you're right. Of course, he did have a running head start.'

Gloria's expression was mischievous.

'Okay,' Patty said, 'I'll bite. What sort of running head start?'

'My maiden name was Storer, as in Storer and Elliot.'

'The investment house?'

'Complete with our own padded cell – I mean *seat* – on the New York Stock Exchange. When Cyrill and I married, I was worth

204

'somewhere in the neighborhood of a hundred million dollars.'

'That's some neighborhood,' Patty said.

'Cyrill was worth maybe a million cents depending on the status of his car payments, but he was full of dreams, and to his credit he had gotten a business degree from Wharton. Actually, that's where we met. I was a year ahead of him. I bought Unity Comprehensive Health for him as a wedding present and out of curiosity to see just how good he could be. The rest is history.'

'Were you involved in the business?'

'Of course I was. I was on the board of directors from the start. I had to protect my investment. It wasn't that hard to have Cyrill believe he was making all the brilliant decisions.'

'He didn't?'

'Let's just say he made some on his own, and lots that he *thought* were on his own.'

'So what's the status of the company now?'

'Well, to all intents, Unity isn't really a company anymore except on paper. We're now well on our way to a merger with –'

'Excelsius Health,' Patty cut in excitedly.

Gloria looked at her queerly.

'Now, that's a piece of information not many people are supposed to have – certainly not people outside our companies.'

Patty reached in her briefcase, passed over Ben Morales's file, and explained how she had come by it. Gloria freshened her drink before opening it, and then scanned each sheet as if she were taking the final exam in a speed-reading course. In just a couple of minutes, she was nodding her head in understanding.

'There are several more cartons of Morales's papers that I haven't gone through yet,' Patty said, 'so there may be more material on all this.'

'Well,' Gloria said with a sigh, 'I tried to stay in the background, but I knew Ben Morales a bit, and most of the CEOs of these other companies, as well, and I knew Boyd Halliday at Excelsius was on the move. But until recently, I didn't know how fast. Excelsius has already absorbed two of these companies, and if you count Unity, it's three. I just read where Steadfast Health, which used to be a pretty well-run outfit, although not that big, has gotten itself into financial trouble and sold out to Halliday.'

'So why did your husband sell out to Excelsius?'

'Oh, he didn't. He never would have parted with Unity. It was like an extension of him. I, on the other hand, was sick to death of the place, if you'll pardon the gallows humor. I had been encouraging Cyrill to get out for more than a year in the interest of kick-starting our marriage, but no go. He had traded me in for the company. Such irony. The day after Cyrill's funeral, his friends and former employees at Unity approached me with an offer I couldn't and didn't want to refuse, and I gave my blessing and control of my stock to them. A couple of days later, the wheels of merger commerce were turning, and turning fast.'

'Gloria, tell me something,' Patty said, now barely able to stay in her seat, 'assuming this serial killer, who has led us to believe he is avenging his mother, picked the CEOs he was going to murder randomly or according to the ease with which he could get to them, don't you think it's strange that two out of four of the victims would never have allowed Excelsius Health to take over their companies had they stayed alive? My research has shown that in this state alone he had about a hundred managed-care companies to choose from.'

'I suppose so, but what about the other two – Marcia Rising's company and that other one? They're not on this list.'

'No,' Patty said thoughtfully, 'no, they're not. Dr. Leaf's widow was not at all involved with his business affairs nor, it would seem, his personal affairs, either. I think it would be a good idea to speak with people at his company – Rising's company, too.'

'You could be way off base,' Gloria said.

Patty gathered her things, stood, and embraced her hostess warmly.

'You're right,' she said, 'I could. You know something, though, that quote I told you from my father, the colonel, about education, isn't the only one he's famous for. There's another. He writes it on the board in just about every class on police work that he teaches and shouts it out at the students.'

'I'm all ears,' Gloria said. 'What is it?'

'It's *I hate coincidences*.'

Gloria took Patty's arm warmly as she led her to the door.

'I hope you solve these crimes quickly, dear,' she said.

'I just might,' Patty replied, her thoughts continuing to whirl. She stopped and turned to her hostess. 'One last thing.'

'Yes?'

'Does the name Clementine mean anything to you?'

Gloria shook her head.

'Nothing,' she said, 'except for the movie.'

'Movie?'

'I'm something of a movie buff – especially westerns. *My Darling Clementine* was an old John Ford film with Henry Fonda as Wyatt Earp. Mid-nineteen forties, I would guess. It's really a classic – maybe the best of the dozen or so movies that have been made over the years about the famous gunfight at the OK Corral.'

'Interesting,' Patty said, no longer surprised by any revelation from this woman, and wondering if there could be any connection at all between the film and the killer. 'Where did that gunfight take place? Wasn't it Kansas?'

'You might be thinking of Dodge City. No, the gunfight at the OK Corral took place in Arizona. *Tombstone*, Arizona.'

Chapter 25

Something big was going on.

Patty knew it the moment she set foot in her office. There was an electricity in the air. People who generally flew out the door the moment their shifts were over were still there. One of them, Brian Tomasetti – a burned-out department lifer but a favorite of hers nonetheless – was actually cleaning his service revolver.

Something was definitely up.

After her meeting with Gloria Davenport, Patty had gone over to see Marcia Rising's husband, a surgeon named Michael Springer who was in practice in Norwood, toward the South Shore. Springer, who still seemed genuinely distraught over his wife's murder, knew a great deal about medical politics, managed care, and his wife's company. What he didn't know was anything about Excelsius Health or any merger plans with Marcia's Eastern Quality Health. Still, it was possible one was in the works. That made two victims connected with the merger list, one maybe or maybe not. The pendulum swung several degrees toward coincidence, but not nearly far enough for her to dismiss the belief that the killings were not the least bit random, and also that they were not the least bit related to the death of anyone's mother.

This was business – pure and simple.

'So, B.T.,' she said, setting a bag of M&Ms down on the keyboard of his computer, 'what's going on here? You're on days, yet here you are.'

'Oh, this is big, Patty,' Tomasetti said, loosening his belt a notch before tearing open the M&Ms, 'real big. I told them I'd man the phones. Sort of control central. Look at me – I'm so excited about this one that I'm cleaning my gun, even though I'm not even out there in the field.'

'That *is* excitement... So?'

'So what?'

Tomasetti poured the last half of the bag onto his desk blotter and divided the candies up by color.

'So what gives? What's going on?'

As she asked the question, Patty felt an eerie tightening beneath her breastbone. She had been on duty all day and had called in any number of times, yet she hadn't heard so much as a whisper about something big going down. Now she felt certain that she had been purposely excluded from whatever it was. Margie Moore, one of the secretaries, swooshed by, packed up for home, and headed for the door.

'Hey, Patty, hey, B.T.,' she said, 'hope this is it.'

'Us, too,' Tomasetti said. 'We'll all be at the top of the pig pile if it is. Have a good one, Margie.'

'B.T.,' Patty asked after the secretary had left, 'does this have something to do with the HMO killings?'

'You're shitting me, right?'

'I'm not shitting you. Now, what's going on?'

'Boy, have they ever cut you out of this one.'

Patty boiled over. Hands on hips, she swept around the desk and stood at Tomasetti's elbow, towering over him with menace that she did not have to conjure up.

'Goddammit, B.T., tell me and tell me now!'

'Okay, okay. Nobody told me not to tell you anything. I thought you already knew, it once being your case and all. I thought you knew. Brasco's set up a meeting with the killer. It's going down in' – Tomasetti checked his Timex – 'fifty-five minutes.'

'That's not possible. The killer's never even made contact with us. Not once, except for those damn letters he leaves at the murders.'

'Well, it wasn't exactly us he made contact with. It was that doctor, the one you've been ... what I mean is –'

'Will Grant,' Patty said, exasperated that if Tomasetti knew, undoubtedly the rest of the squad knew as well – probably her father,

208

too. Just how badly was it possible for her to screw up?

'Yeah, him,' Tomasetti said. 'Apparently the killer told Grant he could put a personal ad in the *Herald* if he ever needed to meet.'

'We took that information off the tap on Grant's phone. I gave it to Brasco and Lieutenant Court myself.'

'Well, Brasco used it and set up a meeting with the killer.'

Patty was feeling more uneasy by the second.

'Where?'

'At a place called Camp Sunshine, believe it or not. It's an old, run-down, unused summer camp on Lake Trumbull, north of Fredrickston. I'm surprised you didn't know about all this.'

'Well, I'm not. Who picked the place?'

'The killer. Brasco allowed him to choose the meeting place so he wouldn't be suspicious. But Brasco's had our SWAT team geared up for like two days now. The moment he gave the word, they infiltrated the area. There's a chopper on standby, too.'

'I know the camp. Brian, the killer's too smart for this. Way too smart. How did Brasco get him to believe he was talking to Will Grant?'

'Patty, I'm sorry. I know this was your case.'

'I appreciate your concern, but don't worry about it. I only look soft. In here where it counts' – she pointed to her heart – 'I'm tough as nails. Now tell me how Brasco convinced the killer he was talking to Grant.'

'VDS,' Tomasetti said simply. 'Voice duplication and substitution. From what I understand, an R and D company on one-twenty-eight has been under contract for this and they've come up with a machine that can take a person's voice and substitute someone else's for it.'

'I know about setups where a man can speak and a girl's or boy's voice can come out. Vice people all over the country are using it to contact predators who want to set up a rendezvous with young girls or young boys they meet online. But you're talking about recording a specific person's voice and then having it speak someone else's words?'

'Exactly. So the killer responds to the ad and calls Grant, and Brasco intercepts the call and uses Grant's voice to say his words. Apparently the killer bought it hook, line, and sinker. You know, just because Brasco doesn't look too bright doesn't mean he isn't.'

'Yes it does. Brasco's using Will Grant without Grant's knowledge, and by doing so, he's putting him in harm's way. I've been on this killer – *these killers* – for months. They never make a careless or dangerous move, even though it might seem like that's what's happening, and they don't care a rat's behind for anyone's life but their own, and that includes Grant's. If Brasco thinks he's outsmarting these people, he's even dumber than he looks, and that's saying something.'

'I never heard you talk that way.'

'I might be just getting started. You have directions to the camp?'

'Yes, but –'

'But what? Brasco said not to let anyone come out there?'

'Something like that.'

'B.T., give me the fucking directions.'

Tomasetti slid a paper from one corner of his desk and passed it over. 'Copy it, and tell them you stole it from my desk without my knowing it, okay?'

'You got it. Thanks, pal. How much time do I have?'

'Maybe fifty minutes now. You've gotta really bust it in that Camaro of yours.'

'Speed is my middle name.'

'I thought that was Danger.'

'Danger's my Confirmation name.'

Patty grabbed the directions, made a quick stop at the Xerox machine, and raced out to the parking lot.

The piper's on the loose and he must be paid.

The killer's proclamation, issued shortly before he assassinated Dr. Richard Leaf with surgical planning and precision, resonated in her mind as she skidded out of the lot and into a tight right-hand turn. There was no shaking the grisly belief that soon, very soon, people were going to die.

By seven forty-five, when he returned to Fredrickston General, Will had given up on recruiting Patty to join the small safari about to explore the hospital for his clothing bag. Several calls to her cell phone had succeeded only in reaching her voice mail, and a wishful call to her place fared no better.

With a dense overcast and intermittent drizzle, night had descended prematurely. Around him, it was business as usual – visitors filing through the revolving glass doors along with a scattering of employees, many of whom Will knew. Two of them grinned uncomfortably and nodded, but most of the others simply averted their eyes and studied the pavement. Even though none of them meant anything special to Will, it was painful to be innocent and to

210

be judged, and it would be an incredible relief to be reinstated. But that reinstatement, he knew, was still anything but automatic.

The board, the hospital, and the Society had been placed in a very difficult position. It would make the decision much easier for each of them if, by some miracle, his Chuck Taylors were found and the insoles tested positive for fentanyl. That possibility seemed remote. The most likely scenario, he believed, was that tonight they would find nothing and would be left speculating about what might have happened his clothing. Even if Micelli's theory about the shoes was right, it was unlikely that someone resourceful enough to frame him would allow the evidence just to lie around. Of course, it was also possible they would have felt confident enough in the sophistication of the frame-up to leave the shoes where they were.

'Good evening, Doctor.'

Jill Leary, a trench coat belted about her trim waist, came up from behind and touched him on the arm.

'Hey, welcome back,' Will said. 'I really appreciate your doing this.'

'No problem. I hope we find something, but as you said in my office, there will be some significance if we find nothing at all. I've tried, but I still haven't been able to poke any holes in your theory, except to say that in hospitals dumb things happen all the time, and yours wouldn't be the first clothing bag that was inadvertently thrown out.'

Will sighed, momentarily and inexplicably consumed by an immense fatigue.

'I suspect we'll be left with that possibility,' he said.

Leary's look was understanding. Guilty or not, it said, she appreciated that he had been through a great deal. Will immediately felt his composure begin to regroup. Kindness and compassion cost so little.

'Let's wait inside for the others,' she said finally. 'I'm sure Sid wouldn't mind.'

Will followed her into the hospital. A few minutes later, Augie Micelli arrived, wearing a rumpled navy blazer, gray slacks, a red power tie, and a dominating cologne. He looked like a premature retiree in Florida or Arizona, but he seemed excited and, best of all, totally sober. His eyes were bright and keen and showed none of the ennui Will had noted when they first met. Micelli was accompanied by a nattily dressed black man carrying a briefcase, whom he introduced as Gil Murray, an assistant DA from Middlesex. Behind Murray was Robert McGowen, a young uniformed Fredrickston policeman whom Will had worked with a number of times in the ER. The Law Doctor guided them over to a deserted corner of the lobby.

'So,' he said, clasping his hands together enthusiastically, 'this mighty task force has been assembled to answer the question of what became of Will Grant's clothing bag. Ms. Leary, thank you for sacrificing your evening on our behalf.'

'No problem.'

'Dr. Grant and I have each spent a good deal of time on the clinical side of hospitals, and so are well aware of the chaos and confusion that can accompany a medical emergency such as his. Officer McGowen assures me that the many cases he has helped haul to the ER here have taught him the same thing.

'Given that a massive amount of the drug fentanyl was in Dr. Grant's body that day, and given that Dr. Grant is adamant in his denial of having taken any, we are forced either to brush him off as a loser and a liar or come up with another explanation. I have chosen to discard the loser–liar alternative and instead, after considering and rejecting many possible scenarios, have chosen to focus on his OR shoes, which, at least as of this moment, appear to be missing. A chemist at one of the pharmaceutical houses that manufacture fentanyl believes that my theory is physically and physiologically possible, provided enough drug is soaked into the insole. Everyone ready?'

'All set,' McGowen said.

'Well then, the supervising nurse in the ICU is expecting us, as is the nurse in charge of the ER. This shouldn't take too long. The idea of having Gil and Officer McGowen along is that if, by any chance, we actually come up with something, it will immediately need to be handled by strict chain of custody. Gil has plastic bags and gummed seals we can all sign, and Officer McGowen will take the bags directly back to the station.'

'Do you really expect to find anything after all this time?' Leary asked.

'The truth is, I don't know what to expect. People in hospitals – in most workplaces, for that matter – tend to ignore anything that isn't directly their job. It's not that hard to imagine a custodian, or nurse's aide, or even a nurse working his or her way around a clothing bag, assuming someone else had placed it there for a reason.'

'I suppose.'

'Any other questions?'

Will found himself wondering about the managed-care bureaucrats who shelved Micelli's career as a physician without so much as the courtesy of an interview. The companies were the Charybdis whirlpool that would suck a physician under even after he had survived the Scylla that was the Board of Registration in Medicine. He was, he saw now, facing the same peril. Guilty or not, his license had been preemptively suspended by the board as a result of his suspension at the hospital. In all likelihood, even if he was deemed acceptable to practice by the board, many of the multiple managed-care panels to which he belonged would remove him as a provider of treatment for their subscribers simply because he once had been suspended. It would be okay for him to practice surgery, they would in essence be saying, but not to earn a living doing it.

His involvement in the Society and that damn debate at Faneuil Hall were sure not to help matters. There probably wasn't a managed-care company within a thousand miles that wouldn't relish the opportunity to bring the hammer down on his career. This was the first time he realized that, regardless of whatever happened today or even down the road, he might well be finished as a doctor.

Easy does it.

Satisfied he had waited long enough for questions, Micelli turned and led the group down the hall to the elevators. In nearly ten years at the hospital, except when accompanying a patient's litter, Will had never used any of the elevators. He suspected that not one of the other three would have passed on the stairs for just one flight, but Micelli was leading this expedition, and there was nothing about the man that suggested he would ever opt for the more physically challenging of any two options. As they headed down the corridor, Will found himself behind the others and next to Gil Murray.

'Thanks for doing this,' Will said. 'I'm really grateful.'

'I would do just about anything for Augie,' Murray replied, his voice a bit like James Earl Jones's. 'I had a back operation a few years ago under general anesthesia, only I wasn't asleep during the procedure and had no way to tell anyone, because I had been given a drug to paralyze my muscles. Some unkind remarks were made about me when my surgeon thought I was asleep. I heard them all. Augie fixed me up with some people who were able to prove that was the case, and he even found an organization named Anesthesia Awareness that's made up of others who've experienced the same thing.'

'I've heard of them,' Will said, cringing at Murray's story.

'It's one of the worst things that's ever happened to me. Augie helped me get a settlement for what I went through, but it's the other things he did that really mattered. He's had some tough times, and doesn't take such good care of himself, but underneath it all he's the best.'

'I'm learning that.'

'On the way over, Patrolman Bob there told me that Augie had helped his dad, as well.'

Up ahead, Micelli was holding open the elevator door, motioning them to hurry up. Loss of a child, loss of self-esteem, loss of health, loss of a hard-earned profession. No one would argue that Will wasn't going through a devastating situation, but the Law Doctor still had him beat.

Nurse Anne Hajjar, usually on the day crew, was waiting for them in the ICU. She was, as usual, radiant and upbeat, even though, she explained, she was working a double because of a hiring freeze on RNs. She nodded to Will, her expression neutral if not a bit cold. He felt a deep pang. They had worked so well together for so long back when life was normal. Now her respect for him seemed all but gone.

Hajjar turned her attention to Micelli.

'So, what are we after here?'

'The truth,' Micelli said.

He gave her a quick capsule.

'No chance,' she said. 'The only thing we are more short of than nurses is storage space. There's a little closet over there where we keep some supplies and cleaning stuff, but I go in there all the time, and I'd have to be as deaf, dumb, and blind as the Pinball Wizard to miss a clothing bag with Dr. Grant's name on it.'

'Is there any other possible place? Wedged way up under the bed Dr. Grant was in?'

Without debate, Hajjar entered the cubicle where Grace was sleeping, knelt down, and peered under the bed. She returned shaking her head.

'No go.'

'Can you think of any other possible space besides that closet?'

Hajjar gave Will a prolonged look. Then, perhaps reflecting on the way things once were between them, she went to the other cubicles and looked under each of the other beds.

'Nada,' she reported.

'Could we check the closet?' Micelli asked.

'Suit yourself. Just you, though. The rest of you will have to wait over there. A couple of our patients are touch and go right now. I don't want any commotion.'

Will watched as Hajjar led the Law Doctor to the far end of the unit and a supply closet that Will knew wasn't any more than six-by-six. The inspection took less than a minute. Without a word, Hajjar returned to her patient, and Micelli came back grinning sheepishly.

'Nothing I didn't expect,' he said. 'Even if we don't find anything here or in the ER, I have documents drawn up for each of you to get notarized stating that fact.'

'Stop by my office after we're through,' Leary said, 'and I'll notarize whatever you need.'

Almost subconsciously, she glanced down at her watch. Will, who was again feeling deflated and peeved with himself for getting so enthusiastic over Micelli's theory in the first place, felt his spirit sink another notch. Jill Leary could and probably should be at home with her kid right now, not offering to notarize worthless documents for him. She was a genuinely caring soul, but there was no way this fruit-less expedition was going to supply the hard evidence he needed to free up the board, the hospital, and the Society to reinstate him. Absolutely no way.

'So,' Micelli said, pumping his fists to demonstrate that his bravado was intact, 'this setback is not totally unexpected. Next we go to the ER, unless any of you has another thought.'

How about we all go home, Will was thinking.

'Ms. Leary,' Micelli continued, 'if you would lead the troops, I have a matter to go over with Dr. Grant.'

He waited until Will had dropped back, then lowered his voice.

'Sorry about the strikeout in the ICU,' he said.

'I didn't expect any different.'

'Maybe the ER will come through.'

'Maybe.'

'Listen, if I'm going to adjust *my* attitude, the least you can do is to stay in this game until it's over.'

'Sorry, Augie, really I am. All of a sudden I just started over-thinking – projecting like hell, getting myself all tied up in knots over things that haven't happened and might not ever happen.'

'Been there, done that,' Micelli said.

'For so long, I just took being a doc for granted.'

'I understand. You know that I do.'

'I'll pull it together.'

'Good. So, what's the deal with Patty Moriarity?'

Will snapped around to face him.

'What about her?'

'She's on our side, right?'

'Right. I told you a little about her. She's the detective who got taken off the managed-care case.'

'Well, she called my office while I was on my way here, but I had the line on call forwarding to my cell phone.'

'Why didn't she call me?'

'She said something about not being able to get through to your cell and not wanting to call you at home. She said to tell you she was off on business and would be in touch either late tonight or tomorrow. She said another thing, too. She doesn't want you to go home until you speak with her.'

'What?'

'You heard me. Don't go home tonight.'

'But why?'

'No idea, but she made it sound as if you might be in some danger if you do.'

'This is crazy.'

'I asked her if you should stay with me tonight and she thought that would be a good idea.'

Why not with her? Will wondered.

'You have room?' he asked.

'I do.'

'I have some business to attend to tomorrow morning, but I suppose I can go from your pad as well as mine. She give you any idea what's going on?'

'Nope.'

'I don't get it.'

'Listen, you'll come to my place tonight. I'll fix you up with a toothbrush and a set of purloined scrubs, and we'll talk.'

They had arrived at the ER. Leary motioned Micelli to the head of the line and he led the expeditionary force into the waiting room. The ER seemed surprisingly calm, especially considering the miles of rain-slicked roadways outside. The waiting room could probably hold twenty-five, but at the moment there were just a mother and her baby, neither of whom seemed particularly ill, and a grizzled man with a hard hat on the seat beside him and an ice pack on his wrist.

'Good news,' Micelli said after a brief trip to the inner sanctum of the ER. 'We can all go in.'

What interest Will had left in the fruitless search for his shoes had been shoved aside by the news of Patty's call and her insinuation that he would be in some sort of danger should he return home tonight.

Barbara Cardigan, the charge nurse, had two decades of experience in the ER and a carefully maintained gruff exterior that Will knew would crack for almost anyone with a legitimate illness or injury. She met the five of them by the nurses' station.

'How are you doing, Will?' she asked, her concern genuine.

'It's been hell.'

'I'm sorry. Well, much as I'd like to, I don't think we're going to be able to help you out. We've certainly had clothing bags left around, but not for more than a day or two. You were brought down from the OR to the Crash Room and intubated there. I wasn't here that day, but Reneé Romanowski was. I just called her. She's certain that you were stripped down here, not in the OR, and that someone put your clothes in a bag.'

Will visualized the scene and found himself feeling embarrassed in front of the others.

'I was in scrubs,' he said, for no particular reason.

'Well, I certainly hope so,' Cardigan said, 'given that you came from the OR. Mr. Micelli, how would you like to proceed?'

'How many rooms do you have?'

'Altogether, fifteen. Two of those have four beds. Five of them have two.'

'And how many of those have closets?'

'I think about half of them do. The rest just have shelves.'

'And there's a closet in the Crash Room?'

'Yes, the largest one.'

Will saw the muscles in Jill Leary's face tighten. Seven or eight closets to inspect followed by a notarizing session in her office to document that they had found nothing. Coming off a long workday, and with her husband and child waiting at home, she had to be desperate to have the safari disbanded.

'I'll tell you what,' Micelli said, as if reading Leary's mind, 'I'm assuming the Crash Room's empty right now.'

'It is.'

'Well, let's all go there together, and if we have no luck, we can split up and each of us can check a closet in the rooms where there are no patients. Perhaps Ms. Cardigan can check the others.'

The nurse nodded her agreement, and the six of them trooped into ER 4, the Crash Room, which was reserved for major emergencies, both medical and trauma. Will, still distracted, was brought back to the moment by the sight of the room where he had so often been one of the central players in a life-and-death medical drama. He was again captivated by the vivid image of himself, lying naked, vulnerable, and unconscious, endotracheal tube down his throat, IVs in his arms, a catheter draining urine from his bladder into a plastic bag, his career as a physician about to slip away.

Goddamn whoever did this to me! Damn you!

The ER used narrower beds than the ICU, each with a wire holder underneath for a patient's belongings. Under normal circumstances, there was no way a clothing bag could remain unnoticed for long. But with a major emergency such as Will's, and a roomful of technicians, nurses, and physicians, it was possible, albeit remotely so, that someone could have shoved the bag aside or even into the closet. At the moment, the accordion door of the closet was pulled shut, but during a code it was often left open to make supplies more accessible.

Micelli and Barbara Cardigan agreed to inspect the closet together. Will gave passing thought to waiting in the hall but instead stood off to one side, feeling somewhat foolish for having gotten so excited about Micelli's theory in the first place.

The lawyer and nurse entered the supply closet, which Will knew was perhaps twelve feet by eight and filled with both medical and janitorial supplies. A minute passed, then another. The four remaining in the Crash Room could hear snatches of an animated conversation coming from within. Finally, Micelli appeared at the doorway, his expression neutral.

'Dr. Grant,' he said, 'why don't you come on in here?'

Will did as he was asked.

The bag was there – heavy, bright blue plastic, somewhat larger than a shopping bag, with white plastic handles. It was on the floor, wedged in a corner behind two mops, a broom, and a bucket. DR. W. GRANT was printed in black Magic Marker across the front.

Will stared at the clothing bag in utter disbelief, as if the numbers on his lottery ticket had just matched the ones shown on TV.

'We haven't opened it,' Micelli said, 'but we each felt it. There are two shoes in there – sneakers, from what we can tell.'

He pulled a small digital camera from his jacket pocket and took half a dozen shots. Then he turned, put his hands on Will's arms, and squeezed.

'I don't believe this,' Will muttered.

'We'll get this bag sealed up, initialed by all of us, and off to the station evidence room with Bob McGowen. As soon as tomorrow, I might be able to have the state lab examining those shoes. One of the women who works there had her renal artery accidentally tied off during a tubal ligation and lost a kidney. Lucky for us, she's still working at the lab.'

'But with the Law Doctor on her side,' Will said, imagining a six- or even seven-figure settlement, 'not for much longer, I'll bet.'

'You've got that right, brother,' Micelli said, beaming. 'You've got that right.'

Chapter 26

With the Camaro's windshield wipers throbbing against what had become a steady downpour, Patty slashed through the night toward Camp Sunshine. Several miles back, she had passed the white *H* on a purple background indicating that there was a hospital somewhere off to her right. Will's hospital. He would be there right now with Augie Micelli, searching the emergency ward and intensive care unit for a bag of clothing that had been taken from him two weeks ago. It felt strange knowing that she was so near to him and that she couldn't simply swing a right and be there, but at the moment she had a more pressing matter to deal with.

Wayne Brasco, operating with zero insight and no feel for the case, and probably with Lieutenant Court's cooperation, had concocted a plan that was either going to fail utterly and without a whimper, or fail utterly and get people killed – quite possibly Brasco himself. Unless she was greatly overestimating the skill and cunning of Brasco's quarry, and she seriously doubted that she was, they would know that the classified ad and phone conversation were bogus and would take Brasco's attempt to trap them as a challenge.

Putting Will in danger by pirating his voice without his knowing was as irresponsible as any police action she had ever encountered. After this night was over, providing Brasco survived, she was going to find a way to make him and their CO answer for what they had done, even if it meant going to her father.

At least Will was safe for the moment. Calling Micelli when she couldn't get through to him had been inspired. It was clear he really cared for Will and would do whatever was needed to ensure that he was out of harm's way until Brasco's grandstanding stunt played itself out.

One very legitimate concern she had was that while Brasco was trying to lure the killer into the open at Camp Sunshine, the killer was poised somewhere within range of Will's apartment, waiting. Now, at least, she could shove that worry to the back of her mind.

There were still unanswered questions about the serial killings of four managed-care executives, but one by one, pieces of the puzzle were falling into place. Misdirection and mayhem. Smoke and mirrors. Boyd Halliday and his killers had been operating that way from the very beginning, and Patty was ready to bet her career that it was going to be that way tonight. Misdirection and mayhem.

Brasco, you jerk!

It was quarter to nine when she skidded onto the narrow two-lane that the map on the passenger seat said would lead to the entrance of Camp Sunshine. Three to four miles to go. She had five or six minutes to cover that distance, but she knew it wasn't going to happen even if she made it to the camp entrance on time. There was no way she would be allowed simply to drive right up to the rendez-vous area and make an impassioned plea for Brasco and Court to forget about their grand scheme and pull everyone back to safety.

The streetlights became more widely spaced, then disappeared altogether. The trim little houses gave way to dense woods, making it even more difficult for the headlight beams of the Camaro to slice through the rain and heavy darkness. Patty switched on her brights, then just as quickly cut them off and actually slowed down. She wasn't going to make it on time anyway, and the last thing she wanted was to be wrong about Brasco's plan, then to compound her stupidity and arrogance by alerting the killer.

This was parkland, she remembered – maybe a state forest. Not too far ahead on the left would be a long, serpentine dirt drive ending at a narrow rectangular parking area demarcated by a ragged border of large, decaying logs. Camp Sunshine. Ten years ago, she and a bunch of classmates had celebrated their fifth high-school reunion at the place. Not that it mattered to their softball, swimming, drinking, flirting, and cookout, but even then, the camp was in a state of impressive disrepair. Of the former sleeping quarters – canvas tents set on wooden platforms – only rotting sheets of flooring remained. The outbuildings were in a similar state of decay and overgrowth.

In addition to the minuscule rent, which was by far the cheapest they could find, the features of Camp Sunshine that had led Patty's reunion committee to choose the site were the natural beauty of the woods, the ball field, and the waterfront. In addition, there were acres of dense, hilly woodland, crisscrossed by narrow dirt trails. The ball field was as well maintained as the rest of the camp was ignored – a vast, grassy space with a rusting wire backstop in one corner, and a barbecue pit. The waterfront, on a lake that was perhaps a mile long and half a mile or less across, featured a sandy beach and a two-story rec hall that, at least at the time of the reunion, was intact and used for outings when the weather made softball impractical.

As Patty turned onto the narrow, winding access road, she wondered about the person or people who owned the decaying camp, which, even nearly a decade ago, was simply begging to be turned into condominiums or some other kind of profitable development. Perhaps there were zoning constraints, perhaps a clause in a will, or perhaps the owners were sentimental eccentrics. No matter. Tonight, serial killers had selected their camp to humiliate the state police and Wayne Brasco. It was never about a vendetta against managed care. It was never about a mother tragically dead. It was never about principle. It was never about Will Grant. It was always about business.

Smoke and mirrors.

Misdirection and mayhem.

Remember Clementine.

Remember Tombstone.

Death to the policeman who thinks he's smarter than we are.

A hundred yards or so down the road, two men stepped out of the forest, their powerful flashlights intersecting upon Patty's face. Blinded, she skidded to a stop, grabbed her shield from the passenger seat, and held it up in front of the lights. At the same time, she smoothly opened her window, hoping that neither of the men thought she was reaching for a weapon. They split up and headed for her car from both sides, their lights still fixed on her face.

'Police,' the man to her left whispered harshly, holding a semi-automatic weapon, possibly some sort of MP5, where she could see it. 'Both hands, let me see 'em.'

Patty lifted her hands palms out, dangling the leather case with her shield and ID from between her thumb and index finger.

'Detective Patty Moriarity, State Police,' she said urgently. 'I've got to get in there. I have reason to believe this is a trap, and the officer in charge is in danger. Maybe others, too.'

The policeman, dressed in black with a black watch cap and greasepainted face, told her to cut her headlights, then motioned her out of the car.

'Kara, you got her,' he said, stepping back and sliding a radio from his belt.

Patty actually managed a wry smile at herself for assuming the two cops were men. A slight woman, who looked absolutely gigantic with a semiautomatic at the ready, moved around the Camaro and kept her at bay from a respectful distance.

'Weapon?' she said stonily.

'On the floor, driver's side. Listen, I've got to –'

'Quiet!'

The woman sidestepped around so she could shine her flash inside the car, then motioned Patty to get her gun and drop it on the ground. Patty could hear the man conversing in hushed tones with, she suspected, Lieutenant Court.

'We're close to being out of time,' she whispered.

'Shut up!' Kara punctuated the order with a menacing flick of the muzzle of her MP5.

Patty sighed and did as she was commanded. No sense getting her head blown off by a cop. Finally, the other officer shoved his radio back into its holder and returned.

'Those people down there aren't exactly your biggest fans,' he said.

'That's because I don't leave the toilet seat up in the precinct loo.'

Patty thought she saw Kara crack a smile beneath her blackface.

'Kara, take her down the road to the others. I'll stay here with B Squad and take care of her car. Be careful.'

'Did they say if anything's happened down there?' Patty asked.

'Nope.'

'I think that's good.'

'Your car'll be on a little road into the woods off this one, about ten yards down there on the right. There may be some camouflage netting on it.'

'Fine. My weapon?'

'Why not?'

Patty retrieved her shoulder holster from the trunk, slid in her Smith & Wesson .38 five-shot, and slipped it on.

'Nice piece,' Kara whispered as they made their way into the darkness.

Fifty feet from the parking lot, another SWAT team member materialized from the heavy underbrush, quickly got the skinny on Patty from her guide, then took charge, leading her across the narrow parking lot, over the rotting logs, and down a rocky, uneven trail toward the waterfront. Thirty yards from the lake, he motioned her off the path and into the woods, raised a finger to his lips, and pointed to a spot nearby, gesturing that she should stay there.

With the forest and dense cloud cover, the scene ahead was impressively dark, although Patty knew that somewhere overhead the moon was nearly full. The rain had given way to a fine mist, which was being blown by a steady wind from directly behind her. Across the lake, isolated lights from scattered houses battled feebly against the night. Closer, Patty thought she could make out the two-story blackness of the rec hall.

'What in hell are you doing here?'

The man's voice, a harsh, angry whisper from behind the trees to her right, nearly stopped her heart. Lieutenant Court. Either the rustling of leaves had masked his footsteps or he was incredibly good at this sort of thing.

'I've unearthed some information about the victims,' she risked saying, knowing that staying on the case after Court had removed her would be grounds for a suspension, if not worse. 'Something's wrong. I think this is a trap. The killers want to punish you and Wayne for messing with them like this.'

Court, dressed like the others, was wearing earphones.

'Moriarity, you are a total screwup,' he said, 'and furthermore, you've been mucking about on a case that I specifically removed you from.'

'I had to finish some things I had started.'

'Bullshit! You'll answer to me tomorrow at the office. Now just stay here out of the way until this thing plays itself out.'

'But –'

He had already started off, moving smoothly and silently through the trees toward the water. Patty hesitated, then followed. *Fired for a penny, fired for a pound*, she was thinking. Ten yards from the shore, just inside the tree line, Court dropped to one knee, adjusting his earphones as if something was coming in for the first time. Patty inched toward him. She was no good to anyone if he wouldn't listen to her, and she had no chance of being listened to if she didn't try.

'Lieutenant?'

Court's glare would have cut glass. He lifted one earphone an inch.

'What is it with you? I told you to –'

'Lieutenant, I really need to speak with you. I went through Ben Morales's office and –'

'Shut up, it's him!' Court hissed. 'Brasco's wearing a wire. He's talking to the bastard right now.'

Patty moved back into the densest shadows, six feet to Court's left. Did he mean the killer was there at the waterfront? If so, she was wrong about everything. The killers weren't shrewd at all, and the only misdirection and mayhem that was going on was between her ears, in which case she and the help-wanted sections were about to become serious friends. Five silent minutes passed. Finally, Court turned to her.

'We've got him,' he whispered, his tone an equal mix of excitement and triumph. 'He's coming in.'

'In from where?'

'It's not clear. He left a two-way radio on the beach for Grant.'

'When did he do that if your people have been here?'

'I don't know. Must have been before the SWAT guys infiltrated the area. Fortunately, we predicted he might do something like that. Our technicians brought the VDS here and hooked it up. Brasco just spoke to him through it.'

'And what did the killer say?'

'He ordered Brasco – I mean Grant – to take the radio, go up to the center of the balcony off the second floor, and wait for instructions.'

'Why the –'

'Shit, there's no way he can get the VDS mike up there. Brasco'll just have to wing it.'

'What makes you think the killer's coming in?'

'He said so. "I'm looking forward to meeting you, Dr. Grant." That's what he said. Now, just shut the F up, will you?'

A chill knifed up Patty's spine. She wasn't wrong after all. Brasco and Court were outmatched – way outmatched. Either this was going to be a Godzilla-size joke at their expense, no harm done, or Wayne Brasco was a dead man.

With Jack Court focused on the rec hall, she edged further away from him to the right, dropped to her hands and knees, and began a silent crawl toward the water. In moments she was at the tree line, facing a sandy beach that was eight or ten feet across. The wind had died off, and the thin mist was gone. The lake was an ebony mirror. Overhead, Patty thought she saw moonlight filtering through a rent in the clouds.

Was he out there in a boat? she wondered. That made no sense. Escape would be impossible if, as was the case, 'Will Grant' had ignored his demand to come to Camp Sunshine alone. SCUBA gear? Elaborate and James Bondish, but risky. Could he be somewhere on land nearby, right now, right here in the camp, thumbing his nose at a legion of highly trained police, setting up for a close-in shot? *Insane.* There was no way the killers she was coming to know would put themselves in that kind of jeopardy. What about explosives? The fatal blast at 3 Serenity Lane was an expert job. Could the rec hall be wired? Wired and waiting to go up like a giant tinderbox? Noisy, colorful, and undeniably effective, she thought, but really not that much of a challenge, and open to discovery if the police took precautions. Still, what other options were there? A big bang – that had to be it. *Bend over, you fraud, put your head between your legs, and kiss your dumb butt good-bye.*

To her left, perhaps fifteen yards away, Patty could see Brasco making his way to the side of the building and up the outside set of stairs to the second-story porch, which ran the full length of the building. She imagined him getting edgy, maybe panicking, as he thought about trying to improvise without the VDS.

Why the second story? Was the killer waiting inside the building? No chance, unless he actually believed it was Will waiting for him, and waiting alone.

This is very weird, she thought. *Why the second story?*

Patty inched out so that she could see Brasco, positioned midway across the porch, staring out like a sea captain searching for land. The gap in the clouds had widened, and moonlight was now pouring through, sparkling off the still water and illuminating the far shore.

The far shore.

Carefully, Patty rose to her feet. Brasco was motionless – a dark statue, silhouetted against the brightening sky.

Motionless ...

Patty panned across the lake. The far shore seemed closer now than she had estimated from the scattered lights – closer even than she remembered. With the right weapon and the right sniper scope in the right hands, Wayne Brasco was nothing much more than a target in a shooting gallery. Granted, a successful head shot at this distance would be Olympian, but any number of rifles, tripod-mounted and fired by someone who knew the physics of long-distance shooting, could pull it off. That was why the killer had picked this spot and why Brasco had been so meticulously set up. A single shot.

Patty squinted as she scanned the far shore. Her imagination visualized the man she suddenly felt certain was out there, grinning as he tightened the bolts holding his Galil or L42A1 in place, or peering through the infrared scope on his FN 30-11.

The CEOs were dead – two or three that mattered, one or two that

225

probably didn't. The mergers, forged in the heat of their blood, were nearly complete. So much misdirection. And now the killer was playing the police like marionettes, sowing the seeds of chaos as he prepared for what was probably going to be his last kill, at least for this operation – the exclamation point on the managed-care murders.

Barely aware of what she was doing, and well beyond considering the consequences of her act, Patty broke past the line of trees and onto the beach, sprinting toward the stairs Brasco had ascended to the porch.

'Brasco, down!' she shouted. 'It's a trap. Get down!'

Totally bewildered, Brasco stood riveted in place as Patty took the wooden stairs two at a time.

'Get down!' she heard herself scream again.

She was just a few feet away when she saw a bright light flash in the darkness across the water. Launching herself at Brasco's mid-section, Patty slammed him backward against the railing at the instant a bullet ripped through her scalp and gouged the bone just above her right ear. The two detectives, one totally stunned, the other barely conscious, exploded through the dry, weakened wood and arced downward, twisting in the air so that when they landed on a rocky corner of the beach, Brasco's full weight was on top. Patty's head snapped against a boulder, cracking the already weakened bone in her skull. Instantly, what little awareness she had left was replaced by a deep, impenetrable darkness.

In slow motion, Patty's rag-doll body toppled off the rock and came to rest face-down in the wet, pebbly sand.

Chapter 27

It was two-thirty in the morning before Augie Micelli stopped celebrating his coup with a wide variety of spirits and lurched off to bed. By that time, Will had pulled out the sofa bed and tucked in a rumpled pair of forest-green sheets printed with an armada of mallards. For the past hour he had more or less been a detached observer of the battle between his need for sleep and his desire to share the moment with Micelli. Of course, the moment he finally killed the lights and settled onto the wafer-thin pullout mattress, he became unable to sleep.

With the aromas of Micelli's alcohol and cigars hanging heavy in the air, Will lay in the darkness, wondering why he hadn't heard from Patty. He had left a message on her machine trumpeting the find in the ER and asking her to call anytime to share the good news and to explain why he was spending the night with the Law Doctor.

Competing with his concerns for Patty were thoughts about what the day ahead held in store. From the moment he spotted Will's clothing bag, Micelli had been on his cell phone, wheeling and dealing. He was now optimistic that preliminary results of the analysis of Will's sneaker insoles might be performed as early as noon. Calls to Sid Silverman and Tom Lemm had brought their promises that if the Chuck Taylors tested positive for any amount of fentanyl, they would immediately urge the Board of Registration to restore Will's license and would then reinstate him at the hospital and in the Society as soon afterward as possible.

While Micelli was making his rapid-fire volley of calls, Will made two – the unsuccessful attempt to reach Patty and a call to Jim Katz. The older surgeon's relief was almost palpable. If the killer was true to his promise, he would be off the hook. After that, only time would tell whether or not his frangible relationship with Will could heal.

Beyond Patty and the vast implications of the overlooked clothing bag, Will wondered about Charles Newcomber and how the odd little radiologist would handle a visit from both him and Susan Hollister. Images of the radiologist – red-faced, terrified, trembling, and perilously close to firing a bullet into Will's chest – brought a fist-size knot to his gut. Susan was as calm and elegant as he was emotional, and if anyone could break through Newcomber's bizarre paranoia, it was she – especially armed with a notarized release from Grace Davis. Still, dealing with the man would be a test.

Will rolled from his back to his side and finally felt the beginnings of sleep settling in. For a time, the blue plastic clothing bag floated through his thoughts like the Goodyear blimp. Then, quite strangely, he envisioned himself as he would from the dirigible, lying in the bed in the ICU, an endotracheal tube connecting his lungs to a ventilator. It was a sickening vision, but symbolically the scene marked the beginning of the hell he had been through, and envisioning it now, so soon after Augie's incredible find in the ER supply closet, meant that he had begun the journey back to reclaim his life.

Finally ... finally ...

As his breathing slowed, and the tension in his neck and shoulders abated, two words echoed in the darkness in his mind: *Who?* ... and *Why?* ...

Where could she be? ... What's happened to her? ...

Will awoke the way he had drifted off – bewildered by a torrent of questions. By the time he left Micelli's apartment to pick up Susan, he was consumed with fear for Patty. She knew where he was staying. Something had to have happened to her last night or she would have contacted him. Worse still, there was no obvious way he could find out if his concerns were founded. Phoning her office got him only an answering service. He left a message for her and then one for Wayne Brasco, as well, feeling that the man now in charge of the managed-care murders would return any call from him.

Will pulled into the lot behind his office, a captive of worry and his own wild imagination. Was there anything else he could do to locate her? What kind of danger did she feel he was in last night? Had it passed? Was it safe for him to go back to his condo? Had she been in danger, too? Would she be angry with him if he tried to call her father?

Susan, looking the total professional in a conservative charcoal-gray suit, kept her phone pressed against her ear and her conversation going as she motioned him to the chair across the desk from her.

'Well, thanks again,' she was saying. 'I really never expected to enjoy The Boss as much as I did. It was just great. We'll talk later, okay? Bye.'

The breathless way she said the last word left no doubt in Will's mind that she was talking to someone special to her.

'So, you're a new Springsteen fan.'

'I want *him* to think so,' she replied, gesturing to the phone, 'but if I had just one last concert I could go to, I'd still take Cecilia Bartoli or Yo-Yo Ma.'

'Let's hope you don't have to make that choice for a long time.'

'Amen to that. Well, the hospital lawyer stopped by and left a notarized authorization she went and got last night from Grace Davis, so we're all set.'

'Amen to that.'

'Are you all right?'

'Why?'

'Well, we're partners and I've seen you almost every day for years and you always look exhausted. Don't take this wrong, now, but today the bags under your eyes are baggier and the droop of your lids are droopier, and you nicked yourself shaving, which you almost never do, and –'

'Okay, okay, enough. The truth is, last night was a real emotional roller coaster that ended at around three or four o'clock this morning with me sleeping on a pullout in the Law Doctor's living room.'

'The Law Doctor! Will, I forgot to ask. Did anything good come of last night?'

'Well,' he said, dragging out the word and managing a self-effacing grin. 'I think you could say that.'

'Yes!' Susan exclaimed, pumping her fist.

Will hurried through the events surrounding the clothing bag. Susan's expression was one of amazement and excitement.

'Incredible,' she said. 'D'you think the insoles will be positive for fentanyl?'

'I don't want to even consider the possibility that they won't.'

'Me neither. So, did you drink too much last night? Is that why you ended up on the couch?'

Will hesitated, then checked his watch. They had half an hour. He hadn't really spoken to anyone about his connection with Patty, but suddenly he wanted to. And Susan, who had supported him in the Society and worried about his isolation and long work hours like a protective sister, was the perfect person on whom to unburden.

'You know Patty Moriarity, the detective?'

'Very cute, very serious, carries a gun.'

'Well, she and I have begun ... um ... seeing each other.'

'Aha! You know, when she was hanging around here interviewing everyone, I actually thought in passing that she looked and sounded like an interesting match for you. The gun turned me off, though.'

'I'm a little embarrassed to say it, but even though at first the notion of it made me edgy, recently it's actually begun to sort of turn me on.'

'I thought you said Newcomber's gun scared you half to death.'

'Correction. *Newcomber* scared me half to death. Having him standing there like an apoplectic frog, his hands trembling as he held a gun on me, merely came close to completing the job.'

'Well, I'm happy for you. You're going through tough times, and having someone has got to help.'

'It would, only she seems to have disappeared.'

'Disappeared?'

'She left a message with Augie Micelli that I was in danger and should stay with him last night, then she never got back to me.'

'I don't know,' Susan said. 'I wouldn't worry too much. Police are always going on stakeouts and clandestine operations and such and –'

'Ah no, young sir. You are too simple. You might have said a great many things about this proboscis of mine. *Mon dieu*, why waste your opportunity.'

The bellowing was coming from the waiting room.

'...For example, thus: Aggressive: Sir, if that nose were mine I'd have it amputated on the spot!...'

There was no question the voice was Gordo's, yet it wasn't.

'...Friendly: How do you drink with such a nose. You ought to have a cup made specially...'

Will and Susan hurried through her office door and down the hall to the waiting room entrance.

'...The descriptive: 'Tis a rock, a crag, a cape!...'

Cameron, gleaming epee in hand, darted about the deserted waiting room with surprising grace, furiously fencing against an invisible adversary. He was sartorially quite subdued this day – tan slacks, white dress shirt, sedate suspenders, blue tie. A navy blazer lay over one of the chairs.

'...A cape? Nay! Say rather a peninsula. The curious: What is that receptacle – a razor case or a portfolio?...'

Amused and astounded as much by Cameron's deftness with the sword as the recital itself, his two partners stood by the wall, arms folded, and watched.

'...The kindly: Ah, do you love the little birds so much that when they come to sing to you, you give them this perch to sit on?'

Cameron noticed them and lowered his sword, his head tilted back haughtily.

'Cyrano?' Will asked.

'Very good, lad,' Cameron replied, his brogue now returned, richer than ever. 'Believe it or not, I've won the role of de Bergerac in my local community theater's upcoming production.'

'That's wonderful, Gordo,' Susan exclaimed. 'Cyrano de Bergerac is a marvelous play.'

'Yes, bravo,' Will said. 'You surely seem to have the skill and the voice. But wasn't Cyrano ... um ... I mean, wasn't he...'

'Thin?' Cameron said, instantaneously changing his accent from Robert Burns to Olivier. 'I, sir, am the consummate actor. I can do British, I can do French – *bonjour, mademoiselle et monsieur*. I can do German – I vas only following orders. I can do Confederate – frankly, Scarlett, I don't give a damn. And by God, I CAN

230

DO THIN!'

He switched accents facilely as he spoke and was right on with each of them. Will suddenly remembered a number of times over the years when Gordo had regaled a cocktail party with stories requiring accents and even impressions. The man was good.

'Well, Gordo,' he said, 'if anyone can pull off a two-hundred-and-fifty-pound Cyrano, my money's on you.'

He smiled and patted his partner on the back, but something had started gnawing at him. When he was retracing his steps through the hospital, searching for the way someone could have gotten fentanyl into his body, and trying to tie the frame-up to the serial killer, he wondered about Gordo simply because he was around that fateful morning. Now another piece had fallen into place – the OR shoes. Gordo had ready access to his locker, and Will kept the key to it on the ring with his car keys. If the man really wanted to, there were any number of ways he could have gotten the key to make a duplicate. In fact, Will felt certain, within recent weeks Cameron had borrowed his car at least once – maybe even twice.

Troublesome, though, in linking Gordo to the phone calls was that even with his voice electronically distorted, the killer had absolutely no accent, and certainly no brogue. There was no way Will could believe the caller was Gordo – no way until now. Opportunity, method – all that was missing to close the circle was motive.

'We should get going,' Susan said. 'In an hour I have some varicose veins to make magically disappear. Hey, Cyrano, knees slightly bent, head more erect, and keep your tip up.'

'Since when did you become interested in my tip, lass?'

'Come on, Will, this is Cyrano de Pigsty.'

With a flourish Will thrust a phantom sword deep into Cameron's gut.

'Keep your tip up, Gordo,' he said.

Over the short drive to the Excelsius Cancer Center, Susan had Will fill in the rest of last night's story, including more about the unsettling call from Patty to Augie Micelli.

'If you're worried, then I'm worried,' she said, 'but I certainly sense that this is a very capable woman who almost surely can take care of herself. If she hasn't called, it's probably because whatever operation she was involved in simply isn't over yet.'

'I hope you're right, and I appreciate your listening to me.'

'Hey, I'm all for young love. Like The Boss sang at the Fleet

Center last night: "I wanna die with you Wendy on the streets tonight in an everlasting kiss." '

' "Born to Run." '

'Exactly.'

'So he *did* get to you.'

'Just don't let Yo-Yo find out.'

The parking lot of the mammography unit of the Excelsius Cancer Center was largely deserted.

'How should we do this?' Susan asked.

'Carefully, that's how. Very carefully. The man's sanity seemed to be hanging by a thread. I know it would probably go smoother if just you went in, but the truth is, Newcomber and I have some unfinished business, and I really do want to face him again. I didn't leave his office easily or without comment, even with that gun waving at me. It was clear that something was terrifying him. The man was screaming at me like a banshee. When I first called him about changing his referral from you to me, he sounded angry way out of proportion to the situation. Same deal yesterday. The thing is, even though I was the one who was there, I'm not at all sure it was me he was frightened of. I tried to calm him down, to convince him I wasn't a threat. I told him Grace's story – how she made it all the way back from the gutter. I begged him to get in touch with me, to let me help him with whatever was wrong, but he just got more and more agitated until it really did seem as if he might pull the trigger.'

'And you want *me* to be the first one through his office door?'

Will turned her to him by the shoulders and perched her chin up on his fingertips.

'Maybe that's not such a good idea after all.'

'No, it's okay,' Susan said. 'I've met him before, remember? Besides, who could shoot someone with such an angelic face as this?'

The entrance to the mammography wing of the Excelsius Cancer Center was on the south side. The waiting room was empty save for two women in their fifties and the silver-haired receptionist who had let Will visit Newcomber on his last visit.

'Dr. Davidson,' she said, 'nice to see you again.'

Will nearly corrected her, then remembered making up the name. He made a major upward revision of his initial impression of the woman's sharpness. Susan's expression said that she had caught on immediately.

'Thank you for remembering me, Mrs...'

'Medeiros. Martha Medeiros. I have a thing about remembering

232

names and faces. Sort of a hobby.'

She tried for a coquettish smile that missed by about four decades. 'This is –'

'I know, I know, Dr. Hollister,' she said proudly. 'Sandra?'

'Susan,' Susan said. 'That's remarkable. Absolutely amazing. It's been about a year since I was here.'

'Thank you. I enjoy shocking people.'

'Consider me shocked.'

'Mrs. Medeiros, we're here to see Dr. Newcomber.'

'Was he expecting you?'

'No, but we just need to pick up a set of mammograms from him.'

'Well, Dr. Newcomber isn't here.' Will and Susan exchanged disappointed glances. 'He never comes in on Thursdays until after one. It's like his day off, only it's just half a day. Dr. Debra Grossbaum is here. Can she help you?'

Susan stepped forward and handed over the release signed by Grace Davis and notarized by Attorney Jill Leary.

'All we need are these films. Can you help us out there?'

'I can try. I think our film copier's broken, though, so you'll have to look at them here.'

Again disappointment.

'We can't take them out?'

Martha shook her head. 'It's a strict policy.'

'Any idea when the copier will be fixed?'

'None. Dr. Grossbaum just made a call about it a little while ago. Let me call Daphna in the film library and see what she can do.'

Martha retrieved Grace's X-ray number from the database, then called the librarian.

After almost five minutes with the phone tucked under her chin, during which she registered two new patients, Martha set the receiver down, a puzzled expression darkening her face.

'Mrs. Shemesh in the library says the copier isn't expected to be fixed until at least tomorrow. No one seems to even know what's wrong with it.'

'That's okay,' Will said, frustrated, 'we can view the films here.'

'Well, that's a problem, too,' Martha replied. 'She can't find them. They're not signed out, so she thinks they've just been misfiled. She's going to keep looking.'

'What about a computerized storage service?' Susan asked.

Martha made another call, then shook her head. 'Daphna says they're talking about getting a service like that, but not yet.

Apparently they're quite expensive.'

'Always the bottom line,' Will muttered.

'Pardon?'

'Nothing. We're just a bit disappointed.'

'Daphna is upset, too. She apologizes and says she'll keep looking. Do you want to wait or should I call you?'

Will glanced over at Susan and shook his head apologetically. At the same time, he could tell she was wondering, as was he, if the disappearance of Grace Davis's mammograms was something more than a clerical error and coincidence.

What in the hell is going on? he could almost hear her thinking.

He wrote their office number down and then, remembering that their receptionist would be quite certain she knew nothing of a Dr. Davidson, he scratched it out and replaced it with his home phone. It was doubtful Martha Medeiros would be calling anyhow. If Grace Davis's films were gone, they were gone for good.

Will passed the number over and then hesitated, hoping against hope that the film librarian would ring in with good news.

'I guess we should have called first,' he said finally.

'I can certainly leave a message for Dr. Newcomber that you were here. Or maybe you can try calling him or stopping by this afternoon.'

'We'll figure something out,' Susan said. 'Meanwhile, feel free to leave him a note that we were here, and tell your records-room person that we'd appreciate her doing everything possible to find those films.'

'I'll do that,' Martha said, coming out from behind the reception counter to bring a clipboard with some forms over to one of the new arrivals. As she turned back, she stopped, staring out the window. 'Now, that's funny,' she said to Will and Susan.

'What?'

'That's Dr. Newcomber's car in the parking lot – that silver Lexus sports car over there. It's his pride and joy. Maybe it broke down and someone drove him home. I didn't notice it when I came in to work at seven-thirty, because my husband dropped me off at the main entrance, but it must have been there.'

Will *had* noticed the exquisite SC model when they arrived.

'Those cars don't break down,' he said. 'Maybe he got here before you came and he's stayed in his office.'

'I don't think so.'

'Could we check?'

234

'I ... um ... I suppose so. Let me call.'

Martha dialed Newcomber's extension, waited a few rings, and then hung up.

Will flashed on the unbridled fear in the strange little radiologist's eyes, on the shaking of the gun in his hand, and on the vibrant flush of red in his cheeks.

'I think we should check in there,' he said, motioning down the hallway. 'Susan, I don't like this.'

Clearly bewildered, Martha hesitated and then finally withdrew a ring of keys from her desk drawer.

Will was still ten feet away from Newcomber's door when the air changed. It was a smell familiar to him after almost two decades of hospital work – an amalgam of feces, urine, blood, and body odor. It was the scent of death. He moved to stop Martha Medeiros, but the knob to Newcomber's office turned in her hand. She swung the door open and stumbled backward, uttering a strangled, gurgled cry, her hand across her mouth.

The rancid odor of well-established death flooded the room.

The portly radiologist sat bolt upright in his high-backed leather chair, held in place by a band of duct tape pulled firmly across his throat. His wrists were similarly bound to the arms of the chair. His dress shirt was ripped open at the front, revealing a fleshy, hairless chest that was pocked by half a dozen or more dark, penny-size sores. Even from across the room, Will could tell they were burns. Still attached by an edge of adhesive to his glistening pate, Newcomber's silver hairpiece flopped down over his left ear. His gray-green eyes, like a taxidermist's marbles, stared sightlessly across the room. Dried blood cascaded around the corners of his mouth from the nostrils of a nose that was quite obviously broken.

Martha's legs had gone out from beneath her. Will eased her gently to the floor and then stayed in the doorway as Susan hurried over to the desk. The fewer people in the room until the police arrived, the better, and this man was far beyond needing medical intervention. Susan didn't bother confirming Will's clinical impression.

'No obvious mortal wounds or injuries,' she said.

'A coronary?'

'Maybe. Will, I think these are electrical burns.'

'Some sort of cattle prod, maybe. It's possible he died while he was being tortured.'

'Jesus.'

From her place on the floor, leaning against the wall, Martha tried

235

to speak, but managed only a piteous whimper.

'Easy does it, Mrs. Medeiros,' Will said. 'We'll help you in just a minute. I'm going to call nine-one-one.'

'Wait, come in and look at this.'

Will checked to make certain Martha was secure against the wall, then crossed over to the desk. Impaled on the pen and pencil of Newcomber's hand-tooled leather pen holder were two cards – plain white, three inches square. The letter *C* was printed meticulously on one, the letter *M* on the other.

Chapter 28

The Excelsius Cancer Center was set on a verdant lot in the bedroom town of Moorland, four miles west of Fredrickston. Within five minutes of Will's 911, the first of what would be nine police cars from three jurisdictions arrived. The Cancer Center was cordoned off, and patients with appointments were told to reschedule. Seated alone in one corner of the mammography unit reception room, Will waited until a graying, pot-bellied Moorland police officer had finished taking a statement from Susan and motioned that it was his turn. On the way over, he stopped briefly to speak with her.

'Just another routine day at the office,' he whispered.

'Poor little guy. So, with those two letters, do you think it was the same person as killed the others?'

'I don't know what to think. This isn't the usual high-level target or even the MO of the managed-care killers, but those two alphabet letters would certainly suggest that's who did this.'

'You still think it's more than one.'

'I do. In fact, it's a little hard to believe Newcomber would have allowed a single person to truss him up like that without putting up a fight. The office looked just like it did when I was here before, and you saw when I slid open his drawer that his gun was right there, so I don't think there was a struggle.'

'I don't know about you,' Susan said, 'but I can handle this sort of thing in the hospital a lot better than I can out here in the real world.'

'I understand. Same here. You think a heart attack?'

'Torture first, then heart attack. I didn't see any wound that looked as if it could have been mortal. I wonder if he survived long enough to tell them whatever it was they wanted to know.'

'Maybe they didn't want to know anything. Maybe they were just doing it for the fun of it.'

'Ugh.' Susan shuddered, then put on her trench coat. 'Well, I've got to get back to the hospital. After this little adventure, I'm really not up for doing any surgery, but my poor varicose-vein lady is already there and, believe it or not, they're holding the OR for me.'

'Give 'em heck,' Will said wistfully.

'Listen, my friend, before you know it, you're going to be back in the OR, beating yourself into the ground again.'

'I hope so.'

'We're all pulling for that to happen.'

All minus one, Will thought.

'Thanks,' he said. 'Any ideas what we should do about Grace's missing X-rays?'

'Not really. I'm not certain there's anything we *can* do. Let's talk about it later.'

'Fine. Thanks again for coming here with me, Suze.'

'You'll understand if next time I beg off, huh?'

'I won't even bother asking.'

She motioned toward the window.

'Looks like my cab's here.'

'I owe you one.'

'At least.'

As Susan headed off, over her shoulder Will could see the portly Moorland police officer speaking with a new arrival – a tall, angular man wearing a neatly pressed, belted tan trench coat. Moments later, the man quickly approached Will.

'Dr. Grant, Detective Court, State Police. If you'll wait right over there, I'll be with you in a couple of minutes.'

Court. Patty's CO. He had to know where she was.

For fifteen minutes Will waited. The crime-scene people came and hauled their equipment down the hall. Soon after, an ambulance crew arrived and wheeled off Martha Medeiros, who was now virtually catatonic. Will recalled the pride in her expression as she boasted about her unusual skill with names and faces. He found himself wondering if the killers thought for even a moment about the spouses, friends, children, employees, and other victims of their zealous beliefs. He knew it was a stupid question.

'So, Grant, another death, and here you are.'

Court had come up from his left and now stood there, staring down at him with piercing, slate-gray eyes.

'Here I am,' Will echoed sweetly.

Court had already set the tone for their exchange, so Will felt there was nothing to be gained by trying to act as if the two of them were on the same side. The detective pulled a chair around to face him and settled in, his keen eyes still probing.

'You going to be able to shed any light on this?'

'I saw those two letters on the pen holder in there, if that's what you mean.'

'So you think your phone pal is responsible for this murder, too?'

'It does seem like a logical conclusion.'

'For someone who drugged his way out of medicine, you are a smug son of a bitch. I can see why Brasco doesn't believe you.'

'I couldn't care less what Brasco thinks of me – you, either, for that matter. Where's Detective Moriarity?'

'Where were you last night at nine?'

'What's that got to do with anything?'

'You going to answer my question, or do you want to see how miserable I can make your life?'

'Where's Moriarity?'

'I'm going to give you five seconds to answer me, then I'm going to walk away. If I do that, you can count on being arrested before you leave this building. Now, where were you last night?'

Before three of those seconds could elapse, a young, acne-faced, uniformed policeman came rushing over.

'Lieutenant Court,' he said with breathless excitement, 'the station just radioed. The victim's got a record, sir. Ten years ago. Molesting a young boy in Fort Worth, Texas.'

Court's glare could have frozen magma.

'You get the fuck home, right now. You're suspended.'

'But –'

'Get out of here. Tell your CO I'll speak with him later, and after that go sit in a corner and think about what you just did.'

'But –'

'Go!'

Will watched as the decimated young man shuffled toward the door, still, it appeared, in the dark as to what he had done wrong.

'A little hard on the lad, doncha think?' Will said.

'He deserved worse for speaking like that in front of a witness. You're next if you keep dicking around with me. In case you couldn't tell, I'm not in a very good mood. Now, where were you at nine last night?'

Will sighed and decided this was not the time to stand up to the man.

'I was with Augie Micelli.'

'The Law Doctor?'

'That's right. Now, where is she?'

'All night?'

'From eight o'clock until this morning.'

'If you're lying, you're toast.'

'There were three or four others with us at nine. They'll vouch that I was there. Now, where is she?'

'She's in your hospital. If you hadn't gone and gotten yourself thrown off the staff, you'd probably know that.'

Shot ... fell ... Camp Sunshine ... blood clot on the brain ... operated on ... intensive care...

Only a few words in Court's abbreviated explanation registered, but they were devastating.

'I need to get out of here,' Will said.

'You'll stay until I'm done with you.'

'Dr. Hollister was in there with me and she's already given a statement. I'm going.'

'Listen, we know all about you and Sergeant Moriarity making dirty together.'

Will nearly leapt at him.

'We're grown-ups,' he managed.

'Fuckups would be a better way to put it. She's in a coma, Grant, so rushing over there won't make any difference.'

'Neither will talking to you,' Will snapped.

Before Court could react, Will sprang up and raced out the door.

'Get back here!' he heard the detective shout. 'Dammit, Grant, this is a murder case!'

Half expecting to hear a gunshot from behind him, Will raced across the parking lot and scrambled into his Jeep.

'I knew it,' he said out loud to himself. 'I knew something had happened to her.'

He screeched into a U-turn and sped out of the parking lot.

Moments later, a dark-blue Mercury sedan pulled out from between two parked cars and followed at a professional distance.

As usual, the main parking lot at Fredrickston General was full, as

239

were the two rows reserved for physicians. Will finally found a place on the street a block away. He entered through the main lobby and, eyes down, melted into the crowd and carefully skirted the lone security guard on duty. Even though the clothing bag and OR shoes had been found, it was unlikely Sid Silverman would lift his ban at the hospital until he absolutely had to.

Like Brasco, Court, and so many others, Silverman had formed his opinion of Will's guilt much quicker than he would ever let it go. Even if the insoles of the red Chuck Taylors were as loaded with fentanyl as Will and Micelli expected them to be, it was likely that many of his detractors would still believe he was somehow responsible. As he hurried up to the ICU, he wondered about those inmates who were awaiting execution on death row in so many states, all the while knowing that they were innocent.

As he entered the unit, Will could see a crowd gathered in cubicle 1. For an instant he thought there was a code blue in progress, but the lack of frantic movement suggested otherwise. Then, over at the bedside, he saw Peter Ng, the slope-shouldered neurosurgeon who for several years had been a member of the Hippocrates Society, albeit not a very active one.

'That Detective Moriarity in One?' he asked the nearest nurse.

'Yes, but, Dr. Grant, we have instructions that –'

'The ban's been lifted. Besides, she's a relative.'

Without waiting for her response, he walked confidently past and into the glass-enclosed room. Ng, watched by two nurses, a resident, and a couple of medical students, was peering through an ophthalmoscope, examining the arteries, veins, and optic nerves inside Patty's eyes.

To the left of the bed, on the X-ray view box, were two films – one showing a panel of CT images, and the other a pre-op side view of Patty's skull. Even from ten feet away, Will could see the fracture – a jagged, three-inch crack, dark against the white of bone. The CT scan, obviously taken before surgery, showed a rather large collection of blood beneath the area of the fracture.

Unwilling to push to the front of the group, Will peered over the shoulder of one of the med students. Hunched over Patty, Ng was blocking some of his view, but he could still discern that she was motionless and connected by a breathing tube to a ventilator, much as he had been at the beginning of this nightmare.

'I am looking for any blurring of the margins of the optic nerves,' Ng was saying, 'and also a loss of the slight pulsations in the veins –

not the arteries, but the veins. Either of these findings would be a warning of the buildup of pressure within her skull that would signify brain swelling. At the moment I see no signs of trouble, but I'm going to keep her on steroids just in case. If she remains stable for the next four hours, we'll pull the breathing tube. How she does from here on out will depend on how long this coma lasts.'

Ng dictated a set of revised orders, which his resident dutifully wrote down. Then he stepped back from the bed and noticed Will. Gratefully, there was nothing in the neurosurgeon's face to suggest that anything had changed in their always-cordial relationship.

'Got a minute, Peter?'

'Of course. Go ahead, everyone. I'll meet you all in the hall.' He waited, then turned to Will. 'Gosh, it's good to see you. You all right?'

His concern was genuine. To his left, Will could see more fully the battering Patty had taken. The entire side of her face was contused and swollen. From this angle, she bore little resemblance to the woman who had made such sweet love with him.

'I'm all right,' he said flatly. 'Someone set up that drug thing. I still don't know who or why, but I'm going to find out. It's been hell, but there's some light at the end of the tunnel.'

'I'm glad to hear that. You know this woman?'

'She's a good friend.'

'Well, she should do all right, but I confess I am a bit worried about why she hasn't woken up.'

Ng reviewed the circumstances of her injury but couldn't supply any details of why she had been at Camp Sunshine or who the fellow officer was whose life she had saved. Will wished he had paid more attention to Court's account.

'You can see her fracture,' Ng was saying. 'The result was a tear in the middle meningeal artery. As you can see on the CT scan over there, we were lucky to be dealing with epidural blood, not subdural.'

Lucky was an understatement, Will knew. The prognosis from bleeding between the skull and the dura – the protective membrane covering the brain – was not nearly as grim as if the collection of blood was *sub*dural – under the dura, between it and the brain itself.

'But you have no idea why she hasn't woken up.'

'From what I can tell, she fell twelve feet from a balcony and landed headfirst on a rock with a man's weight on top of her. I didn't see any actual brain bruising, but given the concussion from such a blow, I'm not that surprised she hasn't woken up yet.' He saw the concern in Will's eyes. 'Listen, this is an epidural, not a subdural, and with no major brain contusion. She's going to wake up, Will, and she's going to be okay.'

'I'm glad she has you for a doc, Peter,' Will said.

Ng took his hand and shook it.

'I'm glad she has you for a friend,' he replied.

For twenty minutes Will sat in the dimly lit cubicle, listening to the soft, dependable whoosh of the ventilator, the steady beep of the cardiac monitor, and the faint whir of the IV pump – once the sounds of his world, now a hymn to his helplessness. To his right lay the woman who had opened his heart in ways none other had for many years. If they ever got out of this mess – if she ever woke up, if he ever found his way back into medicine – he was going to do things differently. It would be the kids first, then Patty, then maybe some sort of exercise program to get back in shape.

The Society could still have a piece of him, but a smaller one. Managed care had to be stopped, but his role in the battle could and would be less. And as long as the twins wanted to share the Open Hearth experience with him, he would continue signing up there, but he was through working eighty hours a week in the hospital just to break even. He was through living in a chronic state of exhaustion just to keep Maxine from siccing her lawyer hounds on him. He was through saying *yes* simply because he hadn't developed the gift of being able to say *no*.

Over the years since his marriage had begun coming unraveled, what he did had completely overwhelmed who he was. He wouldn't wish the nightmare of a suspension on any doctor, but in one way, having to endure his suspension had been a blessing. The wonderful paradox was that he was ready now, truly ready, to go back to being a surgeon because he didn't *need* to.

He reached across and set his hand on top of Patty's. Her skin was cool and dry. The monitor overhead showed a regular heartbeat, but just the same he slid his fingertips around her wrist and assured himself that her pulse was strong.

'Any change, Doctor?'

The man's voice, from just inside the doorway, startled ten or fifteen minutes off Will's life. He pulled his hand back and spun around. Although he had never seen the man before, he knew it was Tommy Moriarity. Moriarity's arms were at his sides, his posture ramrod straight. Even through the gloom, Will could see Patty's eyes and mouth in his, as well as the shape of her face. The policeman was dressed in jeans and a plaid flannel shirt and carried a thin book in one hand.

'She's stable,' Will said.

'Good.'

'I guess you know who I am.'

'I guess you know who I am, too.'

The two men shook hands awkwardly, and Moriarity crossed to the other side of the bed.

'Does she need that tube?' he asked.

'Dr. Ng, her surgeon, just left. If her condition hasn't deteriorated after a few more hours, he's going to have it pulled. She's tripping the machine on her own right now, and the tube could damage her trachea if it stays in.'

'She got hurt saving a fellow officer's life.'

'I heard that, but I don't know who.'

'Wayne Brasco – the man who took over for her.'

Inwardly, Will groaned.

'And he's okay?' he asked.

'Barely a scratch.'

Shit.

'Do you know what happened?'

'Nobody seems to know. There was some sort of sting operation Brasco set up to catch the managed-care killer. Patty showed up uninvited and tried telling people they were on the wrong track and were being set up. Finally, she knocked Brasco away just as a shot was fired. She took a bullet along the side of her head, then hit a rock when she and Brasco fell.'

'The bullet didn't do more than stun her,' Will said. 'The rock is what did the damage.'

'But she's going to wake up, right?'

Will looked across Patty's inert form at her father. For all his gruffness and military bearing, he looked frail and frightened. Still, Will carefully avoided any knee-jerk reassurances.

'Given the sort of injury she had and the location of the bleeding, she could wake up any time. But head injuries are very unpredictable. Until she wakes up, we have every reason to be worried.'

'Thanks for being straight with me,' Moriarity said, rubbing briefly at his eyes. He held up the thin, tattered volume he had carried in. 'This is one of her favorite books from when she was growing up; it's poetry by Emily Dickinson. I thought maybe I'd try reading to her from it.'

'That's a wonderful idea. When someone is unconscious, we never really know what senses are still working.'

'I wanted her to be a professor, or even a lawyer.'

'She's a good cop,' Will said.

'I know.'

Well, why in the hell didn't you ever tell her that? Will wanted to shout out. He stood to go.

'You're a hero to her,' he said.

'So are you, from what I can tell,' Moriarity replied.

'For what it's worth, she knows I haven't done anything wrong.'

'She told me that. At the moment I'm giving you the benefit of the doubt there. But do yourself a big favor, Doc, and don't ever do anything to hurt her.'

Again, Will held back any reflex reaction. Fathers protect daughters. It was as simple as that – at least it should be.

'You have my number,' he said. 'If you have any medical questions, or any questions at all for that matter, please call – just remember that your guys have my phone tapped.'

Will battled back the urge to stop by Sid Silverman's office to see if there had been any news from the lab. Instead, he walked the block to the Jeep through a raw, gray early afternoon and headed home. The piecemeal sleep he had gotten on Micelli's pullout, plus the tension generated by the events of the day, were taking their toll. All he could think of was an hour or two of oblivion on his own bed followed by a shower, some fresh clothes, and a return to the ICU. Given the urgency of Patty's warning yesterday, he wondered if he was still in some sort of danger, or if the events at Camp Sunshine had altered things.

For a time, images of Charles Newcomber's grotesque corpse dominated his thoughts. Was his death in some way related to his history of pedophilia or his homosexuality? Could it possibly have been connected with Grace Davis's films? In view of the two alphabet letters skewered on Newcomber's pen set, no explanation made sense other than that his name had popped up on the screen of the managed-care killers. But knowing what he knew of their motives and methods, Will felt no comfort with that explanation, either.

The Wolf Hollow Condominiums looked as unruffled and serene as usual. There was a prim white guardhouse at the end of the entry drive, but shortly before Will moved into the complex, the condo association had voted down the expense of manning it or installing any of a number of possible electronic security systems. Cautiously, Will drove past his unit, scanning for anything the least bit out of the ordinary. Finally, determined not to spend another night on the Law Doctor's couch, he parked in his space and entered the town house through the rear door. His personal security system was still on. He disarmed it with the twins' birthday and crossed to his mail slot by the front door, his antennae still searching for trouble.

The note was on top of a small wad of bills and circulars – an undistinguished business envelope with *Will Grant* printed in pencil in an unsteady, somewhat juvenile hand. Will's first impulse was to treat the envelope and its contents as evidence and to handle it with a tweezers before opening it with a knife, but he was hardly in the mood to be patient. With some care, he held the envelope by one corner, took it to the kitchen, slit it open with a steak knife, and extracted a piece of typing paper folded in thirds. The writing, also in pencil, was by whoever had addressed the envelope.

For a gift from Charls come alone to the corner of Dennis and Spruce in Roxbury. 8 tonite. Bring $500 cash.

Roxbury.

During his surgical training, Will had done several rotations through Boston City Hospital, which drew many patients from that section of the city. The population there was largely black and poor, and the area's reputation was, simply put, that whites should avoid it after dark.

Bewildered, Will wrote down the address and carefully replaced the original sheet in its envelope. Charles Newcomber had been dead less than a day. Was this note from his killer? What did the foppish little radiologist have to do with Roxbury? Will had a street map of Boston in the car but had only driven through a few blocks of the community while taking the kids on excursions to the Franklin Park Zoo. He had absolutely no idea of the layout of the streets. Was he insane just to bop on in there at night? Should he notify Jack Court about the note? And perhaps the most perplexing question of all: Did he even have $500 in his bank account?

Chapter 29

'What'd you say?'

The elderly black man, dapperly dressed in a sports coat, dress shirt, vest, tie, and plaid walking cap, had been ambling past a row of shops that were all secured with metal accordion gates. Now, in no apparent rush to get anyplace despite the inclement weather, he hunched down by the open window of the Jeep beneath his small black umbrella and squinted in at Will. It was already twenty minutes after eight. Dusk had come and gone, yielding to another in what seemed an unending string of raw, drizzly nights. The tangled, narrow streets of Roxbury, many dating to colonial times, had completely overwhelmed Will's tattered street guide – or at least his ability to read it.

'Dennis Street,' he said, in the exaggerated voice he had unfortunately developed over years of treating older patients in hospitals and nursing homes. '*D-E-N-N-I-S*. I'm looking for the corner of Spruce and Dennis. That's Spruce right over there' – he pointed to the cross street behind him – 'but I can't find any Dennis off it or on my map.'

'Hey,' the man said, 'no need to shout. Just because I been on this earth longer 'n most, don't automatically mean I'm deaf.'

Will managed a grin at himself.

'Sorry, bad habit.'

'You sure these streets are in Roxbury?'

The man – maybe in his eighties – had a creaky, high-pitched voice that reminded Will of a child in a school play trying to portray an old man.

'That's what the guy wrote. Roxbury. See, right here.'

Careful to cover up the part about bringing $500, Will showed the man the note, and he studied it for a time.

'You know what?' he cackled suddenly. 'I think I know why you been havin' trouble. I don't think Dennis is a street at all. I think it's like an alley – Dennis Way, it's called – two blocks, maybe three, down Spruce that way. If there's a sign, and as I recall, there usually is one, it's nailed to one of the buildings, not on a pole.'

246

'Thanks, you're great.'

Will moved to put the Jeep in gear, but the man stopped him with a raised hand.

'I don't think the alley's wide enough for a car,' he said, 'especially this one. You'd best park someplace near and walk.'

'I'll do that.'

'You know what would even be a better idea?'

'What?'

'Go on home and come back tomorrow during the day. Take it from ol' Lionel. At night the – excuse me for cussin' – *darn* gangs own this part of the city. Cabs almost never come here. The cops only come 'round when they have to, and then they only stay long enough to say they did it. I never carry more 'n a dollar with me when I go for my evening constitutional. The Cobras used to shake me down if they were particularly desperate for money, but now they've pretty much given up on me. You go walkin' about these streets – especially back in there where Dennis Way is – an' they'll know you're there quicker 'n you do. It's doubtful that you'll make it out with your wallet or maybe even your car, for that matter. Most of them's pretty good boys, but they don't have much in the way of parentin', if you know what I mean.'

'I'll be careful, Lionel.'

'Careful's good,' Lionel said, 'but it might help for you to be bulletproof, too.'

That does it, Will thought as he drove away from the man down the virtually deserted street and made a slow left onto Spruce, *I am out of here*.

With cars parked on both sides, Spruce was barely more than a lane wide. To either side, Will now noticed narrow alleys, each with a name bolted in some way to the brick facade of a tenement. *Alley 114,* one of them read, *Wright's Path*, another. The fourth sign he saw was *Dennis Way*.

Will opened the passenger window and peered down the alley, which was illuminated by a single low-wattage, hooded lamp jutting out from a building halfway down to the next street. There were two small Dumpsters, several trash cans, and enough loose trash to fill a good portion of them. He reread the mysterious note. If he drove off now, would he ever get another chance to find out what Charles Newcomber had left for him? If he didn't leave, would he still be alive in half an hour?

At that moment, as if by divine intervention, the lights on a parked car pierced the night two blocks ahead. Moments later, it pulled out and drove away. Will raced to the spot, although there was absolutely no competing car on the street. Silently, he promised himself that if the space was by a hydrant, he was out of there and on the way back to Fredrickston. He had mixed emotions that there was no hydrant and so no need to put the deal to a test. In less than a minute, after a brilliant job of parallel parking, he was standing on the sidewalk in a gloomy, windblown drizzle, peering uncertainly down a deserted street in one of the toughest, most dangerous neighborhoods in Boston.

Perhaps whoever had left the note had waited and was gone, he thought, confirming on his Casio that he was a full half an hour late. Again, he thought about leaving. Again, he talked himself out of it and headed cautiously back toward Dennis Way. Although both the street and the alley seemed deserted, he couldn't shake the heavy feeling that he was being watched. He stopped at the mouth of the alley, zipped his windbreaker, and debated whether to stay where he was or move ahead. The note had instructed him to be at the corner of the alley, not down it. He was about to turn and leave when the muzzle of a gun was pressed tightly into the small of his back.

'Don't turn around,' the youthful, almost certainly black, voice said. 'You Grant?'

Will waited until his pulse rate had dropped back below a thousand.

'Yes,' he managed. 'You don't need that gun.'

'I'll decide what I need and don't need. Now jus' head down that alley. All the way down. Eyes straight ahead.'

Will did as he was told, hesitating halfway down as a rat the size of a cat scurried across his path, less than a foot from the toes of his sneakers.

'No collar,' he said. 'I wonder if it's had all its shots.'

The response to his nervous humor was a sharp nudge from behind. They passed under the light and were almost at the far end of the alley when the gunman grabbed him by the jacket.

'Take this off,' he said.

He patted Will down from behind, lingering a beat, it seemed, by the front of his jeans. Then he pushed him out of the alley and onto the sidewalk of the street that seemed to run parallel to Spruce. Finally, he turned Will around and tossed his jacket back. He was, in fact, a teen, maybe sixteen – seventeen, tops – baggy chinos, pricey leather-sleeved jacket with *Chris* embroidered in script over the left breast, ornately stitched Rasta cap. His unlined, richly black face was equal parts pretty and handsome. His eyes, even in the dim light, were bright and intelligent enough, but they were way past being the eyes of a youth, and Will sensed the hard times they had seen. Cradled in the young man's right hand was a snub-nosed revolver – a Saturday-night special. In his left was a large manila envelope, the sort used for transporting or mailing X-rays. The buildings at this point blocked most of the wind and rain, and Will noted with relief that, aside from a few drops, the envelope was dry.

'Did you bring the money?' the teen asked.

'I did. Believe it or not, it wasn't so easy coming up with five hundred on such short notice, but I've got it.'

'I thought you were a doctor.'

'I've fallen on some hard times.'

'Too bad. Stick around here if you want to really learn what hard times are all about. Hand it over.'

'Let me see what you've got for me.'

'Hand it fucking over!'

There was no mistaking the edge in his voice. This was not the time for negotiation. Will did as he was told. The teen flipped through the stack of bills and then shoved them into his jacket pocket.

'That your name? Chris?'

'What if it is?'

'Chris, put that gun away. I'm no threat to you.'

'I'll decide whether you're a threat or not.'

'How did you know Newcomber was dead?'

'I ... I just knew.'

Will could tell he was lying. Despite the gun and the attitude, he began feeling sorry for Chris.

'You didn't know, did you? Well, someone was in the process of torturing him, and he had a heart attack.'

'Why?'

'I don't know. Maybe it was about those X-rays.'

'Shit. He been callin' me twice a day. Eight in the morning, eight at night. He said if he missed a call I was to get this envelope to you.'

His gun still leveled at Will's midsection, Chris had already regain-ed his swagger.

'The five hundred was your idea?' Will asked.

'What if it was? Like the man in the movies says, it's all about the Benjamins.'

'How do you know Newcomber?'

For a second, it seemed to Will as if he was in for a flip answer, or none at all. Then a look that might have been sadness drifted across Chris's face.

'Ol' Charles liked me. I did things for him, he did things for me. You like to have things done for you?'

'I don't think I like the kind of things you're talking about.'

'Hey, don't knock it if you ain't tried it, and don't go talkin like a smart-ass at someone with a gun pointin' at you, neither.'

'Listen, Chris, why don't you just let me have that envelope? You got your money. Now, how about giving me the envelope like Charles asked you to and let me go home?'

Chris hesitated, then passed it over. It was thick with X-rays, although in the gloom Will could tell nothing beyond that.

'Well,' he said, his pulse racing at the notion that in just a couple of minutes he would be behind the wheel of his Jeep heading out of Roxbury and back to his condo, 'thanks for keeping your end of the deal. Charles would be very pleased with you.'

'Don't mean shit to me whether a dead man is pleased with me or not,' Chris said, with forced bravado. 'He's gone, and there are plenty more like him out there anxious to take his place.'

'Is it okay for me to go now?'

'No, Grant, actually, it's not.' The man's voice came from the darkness along a brick wall just inside the alley. It was a voice familiar to Will, although he couldn't at that instant figure out from where. 'Drop the gun, Chris. Now!'

'You fucking bastard,' Chris hissed at Will.

'I didn't –'

'The gun!' the voice snapped.

From the darkness, still looking like something of a bookworm despite the broad shoulders, narrow waist, and heavy pistol he held aimed directly at Chris's chest, stepped Boyd Halliday's executive assistant, Marshall Gold.

Will's thoughts spun wildly as he tried to get his mind around what was happening and why. Nothing made sense.

'I have no beef with you, pal,' Gold said. 'Just put your gun away in your pocket.'

Chris hesitated, then did as he was told.

'Who are you?' he asked.

'He's the man who killed –'

Quick as a rattlesnake, Gold whipped the muzzle of his pistol across Will's face, opening a gash on the side of his jaw and dropping him to one knee. Calmly, his cold eyes fixed on Will through his wire-rimmed glasses, Gold bent down and retrieved the X-ray envelope from the pavement.

'Okay, let's go, hotshot,' he said.

He reached down, grabbed Will by the collar, and yanked him to his feet with little effort. Will felt blood dripping down his neck but refused even to touch his wound. He did use his tongue to probe the inside of his lip, which was cut, and his teeth, one of which seemed loose.

What in the hell is going on?

If Gold had killed Newcomber and left the two alphabet letters, then he was also the managed-care serial killer. It made no sense. Was he trying to mislead police by being a copycat?

'Listen, *pal*,' Chris said suddenly to Gold, 'those X-rays are for sale to the highest bidder. How much you got on you?'

Gold laughed.

'I've got the gun and here you are shaking me down. You are a pile of balls, my little friend, a pile of brass balls. But here you go. Where I come from, having brass *cojónes* gets rewarded.'

He pulled a money clip from his pocket and with one hand worked off what looked like a hundred-dollar bill. Then he flipped it in Chris's direction. It blew a few feet away and fluttered to the sidewalk. The teen made no move to pick it up.

Instead, Chris folded his hands disdainfully across his chest.

'That ain't nearly enough,' he said.

'Well, get used to it, because that's all you're getting. Come on, Grant, you and I have some business to attend to.'

'I don't think that's all our man Chris is gonna get from this dude,' a rich, bass voice said. 'Do you, Rod?'

A man, clearly older and heavier than Chris, stood up from between two parked cars at the moment an even larger man moved out from somewhere in the shadows of the alley. Both held guns pointed at Gold, one of them some sort of submachine gun.

'I don't think it's nearly enough,' Rod said. 'How 'bout you, Smitty? What you think?'

'No way it's enough. I say Mr. Tough here is downright cheap. That's what I say. How about you guys?'

A third man materialized from the night and slid out from behind Gold, pistol ready, then two more appeared from across the street.

'Seems like we never get visitors around here anymore, eh, Biggs?'

A wiry man in his early twenties emerged from a tenement doorway and moved in next to Chris.

'This is Biggs,' Chris said to the two white men. 'He says, "Jump," you ask, "How high?"'

Biggs had narrow, close-set eyes, a broad, flat nose, and a thick, north–south scar that crossed his upper and lower lips just to the right of midline.

'Hail, hail, the gang's all here,' he said. 'Now, Mr. Tough, why don't you jus' put that fine piece of hardware on the sidewalk and kick it over here.'

His eyes still all business, Gold complied. Will sensed that, despite the firepower fixed on them, he was actually evaluating his chances in a shoot-out.

'These X-rays belong to my company,' Gold said. 'This man here killed to get them. I'm willing to pay you well to get them back.'

'That's a lie,' Will said. 'He's the killer. He does it for a living.'

'How much more you got on you?' Biggs asked Will.

'Ten dollars.'

'Hand it over. I find you got any more, I'm gonna shoot off one of your fingers. You, how much?'

Moving with deliberate slowness, Gold slid the money clip from his pocket and tossed it over. Biggs counted the remaining bills, which Will thought might add up to as much as a thousand, and stuffed them in his deep pants pocket.

'You jus' bought yourself some serious consideration, my man.'

'I'll leave him and the X-rays here with you while I go and get some more,' Gold said. 'Twice that much. Then I want them both.'

'I wonder what it is about you that I just don't trust. What you all think, guys? You think we should let him just take off?'

'Bogus.'

'He sucks.'

'You can throw him farther 'n you can trust him.'

'We ain't standin' around here in the rain.'

'The will of the Cobras has spoken,' Biggs said. 'We ain't waitin' around for you or anyone. You want this dude, Mr. Tough, you gotta catch him. Chris, will you feel you kept your part of the bargain if we give this hangdog, say, a minute's head start?'

'A minute'd be fine, Biggs.'

'A minute it is, then. Give him that envelope, Mr. Tough.'

'You're costing yourselves a lot of money.'

'We'll decide what we're costin' ourselves. Now give it to him and lay down on your face.'

'But –'

'Down! ... Okay, now, hangdog, you got a minute. Ready, go!'

'Wait, I –'

'Fifty-five seconds. No, no, not back up that alley, down that way. Fifty seconds. Now get going... Forty-five seconds.'

With Biggs's voice echoing behind him, Will sprinted off down whatever street they were on, which he believed ran parallel to Spruce.

'Forty seconds!'

Frantically, he searched for an alley crossing over to Spruce. Instead, the street began sloping upward and curving to the left – away from where the Jeep was parked.

'Thirty seconds!'

Biggs's voice still seemed to be coming from just a few feet behind him. Will's legs felt as if they were moving through molasses. He looked in better shape than he was, and countless nights on call hadn't helped matters. The muscles he needed for standing at the operating table or prowling the wards of the hospital were strong, but aerobically he wasn't much of a specimen. Already he was breathing heavily, and a sharp stitch had formed in his side. Gold had perhaps five or six years on him, but he was also fit. With the X-rays tucked against his body, Will's stride was choppy and unbalanced. In addition to the dagger in his side, every step sent a railroad spike hammering into his battered jaw.

A right turn. Where in the hell is a right turn?

Initially, he had been grateful they left him his car keys and certain he could make it to the Jeep before Gold caught him. Now he debated whether it was worth abandoning the notion of the Jeep and instead trying to find a place to hide – a Dumpster, perhaps, or a doorway into a building. His minute was over, he felt certain of that, but the bend in the road made it impossible to see if Gold was closing on him.

Ahead on the right he spotted a street sign fixed to the side of a building like the one for Dennis Way. *Alley 122*. A right here, then maybe two more rights and he might find Spruce. It seemed like a better bet than trying to hide someplace. Maybe just the turn would be enough to lose Gold. Still sprinting full bore, trying to ignore his mounting discomforts, he charged into the alley, which was cleaner and less cluttered than Dennis. Ten yards in, he caught his toe in a pothole and fell, sprawling face-first onto the slick pavement. He cried out as skin tore off his knees and palms. Air exploded from his lungs. The envelope of films skidded out of his grasp. He glanced back as he retrieved it and scrambled to his feet. Nothing yet.

Ignoring pain in half a dozen different places, he sprinted ahead. He was nearing the end of the alley when he heard a gunshot from behind him. A piece of brick to his left shattered off. Silhouetted against the dim light at the far end of the alley, still a good distance away, Gold appeared to be on one knee, steadying himself for another shot. Will lurched to his left as the second shot ricocheted off a wall not far from his head. *Damn!* Biggs would never have given Gold back his gun. He must have had a second one hidden somewhere. No surprise. The man was a pro.

The end of the alley was just a few yards away. A car splashed past on what seemed a much wider street than Spruce. Right, then maybe another right, Will guessed, realizing at the same time that he might have gotten completely turned around. Even if he could put a little more distance between him and Gold, would he have a chance to reach the Jeep, jump in, and get it out of a tight parking space? Doubtful. Even if his sense of where he had parked was right on the money, it was extremely doubtful he could make it out in time. Still, however remote, there was a chance.

He pushed himself even harder, blocking out the aches and the hopelessness of his position. Charging around the corner, he narrowly avoided colliding with a man walking toward him. It was Lionel, still on his evening constitutional. Gasping for air, Will grabbed him by the arm and roughly pulled him into the shadow of a brick tenement.

'Lionel, Lionel, listen,' he heard his desperate voice plead, 'I'm in big trouble. Here, take this and hold it for me. Wait in here until it seems safe, then go home. I'll find you.'

'Who –'

Panicked beyond waiting for any reply or working through the potential consequences of what he was doing, Will thrust the envelope into the old man's hands and pushed him into the rear of the unlit, recessed entryway to the building. Then, praying Gold wouldn't realize that his initial move had been to the right, he hunched over as if he were a running back with a football and sprinted across the rainswept street to the left. Another shot snapped off from the alley, then another. Both sounded much closer than had the previous ones. He was across the street now, pounding past a beauty parlor, then a tax office, trying to keep his speed up as pain in his hands, jaw, and knees and the horrific stitch in his side slowed him down. A block passed, then most of another.

'Grant! Give it up!' Gold called from behind. 'Those were warning shots. I can kill you right now, but I won't. Just give me the films!'

The killer was gaining rapidly now. Will knew that, barring the sudden appearance of a patrol car or police station, it was almost over for him. Ahead and to his right was the entrance to an old, unlit cemetery. From what he could tell, none of the headstones seemed large enough to offer a place to hide. Still, the route would take him even farther from Lionel, and if he made it through, maybe there was more activity on the other side.

With no plan other than to keep moving, he cut sharply to his right, between two shoulder-high granite steles and into the graveyard. He hadn't gone more than twenty or thirty feet when he tripped over a low stone nearly obscured in the long grass and pitched forward, slamming shoulder first into a marker that looked to be centuries old. At that moment, part of him wanted to quit, to just roll over and wait. Instead, he scrambled to his feet and stumbled ahead. The far side of the small cemetery seemed to border a fairly busy street. Two cars sped past, then a third. If he could just make it there, he sensed he had a chance.

What little remained of his hope lasted only a few more seconds. Before he reached the low hedges marking the far border of the graveyard, he was tackled from behind with stunning force. His face narrowly missed a stone as he pitched forward into cold, wet mud with Gold's full weight upon him. Another instant and he was on his back, his attacker straddling him, looking furiously about, his dirt-stained face a mask of rage. Squeezing Will's cheeks inward until his mouth involuntarily opened, Gold thrust his pistol to the back of his throat.

'Okay, you son of a bitch,' he rasped, 'where are the frigging films?'

Chapter 30

There was no way Will could tell what was first to work its way into his fragmented consciousness – the free-floating, disconnected images of the hours, perhaps days, just passed, the distinctive odors of animals and disinfectant, or the intense pain. The room was quite long and fairly narrow, with a high ceiling illuminated by two rows of fluorescent tubes and the light from three windows along the wall to his left.

He was naked, lying face-up on a hard, thin mattress. Whether out of pity or anger, someone had thrown a moldy brown army blanket over him. He flashed on the similar sensations of waking up on a respirator in the ICU following his fentanyl overdose. He was absolutely helpless then and terrified of the tube down his throat. This time he was simply miserable.

There was swelling about his eyes that made it difficult to see clearly. His face felt as if it were caked in cement. He could open his mouth, but only at an agonizing price. His nostrils admitted only thin streams of air.

Shakily, he reached up a puffed, abraded hand and confirmed that the cement was, in fact, thick layers of dried blood covering his nose, lips, chin, and chest. Bits of memory continued to drift together, then flutter apart like windblown leaves. He knew that at some point he had been drugged, then hurt, then drugged again. A wiry little man with bad skin and yellowing teeth had cut him or burned him in some way, asking over and over about the X-rays.

Had he told them about Lionel?

Given that he was alive, it didn't seem likely. He had always had a well-documented stubbornness and bull-like obstinacy. Could those traits, so often a source of problems for him, possibly have been enough to resist torture and, at least for the moment, save his life?

Again, the smell of animals worked its way past his swollen nostrils. A farm of some sort? He struggled to focus. He was in a virtually bare room in what seemed to be a house – possibly a farmhouse. Little by little, the fog shrouding his senses and his memory began to lift. The rain ... the Cobras ... the guns ... the envelope ... Marshall Gold hunched over him, his face pinched with rage, the muzzle of his pistol jammed so hard against the back of Will's throat that it seemed ready to tear through to the other side. There, abruptly, the memories ended. Had he passed out? Had the drugs and the pain ablated the final pieces of his ill-fated trip into the city?

The questions kept coming. How had Gold gotten him out of Roxbury to this place? Who was the little man who had tortured him? When they were ready for him to die, how were they going to do it? Would the kids ever know for certain that he was dead, or would he simply become a missing person – a photo in a thick binder or one of many flyers on the bulletin board of a police station? And perhaps most baffling, what were the thick collection of X-rays in the envelope all about?

Gingerly, he tested first his fingers and hands, then his arms, feet, and legs. None of them was pain-free, but none brought the sharp, boring discomfort of a broken bone. It seemed strange that Gold hadn't bothered to tie him down in some way. He rolled uncomfortably to one side and squinted into what might have been morning sun, filtering through the gauze curtains that covered each of the three windows. The unadorned walls of the room were painted light blue, the door and trim around the windows white.

To his right was a small, gouged wooden table, with no chairs. Piled by one of the legs were his clothes. The notion of trying to retrieve them brought a wry, painful smile. Given the agony of even minute movements, the clothes might just as well have been lying on the floor of his closet at home. Still, his nakedness felt unpleasant and demeaning enough to push him to try. It wasn't until he had propped himself on one elbow that he first noticed the burns – small black discs of seared flesh, a dozen or more of them, half an inch or so in diameter, covering his chest and arms in a more or less random pattern. He shuddered. These same burns dotted much of Charles Newcomber's corpse. Whatever instrument was responsible had apparently been more than the radiologist's heart could handle. Will was relieved that the fingers of his own memory seemed unwilling to fully grasp his experience with it.

He rolled off the mattress onto the chilly hardwood floor. Doing his best to ignore the stabs of a thousand daggers, he pulled his way across to the pile of clothing and began arduously pulling on his underwear. As he finished, he noticed that beneath the nearby gauze curtains, the windows were unbarred. He scanned the room, but saw no obvious cameras. If they weren't watching him through some sort of monitoring, and if the room wasn't any higher up than the second floor, he had a chance. He could use a table leg on the window and strips of blanket tied to the table to get to the ground. He leaned against the wall and inched into his jeans, which were filthy and sodden. Apparently he hadn't been in the room long enough for them to dry.

He was turning back to inspect the window when the single door to the room opened. Marshall Gold entered, accompanied by the slightly built man with the pencil-thin mustache and pockmarked face. Gold, handsome and fit in a button-down dress shirt and tan slacks, looked rested and refreshed. He was pushing a well-used, high-backed wooden armchair. His unpleasant-looking companion, dressed all in black, clutched a scuffed leather briefcase to his chest as if it were an infant.

Will had little doubt that the contents of the case had everything to do with the burns on his body.

'Don't bother, Doctor Grant,' Gold said. 'Those windows are half-inch-thick Plexiglas.'

'Is that why there are no cameras?'

Will's voice was sandpaper. He tried unsuccessfully to clear away the raspiness.

'Do you think we need them?'

'I think you're sick.'

'Maybe ... maybe so,' Gold replied thoughtfully. 'I think I'll take that as a compliment. Well, now, my friend, you've given us quite a night.'

'Fuck you.'

'I believe we've heard him say that before, don't you, Dr. Krause?'

Krause nodded.

'A tough nut, Mr. Gold,' he said, his formality sounding like Wint or Kidd, the hand-holding killers in James Bond's *Diamonds Are Forever.* 'A tough nut, indeed.'

'It's too late,' Will said. 'You'll never get those X-rays.'

'I don't care whether we get them or not,' Gold said. 'I care whether anyone else does.'

'How did you get me here?'

Will began to pull his sweatshirt over his head but quickly gave up, exhausted and aching from the effort.

'You mean after you passed out on me, or after the kids spotted us in the cemetery and ran away? Those jerks took my favorite weapon, but not my cell phone.'

'And not the other gun,' Will said as a few more pieces of the hideous night just past fell into place.

'Not the other gun,' Gold said, moving the ominous chair a foot closer. 'Potentially a lethal move. There were only six of them, so I could have just taken them out and walked away with the films. Now it appears that perhaps I should have done it that way.'

'Pity.'

Gold's expression darkened.

'You *will* tell us what we want to know.'

'Fuck you.'

'So, pardon me for saying it, Doctor, but you're really not in very good cardiovascular shape.'

'Take that up with my personal trainer.'

'The point is, you really didn't get very far before I caught up with you. Still, by that time the films were gone.'

'Gone,' Will echoed, holding his hands up in mock dismay.

He glanced at the chair, then at Krause, and decided that from then on he had best keep his flip retorts in check. He had won round one, but at a severe price. Round two was certain to be even more horrible. And if he lost that round, if he gave in and told them about Lionel, it was going to be over for him – no more twins, no Patty, no more anything.

'But where?' Gold went on. 'That is the question that has been troubling me for most of this night. Where? After we removed you from Roxbury, several of us retraced the steps of your flight, in-specting every can, Dumpster, and doorway along the way. Nothing. I don't believe we would have missed a postage stamp let alone an envelope the size of the one you were carrying. You could have had someone waiting for you, but we were watching you from the moment you left the parking lot at the cancer center, to the hospital, then to your condo, to the bank, and finally all the way into Roxbury. There was no one. I'm certain of that. You could have given it to a passing driver, but none of them even slowed to help you – nor would they in that part of the city.' He moved the chair to the center of the room. 'So, how did you do it? There were a few seconds in the beginning when you were out of my sight, then a few more just as you were crossing the street. That's when something happened, isn't it? You gave the films to someone right there, but who?'

'You're way off. I shoved them in a mail slot.'

'We actually checked that. There were none on the route that were large enough. No, sir, you had to have handed it to someone, and the only person I can think of is that old man you stopped just before you parked your car – the one with the umbrella. You stopped him to ask directions, then ran into him again at that corner. He told you his name, didn't he? He told you how to find him.'

'You're way off base.'

'You will tell us who that man is and how you were going to meet up with him again. If you don't, then you will have suffered through a mountain of pain for nothing, because sooner or later we're going to find him. We're just going to go back there and work the neighborhood with enough money until we find someone who will send us to the right door.'

'Then do it.'

'I don't think we're going to have to. Do you, Dr. Krause?'

Krause pulled the table over near the chair and set his briefcase on it.

'I don't believe so at all,' he said. 'We have a bet, you and I, Mr. G., and I never lose a bet.'

Will felt a wave of nausea wash over him. Slick sweat materialized beneath his arms. He had passed out during Krause's last go at him and had awakened with a merciful amount of amnesia. How far would his stubbornness take him this time?

'So, Dr. Grant,' Gold said, 'you have just two choices at this moment. Tell us the name of the man you gave the films to, or take off your clothes for an encore of last night's festivities.'

'Fuck you,' Will managed.

'Your choice.' Gold turned to the doorway. 'Mr. Watkins?'

A black man the size of a pickup truck stepped into the room.

'At your service.'

'Mr. Watkins, our guest is complaining about feeling hot and also about a sudden desire to be up in that chair. Do you think you could help him out?'

'I would love to help him out,' Watkins said.

He reached behind him, brought in a metal bucket and a mop, and lumbered across the room toward Will.

'You only threw up once last night before you passed out,' Gold said. 'Dr. Krause has promised me he won't cut things so close today.'

Chapter 31

Lying in their darkened bedroom, Donna Lee felt her husband's fingertips slip under her T and begin gently kneading the muscles in the hollow of her back and down over her buttocks. She had never been a very deep sleeper, especially over the year since little Davy was born, and she was awake in seconds.

'Honey, can't you sleep?' she asked dreamily.

'I don't want to.'

She stopped herself at the last possible moment from asking what would happen if one of the kids walked in on them and was it worth locking the door. When was the last time they had made love in the early morning? Maybe a couple of years. She rolled from her side to her belly and he responded by massaging her behind in slow, patient loops, one side to the other, the way she loved it – the way that never failed to turn her on.

'Oh, baby,' she moaned softly. 'That feels so good ... so good.'

His hand slid between her thighs and helped her become even wetter than she already was.

She could feel his hardness against her. Responding, she raised her arms over her head, pointed her toes, and stretched her body out as taut and straight as an arrow. The trade-off for fewer surprises in their lovemaking was that each of them knew so well what pleased the other. Not predictable, really, just... comfortable.

She pulled her shirt off and he turned her toward him, kissing her in the way no other man ever had or ever would – pressure just right on her mouth, lips apart, but not too much, tongue exploring, caressing, even as hers explored him.

'Oh, I love this, Jeff,' she said. 'And I love you so much.'

She took him in her hand and stroked him rhythmically until he had grown so large she could barely get her fingers around him, and so hard it seemed he might break. Fifteen years of marriage, and rubbing him this way still excited her so.

'Don't stop, Donna. Don't stop...'

'Donna?'

'Huh?'

'Donna...'

Donna pushed away from her desk and rubbed her eyes. Anne Hajjar, arms folded, was looking down at her mischievously. Like Donna, she was dressed in a set of aqua scrubs and a flower-print hair cover. Beyond her, Donna could see the ICU pulsating the way it always did when the census was near capacity. Today, though, they were again short a nurse, so everything was, if possible, moving even faster.

'What's up?' she asked, trying for a business-as-usual look.

'You were actually out, weren't you,' her longtime friend said, teasing. 'Asleep at the switch.'

'It was my break.'

'Come on, you looked like you were smiling there.'

'So?'

Anne peered down at her, then suddenly grinned knowingly.

'You had sex this morning, didn't you?'

Donna raised herself up regally.

'I refuse to say.'

'You bimbo!'

'Jesus, Hajjar. You're not a bimbo when you make love to your *husband*.'

'I wouldn't know. I divorced mine before I could find out what it was like. Listen, go back to your daydreaming. It's good that at least someone around here is smiling today. I'm jealous as hell and I hate you for Jeff, but I'll still handle the new admission the ER just called about.'

'Nonsense. I'm up for the next one, and I'll do it. I can put Jeff on pause. What do they have?'

'Sixty-eight-year-old man with chest pain. Looks like it may be an evolving MI. There's still a chance they may want to take him to the cath lab to open up a couple of his arteries with stents.'

'So, this guy'll fill us up. Do you want to ship someone out to keep a bed open?'

'If we can do it, sure.'

'Who do we have? Mr. Turnbull?'

'He had runs of extra beats all night, remember? Or were you busy reliving you-know-what during report?'

'Hey, cut me some slack. With three kids, this is not an everyday occurrence. What about Lila?'

'It's either her or Patty Moriarity. All the others are too unstable.'

'I vote Lila. Her cardiac enzymes are down and her pacemaker's working fine, and she's even more of a demanding pain in the neck than she was the last time she was here. Besides, Patty's still in a coma and hasn't even been here for two days yet. Even though she's medically stable and off the vent, Dr. Ng would go ballistic if we tried to ship her out to the step-down unit in this condition.'

'So would Dr. Grant. He was in there with her for a good long time yesterday.'

'Hmmm. Should we be crossing him off the hospital's most-eligible list?'

'I think he crossed himself off the list with the fentanyl.'

'But he may be back on. I just heard he's getting his license back. Something about somebody soaking the insides of his OR shoes with fentanyl.'

'I heard that rumor, too.'

'Who would do a thing like that?'

'I don't know, but I am really relieved there's an explanation for what happened. Will is a very good guy.'

'So, you think Will and Patty?'

'The doc and the cop. How romantic.'

'Were you in with her just now?'

'I was. She's breathing easily and handling her secretions okay. Between the surgery and whatever she went through saving that guy's life, she is really battered. Still, it's probably just me, but I think she seems a little lighter than she did yesterday.'

'Epidurals tend to do better than subdurals.'

'I hope so, because I'm going to be very upset if she doesn't wake up. She's a hero. I want to get to know her.'

'Come on. Let's check her and Lila and make a final decision about who goes.'

'Lila.'

The two friends made their way through the ICU, looking in on each of the glass-enclosed rooms as they passed. They were both seasoned veterans of their profession and were blessed with a sixth sense that often told them a patient was about to go sour, or even sometimes that the ICU was about to be inundated. Today, short a nurse, they were both a bit edgy but comfortable knowing there wasn't a situation that could arise where they wouldn't know how to react.

Patty Moriarity lay serenely still, breathing easily. Patches of gauze were taped over her eyes to protect them against dryness. The right side of her face was gentian with bruising, and in places, streaks of black and blue had made their way across the midline.

'Patty,' Donna said, bending over the bed rail and straightening the oxygen prongs. 'Patty, it's your nurses Donna and Anne. Squeeze my hand if you can hear me.'

'Anything?'

'Nope.'

'She doesn't look as light as I thought she did.'

'My experience with epidurals is that the coma seesaws lighter and deeper, and then most of them just wake up.'

'Okay, that cinches it. Lila is history. She'll do fine in the step-down unit or even on one of the floors. Listen, our resident hero here is due for a neuro check. You want to stay and do that, and I'll get the paperwork started on Lila?'

'Sure.'

'But no reliving your you-know-what with you-know-who.'

'I'm all business.'

With pleasant thoughts of her husband hovering just below the surface, Donna removed Patty's eye patches. Her pupils, which were initially quite dilated from having been covered, gradually became smaller and reacted to direct light by constricting even further. *Good signs.*

'Patty, it's Donna. Squeeze my hand. Please squeeze my hand.'
Nothing.

Donna pressed her thumbnail into Patty's forcefully enough to cause discomfort. Ever so slightly, Patty's thumb twitched. At least Donna thought it did. She repeated the maneuver. Nothing. And again. Same result. Shrugging, she worked each of Patty's limbs and digits through a full range of motion. No resistance. Finally, the nurse ran her thumbnail in an arc heel-to-toe along the bottom of each of Patty's feet. Minutely, Patty's great toes responded with the slightest downward movement, toward the irritant sensation. The Babinski sign, a reflex *upward* movement of the toe, often signifying a disconnection between the brain and the extremities, was absent. It was another positive finding – or at least not a negative one. Patty's neurologic status was no worse than it had been, and if the slight movement to a painful stimulus was real, it might even be better. Carefully, Donna pulled down Patty's lower lids and squirted in a small amount of lubricant. Then she took new patches and taped them in place.

Come on, baby. Time to wake up and smell the coffee.

At the thought, Donna reflexively inhaled deeply through her nose.

Then again. She looked about, quickly going to red alert. Seeing nothing, she hurried to the doorway.

'Hey, Annie,' she called out.

Anne Hajjar poked her head out of Lila Terry's room.

'Patty awake?'

'I wish. Come down here, will you? I smell smoke or something.'

Anne was halfway down the corridor when she smelled it – a faint, chemical odor, more acrid than simple smoke. She stopped short as Donna hurried past her to the nurses' station and grabbed the fire extinguisher. They were moving together, trying to locate the source of the odor when, with two loud gunshotlike snaps, acrid black smoke began billowing from someplace beneath the beds in rooms 2 and 6.

'Call a Dr. Red, Annie!' Donna shouted as she dashed into the first of the rooms, extinguisher at the ready. 'Jeannie, Lesley, get ready for an evac, respirator patients first as soon as we have Ambu Bags to ventilate them and a minimum of three people per patient. Each of the other patients needs at least two with them. Put signs on their beds. Send one through four to the ER, all the rest out to Two East.'

Donna hurried past her. Moments later, the hospital-wide page system broadcast the operator's uncharacteristically urgent voice.

'Dr. Red, to ICU *stat*... Dr. Red to ICU *stat*... Dr. Red to lCU *stat*.'

Dense black smoke had now nearly filled the two patient cubicles and was drifting out into the corridor connecting all the rooms with the nurses' station. Donna felt certain this was an electrical fire of some sort, probably within the wall. She was the charge nurse today, and until someone in authority arrived from security or the fire department, all decisions were hers.

The acrid fumes were making it unpleasant to breathe. There were two Ambu Bags in the ICU and three portable oxygen cylinders. According to the Dr. Red protocol, the respiratory therapist should be up with as many more breathing bags as she could quickly get her hands on, followed by someone from the ER with the ones they had, and finally, just in case, a nurse with the bags from the crash carts on each floor.

Donna pulled on a blue paper mask, handed them out to the other nurses, and then saw to it that those patients not on respirators had them in place.

'Okay, Annie,' she called out, 'let's get portable oxygen into two and six, and move them first!'

Before any patients could be moved, the ICU began to fill with people, and noise. Two medical students burst in along with a surgeon and several nurses. A huge uniformed security guard suddenly appeared on the scene, as well, barking out orders like General Patton at anyone who would listen and trying at the same time to convince people that he was in charge and they were to pay attention to him. The patient in cubicle 6 was removed from her ventilator by one of the nurses. A med student transferred her bags of IV fluids from poles onto her bed. Then they slowly guided her bed through the crowd and out of the unit while a tech from respiratory inflated her lungs from an Ambu Bag hooked up to one of the cylinders of oxygen. One gone.

The number of people milling about was increasing almost as rapidly as the density of the smoke. What seemed like dozens of voices were shouting and issuing orders at once.

'...Oxygen. Hook a portable tank to the bag!...'

'Where are the portable tanks?...'

'...There are none! Just go!...'

'...You can't move him like that. He just had a hip replaced!...'

'...Everybody, just quiet down and listen to me!...'

'...The IV pole! It's falling over. Watch it!...'

The ICU continued filling up with far more nurses, physicians, technicians, and security people than were needed to move the remaining patients. Everyone was talking or shouting or coughing. Certain her voice was just adding to the commotion, Donna quickly gave up trying to coordinate anything and focused instead on getting the very unstable eighty-year-old post-op cardiac patient in cubicle 2 ready for transfer. Across the bed from her, partially enveloped in smoke, rubbing at her eyes with her sleeve, Anne Hajjar did her best to keep up.

'...I've got this!' a man was bellowing. 'Let go, for chrissakes.'

'No, you don't. You don't know what in the hell you're doing!...'

'...You've got to turn off the oxygen, dammit! Turn it off or you'll risk blowing us all up!...'

More bodies, more noise, more turmoil, more smoke. Donna, Anne, and another nurse, all of them sputtering, were maneuvering the bed with their unconscious patient toward the doors as fast as they could manage while still adequately breathing for him.

'Adrienne,' Donna called over to one of the respiratory techs, 'unhook the vent in Two and follow us.'

'You got it.'

'Do you have a room for this guy on your wing?' Donna asked the nurse.

'Two-sixteen is empty. People should be there waiting for us. We have two-twelve as well if we need it.'

'Great. Adrienne, we're going to two-sixteen.'

'God, that was awful in there,' Anne said when they had reached the corridor leading across the hospital to the med-surg wing.

'You can have all the fire drills in the world, but when it isn't a drill, all of a sudden no one remembers anything, and everyone either wants to be in charge or wants to be a hero.'

'People just want to help.'

'I suppose. We could have done better with the five of us who were in there when the whole thing started. Here, let me help you get Martin over to his new bed, then I've got to get back to the unit.'

'What do you think happened in there?'

'Some sort of short in the wires in the wall.'

'I suppose.'

'Well, hang in here with Martin, Annie. I'll see you later.'

Donna hurried back to the ICU. The smoke could now be smelled halfway across the length of the hospital, and she wondered if the entire building might have to be evacuated before the fire was under control. From outside, sirens were wailing. Any moment now, an army of police and firemen would be added to the hellish scene in the ICU. The hallway outside the unit was full of milling people now, many of them newly arrived and some of the others soot-covered and ordering everyone to stay out of the way.

'...There are more than enough people in there!...'

'...Stay away from the doors. Keep back...'

'The firemen'll be here any minute. Move back down the corridor and make room for them...'

As Donna reached the glass ICU doors, they glided opened. A billowing of dark smoke preceded Lila Terry's bed, being hauled out by two nurses and three or four others, some of whom were barely able to keep one hand in contact with the bed.

'Katie, how many patients left in there?' Donna asked as they passed her.

'I don't know. Just one, I think. Better get in there and make sure no one's gotten trampled.'

'Good point.'

The density of the smoke had lessened, or at least had grown no worse. The mob, perhaps finally realizing that it, like the patients, might be in some danger, had begun shoving its way back through the main doors. Donna hurried down the row of cubicles. All were empty except for room 5, and the nurse and two security men were ready to move the patient from there. Black smoke was continuing to pour from the wall sockets in rooms 2 and 6. No flames, no heat, just acrid smoke.

Donna helped see the last patient out of the unit and had returned for a final inspection when the first four of the firemen arrived, including one who was clearly in charge. In seconds, the unit had been emptied of everyone except her. She quickly reviewed the chain of events occurring over what had seemed like hours but in truth had been only slightly more than fifteen minutes.

'You did a great job,' she was told.

She looked around at the bizarre scene.

I guess I did, she was thinking.

She left the unit and returned to the med-surg wing, where she had helped bring the patient from room 2. Anne Hajjar gave her a thumbs-up.

'Martin's tough,' she said. 'He actually looks a little better than he did before the fire.'

'Nice job. The fire people have taken over. I'm going to the nurses' station to find out where all the rest of our patients and staff are.'

Donna took over a small built-in desk and commandeered the phone. After five minutes of calls, she sat in utter dismay, staring down at a page of notes she'd taken. Then, just to be certain, she called each of the floors again. Bewildered, she was rubbing at the irritants and fatigue that were stinging her eyes when Anne hurried over from room 216.

'Denise just came over,' she said breathlessly, referring to the nursing supervisor. 'She says there was never any fire. Apparently someone set off a very elaborate radio-controlled smoke bomb. The fire people have no idea why.'

'I think I know why,' Donna said, her face ashen.

'What?'

'Patty Moriarity is gone, Annie.'

'I don't understand.'

'I mean she's not in the hospital. I've called everyplace twice. From all I can tell, someone wheeled her into an ambulance and just drove away. She's been kidnapped.'

Chapter 32

Cascading images of the twins preceded Will's realization that he was awake – a realization that also meant he was still alive. Like coming out of deep anesthesia, one by one his senses began reporting in. The farm smell mixed with a number of other pungent odors. Once again he was naked on the fetid mattress. No one had bothered to clean the sickness off him, but to his right he could see that there was a grimy white hand towel on the floor and water in the bucket that the behemoth named Watkins had dragged in. A sledgehammer inside his skull was monitoring each heartbeat. Every muscle in his body ached, but it was his fingers where the throbbing was most acute. His fingers! The maniac Krause had done something to his fingers. Now he remembered. He remembered screaming – screaming over and over to blot out the pain.

'No!' ... 'Fuck you!' ... 'Stop! Please stop!' ... 'Go to hell! Go to hell! Go to hell!' ... 'Let go of my hands, you bastard! Let go!' ... 'Noooo!'

Fearing the worst, he withdrew his hands from beneath the army blanket. They were covered with brown, caked blood, but no part of any digit was missing. The source of the bleeding was three of his nail beds – the ones on each middle finger, where the nail had some-how been pried up but not completely removed, and the one on his left index finger, which was dangling obscenely by a single thread of tissue. He could only believe that he had passed out before Krause had gone after the joints themselves. That was the only explanation that made sense. It was certainly doubtful the creep had drawn the line at permanent mutilation.

'Jesus,' he murmured. 'How did this happen to me?'

He raised his brutalized index finger to his mouth and bit through the strand of skin, releasing the nail. The air from his gentle exhale passed across the raw bed and produced the pain of an abscessed tooth. He rolled over, gasping as he lowered his hands into the cool water.

He didn't remember telling Krause about Lionel, but then again, there was still much he could not recall. Gingerly, he washed the gore from his hands. The pain seemed to sharpen his memory. The twins! That was it! He had battled the little monster by forcing his mind to focus on them. Dan and Jess at age one ... at five ... on the swing set in the backyard ... serving clients at the Open Hearth ... throwing snowballs at him and each other. He knew that the moment he told, the moment they had the X-rays, he was as good as dead. The moment he gave in, he would never see the twins again. As long as he held out against the pain and misery, as long as he battled his rodent-faced torturer, there was hope, however slim.

He blotted his hands dry, then reached into the bucket again and rubbed water over his face. His senses cleared still more. Gratefully, the memory of precisely what had been done to him remained cloudy, but one thing now seemed certain. He had beaten Krause again. With the help of his kids and the determination that had pulled him through countless all-nighters in various hospitals, his jackass stubbornness had stood up once more to Marshall Gold's pervert.

As before, he located his clothes under the small table and painfully put them on, crying out every time his wounded fingernails brushed against fabric. Quickly, he learned to keep his hands up near the level of his heart as much as possible. Ignoring the pulsating pain, he crawled to the wall beneath the Plexiglas windows and forced himself to stand. For the first time he got a prolonged look outside his prison. The sky was slate gray. The light filtering through the overcast suggested morning was well along if not gone. As he had suspected, he was being held on the first floor of a large farmhouse – white with black shutters.

From this point of view, he could see two weathered outbuildings, a large, well-used tractor, and the corner of what seemed to be a sizable barn, also white. There was a corral of some sort beyond the barn with hay, a water trough, and several cows – Jerseys, if he remembered right – with hides like tan and white jigsaw puzzles. Not far beyond the outbuildings was a vast, fenced-in field and, beyond that, forest. There was no hint as to where the farm might be located.

Using his elbow, Will tested the window. It was, as Gold had said, thick Plexiglas, firmly bolted to the house. He wondered how many others had been imprisoned there, and why, and acknowledged that if he were ever to escape from this room, it would be through the door. At that moment, as if on cue, the lone door opened and Marshall Gold stepped inside. He was absolutely resplendent in pristine Nikes, a pair of black satin workout pants, and an unadorned gold T-shirt that accented the striking V from his shoulders to his waist. A towel was draped over his neck. It seemed clear to Will that in public, Boyd Halliday's executive assistant went out of his way to dress in conservative styles that underemphasized his impressive physique. No sense tipping anyone off that the mild-mannered bookkeeper also just happened to be a professional killer.

'Grant, good to see you up and about,' he said cheerily.

'Drop dead.'

'I can have my man Watkins bandage up those fingers if you wish. He was a corpsman in the army.'

'That must have been before he discovered pizza.'

'Actually, there's a surprising amount of muscle in there. So, bandages or no?'

'Send him in. Tell him to be gentle, though. I have a very low pain threshold.'

Gold grinned.

'Well, we still want those X-rays and you still haven't told us how you managed to get rid of them and where they might be now.'

'Good. I figured when I didn't wake up dead, I hadn't told you. I guess after he killed Charles Newcomber, you told Krause not to be quite so heavy-handed.'

'Something like that. Let's just say he wanted to get closer to the line, and I wouldn't let him – at least yet. You're fortunate that you have the propensity to pass out. Some people never do.'

'What kind of animals are you?'

'Before he ... um ... suddenly passed out, Newcomber did tell us he had earmarked the films for you. That's why I was following you when you drove to Roxbury.'

'What's so important about those films, anyhow?' Will asked. 'Do they show how your cancer center screwed up and diagnosed Grace Davis as having cancer when they weren't her films?'

Will knew even as he said the words that the explanation really didn't make sense to him. Almost certainly the mammograms weren't Grace's, yet she did, in fact, have breast cancer. One other thing was bothering him. Although he never got the chance to open it, the envelope he had managed to pass over to Lionel was bulky and heavy. It had to contain many more than just one set of mammograms.

'Why we want those films is our business,' Gold said. 'And I promise you, we will have them.'

'Why would I want to give them to you when if I do I'm dead?'

271

'Correction,' Gold said, his pale eyes menacing. 'Soon events will transpire that will obviate the need for those X-rays. When that time comes, we will no longer have a need for you, and you will, in fact, become history. However, if you cooperate now and help us remove the chance that those X-rays might surface at an inopportune time, you have my word that you can go free. You will be no threat to us. Anything you say will be your word against ours, and pardon me for saying it, but at present your word isn't worth too much.'

Will weighed Gold's logic and found it badly flawed. Regardless of what the man promised, there was no way Will was going to be allowed to leave the farm alive. He steadied himself against the wall and clenched his teeth against the throbbing pain in his fingers. Was there any way he could survive another session with Krause?

'Leave me alone,' he said, with more panic in his voice than he had expected. He held up his hands. 'How can you do this?'

Gold sighed theatrically.

'Suit yourself,' he said. 'We haven't time for you to keep passing out on us, so we have decided another approach is called for.'

He returned to the doorway.

'Wat, come on in and put some Band-Aids or something on his fingers. I want him looking and feeling his best for his lovely guest.'

Will's eyes narrowed as he tried to read beneath Gold's words.

Jess! his mind shrieked. *Jesus, they've got Jess!*

He stopped himself from screaming anything out loud just in case he was wrong, although using the kids seemed like the sort of thing Gold would have already considered. Massive Watkins lumbered across to him with a first-aid kit, which he opened and set on the small table. The scissors inside were plastic, as were the tweezers. No help there. Will craned his neck to see past Gold and through the doorway.

Hurry up, Gold! Hurry up!

His heart was threatening to pound through his chest wall as Watkins used peroxide, then applied antibacterial cream and a bulky gauze dressing on each finger.

Come on! Come on!

Finally, the giant packed up the kit and returned to Gold.

'You want me to bring her in?' he asked.

'I think it's time.'

Will gritted his teeth and held his breath. Patty, her head bandaged, eyes patched, nasal oxygen prongs in place, an IV bag resting on the sheet that covered her from neck to ankles, was wheeled into the center of the room on a telescoping ambulance stretcher. The bag attached to her catheter hung down from one of the horizontal struts. She lay motionless, breathing steadily, clearly still in a coma. Will tried not to show how stunned and ill he was feeling. How in the hell had they gotten her out of the ICU?

'What's this supposed to mean to me?' he managed.

'Sorry, Grant, that doesn't work. You two have been an item for a while now. Policewoman sleeps with murder suspect. Everyone knows it.'

'That's bullshit.'

'Okay then, if you don't care, you don't care. Wat, go find Dr. Krause and tell him I want this woman's little finger cut off. Tell him not to worry, because she won't feel it, and besides, she'll still have nine left.' He turned back to Will. 'Next time, though, it could be one of her lips.'

Will felt smothered, unable to breathe.

'Jesus, what kind of monster are you?' he managed.

'Someone who wants information from you and is rapidly running out of patience.'

'You son of a bitch.'

Will knew he was beaten. He gave up his pretense, reached beneath the sheet, and took Patty's hand in his. At that moment, Krause arrived, his narrow, pockmarked face glowing at the prospect of getting back to work.

'Pretty,' he said, leering down at Patty's bruised face. 'Very pretty. You have work for me?'

'It seems so,' Gold said, feigning a helpless, resigned expression, as if giving Krause the green light to begin mutilating Patty was taxing for him. 'Dr. Grant, one last time. Help us get what we need, and I promise you your friend here will be dropped off unharmed someplace where she will be quickly found and taken back to the hospital. I have every reason to despise her, given that she messed up what would have been the greatest shot of my career, but I will release her.'

Will knew that despite Gold's earlier promise of amnesty for him, there was no chance whatsoever the man would let him live, but with Patty in a deep, possibly irreversible coma, she certainly posed no threat. There had to be a way to stall things until he could think of a deal of some sort that would guarantee she would get safely back to the hospital. His mind was working furiously, sorting through various scenarios. None of them provided any deal on which Gold couldn't easily renege. At that moment, minutely but unmistakably, Patty squeezed his hand.

Startled, Will's surgeon's mind and reflexes instantly kicked in. His hand remained virtually motionless but tightened around hers. He bowed his head, shaking it in apparent frustration as he shifted his weight, checking to see if the sheet moved. There was little if anything to be seen, and certainly neither Gold nor the other two seemed alerted to the change. Once again, as if to be certain he knew, Patty's hand tightened just a bit, then relaxed. Watching the sheet as much as he dared, Will returned the pressure.

I know, I know. Just be careful.

'I need some time,' he said.

'Time for what?' Gold asked. 'I think I've made myself perfectly clear.'

'I need some sort of guarantee Patty will be returned to the hospital unharmed.'

'I gave you my word.'

'Gold, cut the crap. You kill people. Ten minutes. Give me ten minutes to see if I can come up with something better than your word.'

'And if you can't?'

Will looked down at Patty and gently brushed his hand across her forehead. Again, immediately, there was pressure from her hand. She was not only awake, she was wide awake.

'If I can't, I'll have to decide if there's even a chance you'd make a promise not to harm this woman and actually keep it.'

'What do you think, Dr. Krause? Should we give Grant his ten minutes, or just go ahead and see what he's really made of?'

'You know my answer to that,' Krause said, surveying Patty from head to toe.

'Ten minutes,' Gold said. 'After that, either we're on our way to Roxbury or I turn her over to the good doctor here.'

Will's stomach turned at the notion.

'Bring me a chair so I can sit here,' he said.

'No problem. Wat, bring Dr. Grant a chair and bring one in for yourself. It's okay to stay over there by the door. Just keep an eye on him. Make sure he behaves under that sheet there.'

Krause snickered. Will ignored him. He was processing the fact that Gold had probably been telling the truth about there being no hidden surveillance camera, although a hidden microphone of some sort remained a possibility. As Krause and Gold moved through the door, and Watkins moved past them, Will bent down and kissed Patty on the temple.

274

'One is yes, two is no,' he whispered. 'Understand?'

One squeeze.

'Ten minutes,' Gold said, tapping his Rolex, then following Krause out of the room.

'If you were me, what would you do, Watkins?' Will asked. 'Should I go out to Roxbury and get those X-rays?'

One squeeze.

'Huh? Oh, sure. I would do whatever Mr. Gold says. He's not a person to mess with.'

Will scanned the narrow room for anything that might have been a bug. There didn't seem to be one, but if he screwed up now and Gold realized Patty was awake, they would have lost the only advantage they had. From what she had said before her injury, it seemed possible she had already figured out that Excelsius Health was behind the murders. That had to be why she wanted him to cooperate. If they somehow got out of this, there was other evidence besides the X-rays that they could use to nail Gold and his boss.

There was slight pressure on his hand, pushing it a half an inch at a time down the thin stretcher mattress until it hit against the catheter.

'You want out?' he asked.

One squeeze.

'What's that?' Watkins asked.

'I asked if you wanted out of all this. You don't seem like such a bad guy.'

'I do my job,' Watkins said. 'Whatever it is. If Mr. Gold tells me to be bad, I can be real bad.'

The catheter was kept from being accidentally pulled out by a round balloon blown up just before the tip. It was inflated not with air but with water inserted by a syringe through a port on the near end. Will found the small syringe taped to the drainage tubing, carefully deflated the balloon, and then slid the catheter out. The corners of Patty's mouth turned up slightly. Not only was she awake, but now she was more mobile.

'Gold says he's the one who shot her,' Will said. 'Did you hear him say that?'

One squeeze.

Impatiently, Watkins checked his watch.

'If Mr. Gold says something, it's generally true. You got three minutes.'

'Is there anything you need?'

'From you?'

One squeeze. Lying virtually motionless, Patty hooked one finger around the IV tubing and touched it to Will's hand. He stood, lifting the sheet enough to see that the IV catheter in her wrist had clotted off. He loosened the tape holding it in place, slid it out of the vein, and kept pressure on the puncture site with his finger. Still more freedom of movement for her.

'I meant is there anything I can do for you that might convince you to let me go?'

Two squeezes.

'Not likely.'

'Suit yourself. I could do a stapling procedure on that stomach of yours. You'd be out modeling bathing suits in no time.'

'I'd rather eat.'

Watkins was checking his watch again when the door flew open. Marshall Gold, showered and now dressed in dark slacks, a sports jacket, and a tangerine turtleneck, strode past the giant to stand across from Will, just inches from the stretcher. With a final tightening on Patty's hand, Will withdrew his from under the sheet.

Don't move, baby, his mind was screaming. *Don't move a muscle.*

'So, I gave you two extra minutes, Grant. What's it going to be?'

'I want your promise again that you'll get her back to the hospital unharmed.'

'You've got it.'

You're lying, you son of a bitch.

'Okay. But I also want your word that the guy with the X-rays won't be hurt, either. He hasn't done anything. I want Watkins there to hear you promise.'

'You really have brass balls to be ordering me around like this in your situation. Okay, okay. If the guy is not a danger to me, I won't hurt him.'

Will hesitated as if he were still considering. He felt sick at the notion of putting Lionel in harm's way, but there really was nothing he could do.

'I gave the films to the man who gave me directions.'

'At the very end of the street, where I lost you for just a couple of seconds.'

'That's right. I gave the envelope to him and told him to take it home and I'd buy it back for a thousand dollars.'

'Then you ran across the street in the other direction.'

'Exactly.'

Gold's expression was absolute glee. In that instant, what little hope remained in Will vanished. He and Patty were dead, and poor Lionel would likely fare no better.

'I knew it was something like that,' Gold said. 'How are you going to find him again?'

'I'm not sure. I know his first name and the area he lives in. I didn't have time to get his last name. I planned to bring as much cash as I could come up with and bribe as many people as necessary until someone told me where he lives. I would guess a lot of people know him. He seemed like a real character.'

'What's his name?'

'I'd prefer –'

Gold whipped a bone-handled switchblade from his pocket, flicked open the five-inch blade, and grabbed Patty's little finger.

'What's his fucking name?' he roared.

'L-Lionel. It's Lionel.'

Gold's fury instantly vanished and he smiled across at Will benignly.

'Lionel. Nice name. Well, let's you and I go and find this Lionel.'

'Marshall, you're not going anywhere. We have business to attend to.'

Will recognized the voice after the first word. He flashed back on the Faneuil Hall debate that had started everything, as Boyd Halliday strode into the room and took up a place at the foot of the stretcher.

'I want those films before tomorrow,' Gold said, speaking to the Excelsius Health CEO more as an equal than an employee.

'I understand, Marsh. I want them in our control, too. But Ed Wittenburg is due here any minute to go over the figures for tomorrow's meeting and to put the folios together, and I must be home by five for a dinner party my wife is throwing for the board officers of our soon-to-be subsidiaries.' He turned to Will. 'Well, if it isn't the darling of the Society. Welcome to the farm, Dr. Grant. Life seems to have been rather unkind to you since we last met.'

Will shook his head derisively.

'Is that what this is all about, Halliday,' he said, 'acquiring companies?'

Halliday looked back at Gold.

'I need you here with us, Marsh. As it is, we're barely going to have enough time to finish our business today, and the meeting is set for ten tomorrow morning. How about sending Mr. Watkins with our friend? He might do better than you in Roxbury, anyhow.'

'But –'

Halliday gestured toward Patty.

'She'll be here with us, right?'

'Yes, but –'

'So there's no chance Dr. Grant will cause Mr. Watkins any problems. Isn't that right, Doctor?'

'Whatever you say,' Will muttered.

'If he does cause even one bit of difficulty, if Mr. Watkins doesn't call in every fifteen minutes on the dot, the good doctor's relationship to this sleeping beauty will be, how should I say, cut short.'

'What companies are you acquiring tomorrow?' Will asked. 'Wait, wait, don't tell me. Let me guess. The companies you'll be acquiring just happen to have been controlled by the four people who just accidentally happened to have been murdered by a killer out for revenge. What a convenient coincidence.'

'Actually,' Halliday said, 'we were only interested in two of them. But patterns can be so revealing. Mr. Watkins, are you ready?'

'Whenever you say.'

'Wat,' Gold ordered, 'before he leaves this room, put a pillowcase over his head and tie it at the bottom. Take it off only when you reach Roxbury. Use the handcuffs for the trip, too, just in case he loses his mind and decides to be a hero. If he gives you any shit at all, just shoot him through the knee, then the balls, and then drag him back here.'

'You got it, boss.'

'We can keep her right here in this room, Marsh,' Halliday said. He reached down and gave Patty's great toe a playful tweak. 'I'm sure Dr. Krause wouldn't mind watching her.'

Chapter 33

'What kind of car is this, Watkins?'

'Lincoln Town Car.'

'Nice. I knew I was kneeling on the floor of something pretty spiffy. Smells new.'

'I take good care of it. Keep your hands up on the seat where I can see them.'

'You're three-hundred pounds of frigging muscle, and I'm

kneeling on the floor of your car with handcuffs on, my fingers all torn up, a pillowcase tied over my head, and my girlfriend being held as collateral. What are you worried about?'

'Mr. Gold tells me what to do, and I do it. And this time he told me you are not to be trusted. So get your hands up on the seat where I can see them, or I'm going to reach down and grab them and put them there, and I don't think you want me to do that.'

Will did as he was ordered. There was an abruptness to Watkins, a coldness, that he hadn't fully appreciated at the farmhouse. Despite his Buddha-like physique and moon face, and the care with which he had bandaged Will's fingers, there was nothing soft about him. If Watkins needed or wanted to kill, chances were he would do so without remorse. Gold knew that. Otherwise, there was no way he would have trusted the man as he had.

They were maybe twenty minutes away from the farm and, at Gold's insistence, Will had spent the entire ride on his knees, his butt crammed under the dash, his face pressed onto the front seat. At first, influenced by any number of hostage movies, he tried remembering turns and listening for the sort of telltale sounds that might enable him to retrace their journey – the tolling of a church bell, the whistle of a train, the jackhammering of road construction. He heard nothing that he could pinpoint. Of course, before retracing any steps, he had to deal with his handcuffs and overpower the gargantuan at the wheel of the Town Car. Quickly he gave up listening for clues and instead forced his mind back to the conundrum of how to guarantee that Gold would release Patty. He had yet to solve that puzzle, and time was running out.

It's not going to happen, jerk. Face it. She's as good as dead and so are you. Gold and Halliday had been several steps ahead of everyone throughout this nightmare. They were not likely to leave any loose ends just because they promised they would.

To Will's right, he could hear Watkins fumbling for something in his jacket pocket. A moment later he dialed a cell phone with a single touch. The check-in call. They were fifteen minutes out, not twenty.

'Mr. Gold, Wat here. Just reporting in. No problems so far... He's doing just fine, sir, just fine, but he doesn't like being on the floor... Okay, Mr. Gold, I'll tell him. I'll speak to you in fifteen minutes. We should be in Roxbury before too much longer... Yes, sir. Whatever you say is the way it's going to be.' He returned the phone to his pocket. 'Mr. Gold says for you to get used to it down there.'

'Isn't he just a sweetie.'

'Shut up.'

'What did he say to you, Watkins? What's the "way it's going to be" mean?'

'Shut up or I swear I'm gonna do some work on those fingers. I bandaged them and I can just as easily unbandage them.'

'You're a real prize.'

Will sank down on the seat, mulling over what Gold might have said. The possibilities he came up with were unsettling. Several of the electrical burns on his body had been itching mercilessly. He asked for permission to scratch and got the predictable response. They were making the frequent turns and stops of city driving now. Watkins had made his second check-in call, this one much briefer than the first, then drove on in silence for maybe ten minutes more. Almost there.

'Okay,' Watkins said, slowing down, 'we're near where you met Lionel. You can untie that pillowcase and take it off. There's a bow in the twine right under your chin.'

'Bless you.'

'Now, slowly, push yourself up onto the seat and turn around.'

'What about these handcuffs?'

'Just keep your hands in your lap.'

'How will I fasten my seat belt?' Will waited in vain for Watkins to respond to the humor. 'Okay,' he said once he was upright and had worked the stiffness from his shoulders and a painful cramp from his hip. 'That's where I stopped Lionel to ask directions, right over there, but I think it's too early for his evening walk.'

'Mr. Gold wants us to check in some stores. He says if this Lionel is the way you described him, someone will know who he is.'

'Smart man.'

'You're going to come with me, but you're going to keep your mouth shut unless I ask you to speak. Try anything, and Mr. Gold has instructed me to shoot you and whoever we're talking to. You know I'll do that, right?'

'Right, chief.'

'Wiseass.'

Half a block down, Watkins found space by a meter and skillfully maneuvered the boatlike Lincoln into the spot. Then he lumbered around to Will's door, undid the manacle on Will's left wrist, and clicked it onto his own.

'What direction was this man coming from when you stopped him for directions?' he asked.

'From there.'

Will pointed across the street at a row of modest stores. The late afternoon was gray and breezy but not all that cold. Still, there was little foot traffic along the block. Watkins nodded toward a florist's on the corner – Bethany's Flowers.

The woman behind the counter of the fragrant shop was in her late thirties with a neat figure, black-framed spectacles, and pleasant eyes. She glanced minutely at the handcuffs joining the two men, then back to their faces, clearly unsure as to which of them was the alpha male. Will expected she would be both surprised and pleased to realize that for once in such situations, it was the black one.

'My name is Joe Dunn,' Watkins said, flipping open his billfold to reveal a bogus ID. 'I'm a private investigator and part-time bounty hunter. This man is my prisoner.'

'Carol. Pleased to meet you,' the woman said without fear, her expression now one of respect.

'Before I take him in and waste everyone's time, I need help in identifying for certain that he's the one I've been after. People have told me that an older man named Lionel can do that and that he lives around here. There's a hundred-dollar bill in it for anyone who can point me to him.'

'Lionel's his first name?' she asked, carefully avoiding any eye contact with Will.

'Yes, ma'am. I don't know his last. Here's the hundred.'

Watkins slid the bill out just far enough for Carol to confirm the denomination. Still, she shook her head.

'I guess he doesn't buy flowers,' she said.

'Well, thank you very much, anyway,' the huge killer said, as civil and composed as a diplomat.

It seemed to Will that some connection had formed between Watkins and the slender florist.

'Wait,' she called out as they approached the door. 'Let me call my mother. She's Bethany. This used to be her shop. She knows almost everyone in this neighborhood.'

She took the phone out from under the counter and dialed.

'You're doing fine,' Watkins whispered harshly. 'Just keep it that way.

'You know, you're really quite charming when you set your mind to it,' Will replied, winking at Watkins conspiratorially. 'I think she digs you.'

'Shut up.'

'I told you my mother would know,' Carol called out from behind the counter. 'She thinks the man you want is Lionel Henderson. He's a widower. Very dapper dresser, Mother says. Goes to her church, but not too often.'

'That sounds like him,' Watkins said. 'Find out if she knows where he lives.'

Carol asked her mother, then hung up and searched through a low, two-drawer file cabinet.

'Mother says he's bought flowers here. If he has, she probably has him on file. She kept incredibly accurate records for promotions or Christmas cards or whatever. I'm not doing nearly as well at that as she – wait, here he is. Lionel Henderson, two-thirteen Spruce Street, apartment six. Just down the street that way.'

She wrote down the name and address and handed it to Watkins. Will read the attraction in her face but still had trouble understanding it. Perhaps nearing forty she had pared down her requirements. Perhaps his knowing that the behemoth killed people for a living had something to do with his underappreciating the man's desirability.

'Here you go,' Watkins said, taking the card and handing over the Ben Franklin.

'Don't you want to wait and see if it's the right man before paying me?'

'If it's not him, you can still keep the money for being so ... helpful.'

'That's my card. The number of the shop is on the other side.'

Oh, enough already!

Will twisted his wrist to stop the manacle from chafing, and his captor shot him a sideward warning glance.

'Perhaps we'll see each other again,' Watkins said, continuing the dance.

'That would be very nice.'

The florist and the thug, Will thought savagely as they headed out to the street. The walrus and the carpenter may no longer be the most bizarre pairing ever. They paused long enough for another check-in call to Gold and then headed down Spruce.

Number 213 was a deteriorating four-story brick tenement, absolutely nondescript except for three cement gargoyles jutting out from just below the roof. In the gloom of approaching dusk, it was impossible to appreciate the detail of the sculptures, but from what Will could tell, they were as unique as they were incongruous. He wondered briefly about the building in its earlier days, proudly displaying its unusual art. Then he pictured himself in *his* earlier days, poised beside the operating table, ready to lead a team of technicians, nurses, and physicians into battle.

The foyer of the building was surprisingly clean, with mailboxes that were locked and a row of a dozen or so bells, identified by black plastic labels. The inside oak door was also secure.

'L. Henderson,' Watkins said. 'Here it is. Apartment six, just like the nice lady said.' He undid the handcuffs. 'Don't do or say anything stupid. Just follow my lead. I don't want to have to kill you, but if I do have to shoot, it will be to your spine first, then your knee, then your balls. Got that?'

He reached into his jacket pocket, assuring himself, it seemed, that his gun was positioned just the way he wanted it to be.

'Watkins, just remember,' Will said, 'your boss promised you wouldn't hurt this guy. He's an old man and he doesn't have any idea what this is all about. He was just in the wrong place at the wrong time.'

'Yeah, sure,' Watkins mumbled, pressing the bell.

Don't be home, Lionel! Will screamed silently. *Don't be home!* He knew it made little difference. Sooner or later, the dapper little man would return, and Watkins would be waiting. Still, Gold wanted the X-rays ASAP, and that was more than enough to root for any delay.

Watkins pressed the bell again. Nothing.

'I guess we'll just have to –'

There were sounds from inside the door, and moments later Lionel opened it. His gaze was drawn first to the huge black man, but quickly he fixed on Will. Recognition took only a second.

'Well, if it isn't the mystery man.'

'Will. My name is Will.'

'You all right? You don't look so good.'

'I'm fine, Lionel.'

'I never thought you'd get away from those Cobras. I'll bet they tried some sort of double cross, right?'

'Exactly.'

'That's just like them. Well, at first I didn't know how you'd find me, then I remembered telling you my name. Ain't too many Lionels around here.'

'My name's Dunn,' the killer cut in, 'Joe Dunn. You have a reward comin' to you for keeping that envelope safe.' He smiled his most disarming Buddha smile. 'You do have it, right?'

'Oh, I have it, all right.'

'Well, then, may we please come up and do some business?'

Lionel looked from one of them to the other, then erroneously decided they were no threat. He led them up a flight and into a little apartment that was as fastidiously kept as the man himself. The living room – an overstuffed sofa and easy chair set in front of an ancient console TV – was decorated mostly with framed photographs of various permutations of a large family. The dapper groom in the handsome wedding photo gracing the top of the TV was clearly Lionel, his arm around the waist of a lovely young woman who exuded charm and dignity. To one end of the living room was a closed door that almost certainly led to the bedroom. To the right was a neat, surprisingly large eat-in kitchen.

'Why don't we go into the kitchen?' Lionel said. 'I can make you both some tea if you like.'

'That would be f –'

'We'd really love to stay for tea, Mr. Henderson,' Watkins cut in, 'but we have a doctor waiting to see those X-rays.'

'Is that what's in that envelope? X-rays? I thought about bringing it to the police, but they haven't been much help to folks from this neighborhood, and the Cobras have a way of finding things out, so I decided that –'

'Please, sir,' Watkins pleaded, 'the envelope?'

Will wondered why Watkins wasn't speeding things up by flashing the reward money the way he had in the florist's shop. The only explanation he could come up with was disturbing – very disturbing. The big man needed to play the reward card to get through the door, but now that they were inside, there was no longer any need. The moment they had the envelope, the moment Watkins was sure the films were there, Lionel was a dead man – and quite possibly, Will was, too.

It was at that moment Will noticed the knife resting on the counter – a large carving knife, it appeared, although it was mostly obscured behind a plump tomato, a head of lettuce, and an as yet empty salad bowl. There was no sign that Watkins had seen it. Will felt his pulse accelerate as he forced his eyes away from the weapon and moved a nonchalant six inches to his right, cutting down Watkins's angle of sight.

'Like I told you, Mr. Dunn, I've got it,' Lionel was saying. He turned to Will. 'You sure this is okay? You really don't look so good.'

'No, no. I'm fine. Really I am. Ol' Joe here is my friend. The reason I don't look so good is that I've had like the flu. I haven't been sleeping too well lately.'

'Oh, okay. Well, you two just wait here.'

He headed over and opened the bedroom door.

'You're doin' fine,' Watkins whispered to Will, 'just fine.'

'Watkins, don't you hurt him.'

This time the giant didn't even bother to respond. Will risked a glance at the counter, gauging the best approach to the knife. If he even got the chance, it would be only fleeting. He was going to have to take it and move decisively. There was little doubt that both his and Lionel's lives were at stake.

'Here you go,' Lionel sang cheerfully. 'I hid it under my mattress in case the Cobras came callin'.'

'You did good,' Will said. Then he added, stalling as he tried to create even a momentary advantage, 'Joe, my friend, it's not that I don't trust Lionel, but you never know. One thing I *do* know is how angry our pal Mr. Gold can get when things aren't exactly the way he wants them. I think you'd be making a big mistake if you didn't let me examine the contents of that envelope to ensure that everything that's supposed to be inside is there.'

'Hey, wait a minute,' Lionel said. 'You can trust me. I never even looked to see what was inside that envelope.'

'It's not just you, Lionel. The Cobras could have messed with it, too. I know exactly what should be in there.'

Clearly nonplussed, Watkins hesitated, then decided that of his two choices, more trouble could result for him by not checking inside the envelope and bringing Gold a sheaf of cardboard. He gave Will a good look at the way his hand was thrust into his jacket pocket.

'Quickly,' he growled. 'We don't have much time.'

His pulse hammering, Will settled onto a chair and slid the thick stack of films out onto the table. It looked as if all of them were mammograms. At least one man had died because of them, and both he and Lionel Henderson were on the brink. *Why?*

He was about to spread the X-rays out when he saw the corner of a white envelope protruding from the stack. He covered it with one hand and, in almost the same motion, grasped half of the films with his other, allowing them to slip through his fingers and onto the floor between Lionel and Watkins.

'Clumsy bastard!' Watkins exclaimed.

'Now, listen here,' Lionel said, 'Cussing is not allowed in my *home*.'

He glared at Watkins, then dropped to his knees and began gathering up the glossy X-rays. They had scattered over quite an area and were awkward for him to handle. Watkins reflexively bent over and grabbed a few before sitting up and warily turning his attention back to Will. But during those precious seconds when the killer's attention was diverted, Will pulled the business-size envelope out, folded it in half with one hand, and stuffed it into his pants pocket.

'Come on,' Watkins growled.

'Sorry. Sorry, Joe. Thanks, Lionel.'

'No problem. No problem. Eighty-one and I can still get down and do my own floors. But I can't believe you suspected I might have messed with the stuff in that envelope. I never even looked to see what was in there.'

'Sorry,' Will said.

'Dammit, Grant, let's go. Are they all there or not?'

There was a small wall lamp tacked up just to Will's left. Once the shade was removed, the light, though not great for a detailed reading of the mammograms, was adequate. Will quickly arranged the films in stacks by patient. There were ten different patient names altogether. Grace Davis was one of them. Even though the cancer was there in the upper outer quadrant of her left breast, the absence of a BB assured him the film wasn't hers. The next two sets also showed cancers, one in the right upper outer quadrant, and the other a rather large mass just lateral to the right nipple, with bright white flecks of calcium throughout – often an ominous sign. The fourth stack of films held the key. The name on those X-rays was different from the patient of stack three, but the cancer was identical. Will was absolutely certain of it. Same location, same size, same pattern of calcium deposition. In fact, even the pattern of the blood vessels and other markers in the rest of both breasts were the same.

Watkins shifted edgily and jerked his head in a demand that Will hurry up.

Stack five was identical to Grace's films. In all, although the mammograms were labeled with ten different patients' names, dates, and clinic numbers, there were actually five identical pairs of films. Will suspected that the variation in the films coincided with the size and shape of the patients' breasts. He also began suspecting something else – that none of the X-rays actually belonged to the women whose names were on them. If he was right about those two possibilities, a third one, sickening almost beyond imagination, seemed quite likely, as well. None of these women, all of whom were probably treated for cancer at the Excelsius clinic, actually had the disease.

Will slumped back in his chair, trying to get his mind around what he was seeing. One thing seemed certain: As with everything involving the Excelsius HMO, at the root of the films and the deception, one way or another, was money. Watkins stood.

'That's it,' he said. 'Are there any problems, or are these all the X-rays?'

'No, no problems,' Will replied.

'So,' Lionel said, 'there's a reward in it for me, is there?'

Watkins turned toward the little man and, in what seemed like slow motion, Will could see what was about to happen. There would be no gunshot; no telltale bullet hole in Lionel's body; no suspicion of foul play; no police questioning neighbors and others such as Carol in the flower shop. Watkins was going to do this with his hands. In the end, there would only be a frail old man dead at the bottom of the stairs, his neck broken by the tragic fall.

Watkins had reached the bewildered Lionel and was raising his huge hands toward the man's neck when Will moved. With one step he was at the counter, grasping the carving knife. Before Watkins could effectively react to the movement behind him, Will leapt at him, locking his palm under Watkins's chin. On his tiptoes, powered by a massive adrenaline rush, Will yanked back with all his strength and pressed the blade of the knife firmly against the giant's exposed throat.

'Move and I'll kill you!' he snapped, tightening his grip even as he felt the enormous power of the man he was trying to hold in place. 'I know exactly how to do this, Watkins. Believe me, I do. One slice. That's all. It's a terrible way to die.'

He added some pressure for emphasis and felt the killer wince as the blade broke skin.

'What in the heck are you doing?' Lionel cried.

Watkins's body stiffened. For an eternal few seconds, Will could sense him sorting out the odds. Then the tension in his body lessened.

'You're crazy,' he said.

'The gun. Ease it out of your pocket and drop it on the floor.'

Muttering threats and obscenities, Watkins did as he was ordered.

'You're signing your girlfriend's death warrant,' he said.

'Lionel, get out of here now,' Will ordered. 'Don't tell anyone; don't go to the police. Just get out of here, get off the street, and don't come back for two hours. Watkins, give him your wallet... Now! ... Lionel, take all the money in it. You've earned it. Now, get out. Quickly!'

The little man hesitated, then took the stack of bills from Watkins's wallet, grabbed a jacket from the back of a chair, and hurried out of the apartment.

Watkins slowly, dramatically lifted his hand and checked his watch.

'You really fucked up, asshole,' he said, careful not to move any further against the knife. 'I'm five minutes late. Your little honey's probably dead already.'

'Call Gold,' Will said.

'No way.'

Will tightened his grip across Watkins's chin, but this time the killer didn't react at all.

'I said call in!'

'Drop the knife.'

At that instant, Watkins's cell phone began ringing.

'Answer it.'

Watkins laughed derisively. Another ring.

'Five rings and the recording starts,' he managed.

Three.

Will stepped back and threw the carving knife to the floor.

Grinning, Watkins flipped on his phone.

'Sorry, Mr. Gold. We were getting the envelope and I lost track of the time. No, he's right here. He had a little accident and banged his face, but he'll be all right... Yessir. I'll bring him. We'll be back soon. No problem. He's been acting up some, but I know he'll behave from now on.'

Watkins flipped the phone shut and dropped it in his pocket. Then, without warning, he swung from his hip, smashing Will flush in the face. Will heard his cheekbone snap an instant before the pain exploded from it. He was sputtering on a gush of blood down his nose and throat before he hit the floor.

Chapter 34

Discipline ... Discipline ... Don't move ... Not a flicker ... Not a twitch ... Breathe in ... Hold it ... Hold it ... Breathe out ... Hark, the herald angels sing, glory to the newborn king ... Discipline ... Discipline...

For most of a year during college, Patty and one of her roommates had taken yoga classes together. They had both dropped out, partly because of the pressures of class work, but also because each had met a man.

What in the hell was his name? she wondered now. He was supposed to have been The One. Now she couldn't even remember his name. Why hadn't she stayed with yoga?

Breathe in ... Hold it ... Hold it ... Breathe out ... Slowly ... Slowly ... Don't move ... Don't move ...

At least an hour had passed since Will was sent off with the man named Watkins – probably closer to two. Boyd Halliday and Marshall Gold had departed just a few minutes after that for an important session with their lawyer and hadn't returned. Before they left, they had said enough for her to know that tomorrow at ten there was a meeting scheduled at which the Excelsius takeover of several companies would be completed. The new conglomerate, still to be called Excelsius Health, with Halliday as CEO, would instantly be among the largest health-care providers in the east, if not in the country. Power and money. The managed-care killings, believed by almost everyone to be about revenge and retribution, had never been about anything except power and money. Now, unless she or Will could do something, the body count of those sacrificed on that altar was about to rise.

Patty had begun experiencing momentary glimmers of consciousness for a while before she was taken from the ICU, but it wasn't until she was being transferred from her bed to the stretcher that she had started to come around on all levels. By the time she was secured inside the ambulance, the conversations around her were increasingly penetrating the darkness that had enveloped her mind. In snatches, she heard about her brain surgery and her persistent coma. Some sort of a diversion – maybe a fire – had been set off in the hospital solely for the purpose of getting her out of there. She had no idea where she was being taken, or why, but what she did hear told her that the best she could do was to remain still – absolutely still.

As the ambulance ride wore on, beneath the patches that covered her eyes, she opened and closed her lids. Then, carefully, concealed by the sheet that was draped over her, she tested her arms and legs. From what she could tell, everything was working. But she also knew of the phantom pains of amputees and the phantom movements of paralyzed limbs in stroke and spinal-cord victims.

Breathe in ... Hold it... Hold it ... Breathe out ...

Since Will and the others had gone, she had been alone with the torturer Krause – the man Gold had referred to as the good doctor. He was seated toward the door, maybe ten or fifteen feet from where she lay. Several times he had come over and stood beside her, breathing heavily and, she sensed, touching himself. First it was just a few seconds at a time, then a minute, then even more.

Good, she thought, stoking her anger, *the more you get turned on, the better. Creep.*

As the visits to her stretcher became longer, they also became more frequent. It was as if Krause was battling his own instincts – and losing. Each time Patty tried, through the man's breathing and the sound of his movement, to create a mental picture of him and to focus in on his position and posture. She felt certain from his footfall and at what height she placed his mouth that he was slightly built and not very tall. Finally, perhaps unable to control himself any longer, the good doctor pulled her sheet down below her breasts and stood by her shoulder, staring down at her. She was wearing some sort of hospital pajamas, or perhaps a set of surgical scrubs, but still she felt naked, exposed, and vulnerable.

'How beautiful you are... How beautiful.'

His breath reeked of cigarettes and garlic. His voice was raspy and rather high-pitched. She honed in on the image of a very thin, wiry man, maybe five-six or seven, and for no objective reason whatsoever, decided that he fancied himself an intellectual and a poet.

Krause replaced the sheet, and Patty silently sighed relief. He had stopped short of uncovering her hands and the loose IV tubing that rested beneath them. The clear plastic tube was the only accessible weapon she had, but applied quickly and with the proper leverage, she felt it might be enough. The green polystyrene oxygen tubing was a bit thicker, with perhaps less give, but it would be impossible to get at without lifting her arms and risking the loss of the small advantage surprise was going to give her.

Strangulation, from the front and back, was a maneuver they had studied at the academy, mostly so that they could learn how to defend themselves against it. She had never paid that much attention to technique when she was the attacker. Now she wished she had. It frightened her that any move she made would have to be done with the patches covering her eyes, but she sensed, right or wrong, that this unpleasant little man was physically weaker than Gold or Watkins, or even Halliday. If she was going to defeat any one of them, he was the best bet, and if he gave her the chance, she was going to take it.

She had barely completed the thought when he was back. Again the sheet went down. This time, after muttering how beautiful she was, he bent down and kissed her lightly on the lips, at the same time setting his hand on her breast. It was all she could do to keep from cringing. Instead, her resolve grew. Krause was testing now, perhaps seeing how much he could get away with without waking her up, perhaps fearful of being caught by Gold or Halliday should he linger too long. However, excitement and his perverse nature clearly had a grip on him.

Not knowing whether he was watching her or not, Patty had not yet dared to move enough to wrap the IV tubing around her hands. If she tried and he was looking at her, it was all over. Still, she felt she was running out of time. She had to sense the opportunity and make her move.

'You're so beautiful,' he was whispering again, increasing the pressure on her breast. 'Just so beautiful.'

His vocabulary was woefully limited, Patty noted, distracting herself from being touched by him. If he *was* a poet, he was a very bad one.

Finally, after what seemed an eternity, Krause lifted his hand from her breast and again drew the sheet up. She listened to his heavy breathing and envisioned him standing there, a hand down his pants, fondling himself. Then she heard the scuffing of his shoes as he turned away from her to return to his chair. For a few precious seconds, his back would be to her. He was too stimulated to keep away for long. When he returned, she had to be ready. It had to be now.

Keeping her movements minimal, she located the IV tubing, gripped it, and using quick, minute circles, wound it around each hand. The polystyrene garrote she had created, nearly two feet long,

291

rested across the tops of her thighs. Now she had to pray that Krause's lecherous ambitions remained above her waist. Across the room, from near the door, she could hear him breathing, clearing his throat, and shifting in his chair. She tried envisioning his movements as she rehearsed her own in her mind.

Many times since joining the force she had asked herself whether she was capable of shooting to kill in order to protect herself or others. Always, the answer had been yes, but in the scenarios she created, firing her weapon to kill had always been reflex and instinctive. This time, the kill would be premeditated, deliberate, and at close range, and once she was committed, there could be no hesitation, no turning back. She tested the strength in her arms by pressing them tightly against her sides while clenching and unclenching her fists. Then she continued her deep breathing, allowing images of Gold's victims and their families to flow through her thoughts and keep her still.

Several minutes passed. Krause's breathing seemed more rapid now. Was he masturbating? He began humming to himself – a bizarre, tuneless incantation that Patty found quite chilling.

Come on! ... Come on!

Finally, he stood up and returned to her.

'Oh, baby, you are so beautiful,' he whispered. 'So beautiful and all mine.'

He lowered the sheet to her waist and pulled her top up above her breasts. She sensed him devouring her with his eyes. Then she felt the heat of his breath as once again he bent down and set his lips on hers. In seconds he would put his hand on her breasts again. Getting the tubing past his arm and around his neck would be much more difficult. It had to be now – right now!

She drew her hands up clear of the sheet. Then, just as Krause was reacting to the maneuver, she swept the tubing around his neck and pulled his face down against her breastbone, tightening the loop with all her strength. As she had envisioned, holding him tightly against her reduced what he could do with his arms. He flailed at her face but was unable to land a blow with any real force behind it. The patches were torn from her eyes, sending a painful blast of light through her widely dilated pupils. One random swing hit directly on the incision and bone flap on the side of her skull. She cried out, but intensified her grip even more. The tubing felt as if it was going to tear through her palms, but she battled the pain and pulled even harder. It strengthened her to realize Krause hadn't uttered a sound. His airway was completely occluded, as were his carotid arteries.

Harder ... Harder ... Don't let up no matter what... Don't let up.

The blinding light was rapidly giving way to movement and color. She could see his jet-black hair, then one blurry ear, then her own hand, blanched and bloodless with the effort of killing him. Krause struggled to straighten up, but instead lurched to one side and fell onto his back on the floor. Patty was pulled off the stretcher and landed heavily on top of him. The tension in her grip held. Instantly, what little leverage he had vanished. His arms went limp and flopped to the wooden floor.

Patty was looking directly into the torturer's bulging, bloodshot eyes when he died. She heard, then smelled, then felt his bladder and bowels give way. The tension in his body ceased. His jaw went slack, and a trickle of blood emerged from the corner of his mouth. Still, she maintained her grip on the tubing, holding fast until she could no longer bear the throbbing in her hands and arms.

Ignoring as best she could the shell bursts going off in her skull and the stench of violent death, she rolled off Krause's corpse and lay on the floor nearby, gasping for air. Finally, she propped herself up unsteadily on one elbow and took her first careful look at the man she had just killed. If she was feeling any remorse at that moment, any at all, she certainly couldn't identify it as such. Krause had a narrow, rodent-like face, with burned-out acne and irregular, cigarette-stained teeth. His blood-red eyes still bulged almost out of their sockets.

'Beautiful,' Patty muttered. 'Just beautiful.'

With difficulty she grasped the frame of the stretcher and hauled herself upright. Her legs held her there, but not without some conscious effort. Across the room was the chair from which Krause had so vigilantly guarded her – high-backed with a caned seat and no arms. There was a copy of *Penthouse* on the floor beside it, along with a glass half-filled with what looked like Coke. Draped across the back of the chair was a black sports coat, and hanging over the coat, nearly invisible in its black shoulder holster, was a gun. Suddenly energized, she hurried over. It was a Colt .38 Special – reliable, but with a bit less stopping power than she would have liked. Still, in her hand and at close quarters, it was certainly enough.

Expertly, Patty flipped the cylinder open and assured herself that the six chambers were full. Then, hefting the revolver in her hand, she managed a thin, bitter smile. The odds on their making it out of this mess had just shortened considerably.

★   ★   ★

293

Patty checked the windows and satisfied herself that without tools, there was no way out of the room except the door. Through the dense overcast, the gray afternoon light was fading. Four-thirty, she guessed, maybe five. Boyd Halliday would probably be gone by now, hurrying home to join his wife at the dinner party they were throwing for their new business associates. She had heard stories of managed-care CEOs with villas in Majorca and stables of rare antique cars. What sort of place did Halliday live in, she wondered. Would any amount of money, any amount of power, ever be enough for him? She scanned the buildings and grounds outside, trying without success to get some sense of where the farm might be located.

With Will unaccounted for and no definite idea of the firepower beyond the door, she decided that her best chance was to stay in the room and wait. The odor emanating from the body on the floor was testing that decision, but she knew that she held the advantage so long as the first person to arrive could be induced to move through the doorway and into the room – especially if that person was Marshall Gold.

The aromatic Dr. Krause was quite literally dead weight. She gave thought to somehow pulling him up onto the stretcher, covering him with a sheet, and then flattening herself against the wall behind the door. Quickly, though, she passed on the notion of hauling him up that far as a physical impossibility. Instead, staying tensed for the slightest noise outside the door, she rolled the body on its side and left it where it was. Next, she brought the chair over, and laid it on its side, adjusting Krause into a sitting position against it. Using the oxygen, IV, and catheter drainage tubing, and Krause's belt, she lashed the body to the chair. Surprised and utterly grateful that the chair legs didn't shatter, she hoisted her creation upright with surprising ease and dragged it to a spot about ten feet in from the door, facing the stretcher.

With the good doctor's sports jacket draped over the back of the chair, the illusion was nearly complete, and quite good if she did say so. It became even better when she added the finishing touch of the small table that stood near the ratty mattress she assumed was Will's bed. Setting Krause's arm at a jaunty angle on the top, she wrapped his fingers around the half-finished glass of Coke. The position also helped brace the body against toppling over prematurely.

'Voilà!' she whispered proudly. 'C'est si bon.'

The lure, calculated to draw her first visitor at least several steps into the room, was in place. There was little she could do with the

294

stretcher other than to put the thin pillow under the sheet, but by the time anyone got that far, hopefully she would be in charge.

The door to the room opened inward. Patty checked Krause one last time, then positioned herself against the wall so that it would swing toward then past her. The extra half second might make a difference. Now there was nothing to do but wait. Inside her head there seemed to be a serious synergy between her concussion and the massive pounding of her heart created by her battle with Krause. She was feeling vague and sluggish one moment, sharp and focused the next.

Images of her father and of Will, of Lieutenant Court and Brasco, of Marshall Gold's victims and their families flowed through her mind as she crouched on one knee and waited. It was going to be over soon, she told each of them – very soon. Finally, she heard footsteps outside the door. An instant later, it swung open and Marshall Gold strode into the room.

'So, Doc,' he said cheerfully, 'how's our prize patient?'

He reached Krause's side and actually touched the corpse on the shoulder before realizing that the stretcher was empty. At the same moment, the body and chair toppled over, taking the table and Coke with them. The glass shattered on the floor.

'Welcome back, Mr. Gold,' Patty said, standing and kicking the door shut. 'Keep your hands where I can see them.'

Patty was totally unprepared for Gold's reaction. Without a moment's hesitation and with a furious bellow, he charged her. Teeth bared, he covered half the distance between them with a single step and launched himself, arms outstretched, at her head. His hands slammed ferociously against her shoulders, driving her backward and off her feet. She was in midair, almost parallel to the floor, when she heard a shot. She landed heavily on her back, air exploding from her lungs. Her head snapped against the polished wood with stunning force, sending an explosion of white light through her brain.

She lay there dazed, unable even to lift her arm to fire, helpless to keep Gold from finishing the attack. Then she realized he was screaming.

'You bitch! You fucking bitch! Goddammit! Oh, shit! My leg! You bitch, you bitch!'

Desperately, he grabbed her ankle, but Patty kicked at him and pulled free easily. His face, twisted with rage, was ashen. He was clutching at a spot just above his right knee. Blood was seeping between his fingers.

Bone, Patty thought. The shot had to have shattered his femur. She pushed herself out of his reach and lay there, propped on one elbow, breathing heavily.

'Next time I'm going to aim,' she said.

It was a while before the dizziness and the pounding in Patty's head allowed her to move. During that time, she twice thought she saw Gold's hand drift toward his left ankle. Her eyes riveted on him, her revolver aimed at his mid-chest, she crawled around to his feet and felt up inside his pant legs. Even though she tried to be gentle on the right, he cried out with even the slightest movement. His gun, a slender .9mm Glock, was strapped just below his calf on the left. She removed the bullets from the Colt, then sent them and the revolver skidding across the floor to the far end of the room. Now, with the Glock, she had some serious firepower. Warily, she patted Gold down, even though there was precious little else he could have hidden beneath his turtleneck and form-fitting slacks.

He seemed to have regained some composure, although the pallor around his mouth said that he was in some degree of early shock.

'Who else is in the house?' she demanded.

'Go fuck yourself.'

'Those are really nice shoes. How about I just tap that right one on the sole?'

'Why not? You asshole cops are no better than Krause there, anyhow. Go ahead. Do it, bitch.'

Jarred by Gold's words, Patty stood up and stepped back, glaring down at the man who had brought so much terrible pain to so many.

'Not tonight,' she said softly.

She moved cautiously to the door and listened. If anyone else had been in the house, surely they would have reacted to the gunshot. All she had to do now was find a phone and call 911. Was there danger in leaving Gold here unguarded? It would take a hell of an actor to fake the signs of early shock, but if he were acting and the bullet hadn't shattered his femur, there was plenty of danger. At that moment, from somewhere nearby, a door opened and closed. Moments later, a man called out Gold's name.

'Mr. Gold. Mr. Gold, we're back. I have the package. I'll bring our friend into the blue room.'

Watkins!

Patty pushed the door closed and again flattened herself against the wall.

'One word, Gold,' she whispered fiercely, 'one sound, and I'll put a bullet into your face. I swear I will.'

'Fuck you,' Gold moaned, but there was little force behind the words.

The door opened and Will, his wrists handcuffed and a blood-soaked pillowcase over his head, was shoved rudely onto the floor.

'Get in there, jerk,' Watkins said, stepping in after him, his boot drawn back, poised to land a kick.

Patty came at him from behind and jammed the Glock against the base of Watkins's skull.

'Police. Down on your knees!' she snapped. 'Put your hands on your head or I'll blow it off. Now! I mean it, dammit!'

In slow motion, the giant complied.

Will pulled the pillowcase off. His face was a bloody mask, his left eye swollen shut. Blood was still oozing from his misshapen nose.

'He's got a gun in his right jacket pocket,' he said thickly. 'The keys to these are in his pants pocket.'

Keeping the revolver in contact with Watkins's skull, Patty pulled his jacket off and threw it aside. Then she forced him onto his belly, had him retrieve the key, and helped Will remove the manacles.

'Hands behind your back! Will, can you put those on him?'

'I can do anything you want,' he said, looking from Krause to Gold and back. 'Bad things happen to people who don't.' He snapped the handcuffs onto Watkins. 'I think I'll swallow this key and bring you a week's worth of my dung so you can look for it.'

He dropped it into his pocket.

'Do you need help right away?' Patty asked.

'My cheekbone is broken and I'm a little dizzy, and I can't see so good out of this eye, but I'm not in any immediate trouble. Patty, I can't believe you pulled this off.'

'I don't think I've told you yet, but I have quite a nasty temper.'

'I don't think I'll have much trouble remembering that.'

'Find a phone and call nine-one-one. Take Watkins's gun just in case. Make sure the safety's off and don't shoot yourself by mistake.'

Will retrieved the pistol, had her check that he had released the safety, and headed off. Patty surveyed the human wreckage around her – one handcuffed, one disabled, one dead. What would Tommy Moriarity say if he could see her now? Probably that she had violated some protocol or procedure and had just lucked out. She smiled. At least there'll be photos of the scene from the crime-lab people. Maybe she could have one matted and framed for Father's Day.

She was still smiling a few minutes later when Will returned. He stopped in the doorway, staring at her strangely, not moving or speaking.

'Will, are you okay?' she asked. 'Did you make the call?'

Will stepped into the room, followed immediately by his partner, Susan Hollister, her hair still wet from the shower. The powerful automatic weapon held expertly in her right hand was aimed directly at Patty's heart.

Chapter 35

'Sit down, you stupid bitch! Right there! Now, or I swear I'll just blow you apart! Did she do this, honey? Did she do this to you? God but this room stinks. Krause? Is that smell from Krause?'

Not even in the most critical surgical situations had Will ever seen anything approaching such fire in his partner. There was a pressure to her speech and a detached, chilling wildness in her eyes that left no doubt she would carry out any threat instantly and without remorse. She knelt next to Marshall Gold, stroking his face and hair with her left hand while keeping her submachine gun leveled at Patty with the other. Gold had quieted down considerably, but Will wondered if his demeanor might be a reflection of persistent, even worsening shock. He suspected Susan sensed the same thing.

'Will, get over here and tear off his pants leg,' she ordered. 'Hurry, or I'll cut your girlfriend in half.'

She punctuated the order with a burst of bullets that splintered the floor between Patty's legs. One actually grazed her. Blood instantly began seeping through a rent in her pajamas, just below the knee. Will started moving to help her, but she stopped him with a raised hand.

'I'm okay, Will,' she said, her voice meek and whiny. 'Just do whatever she says.'

Will remembered the fearlessness with which Patty had dealt with the two toughs by Steele's Pond, and could only imagine how, in her condition, she had managed to take out both Krause and Gold. Sounding fearful and subdued at this moment was purposeful. He was certain of it. Patty knew, as did he, that there was no chance either of them would be allowed to live. In truth, there never had been. She was sizing up both Susan and the situation, searching for an opening – any kind of an opening – that would give them a chance at the gun.

The best he could do to help was to keep Susan as calm as possible and make himself essential by helping to stabilize Gold. When the moment was right, he would try to heighten the tension and create chaos in the room. At that point, he and Patty would have only seconds for some sort of coordinated, unscripted attack before one or both of them were dead. He inserted two undamaged fingers into the bullet hole in Gold's trousers and, with difficulty, ripped the leg off. Gold, still awake though definitely slowed, moaned in pain at even the slightest movement.

'Careful, Will,' Susan warned. 'You and I both know you're not that clumsy.'

'That's when my fractured cheekbone isn't throbbing and I have all my fingernails.' Will showed her the bandages.

Gold's leg looked bad – very bad. There was a massive amount of swelling in the thigh beneath the wound – a unit of blood, Will guessed, possibly even two. Almost certainly the femur had been shattered, and the femoral artery had probably been severed, as well.

'Use his belt. Put a tourniquet on.'

'Rather than jostle him any more than necessary, I'll use mine... So, it was you and Gold all the time. And here I thought you were just a mild-mannered surgeon.'

Susan laughed.

'Compared to the life I've led, surgery has been a big yawn. Over the last six years this man has taught me things and taken me places surgery never could.'

'You're the one who sabotaged my shoes.'

'I had to. Otherwise you would have operated on that Davis woman, and we just couldn't have that.'

'Because I would have discovered that she didn't have any breast cancer at all. I get it now.'

'We had a bit of a problem because we had developed you so carefully as our public spokesman, but something had to be done quickly to get you out of the OR. Killing you would have been so messy and so final, and would have started people wondering if they were wrong about you and the Society and the managed-care killer all being on the same side.'

'So, after you crucified me and took the Davis case back, you threatened Jim Katz to try and get me reinstated at work.'

'As long as the attention was diverted from Excelsius, you were serving your purpose. Your pal the Law Doctor actually helped us out by planting those shoes in that ER closet.'

'He planted them?'

'Of course. What kind of a dummy do you take me for? I would never have just left your Chuck Taylors lying around the hospital. The lawyer made a calculated guess about how we got the fentanyl into you, and he guessed right. I'm sure the insoles of those shoes will turn out to be loaded with fentanyl. It's not that hard to get.'

Will couldn't help but smile. Augie realized that the only one who could prove he had hidden a pair of counterfeit, fentanyl-soaked sneakers in the ER was the person who had actually framed Will. The man had rolled the dice for him with both his law and medicine careers at stake, and he had won.

'So, how many women got treated for breast cancer they didn't have?'

'Enough to force Steadfast Health into selling out to us. They were paying over a hundred thousand a case. With more and more women getting breast cancer these days, it wasn't hard. Besides, we had a one hundred percent cure rate.'

'But Halliday couldn't do that with every other company he wanted to take over.'

'No. It was a brilliant idea that worked, but we needed to develop a more ... *direct* method.'

'Jesus. Listen, Susan, this belt isn't tightening enough. He's still bleeding. I suspect his femoral artery's torn. If so, this leg's in trouble. *He's* in trouble. I think we should use that IV tubing tied around Krause over there, and maybe break off the leg of the chair to twist it tight. Rope would be even better. He's really getting shocky. You've got to get him to the hospital.'

'Watkins, get up and help us,' Susan ordered. 'My medical bag is in the trunk of my car. Get the bag and also some rope. And I need something like a tire iron to tighten the tourniquet.'

'Look at me, Dr. Hollister. I'm handcuffed. He's got the key in his pocket.'

'Will, unlock his cuffs... Now!'

Susan swung her machine gun toward him, and Will saw Patty instantly change her stance so that one leg was beneath her now, ready to shove off. It was time to raise the ante. Without thinking twice about it, he pulled the key from his pocket and swallowed it.

'I told him I was going to do that,' Will said lightly, hoping to lessen Susan's anger and the tension in her index finger.

'God damn you!' she shrieked, her cheeks crimson.

From the corner of his eye, Will saw Patty shift again.

'Don't worry, Dr. Hollister,' Watkins said. 'I've got another key in my room, in the drawer right by the bed. I can get it.'

The giant began struggling awkwardly to his feet, lost his balance, and tumbled heavily onto his side. Another distraction. It had to be now. As Watkins was righting himself, Will kneed Gold's thigh at exactly the fracture point. The killer bellowed with pain and took an ineffectual, floppy swing at Will. Reflexively, Susan turned toward them. In that instant, Patty sprang forward, viciously swinging her bare foot upward in a punting motion against Susan's wrist. The machine gun flew out of Susan's hands and landed at the base of the wall, a dozen feet away. Will, who was on one knee, was trying to stand when Watkins slammed into him like a semi, driving him back against the wall. Powered by adrenaline, Will hammered at the man with his fists and feet and managed to pull himself upright.

Patty followed her kick by trying to dive over Susan toward the gun, but the surgeon moved with the quickness of a gymnast, striking her with a backhand fist flush against her skull flap, while in the same motion spinning and lunging toward her weapon. Patty cried out from the blow and dropped to her side. Dazed, she remained composed enough to grab on to one of Susan's legs. Absorbing kicks to her face and chest, she hung on for a few precious seconds, but there was no way she could beat the woman to where the machine gun lay.

'Run, Will!' she shouted, losing her hold and rolling over and over toward the open door. 'Run!'

Will grabbed her by the arm as he raced past and dragged her to her feet and through the doorway. They were sprinting down a long corridor toward what seemed to be the back of the house when they heard a burst of gunfire from behind them. Will risked a glance over his shoulder. Susan had fired wildly from inside the room and hadn't yet reached the hallway.

'Straight ahead,' Patty gasped, pointing to a windowed doorway that led outside.

They charged past a richly appointed conference room and a vast, gleaming, brilliantly lit kitchen. Neither held any hope of protection or concealment. Getting outside was their only chance. Will dropped back a step to allow Patty to reach the door first. If only one of them was going to make it, he wanted it to be her.

Please don't be locked. Please ...

Patty had already considered the possibility. With her left hand, she slid the dead-bolt lock aside and simultaneously pulled open the door with her right. The aluminum storm door, with a full pane of glass, was also locked. Without hesitation, she drove her knee and forearm into the pane, shattering it outward onto a small unlit porch.

'Stay low!' she screamed.

Without hesitating, she stepped onto the shards of glass with her bare right foot, then leapt over three stairs and onto the lawn, finishing with a perfectly executed roll. It was an incredibly athletic move, and not one Will had any chance of duplicating. Instead, he pulled the inside door nearly closed behind him and was carefully stepping through the storm-door frame when a staccato of bullets snapped into the wood. One of them ripped into the muscle overlying his right hip. He fought through the intensely burning pain and drove ahead. Susan had to be wondering whether she could chance leaving her lover to go after them, or whether any risk was worth taking to keep them from getting off the farm alive. The longer they could keep moving, the more they could increase her indecision, the less effective she was going to be.

By the time he reached Patty, she was braced against a tree, pulling a two-inch-long stiletto of glass from the sole of her foot. He moved to help, but she waved him off, then raced with him toward the barn. The night was black and raw, the grass unpleasantly cold and slick, and she was barefoot and battered. Still she ran. It was as if by example she was willing him not to be hesitant or afraid.

Ignoring the searing in his hip, he hobbled along beside her until they had rounded the small corral and flattened themselves against the far side of the barn. Clouds of their breath hung in the chilly blackness as they gasped for air. Ahead and to the left of them, all was dark and quiet, but to their right, not too far away, were the lights of another house.

'What... happened ... to your leg?' Patty asked between breaths.

Will needed several seconds before he could answer.

'My hip ... well, my butt really ... I took a bullet there ... for the home team.'

Patty squeezed his arm.

'Be tough.'

'That was ... amazing what you ... did back there. Does your ... foot hurt ... badly?'

'It'll hold me.' Patty inched back to the corner of the barn and

302

peered around it. 'She's out there, just beginning to move this way.'

'I guess she decided that getting us is more important than staying with Marshall.'

'That choice is a no-brainer. If we get away, life as they have known it will be over.'

'Let's hope so. What do you think that house is over there?'

'Probably belongs to the farmer who actually works this place.'

'Maybe he doesn't know what his landlord does when he's not looking like a respectable health-care provider.'

'Maybe. It's either go there or head across the fields and try to find a way out of here.' Patty risked a second look around the corner of the barn. 'Watkins is with her now. No handcuffs. We've really got to move.'

'You've got to take my sneakers.'

'I don't –'

'No argument!'

She sighed and did as he insisted, muttering about clownshoes. Moments later, she shuddered and then began to shiver intensely. Will held her, and for a few seconds she allowed him to. Then she pulled away.

'If I had known we were actually going to make it out of that room,' he said, 'I would never have taken my jacket off. Hopefully the people in that house over there will help us out. Your hands are like ice.'

'They're okay. My head's the problem. It's like a kangaroo's in there, bouncing through a minefield, setting off explosions.'

'That settles it. Let's go meet the farmer.'

Much of their path to the house was obstructed from their pursuers by the barn. Over the final twenty-five open yards, they kept low and moved steadily ahead until they were flattened against the house. In the distance they could still hear faint snatches of Susan's voice and see the beam of a flashlight piercing the night. They turned and were peering through the window into a small, cluttered kitchen where a grizzled man in his fifties sat at the table in overalls and a narrow-strap T-shirt, drinking beer from a bottle and watching a small countertop TV. Beside him, a disheveled, silver-haired woman sat in a wheelchair, a beer in the cup holder by her right hand.

'American Gothic,' Will whispered. 'They look friendly enough. I think we should go in.'

'I don't know.'

'Do you have any other ideas?'

'We've got to get away from here quickly, or get inside and make a nine-one-one call.'

'I think those two will be able to help us. I'm a great judge of character by people's faces.'

At that moment, they heard the phone start ringing inside.

'Shit!' Patty whispered.

The farmer's conversation lasted only a few seconds. He hurried out of the kitchen and returned with a shotgun, which he held on to as he pulled on a red-and-black-checked hunting jacket, and a rifle, which he handed to his invalid wife.

'I forgot to add that sometimes I'm a *lousy* judge of character,' Will said.

They stayed pressed into the shadows and worked their way to the far end of the house. There was a broad expanse of fields, perhaps a quarter mile or more, between them and the forest.

'We've got to try it,' Will whispered.

At that moment, the farmer, shotgun at the ready, clunked across the back landing and made his way into the field a short distance from where they were standing. The move effectively cut them off from any kind of race to the woods.

'Now what?' Will asked.

They were peering back at the barn, expecting any instant to see Susan and Watkins come around the corral and the other corner, cutting them off even further from any escape.

'We have one chance,' Patty said.

'What?'

'The tractor. Did you see it? Just past the barn. If we can somehow get around that side of the barn and onto it, we can try and drive it around the house and down the drive.'

'What about the key?'

'People always leave the key in tractors, especially on a place as isolated as this one. And if there's no key, I'd be surprised if I couldn't hot-wire it.'

'Of course. How stupid of me not to think that you knew how to hot-wire a tractor. You are really a remarkable piece of work, do you know that?'

'Right now I'm a freezing cold, miserable piece of work. Let's head back to the barn before Susan and Monstro show up. From there, maybe we can make a run at the tractor. If they leave the barn unguarded, maybe you can even find a pair of boots inside.'

'My feet are okay for the moment.'

They moved back along the shadows, shielded from the farmer by the house and from Susan and Watkins by the barn. Just a dozen or so yards ahead, washed faintly in some of the light from the old farmhouse, they could make out a split-rail fence enclosing a fairly large corral, which featured a water trough and filled hay bin. Patty put a finger to her lips and motioned in that direction. Seconds later they were crouching by the fence. Initially, Will thought the corral was empty, but then he noticed four cows standing huddled together at the far end.

'We should cut through,' Will whispered.

'You're barefoot.'

'I've got socks on. Besides, I've stepped in shit before.'

'You really are a piece of work.'

'Maybe it's contagious.'

They hunched down and carefully slid between the middle and highest railing into the corral. For the moment, at least, they were hidden from the barn by the shoulder-high hay bin.

'Patty, look! Talk about American Gothic.'

Propped against the far side of the bin, nearly as long as the bin was high, was a pitchfork. Just as Will seized the handle, they heard Susan's voice, close enough to make out her words. She had come around the side of the barn and seemed to be headed directly toward them. With the submachine gun pointing their way, she was speaking on a cell phone as she moved cautiously forward.

'Quick, over there,' Patty ordered, pointing to the cows.

Keeping low enough to be partially screened by the fence, they hurried across to the massive animals and worked their way among them. There was some slight, irritated movement from the beasts, but otherwise no reaction to the intrusion. Susan had reached the far corner of the corral, no more than thirty feet away.

'Watkins, I don't see anything out here,' she was saying. 'Just cows. You watch the front of the barn. Call Sanderson and tell him it's his ass if they get past him. Then call your people and tell them to get the hell out here now! Those two are still around here someplace. I'm positive of it. I'm going in to check on Marsh and get another flashlight. I'll be right out. Stay sharp.'

Will pressed his face against the cow's flank and patted her silently as she shifted nervously from one foot to another.

Easy, Bossie, easy does it. Come on, Hollister, leave. Leave!

He didn't dare to raise up and look. To his right, Patty seemed completely concealed between two cows. An endless minute passed. *Is*

Susan still there? Dammit, he never should have told her about Newcomber. He was so certain Gordo was behind everything that he just didn't think things through.

Finally, moving with exquisite slowness, Patty crouched down, peered out under the cow to where Susan had been, and then gave him a thumbs-up sign. They crossed the corral and slipped out through a gate. Patty, now limping even more noticeably, moved close to him and took his arm with one of hers, then appropriated the pitchfork to use as a walking stick.

'If we split up,' she said, 'and you go that way toward the forest and I go that way, one of us might make it.'

'No go. We're getting out of here together. Besides, neither one of us is moving very well. We look like that painting of the Spirit of Seventy-Six, only no one's bothered to bandage us up. Now, let's get to the tractor. You can really hot-wire it?'

She shrugged at him modestly.

'I can try. It may be tricky in the dark.'

Rather than cross between the main house and the barn, they chose to work their way back around the barn and the small, empty corral on the other side. Taking that route, they would be in clear, easy range of the farmer, Sanderson, should he spot them, but they would be concealed from Watkins until they were no more than twenty-five yards or so from the tractor, and also from Susan when she reemerged through the back door. No matter what, they knew that there was little chance of their making it unseen to the tractor, getting it started, and avoiding the bullets of two heavily armed professional killers.

'I don't like these odds,' Will said.

'We can do this.'

Cautiously, more than grateful for the heavy overcast, they hobbled along the vast wall of the barn until they had reached the corral. To their right, past Sanderson's house, they could just make out the silhouette of the farmer as he patrolled the broad, grassy field that separated the working farm from the forest. To their left, well beyond the far corner of the corral, facing the entrance to the barn, stood the tractor. With five-foot wheels in back, three-foot wheels in front, and a snout like a submarine, it was larger than Will had initially appreciated – certainly large enough to tow serious attachments for threshing or plowing and also, he hoped, to generate some speed with the two of them on board. If they could somehow make it out to a paved road, there was at least a chance of piling up some distance before Susan or Watkins reached their cars and caught up.

With Will keeping an eye on Sanderson, and Patty watching for Watkins, they reached the end of the corral.

'I know it's weird,' Will said, 'but after all that's happened, after all I've been through and dealt with, all of a sudden I'm scared stiff.'

'That's because all of a sudden we have a chance. I'm thinking that these are not the people I want to have end my life.'

'Amen to that,' Will whispered, slipping his arms around her. 'Well, I guess we've got to go for it.'

'We do.' She took his face in her hands. 'You're a hell of a guy, Will Grant – very brave and a terrific lover, too. That's a combination I like.'

Their kiss was brief, but intensely sweet.

'How long did you say it takes to hot-wire a tractor?' he asked.

'I didn't. Let's hope we don't have to find out. Listen, though, one thing – you've got to drive. Even in your sneakers I can't step down very well with my right foot. If any of them get in our way, you're probably better off trying to run them down than avoid them. Sometimes people don't react well with something coming at them head on.'

'Got it.'

'I'll do what I can with this.' She held up the pitchfork. 'Okay, Doc, ready ... and ... now!'

There was no sense trying to conceal their movement any longer. Hand in hand, they loped awkwardly across the grass as rapidly as Patty could manage. Just as they reached the tractor, the dense night was pierced by a piteous, screeching wail coming from the farmhouse. Susan.

'The key,' Will said. 'It's here.'

'Thank God,' Patty muttered.

Will scrambled up onto the broad seat.

'There's not much protection up here.'

'Try praying.'

Ahead of them, Watkins had appeared at the doorway of the barn and, without looking in their direction, started toward the commotion in the house.

Patty balanced herself on the metal step, hanging on to the seat with one hand and the pitchfork with the other.

Will turned the key, and with a brief cough, the powerful engine kicked over, thrumming loudly.

'How do I make it go forward?' he asked, suddenly panicked.

Patty, anticipating the problem, grabbed the shift lever beside the seat and snapped the huge tractor into gear.

'I was the Four-H queen in junior high!' she explained.

'Amazing.'

Watkins had swung around and was lumbering toward them, his gun drawn, when the tractor lurched forward.

'Duck down!' Patty cried. 'Head right at him!'

They were gaining speed when Watkins began firing. Bullets clanged off the grill, and one splintered the top of the steering wheel. Will was crouched awkwardly on one knee, peering along the side of the engine casing, reaching overhead to steer by one hand, wondering how long he could survive a bullet between the eyes. To his right, Patty was now hanging off to the side of the tractor by one arm, completely exposed to the gunfire, the pitchfork extended forward like a lance.

'That's it!' she hollered. 'Right at him, Will! Then keep him on my side!'

For several frozen seconds, the massive killer looked confused. Then, with the tractor bearing down on him, he took several clumsy steps to his left, stumbled, and fell to one knee. Although he still had a grip on his pistol, he never got the chance to fire it again. As the tractor rolled past him, Patty drove the pitchfork straight through the softness beneath his chin and then upward, almost to the hilt, in his brain. His death was instantaneous.

'Stop, Will!' she yelled.

Will slammed down on the brake. Clambering off the tractor, Patty retrieved the pitchfork, grabbed Watkins's gun, and was quickly back on the step as Will again accelerated.

'I think that way,' he said, pointing.

'You're in charge.'

'Boy, am I glad that isn't true.'

Will swung the tractor to the right in a wide arc that would take them around to the front of the house. At that instant Susan appeared on the back porch brandishing the submachine gun and screeching at them hysterically.

'You killed him, you bastards! You killed my Marsh!'

She rattled off a burst, then raced down the stairs, but the tractor was moving away to her left, and it seemed as if none of the shots had hit. Firing like a commando as she ran, Susan took a line that would cut them off before they made the far side of the house.

'What should we do?' Will called out over the wailing engine.

'Just hold us steady,' Patty answered. 'Real steady.'

She gripped the seat with her left hand and lay her right arm down across her left, sighting down the barrel of the pistol.

'Payback time,' she murmured, as she cracked off a single shot.

Through the gloom, thirty yards away, Susan cried out and fell, clutching her thigh and cursing. She was up with incredible quickness, though, hobbling after them, almost dragging her leg. But what chance she had to cut them off was gone.

Will swung the tractor to the left, alongside the house.

'That was an unbelievable shot!'

'It was a terrible shot. I was aiming at her chest. Take me past those cars. If she gets ahold of the keys to any of those, she'll catch us in no time.' Will stopped beside Watkins's Lincoln. Patty limped over to it and drove the pitchfork through the tire.

'Why don't you just shoot it?' Will called down.

'I may need what's in here.' It took two tries, but she stabbed through the left rear tire of Susan's nifty Porsche. Then she climbed back onto the step. 'Over there, the Jaguar!' she cried.

They were still twenty feet away from the car when Susan appeared at the corner of the house. She was bathed eerily in the light from the windows, her lips pulled back in a snarling, wolflike rictus as she fired.

'Go!' Patty cried.

She fired once at Susan and once at the Jaguar's tire, missing both times. The third shot produced only an impotent click. With the cracks from Susan's gun growing fainter, Will steered the tractor around two huge oaks and back onto the gravel driveway. One of the only things he remembered from the drive to Roxbury with Watkins was the right turn he took at the base of the drive.

'Even Boyd Halliday might have difficulty explaining that mess back there,' Will said as he made the right and they rumbled off down a narrow, deserted country road.

He was feeling absolutely buoyant.

'You have this thing wide open?' Patty asked grimly.

'Full speed ahead. Why?'

'I don't think we can chance being on this much longer. Dammit, I should have taken more time for that shot at the Jaguar's tire.'

'Nonsense.'

'Just the same, assuming Hollister limps inside, finds the keys to the Jag, and limps back out, she'll be on top of us before you know it. Then there's the people she told Watkins to call. They could come driving down this road at any second.'

Will rapidly deflated.

'So what should we do?'

'I'd rather take our chances in the dark in the woods than out here on this noble steed. You want your sneakers back?'

'No way. You've earned them. Besides, given where my socks have been, I don't think I want to risk even touching them.'

'We should get off this thing soon,' she said. 'One more minute, two at the most. I'm out of bullets, but I guarantee you that your pretty practice partner has plenty. I'll get off and move inside the tree line. You drive about a hundred more yards, then ditch the tractor, get into the woods, and work your way back here. I'll go straight in, twenty or twenty-five yards. That's where we'll meet.'

Without questioning, Will did as he was told, nosing the tractor off into the edge of the woods, then gingerly hiking back to where he estimated Patty was waiting. In just a few minutes, he heard her harsh whisper, calling him to the right. He was holding her tightly, concealed in a dense grove of young beech trees, when they heard a car skid to a halt by the tractor. Another minute and it accelerated, headlights slicing through the blackness as it sped past them toward the farm.

'Once again the woman in the pajamas proves her worth,' he whispered, genuinely impressed as he had been so many times this night. 'You are the master. Speak, and so it shall be.'

'Well, I say we head diagonally away from the tractor and away from the farm. They'll be back as soon as they meet up with Hollister. If we can put some distance between us and that road, I think we've got a chance. It's cold out here, but not cold enough to kill us. As long as you can walk, if we just keep putting one foot in front of the other, sooner or later we've got to run into some sort of civilization. Massachusetts isn't that big. Your feet okay?'

'I can manage. How about yours?'

'The right one where I stepped on the glass is starting to kill, but I can handle it. The sneaks are a godsend.'

'And they really look good on you, too.'

As rapidly as they could manage, they pushed deeper and deeper into the forest. At one point early on they both heard voices, but those quickly died away. Soon, there was only silence, intense darkness, and the damp chill of night. After an hour, they sank down at the base of a tree and held each other.

'Should we keep going, or try to wait until morning?' Will asked.

'I don't mind resting for a bit, but I think we should push on.

Halliday has a big meeting in the morning. He spoke about it when he thought I was in a coma. A number of companies are going to sign themselves into a merger with Excelsius. The way corporate lawyers operate, these sorts of business dealings are much easier to stop before they happen than they are to untangle afterward. If we can't stop it, Halliday may not only get away with murder, but he'll get away richer than ever.'

'I see what you mean. We really have no proof of anything. We may not even be able to find our way back to the farmhouse.'

'I think with a chopper we'll be able to, but I'd be surprised if Hollister and Sanderson and the rest didn't have the place cleaned up by then.'

She sighed.

'What? What?'

'I have a feeling it's going to come down to our word against Halliday's. Without those X-rays we don't have much in the way of hard evidence. I suspect the fake slides have already been taken care of, and the pathologist who cooperated with Hollister and Newcomber dealt with one way or another. So at the moment, there's nothing tangible to connect Excelsius and Halliday to the killings, or even to the breast-cancer scam.'

'We'll come up with something,' Will said. 'That bastard isn't going to get away with what he's done, even if he wasn't the one who pulled the trigger. Come on. If you're up for it, let's keep going.'

Will helped Patty to her feet, then kissed her softly.

'You're right,' she said. 'One way or another we'll get him. Just the same, I hate that we don't have one hard piece of evidence... Will? Will, are you all right? What did I say?'

Will was smiling down at her in an I-know-something-you-don't-know way. He had just brushed his hand across his pants pocket and remembered, for the first time since Roxbury, what he had thrust in there. He slid his hand into the pocket and slowly withdrew the creased, damp, sweat-stained letter Charles Newcomber had sent him in the envelope of mammograms. He had no doubt that it contained the link between Halliday and the cancer scam.

'Merry Christmas, Sergeant,' he said.

Bullock and Carruth, widely referred to as B&C, had been the brightest star in the Boston legal firmament for 150 years. Ed Wittenburg, in his twenty-fifth year with B&C, was the senior partner in charge of acquisitions and mergers. Now, he looked across the fortieth-floor conference room, past the massive floor-to-ceiling windows with their grand view of the harbor islands, and silently asked Halliday when the show was going to get under way.

Janet Daninger was worried. She had come over to Excelsius Health along with Halliday and Gold after Halliday had been wooed away from Bowling Green Textiles to become the new CEO. Marshall Gold had been his executive assistant at Bowling Green, just as he was now. It was absolutely out of character for Gold to keep his friend waiting – especially for a meeting as significant as this one, which represented the pinnacle of Boyd Halliday's career to this point. Janet smiled inwardly at the objections from those who initially opposed his appointment as CEO by pointing out that successfully repositioning a textile manufacturer did not necessarily translate into dealing with the highly competitive and volatile managed-care industry. How wrong they had proven to be.

'Try once more, Janet,' Halliday said. 'I think we've got to get going. It's just that Marshall did so much to ensure that this day came to pass, it seems only fitting that he should be here.'

He turned to the twenty men and women seated a comfortable distance apart from one another around the massive mahogany table. In front of each of them was an elegant name plate with their name and the name of the company they would be bringing into the Excelsius family. Premier Care, Unity Comprehensive Health, Steadfast Health, Coastal Community Care. In front of each of the attendees was an inch of documents, flagged where signatures would be needed. Beside those documents was a glossy brochure, trumpeting the new corporation: Excelsius National Health.

'When ENH stock comes out,' Halliday had told Janet with a wink, 'I recommend you have those in your family buy a share or two.'

Now he fidgeted for another minute, until he sensed the increasing restlessness of those in the room, then he cleared his throat and stepped to the table. Over more than a decade together, he and Marshall Gold had functioned as a unit, with virtually no philosophical or professional differences. Marshall's missing a meeting as monumental as this one would be a first.

You'd better have a damn good reason.

'Ladies and gentlemen, I'm sorry for the slight delay. I was waiting for Marshall Gold, my executive assistant, whom I believe most of you know. He's tying up some loose ends relative to this meeting, and I'm sure he'll be here shortly.' He took a deep, proud breath. 'And so, without further ado, it's time for us to make history. By the time we

312

adjourn this meeting, each of us will be an important part of one of the largest, most influential health-care delivery companies in the nation, indeed, in the world – Excelsius National Health. The two-thousand-dollar custom-made diamond and gold Diablo de Cartier fountain pen on top of each stack of documents will be your souvenir of this day, but another pleasant and constant reminder of it will also be your bank accounts.'

The laughter from around the room was generous.

'Now, then, if you will each take your pen and refer to item one, we –'

The elegant double doors at the far end of the conference room swung open.

Welcome, Marshall, Halliday almost exclaimed. Instead, he watched in stunned silence as Will Grant and Patty Moriarity stepped shoulder-to-shoulder into the room. They were showered and dressed in clean, casual clothes, but nothing could hide the fearsome bruising covering their faces. Will's left eye was completely swollen shut, and his hands were bandaged. Patty's eyes were enveloped in violet, with gentian streaks running down her cheeks and over her jaw. Both were limping.

Moments after they entered the room, a third person followed – a tall, distinguished man, marching ramrod straight, wearing the uniform of a colonel in the state police. Tommy Moriarity remained there, unmoving, as Patty and Will split apart and slowly rounded the massive table, giving each of the people seated there a slow close-up of the battering they had taken. When they reached Halliday, Patty handed him a folded piece of paper ... then another.

'Boyd Halliday,' she said, 'this is a warrant for your arrest.'

'On what charges?'

'The DA is just getting started on those, but the one you have in your hand is for fraud and accessory to murder. I can promise you that there will be others. The fraud part is outlined in that letter from a certain radiologist at the Excelsius Cancer Center.'

'Would you like us to add copies of these documents to those already in front of your business associates?' Will asked.

Boyd Halliday raised himself up and stared stonily out the window.

'That won't be necessary. Ed, will you come here, please, and make certain these people don't violate any of my rights.'

No one around the table moved as Ed Wittenburg held whispered conversations first with Patty, then Halliday. Finally, he stepped aside as Patty handcuffed Halliday's wrists behind him and led him from the room, joined at the doorway by her father.

Will, bracing himself on the back of a chair, turned and faced the others.

'I hope most if not all of you are completely in the dark about what is happening here,' he said. 'In time, much will become clear to you. For now, all I can say is: The stakes in the struggle between organized medicine and managed care have just gone up considerably. None of us should be taking care of the health problems of others until our patients' or clients' concerns come before our own. I challenge each of you to go back to your companies and figure out just how to put those words into practice. Oh, and meanwhile, feel free to keep your souvenir pens.'

Epilogue

Winter sun glistened off the surface of Lake Michigan and the new, powdery snow that blanketed much of the city. Physicians, more than 25,000 of them, streamed across neatly shoveled walks and into McCormack Place South on the vast convention campus. The healers, including several thousand chiropractors and hundreds of optometrists and podiatrists, represented every specialty and medical organization, as well as every state. Organized by the Hippocrates Society, the gathering was unprecedented in its spirit of cooperation and its mission, which was to carve out the framework of a single-pay, national health-insurance plan and to back up its demand for implementation by Congress with the threat of a slowdown or even a general strike.

'It's going to happen,' Will said. 'Can you believe it, it's gonna happen.'

'Thanks to you.'

Patty tightened her grip on his arm and led him over to a spot where they could look out across the lake.

The magnitude and cruelty of Excelsius Health's perfidy had galvanized physicians in ways that had previously been unimaginable. Almost overnight, chapters of the Hippocrates Society sprang up in cities across the country, and membership swelled. The AMA threw the force of its 260,000 members behind the search for a solution to the crisis. A widely publicized and completely televised congressional hearing uncovered unacceptable business practices on the part of a number of health-care provider companies. Patients and physicians at the hearing were joined on the witness stand by employees of a number of those companies, suddenly anxious to share shortcuts they had encountered that adversely affected patient health. Subsequent to that, a significant number of congressional seats had gone to candidates advocating immediate action on revamping the health-care delivery system toward federal control.

Meanwhile, desperate corporations were quickly restructured. CEOs were replaced. Other officials simply took off, some of them absconding with tens of millions in ill-gotten profits. Sentiment against continuing the status quo in health care grew like a tidal wave. The uninsured middle class became martyrs to the cause of change.

The Society national steering committee, charged with organizing the Chicago conference, had originally planned for ten to fifteen thousand attendees. Twenty-five thousand was beyond anyone's wildest imagination, but adjustments had been made.

'I really love Chicago,' Patty said dreamily.

'And *I* really love ... Chicago, too.'

'You know, I hope the day you realize you're not very funny isn't too hard on you.'

'Okay, that's it. I've taken enough verbal abuse. If you don't think I'm funny, then the wedding's off.'

'You can call it off if you want, but you're going to have to tell my father.'

'On second thought, I think I'll opt for the verbal abuse.'

'Wise move.' Patty guided him back toward the convention center. 'I just wish your old partner, Susan, could be here with us. She worked so damn hard in the interests of better health for all.'

'Especially for folks like Charles Newcomber.'

'Ah, yes. And let's not forget all those women from Steadfast Health whom she helped to experience the joys of learning they had cancer and undergoing surgery and chemo. God, but I wish that bullet I fired at her had actually gone where I was aiming.'

She pointed to the center of her chest.

'What goes around, comes around,' Will said. 'It ain't over.'

'I hope not, baby, but take it from a cop, bad guys *do* get away.'

And Susan Hollister had most certainly vanished.

Even with lawyer Ed Wittenburg's help, it had taken the state-police chopper most of the day to locate the farm. When they finally did, Susan was gone. There were bullets and bullet holes everywhere, but the bodies of the torturer Krause and Marshall Gold and his man Watkins were gone. The farmer and his wife were questioned extensively and threatened with charges, but neither caved in, and they were ultimately sent back to their farmhouse.

The Excelsius pathologist who had been paid to cooperate with Hollister and Newcomber by labeling cancerous slides with the names of women who were 'given' breast cancer agreed to a plea bargain, which helped to send Boyd Halliday to prison, though not nearly for as long as Patty and Will felt he deserved. The pathologist's statement also led to the indictment in absentia of Hollister. The lawsuits from patients were just beginning, but soon after Halliday's arrest, Excelsius Health was dissolved. It would be years before the finances of the conglomerate were untangled and settlements awarded. In addition to the individual suits, Augie Micelli was assisting a top Boston law firm in a class action against the former health-care giant.

It was the opening session of the four-day Consortium for Effective National Health-Care Coverage, and the vast convention hall was rapidly filling up for the keynote address, to be delivered by Diana Joswick, a Texas anesthesiologist and the recently elected president of the Hippocrates Society. A banner proclaiming AFFORDABLE HEALTH CARE FOR ALL stretched across the wall behind the dais. The atmosphere was electric. Will had tried to decline the Society's request that he be seated on the dais with Joswick and other notables, citing his resignation for personal reasons from all but general membership in the organization. In the end, though, for the sake of unity, he demurred. At his request, seats in the center of the third row had been set aside for Patty and Augie Micelli.

'There's Augie,' Patty exclaimed, pointing.

Will followed her into the row and settled temporarily into an empty seat next to hers. Micelli, much lighter and healthier-looking than he had been the day he first met Will, was beaming.

'This is a bigger happening than frigging Woodstock!' he gushed. 'Talk about making a difference. You two have changed the world.'

'Let's not get carried away, Augie.'

'Who's getting carried away?'

'You look great,' Patty said. 'How many pounds?'

'Nineteen and three-quarters, but who's counting? It's amazing what cutting alcohol out of your diet can do for the old waistline.'

'How long has it been?'

'Since I left for rehab? Eight months tomorrow.'

'Has it been hard?'

'Reasonably, but I'm still not ready to cave in. I keep telling myself that anyone who can come up with as much fentanyl solution as I did in as short a time can stay away from a drink for a day at a time. All those AA people I used to make fun of have helped, too.'

'In time, maybe you'll consider going back into practice.'

'Not until this mess is straightened out I won't.' Micelli gestured toward the banner. 'Plus I still have some big-league suin' to do.'

'Medicine's ready for you as soon as you're ready for it,' Will said.

'Go, they're waving for you up there,' Micelli replied.

'I still don't feel comfortable being –'

'Just go!'

Will took his place on the dais. He had been reasonably prepared for his introduction, in which he was presented as a physician whose courage, spirit, and dedication defined what the Hippocrates Society was all about. What he was not prepared for was the ovation – 25,000 standing spontaneously and applauding, whistling, and shouting out for fully two minutes. Below him, Patty was beaming and laughing out loud at his discomfiture.

Finally, the tribute subsided and Diana Joswick was introduced.

'Never in our history,' she began, 'have our medical students and residents been better prepared for the rigors of taking care of patients. But ironically, never has the care their patients are receiving been poorer. Hospitals are no longer safe, accessible havens for the ill and injured. Getting admitted to one is often more difficult than getting into an Ivy League college. Cost of care has become our standard of care. The stethoscope and careful physical exam have been replaced by paperwork and excessive documentation. And all of this for only one and a half trillion dollars a year – many, many times what the very effective and accessible Canadian health-care system costs.

'Health care in America, the most affluent and resource-blessed nation in the history of the world, is a disgrace, and expecting change to come from insurance executives, who are the oilmen of medicine, is just not going to cut it. That is like asking the fox to build improvements in the chicken coop. It is time, my friends, to step forward and be heard. It is time to step forward and be counted. It is time we made health care something other than an oxymoron.'

Applause reverberated throughout the cavernous hall, as it would again and again throughout her forty-minute address.

Five thousand miles to the south, in a barrio of the village of Talavera, in the state of Guaira, in south central Paraguay, the assassin sat slumped on a rickety wooden bench near the corner of a cantina, asleep to all appearances. In truth, beneath the broad brim of her straw hat, her dark hawk's eyes were open a slit and fixed on the doorway of the building across the street – *Clinica Médico*.

Beneath her loose cotton robe, her right hand, inside a rubber glove, was loosely wrapped about a snub-nosed .38. Not daring to try to bring a gun into the country, she had settled for the best the shop-keeper in Asunción had to offer. The pistol, which he said was Russian, felt cheaply made, and the price was inflated, but no matter. He had let her fire it at some bottles, and her plan called for only close-range shots – very close range. The .38 would be enough.

An hour passed, then most of another. Nothing. For three days she had watched from the bench, noting the comings and goings of her prey. For three days, the doctor had arrived at the clinic almost precisely at nine and remained alone inside until she opened the door to patients at ten. Casually checking through a side window, two days in a row, the hunter had watched as her quarry performed advanced martial-arts forms in the small waiting area. Power, balance, speed.

Had something gone wrong today? Had she taken the day off?

The assassin was casting about, looking for signs of trouble, when she spotted the doctor approaching casually through the dust and hazy mid-morning heat, nodding to a woman hanging out clothes, waving to a fruit vendor. Relaxed. Happy. The woman on the bench clenched her jaw and tightened her grip on the pistol. She had waited long enough – it was time. Even though the doctor was two hours later than usual, she showed no indication of opening the clinic to the public right away. For five minutes, ten, the door remained closed. The doctor was alone inside, probably practicing her forms. Finally, her hat still pulled low across her eyes, the assassin rose, ambled across the street, and knocked on the door.

'Esta cerrado,' the doctor's voice, slightly breathless, called from within. *We're closed.*

Another series of knocks.

Come on ... Come on ...

Footsteps from within.

That's it... Soon now, very soon.

The door opened, first a bit, then all the way.

'Hola, buenas dias. ¿Enque le puedo servir?'

'May I please come in?'

There was surprise on the doctor's face at hearing English.

'I suppose. I'm very busy right now.'

She stepped back and allowed the assassin two steps into the waiting area where she had been working out.

'Dr. Hollister, we've had a hell of a time finding you.'

The assassin brushed her hat up away from her eyes.

Recognition took a few seconds. By then, the .38 was in position. 'Grace Davis?'

'Your grateful, devoted patient.'

Grace could see Susan Hollister's hands tense and knew the professional killer could take her in an instant. She and her husband had given up more than eight months of their lives and all of their savings, pointing to this moment. Throughout their hunt, Grace pictured the confrontation over and over in her mind – pictured it and wondered if she could do it, if she could actually pull the trigger, if she could actually kill. Now it took less than a second to find out. As Hollister swung her foot up in what would have been the equivalent of a decapitating kick, Grace fired into her spinning form – once, then again. Hollister's lethal pirouette stopped in midair. She stumbled back against a table and fell heavily, blood expanding from two rents in the side of her white T. Her eyes widened as Grace stepped forward, the barrel of the .38 leveled at her forehead.

'Don't do it,' Hollister gasped. 'Don't –'

The third bullet, fired from less than three feet, entered the center of Susan Hollister's forehead and exited the back of her skull with enough force to embed itself in the clay floor.

Grace Peng Davis stripped off her robe and dropped it next to the body along with the gun. Then she exited through the back door of the clinic and calmly made her way along the street leading out of the village. A block down the road, Mark Davis pulled over in a rented Kia.

'Is it over?' he asked as his wife climbed in and he pulled away.

Grace bit down on her lower lip and nodded. Her eyes were full. 'Take me home,' she said.